LEGACY

Catriona King

This is a work of fiction. Names, characters, places and incidents are used fictitiously and any resemblance to persons living or dead, business establishments, events, locations or areas, is entirely coincidental.

No part of this book may be used or reproduced in any manner without written permission of the author, except for brief quotations and segments used for promotion or in reviews.
Copyright © 2020 by Catriona King

ISBN: 9798641644035

Photography: Image by Bruno Passigatti
Artwork: Jonathan Temples: creative@jonathantemples.co.uk

Editors: Andrew Angel and Maureen Vincent-Northam

Formatting: Rebecca Emin

All rights reserved.

Hamilton-Crean Publishing Ltd. 2020

For My Mother

About the Author

Catriona King is a medical doctor and trained as a police Forensic Medical Examiner in London, where she worked for some years. She returned to live in Belfast in 2006.

She has written since childhood and has been published in many formats: non-fiction, journalistic and fiction.

'Legacy' is book twenty-three in The Craig Crime Series.

Each book can also be read as a standalone or in any order. Details of the main characters and locations are listed at the end of each book.

The Craig Crime Series So Far
A Limited Justice
The Grass Tattoo
The Visitor
The Waiting Room
The Broken Shore
The Slowest Cut
The Coercion Key
The Careless Word
The History Suite
The Sixth Estate
The Sect
The Keeper
The Talion Code
The Tribes
The Pact
The Cabal
The Killing Year
The Running of The Deer
The Property
Crossing The Line
The Depths
The Good Woman
Legacy

The twenty-fourth novel in the series will be released in late 2020.
The audiobook of the first Craig Crime novel, A Limited Justice, is now available on Amazon ACX.
The author has also released a science fiction novel set in New York City: The Carbon Trail.

Acknowledgements

My thanks to Northern Ireland and its people for providing the inspiration for my books.

My thanks also to: Andrew Angel and Maureen Vincent-Northam as my editors, Jonathan Temples for his cover design and Rebecca Emin for formatting this work.

I would also like to thank all the police officers I have ever worked with for their professionalism, wit and compassion.

Catriona King
April 2020

Discover more about the author's work at:
www.catrionakingbooks.com

To engage with the author about her books, email:
Catriona_books@yahoo.co.uk

The author can also be found on Facebook and Twitter:
@CatrionaKing1

Chapter One

December 2019.

Silent is an interesting word because of its clarity. In its purest form it means one thing, the absence of sound; but that purity is often lost in common use.

Is the meaning of 'they were silent' absolute but 'the forest was silent' less so? And could either of those statements ever really be true?

How can a forest be silent unless the cries of birds and animals, the sibilance of breezes and the rustling of the leaves on its trees are eliminated completely? Similarly, how can a human being be silent unless they have ceased to breathe?

But if that is the requirement for someone's true silence then several people in Belfast were about to hit the mark.

****

Katy Stevens' Apartment. Laganbank, Belfast. Sunday 15th December 2019. 10 a.m.

"It'll take us months to get the new house right, Marc."

Marc Craig nodded automatically at his wife's words, having learned after just a year of marriage that even if he hadn't registered enough of what she'd said to respond meaningfully the gesture gave him time to catch up as she moved on. It was a form of marital holding pattern that he'd implemented soon after their honeymoon, in the same way that air traffic controllers instruct planes to circle to give them time to recheck whatever it was controllers checked.

All caught up, Craig knew that the house to which Katy had referred was the solid but neglected Victorian schoolhouse on Belfast's Stranmillis Road that they'd purchased months before as their first family home, but had only finally decided to make habitable after his Italian mother Mirella, who'd been made to jump through the endless and punitive hoops of applying to remain after Brexit in the country where she'd lived for fifty years, had *finally* had her application for settled status approved.

That meant his parents *weren't* decamping fifty miles south to the Irish Republic as previously mooted, and so he, Katy and *her* widowed mother were also staying put in Belfast; Maureen Stevens being so close to her only daughter that it would have been unthinkable to have left her behind if the caravan had headed south.

Those worries now behind them, the main reason the detective hadn't registered his wife's words fully right away was because he was busy juggling his ten-month-old son and a Sunday newspaper, an inconvenient broadsheet that was in danger of getting sprayed with oatmeal if he did *anything* too fast.

It was his own fault of course; if he'd put Luca in his highchair to entertain himself instead of bouncing him on his knee he would never have been faced with the dilemma, but then he saw so little of his son during the week because of people in Belfast murdering each other that affection had trumped his common sense.

Spotting the situation Katy swooped and rescued her offspring from a face full of newsprint, continuing her train of thought as she placed him in his playpen.

"It'll be a death-trap for Luca until the builders have finished so we'll *have* to stay living here until it's done. Unless you fancy moving in with the folks?"

This time Craig *did* respond immediately. "*No way!* I moved out when I went to Uni and I'd feel like a kid again."

Not to mention that, much as he adored his mother Mirella, returning home to the chaos created by the Italian Tornado and being expected to shovel down three thousand calories every night would make him fat and homicidal within a month.

Having deposited her son inside his little kingdom Katy shot her husband a wry look.

"Did I specify *your* folks?"

Craig's eyes widened in alarm. Much as he liked his mother-in-law, moving in with her was a minefield he wasn't entering without protection. Before he made the profound mistake of saying as much, salvation came in the form of his mobile ringing and his best friend's name flashing up.

He took the call over to the window, gazing across the fog obscured River Lagan as he answered.

"Morning, John. How's it going?"

John Winter, Northern Ireland's lead pathologist and the detective's best friend since they'd been twelve, was currently staying in his old bachelor pad with his toddler daughter Kit while he and his estranged wife undertook counselling, the aim of which was to try to deal with her obsession with making their daughter so perfect that the little girl's life had become hell.

"Fine. Apart from the fact I'm attending the therapy sessions alone now. Natalie's being impossible and refusing to go."

Another minefield that needed dodged.

Craig responded with a brisk, "Great. Excellent" as he mused that the fog resembled a grey duvet he'd had on his bed at eighteen and wondered idly where the item was now.

"So what can I do for you today, John?"

Smirking at his friend's neat sidestep, the pathologist got to the point.

"I was just wondering if you'd mind taking care of Kit for a few hours. I need to go to the lab and finish a report."

"Sure. Bring her down. I'm on call, but short of someone getting bumped off I won't be going into work today."

It was a master class in tempting fate.

****

Northern Ireland (N.I.) Bank. Royal Avenue, Belfast City Centre. 12 p.m.

Noel Lovett loved his job as Chief Security Guard, which was just as well given his name. No matter how many times the East Belfast man repeated, "It's Love-*ett* not Love *it*" the lazy mouths of his home city constantly repeated the mistake. It had led to a life of him being asked, "*Do* you love it then, Noel?" and "*How* do you love it, Noel?", questions that in adolescence had made him growl but now at the ripe old age of sixty he merely responded to with a weary smile.

But he *did* love his job as it happened, his earlier career as a beat cop ending in optional redundancy at forty-two with a solid pension when the RUC had become the PSNI, leaving him with only the challenge of what he, as a divorcee disinclined to take the long walk up the aisle again, would do all day to fill his time.

He'd had a list of requirements for any new job: no night

work, a smart uniform to save him having to plan what to wear every day, preferably one with an elastic waistline to accommodate his love of food and increasing bulk, and *absolutely* no being outside in the cold and rain. So when he'd been offered the role of a day-time security guard at the bank sixteen years before he had jumped at it, and now he was the boss of ten men with a sizable hike in pay. These thoughts and others, such as that there were sandwiches and a flask of gourmet coffee in his lunchbox that he would be having as soon as he'd finished his rounds, were running through Lovett's head as he did his initial bank walkthrough of the day.

He'd taken the handover from his night-time counterpart Mickey Dorsey thirty minutes before so he didn't expect to find even a wastepaper bin unchecked on the main floor, but as Chief Guard he had some specific duties and he decided to perform them first. He didn't always, preferring to shake his routine up now and then and enjoying the knowledge that as the boss he could. He'd taken orders for years, seemingly from younger and younger men, so now he liked to march to his own tune.

That desire showed itself in Lovett's showy strut as he circled the bank's extensive marbled reception hall and in the way he swung his baton rhythmically as he did, but it displayed itself even more ostentatiously in the manner in which he jangled the ring of keys at his belt as he approached the lift to the bank's other floors; they were passkeys to the *real* kingdom, with copies held only by a select few.

Three floors above reception and three below, the upper ones holding mostly offices full of inert computers and quiet telephones, catching up on their sleep before the exertions of the coming week. The lower floors were however a different story and as Lovett exited the lift on the first of the basements he was assailed by a wave of noise. A loud whirring and droning generated by the wall-wide ranks of computers that filled the space, their multicoloured lights flashing with every overseas transaction and fluctuation in exchange rates, the merchant banking component of the financial institution ensuring that they never slept.

The guard paraded manfully between the high banks of machinery, up and down the first row, up another and so on, until satisfied that no intruder had invaded his small fiefdom he descended again, to perform his checks on the bank's two sub-basements before lunch.

But the first sub-basement, a bright-white, sterile chamber that held three of the bank's six vaults, their circular, brushed-steel doors arranged like giant coins along one wall, was to allow him no such comfort. As soon as Lovett stepped out of the lift a prickle of alarm ran down his spine; his instincts instantly telling him that something was wrong although what it was he couldn't have said.

A sweep of the area revealed nothing visibly amiss with the secure storage facilities, and on closer inspection their doors' steel lever handles were properly aligned and their electronic keypads read 'locked'. But twenty years of watching his back on the mean streets of Belfast during The Troubles, when every day could have been his last, had endowed Noel Lovett with finely tuned senses, and those made him alert for when *anything*, however tiny, was off.

And it was off now, he could feel it in his bones, but rather than flee in panic at what might be coming like the average person the guard did what he had done a million times as a cop. He fixed in place and slowed his breathing, then he moved very deliberately through the chamber scrutinising his surroundings as he went, at first with wider scans and then methodically inch by inch.

The guard's inspection revealed nothing but three vaults with locked doors and keypads and an iron grille that he could bring slamming down between them and the lift if he flicked a switch. He decided not to, not yet, not until he had run through all of his other senses to see what he could find.

So next he listened, closing his eyes to focus only on the basement's soundtrack. The rhythmic beeping of the vaults' keypads that would turn to sirens if a code was entered incorrectly, the light hum of the neon strip light above him and the vague hiss from the lift's resting hydraulic drive. But there was nothing else audible, nothing that wasn't there every day; nothing that sounded *wrong*. Taste was redundant in his detection because there was nothing thick in the air to taste, and touch would come later but not without sterile gloves.

That left only smell and Noel Lovett knew as soon as he'd thought the word that *that* was what had set off his alarm. Not an unpleasant smell in any way, and not one of the nasty bodily ones he'd grown familiar with as a uniformed copper; this was an aromatic and very pleasant scent. He'd named it within seconds; Cedar wood. But how? *He* was a traditionalist who only ever wore Old Spice and it definitely hadn't been present when he'd made his rounds the day before.

No one else should have visited the vault floors since Friday evening when the bank staff left for the weekend, so unless one of his guards had entered unauthorised...

Lovett shook his head as if he was actually arguing with someone. No, that was impossible; only he and the bank's manager held keys to the lift and Mervyn Gambon always notified him if he'd had to enter unexpectedly at a weekend. Someone else *had* to have entered the floor since his visit the day before, someone who had worn a Cedar wood scent!

For a seasoned cop who trusted his instincts it was enough, and one hour and the discovery of a dead body later Craig's peaceful family Sunday came to an abrupt end.

Chapter Two

N.I. Bank. Sub-Basement One. 3 p.m.

"Have you *seen* how thick that door is, boss?"

Craig didn't look up from his position beside the corpse splayed on the vault's floor, answering his deputy D.C.I. Liam Cullen absentmindedly instead.

"Has to be. The walls as well. There are a lot of Hatton Garden wannabes around."

The D.C.I. gave a long sniff and an ostentatiously loud cough before making his next point.

"Yeh, but how the hell did they get in here then?"

He glanced around the windowless space pointedly as he said the words.

"If you mean because they didn't bore a hole in the wall or cut through the metal, Liam, most thieves don't do that anymore. Codes are the open sesame nowadays. Anyway, be quiet and let me concentrate for a minute."

It earned him another cough and a muttered, "You're heartless. I've a really bad chest and you didn't even notice."

Craig gave a weary sigh. "I could hardly have failed to with all the spluttering you've been doing, but I'm not your mother. There's a chemist down the street where you can buy a decongestant when we've finished, but for now zip it please."

He refocused on the dead person that they'd been summoned to see; running his dark gaze up from the young man's brown booted feet, past his artfully worn jeans and sports logoed hoodie to the top of his dark-blond gelled head for the umpteenth time in an hour. Not to identify what had killed the youth, *that* was glaringly obvious from the hole in his head, but as if something that had happened before that fatal event might just reveal itself if he focussed hard enough.

The detective's murder-divining was interrupted by the appearance of a man he'd seen just a few hours before, this time carrying not a toddler but a medical bag, and wearing, as they all were, a white forensic suit.

"Hello again, John." Craig jumped to his feet. "Sorry to disturb your report writing."

The medic shrugged and nudged his black wire glasses up the bridge of his narrow nose. "Can't be helped. I don't expect your victim chose to die. Hi, Liam."

"Hi yourself, Doc. I've got a chest cold."

The announcement got the unsympathetic reaction the D.C.I. had come to expect. Unless you were dead or about to be professionals who worked on murders didn't even blink.

"Nice for you, I'm sure." He indicated the young man lying at their feet. "Does anyone know how he got in here?"

A defiant sniff preceded Liam's reply. "NO, we don't know how he got in here, but Harry Houdini couldn't have pulled a neater trick." He scowled at Craig. "And just so you know, you're as heartless as your mate here. And you a doctor too."

"I'm a dead people's doctor so come back and see me if your cold kills you, Liam." The pathologist turned to Craig. "My guess is your victim wasn't killed here. No blood or brains."

Craig shook his head. "They could have masked the room and cleaned up. Also, he might have committed suicide. There's a weapon over there."

John glanced to where he was pointing and saw a handgun lying on the right hand side of the small space. He conceded the point with a nod.

"Right then, it's my job to sort out the possibilities, so the pair of you should bugger off and let me work."

He took up Craig's now vacated hunkering position and started to examine the body, while the detectives exited the vault and found themselves sharing the outer sub-basement chamber with some waiting CSIs who, seeing that Craig had ordered the other two vaults on the floor opened as well, and found them thankfully free of dead bodies, were craning their necks to sneak covert looks at the valuables inside.

Knowing the investigators' presence would inhibit their free and frequently un-PC exchange of ideas, the policemen ascended in the lift to a first floor office, where Liam draped himself across two chairs like a dying swan as he thought aloud.

"He shot himself."

"Or it was made to look that way."

The D.C.I. shrugged. "OK, so suicide or faked suicide. But why? And why here? Also, who the hell is he? And more importantly, how did he get into the vault? Those things are made as single units without joints and there's been no holes drilled, the doors are a foot thick and the keypads on all three are intact."

All good questions and Craig decided to take them in turn, apart from the first and third.

"Whether the suicide was genuine or mocked-up will have to wait for John's post-mortem, and the reason for it and victim's name will come later, but *why here* is an interesting question. And how *did* he get in?"

He stroked his chin for a moment in thought, his stubble reminding him that he hadn't shaved. A weekend perk.

"Why would anyone choose to die in a bank?"

"Theft gone wrong?"

"That's one possibility. So, maybe he was part of a gang and they killed him, but if so where are the others? Revenge against the bank could be another option. Committing suicide here to make a statement and try to discredit it in some way. But it starts another list: revenge against what? Individuals? Capitalism generally? Has the bank been investing in something unethical that the victim objected to perhaps-?"

His deputy interjected. "So some kind of Crusty protest you mean? Like that Swampy guy? Or the lot who blocked the roads in London over the climate?"

Craig shrugged. "Perhaps. Although his grooming suggests more an armchair protester than one on the frontline. But people *have* risked themselves in ideological or political protest before in lots of ways. Self-immolation, hunger strikes, standing in front of a tank-"

Liam waved him down. "OK, I get it. So maybe murder or protest stroke revenge against the bank. To be confirmed. But none of that tells us how the hell he got inside that vault."

Craig nodded. "Or inside the bank in the first place. They've had twenty-four-seven security guards here since that big robbery a few years back." He sighed heavily. "And now *we* get to interview them all."

Liam forgot he was supposed to be dying from a cold for a moment and chuckled. "It was some pickup by that guard Lovett though, wasn't it? Guessing something was up just because he smelled Cedar wood."

Craig smiled admiringly. "It was, and he was right. The smell is still strong inside the vault, although it isn't coming from our victim so someone else was definitely in there with him. The fact the vault's very warm probably helped the scent linger, but we still need details on why Lovett didn't think it could have filtered down there from say this floor or even the street level one, so get someone to ask him please."

Liam shook his head. "I already did. Each floor has its own air supply and is sealed off from the others to prevent fires spreading. So if a scent's on the vault floor that's where it originated."

"Interesting. It lingered there because of the air system and small area, whereas any scent left in reception, if they entered that way, probably faded quickly in the larger space. OK, let's return to your earlier point. How *did* our victim enter the bank, the sub-basement and the vault when it takes keys to access everywhere?"

That discussion would have to wait a while, because just then the lift doors opened and John Winter stepped out.

"Grab a pew and enlighten us, John. Did our victim kill himself or was he killed?"

Before the medic answered he took a bottle of pills from his bag and threw them for Liam to catch.

"Decongestants. I went out to the car for them so don't say I never do anything for you. Unless you start coughing up muck, in which case you'll need antibiotics, they *should* make you dry up."

No-one missed the words' double meaning and they earned him a wry, "Thanks" from the D.C.I..

The pathologist considered Craig's question for a moment before replying.

"OK. Here's what I can tell you so far. We have a Caucasian male in his late teens or early twenties who was shot through the right temple at zero range-"

"The barrel was pressed against his head?"

"That's what the burns and preliminary powder tests say, but I'll need to check for bone bevelling to be absolutely sure. But after your comment about masking don't ask me whether death occurred here or elsewhere yet. At the moment I'm inclining against here because of the lack of fluids but that could change with what the CSIs find. As to whether our victim pressed the gun against his temple or someone else did, well that could depend on whether the gunshot was his actual cause of death."

Craig arched an eyebrow but didn't interrupt.

"If the gunshot *was* his cause of death and the boy did it himself, then he must have been right-handed or at least ambidextrous."

Liam pulled a face. "Not many of those about and most still have a favoured hand."

"Very true. So, *if* the boy shot himself then his *favoured* hand was definitely his right, but I'll need to check a lot of things out at the lab before I can confirm. And if he *wasn't already* dead from some other cause and someone *else* shot him either here or elsewhere, that's definitely murder and it'll be over to you."

Craig thought out loud for a minute. "If you're not convinced the shot killed him we could be looking at a faked scene, which could explain the lack of blood but raises the question of why. But leaving that aside for a moment, the gun was found on his right hand side, which means-"

"It *could* have fallen there in a suicide *or* any clever murderer could have planted it there, but I'll check possible trajectories with the CSIs."

Craig nodded. "It's an old-fashioned bugger so although the shot itself might have had low momentum the recoil could have been substantial, so part of me says it should have landed further away than where we found it if he'd pulled the trigger himself."

Liam shrugged. "It could've hit the vault wall and bounced back, boss. Space is pretty tight in there."

As the debate lapsed John picked up his report.

"OK, so getting back to our victim. His hair, teeth and nails suggest good nutrition and his skin was cared for, so I don't think we're looking for someone who lived on the street. Although-"

"That'll have to wait for the PM. We know, Doc."

The medic sniffed huffily. "I don't know why you don't just take my job, Liam, since you already know everything I'm going to say."

"Ooh, who got out of bed the wrong side this morning then?"

The medic gestured sharply at Craig.

"Blame the mattress in his apartment. Honestly, I don't know how you slept on it all those years, Marc. It's like a bloody brick."

"I didn't. I fell asleep on the couch most of the time. But since it looks like you'll be staying there for a while write a list of whatever you need and I'll sort it out. Now, can we *please* get back to the dead boy? Well-nourished, young and not homeless. Anything else?"

"He has a transparent brace on his bottom teeth so there'll be dental X-rays somewhere."

"And those things cost, so he definitely wasn't broke."

John agreed. "His clothes labels back that up. They're not designer but almost, so top-end high street would be my guess. So either *he* had money or someone else was paying his bills."

"His parents probably."

It was said mournfully; Liam was feeling the cost of having two growing kids.

"Possibly. OK, back to the braces. The good thing is they sometimes have serial numbers which could help with an ID, so I'll check that at the lab. I didn't strip him here obviously but I couldn't see any obvious tattoos, although confirmation of that will have to wait. What's important for you two to know now is that there are no signs of struggle or assault. So again, either suicide…" He paused, looking thoughtful for a moment, "…or I suppose he could have been drugged before someone forced his hand up to shoot himself-"

Craig shrugged. "He could have volunteered as well. To be martyred for some cause. Although killing yourself somewhere so hidden certainly limits any possible impact on public consciousness or media coverage. You don't make much of a political statement killing yourself in a hole in the ground."

"Wall, boss. A vault's a hole in a *wall*."

Craig rolled his eyes. "Thanks for wrecking my point."

The thwarted quip was clearly Liam's revenge for his earlier lack of sympathy.

John was still on the why of their victim's death. "OK, even supposing someone would be prepared to sacrifice themselves like that, and I concede that the rare individual does, there might *still* have been a final moment of fear where he'd changed his mind and the gun had slipped, or if he'd decided to fight off someone forcing his hand."

Craig nodded. "So what you're saying is the whole scene's too bloody neat. I agree. We've basically got nothing but questions at the moment, and with the location being so unusual we can't rule anything in or out."

"Except that he was someone's kid and he's dead, boss."

There was pathos in Liam's tone, as if he was imagining his own son or daughter lying in the vault in a decade's time. A shudder confirmed it.

"You're right, Liam. That's why we need to ID him fast."

John rose wearily to his feet. "OK. I can PM him this

afternoon if Katy will take care of Kit."

"I'll call her and check."

A minute later the pathologist had his guarantee that his daughter would be safe and he left to continue his part of the hunt, while the detectives headed to the basements in search of people to interrogate.

****

County Galway. The Republic of Ireland.

"Irina's just called to say that Dylan's been found. The police are at the bank now."

The young man seated on a couch across the room glanced up from his phone in surprise. "So soon?"

Gretchen Bakker sat down beside her other half, nodding. "I was surprised too. I was sure nothing would be heard until the week began, but perhaps the northern cops are better than we thought."

Kurt Nilsen set his mobile on the table beside him and relaxed back in his seat.

"I never thought that they were bad, elskling. After all, they must have learned *something* during their long troubles. And we know that the lead detective's good. That's partly why we chose him after all. But I *am* still surprised the bank discovered the body so fast when it's a Sunday. It's a sleepy time in that little town."

He turned his attention back to his smart-phone. "But today, tomorrow, it does not matter. None of them will understand our message until *every* piece is in place. And by then we'll all be very far away."

****

N.I. Bank, Sub-Basement One. 6 p.m.

After an afternoon of interviewing bank personnel Liam was just about to raise the important matter of food when he heard Craig's mobile ring half-way across the chamber. He'd missed lunch so an expletive at the thought of yet more missed vittles was just about to hit the air when the D.C.I. realised that despite being only inches away from the offending phone his boss, seemingly engrossed in whatever

Noel Lovett was telling him, hadn't registered the sound at all.

That left him with a dilemma. Pretend that *he* hadn't heard the old-fashioned ringtone either and hope the caller didn't try again before they'd had *at least* a sandwich and coffee, or, given that it might be something important, point the ringing out to Craig with some insult about going deaf.

Cursing his religious upbringing and resulting giant conscience the D.C.I. did neither, instead tutting at himself and calling out politely, "Your mobile's ringing, boss" while allocating additional blame to his wife as he did so for civilising him. Fifteen blissful years before he would just have yelled, "HEY, THICKO, PICK UP YOUR PHONE!"

Craig lifted the device and read its screen, immediately puzzled as to why Teresa Harding, a Fraud Squad D.C.I. that he only knew from courses and the last of those two years before, would be calling him ever, but especially on a Sunday afternoon.

There was only one way to find out and Liam meandered across to listen in.

"Hello, Teresa. Long time no speak."

As the D.C.I.'s light tones hit the air in response Craig smiled, remembering the amusement that her voice, whose uber-high soprano really belonged to a teenager, had caused each time she'd asked questions in a group. Even though it matched her slight appearance it wasn't the usual authoritative sound most police officers employed or aspired to, but it really suited her.

"Good afternoon, sir."

He was taken aback by her term of address and then remembered again that he was a DCS.

Even so.

"Marc, please."

"OK then, sir, and I'm Terry now. Sorry to bother you, especially on a weekend, but I'm on call today and heard you were at N.I. Bank."

"I am. Liam Cullen's here too. But we were called to a suspicious death not a theft, so what's the Fraud Squad's interest?"

"There's no such thing as the Fraud Squad now."

Liam's eyebrows shot up. When the hell had *that* happened? He really couldn't cope with the force's constant rearranging of names and sections, it was becoming like his local SuperMark. *It* was the hell for switching its sections around too, and just when he'd finally learned where his favourite foods were in the aisles!

"It was amalgamated with Robbery, that's my bit, in the summer, so we're called Fraud and Robbery now. Anyway, I take your point about me calling, but it was actually to pass on something that I thought might interest *you*. There's been a theft at an art gallery on the Lisburn Road and the owner of the gallery has connections with N.I. Bank."

Craig glanced at his deputy and frowned, trying to make the link. Did she mean the owner had bought shares in the bank? Could people even do that? Or was it something else?

Before he could ask the Robbery D.C.I. went on.

"I'd really rather not have this conversation on an open line, sir, but as you're working today perhaps you could pop up? I'll be at the gallery for a few hours yet. It's number nine-hundred-and-fifty Lisburn Road-"

Hearing the address Liam cut in.

"Is that big burger place near you? The one that's laid out like an American diner?"

"Eddie Rocket's you mean? Yes, it's just down the road a stretch."

"Brilliant."

Craig smirked. It seemed their decision had been made.

"OK, Terry, depending on the level of Liam's hunger we'll be with you in thirty or sixty minutes."

As he hung up Craig frowned again. "What do you think 'connections with N.I. Bank' means, Liam? That the gallery owner has deposits here?"

Instead of the glib response that he'd expected his deputy's small eyes grew wide and he swung around to face the vault.

"Did anyone check everything's still in there?"

"What?"

A second later Craig caught his drift and raced back through the open vault door to where the CSIs were now hard at work.

Two walls of the enclosed space were covered in small rectangular steel plates, so familiar from heist movies that he hadn't even registered them, each one carrying a number and forming the front of a deposit box of uniform size. The third wall was patterned with a similar but less regular mosaic, for people who could clearly afford boxes two, three and even five times the size of the first. Added to that, propped along each wall were stacks of wooden trunks and crates, presumably filled with valuable items too large to fit elsewhere.

Craig sighed wearily. It could take days to check that everything that should have been there still was.

He gestured around the warm space shaking his head in disgust. "I was so focused on the body I didn't even notice this lot. To be honest, I completely forgot valuables were stored here."

Liam smiled. "That's 'cos we're Murder, not regular plods."

"Nice, but still no excuse for it not even occurring to me."

After a lengthy scan of the vault revealed nothing that obviously shouted theft Craig realised that it never would to them; unless someone with an inventory examined every deposit box they couldn't possibly know if something had been taken, or perhaps even left behind for them to find.

"Liam, the bank manager's upstairs, so get him down here. And tell him to bring the list of everything held in the vaults."

When Mervyn Gambon appeared a minute later Craig realised that the pursuit was likely to prove even more onerous than first thought. The middle-aged manager, who was dressed in what was probably the closest he ever got to casual wear; a pair of dark chinos with ironed seams and a woollen jumper in that unfortunate shade of mint green so beloved by golfers which hinted that his Sunday had probably been designated for letting what was left of his sparse hair down at some club, was grasping a clipboard so plump with sheets of paper that if they represented only this vault's inventory they could be there all night.

The detective pointed an accusing finger at the pages.

"They're *all* items lodged in this vault?"

When Gambon smiled and shook his head Craig's hopes soared momentarily, only to be dashed again when the manager opened his mouth.

"Not just this one. *It's* covered by the top three pages. But there are the two other vaults here and then there's the lower floor."

A sub-sub-basement? Why hadn't Noel Lovett said? Why hadn't *he* thought to ask?

Craig hardly dared ask his next question but he knew that

he had to, and its terseness spoke worlds.

"How many vaults do you have in the bank in total?"

In truth it hadn't even occurred to him that there would be more than the three on this floor. It seemed that he'd seriously underestimated the wealth in their small State.

"Six. Three here and three downstairs. This vault is the smallest. I was planning to go through them all in turn and check that nothing was out of place."

Just then Liam had an even more worrying thought than his boss.

"Open the lower ones now."

"Well, I was going to check this floor first, after your CSIs had-"

"Now!"

Craig's add-on, "Please" didn't prevent Gambon sulking and muttering all the way to the lower basement, where only one small vault door was immediately visible when the lift doors slid back. Making a sharp right turn the manager headed down a narrow corridor to one side of it, that to a burglar would simply have looked like a design feature or a dead end. In a moment the men had entered another chamber containing two larger and even more substantial vaults than the first. The detectives met each other's gazes in silence, understanding why the other had been so terse. There could be more bodies in the unopened vaults.

Craig kicked himself for not thinking of it before and then turned rigid with fear; one of the reasons he'd always resisted getting married and having a family was that he'd worried it might make him lose his focus, so what if *that* was why it hadn't occurred to him to check the other vaults? The excuse that they hadn't been told about the extra basement was dismissed instantly, as if telepathy should be a basic skill that he possessed.

During the breath holding, heart slowing minute while they awaited codes, voice and thumb prints being entered at the first of the large vaults, Liam blamed their lapse on it being a Sunday while Craig kept beating himself up for his mistake. His deputy threw in a prayer that they found no more victims, in truth partly because of the time it would delay his meal.

When the huge steel door was finally pulled back to reveal nothing but valuables there were multiple sighs of relief, but unfortunately the second of the large vaults offered no such comfort. Lying on its grey tiled floor in an almost identical tableau to their first was a second victim, this time a young woman, dead from a seemingly identical shot to her temple although this time with the bullet hole and gun on her left hand side.

Craig fell grimly silent, shutting out Gambon's shocked gabbling as Liam ushered the manager out to check the last of the floor's vaults, which thankfully held nothing but wealth.

As he phoned another member of his Murder team and then called back pathology, Craig's doubts that they were dealing with suicidal martyrs grew; but not half as much as his doubts about his skills as a cop.

Chapter Three

The Fervier Art Gallery. Lisburn Road, Belfast. 7 p.m.

D.C.I. Andy Angel had half-expected an interruption to his peaceful Sunday afternoon and he knew it could have been far worse than being sent to an art gallery. After all, being on-call meant just that, and the idea that it was really endless television watching at the taxpayers' expense was just some politician's election slogan when they were trying to look tough on costs.

The Murder detective chuckled to himself; if the government *really* paid cops for every hour they worked they would earn more than the Prime Minister and clearly in someone's hierarchical view of the world that would *never* do.

In fact he *hadn't* been watching TV when Craig had rung and asked him to meet Terry Harding at the gallery he'd been painting, and as a minor collector of Irish art and an enthusiastic artist himself an excuse to view other people's work was always a thrill.

So there they were, two Chief Inspectors staring at a blank white wall where a painting should have been, the only evidence that it had ever hung there its abandoned mountings and a five o'clock shadow of dust around their edges that a CSI was just about to brush away.

"When was it discovered missing, Terry?"

He knew Harding from all the interminable courses that Inspectors and Chief Inspectors had to attend to earn their annual assessment ticks and they had always got on well.

She smiled at him, her extreme slightness making her one of the few women who made the cerebral but weedy D.C.I. feel really strong.

"And *how* was it discovered, Andy? That's interesting too. It was noticed missing this morning by the gallery's owner as she and her family drove past to church."

"Really? From a moving car?"

Someone clearly had eagle eyes.

"Yes. Well, to be precise it wasn't the owner herself who noticed, because she was doing the driving; it was her eighteen-year-old daughter. Apparently the girl really liked the painting and looked out for it whenever they passed. That's why it was displayed so prominently in the window."

The now-blank white wall, or false display wall to be accurate, held pride of place in the gallery's front facade, so Andy *guessed* he could understand how the girl had spotted the piece missing from the road. Still, it was quite a feat.

When Harding turned towards the back of the long, narrow gallery he followed, talking as they walked.

"You told the chief the gallery owner had connections with N.I. Bank."

"Yes, that's why when I heard on the grapevine that your lot were investigating a body there I thought I should tell him. Given that everything seems to have happened on the same day."

"Good call. What sort of connections?"

She nodded to some chairs and sat down. "The gallery owner is called Hortense Fervier-"

"French?"

"By descent perhaps, but her accent says she was raised here. Anyway, she comes from a wealthy, *seriously* wealthy family. They own a house on the Malone, the Kilgallon Estate at Lough Neagh and businesses and apartment blocks in Belfast, Galway and Dublin."

"Where did their money come from originally?"

A shrug told Andy he would need to find that out for himself.

"Anyway, I know from speaking to our art theft guy that the Ferviers store any art that isn't on public display or in their various homes in the vaults of that bank. Ms Fervier told me they have around forty items there at the moment."

Andy's dark-blond eyebrows shot up. *"Forty!* Bloody hell, that's quite a collection. We'll need all the titles to check that they're still in the vaults."

"Sure. But just so you know, they have around another fifty pieces held privately in extended family members' homes. There's also other artwork: bronzes, charcoal sketches and marble sculptures that rotate between Irish museums and the Ferviers' commercial properties in a sort of travelling exhibition. I've told Ms Fervier we'll need the full list of everything by tomorrow, and then I'll be checking *their* insurance and security details as well as the items' held here and at the bank."

"I don't fancy your chances of getting it without going

through the courts."

She looked downcast. "You're probably right, but I had to ask. She *seems* to be considering giving it but I can't compel her. Only our interest in the gallery and bank art is really legitimate for the case."

"On the bright side. It might save you some work if she doesn't." The Murder detective gestured back at the empty wall. "So the painting that was stolen..."

Harding produced her smart-phone and pulled up an image, passing it across for him to see. Andy held his breath at the painting's beauty. It was a study of a mother and child in oils and its light and shade made the figures seem alive.

When he spoke again he struggled to keep the awe from his voice.

"Is that a *Vermeer*?"

"Apparently so. I don't know much about art myself but it *is* lovely."

"If it's real it's also a piece that unless my memory's off was believed to be lost-"

Terry's eyes widened. "What do you mean *if* it's real?"

"Forging Vermeers was a specialty of a guy called Han Van Meergeren last century, and some of his copies were so good even the Nazis with all their paid experts bought them thinking they were real. One was found at Hermann Goering's home after he was arrested. Anyway if this painting *is* the real deal there should be a certificate of authentication. It might just have been thought lost because it hadn't been seen publically for a long time, so perhaps it's actually been in the Fervier family for generations."

She nodded and took back her phone. "That was my understanding. It wasn't for sale so I think they were just exhibiting it to attract people in to browse."

He smiled at the old trick.

"An expensive lure. That figures. It entices people while also sending out the message 'Don't even bother walking through our door unless you have loads of dosh'. But still... displaying something so valuable on a main road." He rolled his eyes. "Idiots."

But since he'd raised the subject of filthy lucre.

"Exactly how valuable *was* it? What was paid for it at auction and what was its insurance valuation?"

"Fervier said she didn't know what the family had paid for it they'd had it for so long, but it was insured for twenty million."

"*Shit!* Now, that *is* a theft. How *did* they steal it by the way?"

The Robbery detective sighed.

"I'm still trying to work that out. There are no obvious signs of a break-in and none of the alarms were tripped, so we could be looking at an inside job. Handily there are only three employees to check on."

"An inside job could mean family too don't forget, and I bet there are plenty of broke or resentful distant cousins who wanted to get their hands on that beauty."

As her jaw dropped at the implied workload the Murder detective rose to his feet.

"Sorry to leave you with all that work, Terry, but I'm just here to see how the theft connects to our murder case." He glanced at his watch. "On that note, I'll just nip outside and make a call."

A call to see whether Craig needed him down at the bank or he could spend a leisurely hour viewing the rest of the gallery's displays and calling it work.

****

Andy's viewing time was limited to thirty minutes, the time dictated by Craig's call to the labs to ask John to return and assess their second victim. The pathologist's response was that as he was up to his elbows in stuff that Craig *really* didn't want described to him he would be sending his deputy instead, the abnormally young looking for his forty-odd years Mike Augustus.

Augustus also just happened to be the other half of Craig's inspector, Annette Eakin, so his sojourn in the bank's sub-sub-basement began with him passing his mobile to Craig before he got to work.

"Annette's on the line and she wants to speak to you. I'll go ahead and start. Which vault is it?"

While Liam led the pathologist to their second victim, Craig greeted his inspector apologetically.

"Sorry to muck up your family weekend, Annette."

A warm chuckle came down the line. "Well, I don't suppose you killed our victims yourself, sir, so don't worry about it. I really just wanted to ask if you needed me there as well."

"That's kind but you're not on-call."

"I would only be sitting here reading a book. I can get one of the kids to babysit Carrie if you do need me."

Carrie being the couple's toddler daughter and 'the kids' being Annette's two older children from her long defunct marriage who were both at local universities.

"They'll just be snoozing off a late night at some dance club or other, and they can just as easily do that in front of our TV as in their flat."

"And eat better food too I'm sure. It's a kind offer, Annette, and I may take you up on it later, but we need to get the forensics and PMs out of the way first. Can I call you back in an hour or so?"

"Just let me know."

As the call clicked off Augustus emerged from the vault with a question.

"Did the first body look the same as this one when it was found, Marc?"

"Exactly, except with the male the bullet wound and gun were on the right hand side."

"OK then. I want to call John. I have to send him a photo so I'll need better reception."

As he took the lift up to street level in search of it Liam stared pointedly at his watch and Craig knew the word 'food' was about to follow. In fact he was wrong; this time the D.C.I. opted for the less elegant "Scran" and accompanied it with a desperate look.

Craig was hungry himself so his response was more sympathetic than earlier.

"Just a little longer, Liam. We'll be heading to meet Andy at the gallery soon and all three of us can get something in your burger bar."

"Well, don't be surprised if I die of hunger before then, boss, and me with a cold and all. My stomach thinks my throat's been cut."

A scan of his deputy's well-covered frame said exactly what Craig thought of *that* comment, but further debate was prevented by Mike reappearing, nodding as he did.

"John agrees with me. This is all too damn neat. The bullet holes in both temples are positioned identically, and the guns are the same distances from the bodies to an inch."

"You're saying they definitely didn't shoot themselves."

The pathologist shook his head. "No. I mean yes, they

23

didn't. Even if we find gunshot residue on their hands to show that our victims pulled the triggers I'm pretty sure they had help doing it."

Craig glanced around for somewhere to sit while the medic elaborated and found a set of metal equipment boxes some kind CSI had left there that looked like they would bear their weights.

He sat down gingerly, motioning the others to do likewise, and nodded Augustus on.

"Explain, please."

"OK. Imagine I'm going to shoot myself in the head."

Liam chortled; his day had suddenly got much more entertaining. As Mike mimed the action he decided to clarify a point.

"What sort of gun are you killing yourself with?"

"Well, the ones left behind were revolvers so let's say one of those. But is that *really* important to my reconstruction?"

The D.C.I. gazed at him solemnly. "*Very*. I need to *be* the gun."

When he closed his eyes, held his palms up and chanted, "Om" Craig gave a smirk.

"He's playing you, Mike. Just go on."

The medic pressed two fingers at a right angle to his left temple.

"OK, so I'm left-handed, like our second victim was *apparently*, who by the way was a well-nourished Caucasian female of around twenty who looked like she came from money, but I'll go into that in a moment. Back to the shooting. *Because* I'm left handed I could only just about manage to shoot myself in the right temple if my arms were long enough, but the angle would be off, and to be really accurate I *have* to shoot myself in the left. The opposite applies if I'm right hand dominant. But even so, if I have a gun pressed against my temple either intending to shoot myself or with someone else intending to shoot me I'll be nervous, no matter *how* much I want to die. Agreed?"

"Nervous is one word for it. Terrified would be mine."

"Shitting yourself more like, boss."

"Thanks for the poetry, Liam."

Augustus smiled. He always enjoyed working with the two detectives because of their banter; it made a nice change from corpses and boring seminars.

"OK, so I'm about to shoot myself in the left temple or

someone else is and I'm really nervous, which means that it's unlikely I'll be able to keep the gun or my head absolutely still even if I'm determined. And when the moment of pulling the trigger comes, I've *never*, not even in ex- soldiers who were accustomed to violence, seen someone who didn't instinctively either pull the gun away slightly or angle it up. Which means either there won't be a perfect contact burn or the bullet will enter the skull and brain at an angle."

Liam frowned. "How do you know it didn't? You haven't seen inside the girl's head yet, and did you already test for GSR?"

"No to both, but John has on *his* victim. That's partly why I phoned him."

"And?"

"Your male victim has a perfectly circular burn on his right temple that matches his gun barrel exactly, and the bullet entered in a straight line through the temporal bone and into the brain. Perfect contact and angle, and my victim's entry wound looks exactly the same. John's never seen it in a suicide before and neither have I."

Craig rubbed his chin thoughtfully for a moment before speaking again.

"So...you're saying that even if someone held our victims' hands, which were holding the guns, and *forced* them to shoot themselves, the wound simply *couldn't* be that perfect?"

"Not even if the killer's finger was inserted above the victims to press the trigger down. Not unless the victim had been completely immobilised. And John says your male victim was muscled so it would have taken someone very strong to immobilise him. The female would have been easier."

Liam frowned again. "And they wouldn't have just had to control their shooting hands, boss. Their other hands and both feet would have needed restraining or they'd have tried to fight back. Not to mention how the hell did they keep their heads still? Put them in a vice?"

"Good point. Any signs of restraints or struggle with the girl, Mike? John said there were none on the boy."

"Not that I can see on first look, but I'll check at the PM. That's a good catch though, Liam, and means that if we find no signs of bindings we'll need to check for the full range of drugs. If both victims were unconscious when they were shot that could explain a lot."

The D.C.I. accepted his praise and then undermined it. "But not everything. How could they have pulled the triggers if they were stoned?"

Craig was more convinced. "Revolvers have large enough trigger guards for a second finger to be slipped through to press on the first and if the victim was drugged and still..." He turned back to the pathologist. "Who's leading for forensics today, Mike?"

"Des, I think."

Doctor Des Marsham was head of the country's forensic service and worked out of the same laboratories as John.

"Good. Ask him to do ballistics once you've got the bullets and the usual GSR and whatnot, and then I'll need to know exactly how the shooting might have worked. Tomorrow afternoon would be good for the logistics."

The medic gave him a sceptical look and rose to his feet. "I can always *ask*. OK, I need to get back to our victim now. John said he'll be finished his PM on the boy around eight-thirty, but if you'd rather get the prelim reports on both victims together then call down around ten."

Liam rubbed his hands together gleefully. "Excellent. Time for a short gallery visit followed by a lonnnng munch."

****

The Fervier Art Gallery.

The Murder detectives' gallery visit took longer than anticipated, not only because Andy was reluctant to leave his private tour of its paintings, some of which, those by Irish artists including Lavery and Henry, Craig would cheerfully have stolen himself, but because Hortense Fervier had arrived at the street level exhibition space just a minute before them.

Liam's pre-prepared objections to dallying died on his tongue when he saw the proprietress, who at a statuesque six foot with an additional three inches of heel was staring both of the new entrants in the eye. Combined with her snow-white hair swept into a high chignon and a baked-in suntan that smacked of decades of summers spent somewhere costly, Fervier looked like a queen whose coach had taken a detour through Belfast on its way to the Cote D'Azur. In fact, she didn't look like someone who belonged in Ireland at all.

Her regal appearance was backed up by an extended hand that she clearly expected to be either bowed over or kissed. Liam watched as his boss met the expectation halfway, taking her tanned hand lightly and giving a polite nod, and guessed that being half-Italian probably made Craig comfortable with all those, to the Crossgar man, fancy pancy ways.

"Madame Fervier?"

"I am. And you are?"

If a voice could slice through steel they'd just heard it.

"Chief Superintendent Craig and Chief Inspector Cullen."

She would have to make do with Liam's cursory jerk of the head.

"Very well. What are you doing to recover my painting, Chief Superintendent?"

Craig shook his head firmly. "Your painting's theft and recovery rests with D.C.I. Harding." He smiled past her to Terry who was standing in silence, clearly waiting to be acknowledged by Fervier at all. "The rest of us are from the Murder Squad."

"Murder!"

Liam was pleased to see her equilibrium take a jolt.

"Yes, but not here. We merely came to retrieve our officer."

It was Andy's cue to exit past him to the street, followed by Liam. Craig had obviously decided that anything he needed to discuss with Terry would now be discussed in the privacy of the coordinated crime building where both their offices lay.

After smiling a polite, "Good day, Madame" he joined his men outside, and as soon as they could no longer sense Fervier's gaze drilling into their backs Liam jerked a fat thumb down the road.

"Burger time, lads."

By tacit agreement nothing more was to be said about the murders until after they'd eaten, but as they were waiting for their food to arrive Liam decided that it *was* time for some laughs. He might not show it but two dead kids in one day had affected him and he needed to blow off some steam.

"I thought you were actually going to kiss her hand, boss. Maybe even snap your heels."

Craig gave him a wry look. "Now, you *know* I only snap my heels when I'm wearing my jack boots."

"The ones with the spurs you mean."

"Ha ha. She *is* formidable though, isn't she? She reminded me of a Countess I met once in Italy."

Andy's interest was piqued. "Does your Italian family often move in circles like that?"

Craig blushed. They knew little of that side of his family except that his mother Mirella had been a concert pianist and her family travelled between Tuscany and Rome several times a year.

He gave a dismissive shrug.

"Every other person in Italy is royalty, mostly hereditary titles with no money attached, so there are a lot of impoverished aristocrats floating about dreaming of their past glories. It's hard not to bump into a few now and then."

But Liam scented blood. "*Aristos?* That wouldn't have included your mum's folks would it?"

As the D.C.I.s laughed Craig's colour deepened and he muttered, "How would I know?" in response, adding hastily, "No. All my Italian relatives work for a living. Mostly as doctors and musicians for some reason."

Liam was unconvinced. "I don't believe you. That's it; I'm calling you Baron Craig from now on."

Craig rolled his eyes, knowing that his deputy would tire of the title after a few hours; Liam had the attention span of a goldfish for anything that he wasn't incredibly interested in. But just in case he *didn't* tire of this particular fancy he decided to create a diversion by breaking their pact and discussing the case.

"Let's discuss Madame Fervier while we're waiting for the food. Andy, what's the gallery's connection to the bank? She can't be a shareholder. I asked the manager and the bank has none but the government."

The D.C.I. had been busying himself lining up the condiments but he abandoned his pursuit to reply.

"Apparently the Ferviers store around forty paintings in its vaults. The ones that aren't being exhibited in the gallery or around their various homes and businesses."

A follow-up question was prevented by their burgers arriving and for ten minutes nothing was heard but chewing and satisfied sighs. When they'd finished eating Craig picked up his thread.

"Homes and businesses plural?"

As Andy elaborated, Liam put in orders for hot drinks

and a bowl of apple pie and cream, making his fellow D.C.I. wonder where he would put the reheated dinner that he would doubtless be expected to eat when he got home. Craig didn't wonder at all; Liam's appetite was so legendary it would form the basis of a Celtic saga someday.

As the scale of the Ferviers' wealth was laid out he grew decidedly uneasy.

"That's a *lot* of money for one family. Give me some background. Are they Huguenots?"

The Huguenots were a Protestant grouping in sixteenth to eighteenth century France. Largely Calvinist, they suffered severe persecution at the hands of the Catholic majority led by Louis the fourteenth and then the fifteenth, which resulted initially in many thousands emigrating, mostly to South Africa, North America and northern Europe. After a period of relative religious tolerance in France under the Edict of Nantes, its revocation resulted in a further wave of Huguenot emigration in the late seventeenth and early eighteenth centuries including to Ireland.

"Pass. But I'll find out."

The question made Liam curious. "So what are you saying, boss? Unless they came to Ireland centuries back why are they here now?"

The question made Craig roll his eyes. As the child of an immigrant he would never dream of questioning anyone's right to live wherever they chose to in the world.

"Catch a grip, Liam! That's not what I meant and you know it. But in one day we have two murders and the theft of a valuable painting, and that painting's owner Hortense Fervier *just so happens* to store her other paintings in the very vaults where our bodies are found. There are over seventy banks to choose from on this island and half a dozen in Belfast alone, so that's too much of a coincidence for me. It's enough to make me ask questions about where the family got its wealth e.g. have they been growing it here over centuries or did they import it more recently? We need to dig on its and their origins. There's something off here, I can feel it in my bones."

Andy nodded eagerly. "I'll take that bit if you like, chief. I'd love a dig around in the Ferviers' archives. I bet they own some amazing pieces of art."

"Exactly the person I was thinking of."

Andy's visual skills made him the natural choice for the

job.

"But liaise closely with Terry, please. I don't want Robbery thinking we're invading their turf. While you're at it, Andy, keep a tab on what the bank's inventory checks reveal. If something was taken from those vaults or left there it could be significant to our case."

Liam spotted his apple pie approaching and sat forward eagerly, and then he had a thought that dampened his glee.

"Are you saying those kids were just killed to cover up some thefts?"

Craig made a face. "I don't know *what* I'm saying yet, Liam, but it's a hell of a place to leave bodies if the vaults didn't mean *something*, isn't it? I mean, breaking into a vault just to deposit a corpse is-"

He was cut off by a guffaw.

"Deposit, like bank deposit. Good one, boss."

"Not what I meant but I'll take any praise I can get. Anyway, my point stands."

Seeing that he'd already lost his deputy's attention to his pudding Craig turned to his other D.C.I., who expanded on the point.

"You mean why bother with the bank at all, chief? Why not just kill them at home? Or if the bank *is* significant then why not just do it upstairs in the reception area? Why go to all the bother of getting the vaults' codes and prints and sneaking in there, not to mention how had the killer managed to get hold of them? But actually there's another point on that. I know what the pathologists think, but were our Vics *definitely* killed elsewhere and dumped in the vaults, or was it just staged to look like that? Like a double bluff."

The last question prompted Craig to exit the café to call forensics; politeness saying it wasn't fair to discuss any gorier points while Liam was finishing his meal, although in truth it wouldn't have bothered the D.C.I. at all.

"Des?"

The response was a typically dry, "Who else owns this mobile?" that Craig completely ignored.

"Sorry to bother you, but Mike's probably brought you up to speed on our killings."

It was said more in hope than expectation, and the fact that he could hear a whistle blowing in the background added to his doubt.

"Are you at a football match?"

"Aye. We're running late. Martin's Sunday five-a-side's just ending..."

Martin was the scientist's ten-year-old elder son, who was already displaying significant talent at every sport that involved a ball.

"...but yes, I do know about your bodies." There was a short pause while the football dad swallowed something before carrying on. "Mike's just brought me up to speed so I'll be heading for the lab in an hour. Do you need me to look at something before then?"

"Mike will give you our list of queries, but could you commune with your CSIs at the bank before then and ask them a question, please. John and Mike seem to think our victims were killed elsewhere and the bank scenes were staged, but are there any *definite* forensic signs to say yay or nay?"

Craig knew the forensic expert's bushy eyebrows would be rising in curiosity but his response gave nothing away.

"Right-ho. I'll call them now to check for blood spatter."

"Brain too. They were both shot in the head."

"OK, I'm *really* glad I got to finish at least one pizza slice before you said that. You've just put me off the rest."

Craig heard what was left of the meal being dumped in a bin.

"Sorry about that. Right, I'll let you go now. I hope Martin scores a goal."

As he hung up he wondered if Luca would play football one day and *he* would be the dad standing on the sidelines cheering him on. The thought made him re-enter the café wearing a stupid grin.

"OK, Des will check for definite signs that the scenes were staged or not. Any other thoughts, you two?"

Liam had finished his pie and was thinking well of the world so he decided to contribute again.

"The killer can't have expected us to find the bodies today, boss."

Craig was about to ask why not when he realised that his deputy was right.

"Ah... very good, Liam. You mean because the bank isn't normally open on a Sunday no-one should have been checking the vaults."

"Correct."

Andy cut in.

"So that means that if there *is* a link between the Ferviers' stolen painting and the murders the killer probably didn't think that we'd make it, because the events *should* have been discovered a day apart. It could have introduced an element of doubt in the murders' timelines too."

His counterpart nodded smugly. "That's it. The only reason the boss got curious about the *Ferviers* was 'cos everything seemed to have happened at the same time."

Craig chuckled. "I'd love to take the credit but it was actually Terry who made the link. But I agree the killer didn't expect us to find the bodies today, although whether that will help us catch them only time will tell."

He took a deep sip of his coffee and realised too late that it had milk in it. He was an espresso man and to him any form of milk in coffee was a capital crime. Andy seized on the pause created by his boss' disgust to comment again.

"OK, so we have two young, dead people. Both well-nourished, and both looking as if they came from decent circumstances. That means someone's likely to notice them missing pretty soon."

Craig nodded; pushing his offending cup so far away his deputy thought it might end up on the floor.

"Hopefully. And that means they may *already* have reported them missing." It gave him an idea. "Liam, Annette offered to help out, so call and ask her to chase the cop-shops for missing persons' reports. Tell her to phone Jack and the rest of the Belfast ones first, since the bodies were found here. She can make the calls from home."

Jack Harris was the long-suffering desk sergeant at Belfast's High Street Station and his suffering was borne less patiently at some times than others. The current stats stood at ten to one.

"Will do."

"Andy, follow up on that with her, please. We'll be up to our eyes in other things."

While one D.C.I. made his call the other picked up his thought again.

"OK, so a missing person report or something that the Docs might find could ID our victims, and-" The arty D.C.I. halted abruptly, realising that he'd just exhausted his store of ideas. "Nope. That's me done. I've got nothing more."

Craig turned back to his deputy. "Liam?"

"Hang on a second."

He signed off his call and picked Craig's question up smoothly.

"We've gone as far as we can until we get a missing report, something from the PM or forensics, boss. Or until something hinky comes back from the inventories."

"Or Andy finds something on the Ferviers or their art. Agreed. So let's get more coffees, mine without milk this time, please, Liam. Then you and I will head for the lab and Andy and Annette can continue to dig."

Chapter Four

Amsterdam.

Marianna Visser scrolled through her emails nervously, until suddenly she spotted the name that she'd been waiting for weeks to see and clicked eagerly on their message.

The man who stood behind her, his muscled, tanned hands resting lightly on her shoulders, held his breath as the words 'I believe this is yours' appeared and then as an image downloaded so slowly that he wanted to punch the screen, until he saw its final, high resolution glory and then he gasped.

"It's your father's watch! They found it!"

The elderly woman shook her head excitedly. "Wait, wait, there are more pictures!"

Moments later they were gazing at full-screen images of a heavy, antique-gold carnival mask, a diamond necklace that even through the screen's pixels sparkled so brightly it made the couple catch their breath, and a harpsichord whose deeply patinaed Linden wood and keys of pure ivory placed its origin over two hundred years before and its provenance unmistakably from the court of Marie Antoinette of France.

Adlar Visser grinned, triumphant but still stunned. "We were right! We were RIGHT! And now they've proved it! I don't think I'd ever *really* believed it until now."

His wife reached her arms up excitedly and wrapped them around his still broad chest.

"I always knew we were, my love, and this is just the beginning. Don't forget the rest of the things on the list. In just a short time they will *all* be making their way home."

****

Northern Ireland's Pathology and Forensic Laboratories. Saintfield Road, Belfast. 10 p.m.

"Anything for us, John?"

As John Winter was standing by his chrome coffee maker when Craig entered his office asking the question, he was momentarily confused as to whether the detective was referring to their victims or hot drinks. But knowing his friend's hardcore caffeine habit he shot a jet of espresso into a cup pre-emptively and passed it across before taking his own, far less palpitation generating, cappuccino to his desk.

"I didn't mean coffee, but thanks anyway."

Liam crossed his arms in a huff. "Yeh, and thanks for not asking *me* if I wanted one."

"You never drink coffee!"

"That doesn't mean I don't like to be asked! Or do you only serve Barons around here now?"

Not even John with his overdeveloped good manners was prepared to apologise for a hypothetical insult so he merely snorted and sat back in his chair, completely missing the D.C.I.'s joke about aristocracy. Liam wasn't worried; there was no time limit on slagging Craig about his mythical ancestry so he could wait.

After a few sips of foam the pathologist indicated a file on his desk.

"OK, so you'd like to know if I have anything on your first victim."

"Or both victims if you've been quick."

"Mike's finishing the girl's PM now so we can pay him a visit when we've finished our chat."

Craig knocked his coffee back in one hit and set the miniscule espresso cup on the desk to the sound of his deputy tutting.

"Ach now, look what you've gone and done, Doc. He'll be hyper all night, and on a Sunday too. If I get a call at five a.m. I'm forwarding it to you."

The pathologist shrugged.

"I don't know how you can tell the difference considering he's always hyper."

The words prompted Craig to rap the desk hard.

"I *can* hear you, you know. Sunday or no Sunday, Liam, there's no rest when we're on-call, so let's have your report please, John."

The medic slid a sheet from the file across to him, tapped his computer and began reading the original from the screen.

"Jack Doe-"

"Why not John?"

"Because the victim's young and Jack's trendier. I've also called the girl Jessica instead of Jane. Anyway, Jack Doe is a Caucasian male of between seventeen and twenty years, much nearer the lower end because his bone epiphyses were still fusing and he only has one wisdom tooth, so I'd settle around eighteen or nineteen. Sadly his dental brace didn't have a serial number so it gave no help ID-ing him, but there'll be X-rays out there somewhere to match his against once we have a possible name. Meanwhile Des is running them against the central database to see if anything pops."

"Fine. You mentioned good nutrition earlier too."

"Yes, and he worked out as well. Quite a lot I'd say judging by his muscle definition."

Liam gazed down mournfully at his torso. "*I* used to have muscles."

It brought a snort from the medic. "Clearly you still do or you'd be a heap on the floor! But I take your point. Maintaining muscle definition takes a lot of work, especially as you get older."

The D.C.I. stared enviously at his boss. "The Baron has definition."

When once again the title seemed not to register Craig hurried them along.

"That's because *he* gets off his ass sometimes and goes to the gym. Carry on, John."

But the pathologist made a rewind motion instead, telling Craig that this time Liam's jibe *had* sunk in.

"That's the second time you've said Baron, Liam. Is that the boy's name?"

"Nope. It's the boss' name. Baron Craig of Rome. Didn't you know we were in the presence of an aristocrat?"

Craig rolled his eyes. "Ignore him. He's been at the e-additives again. Carry on with your report."

The words were accompanied by a covert scowl at his deputy that just made him grin, but John Winter's curiosity was piqued and once *that* had happened there was no escape.

"We'll be coming back to this Baron business, Marc, but returning to your male victim. Based on his muscled appearance I've asked for blood steroid levels, in case he was a user, along with all the usual tests of course. He did have quite small testicles and they *can* atrophy with steroids so the idea isn't completely left of field. And speaking of genitalia, he wasn't circumcised and there was no sign of sexual assault or any sexual event just prior to death. I've taken all the usual swabs."

Craig saw his deputy's mouth open to comment and then

close again, clearly deciding that a discussion on gonads was a step too far for a designated day of rest.

"That's interesting. If he *was* a steroid user then he might have been aggressive. Roid rage. But even if he wasn't, with that level of musculature he wouldn't have been easily subdued."

"Well, there were definitely no restraint marks, so I've asked for drug levels in case he was roofied. I *can* say there were zero signs of him being a regular drug user; no injection marks and his veins and nasal mucosa were fine. But any weed, coke or narcotics he *might* have taken regularly will show up on his hair samples and bloods. I swabbed both his hands for powder residue, and the bullet I removed from his brain *could* have been shot from the gun you found but Des will need to check the markings to be sure."

Both detectives nodded.

"So he shot himself, boss."

"We can't say that yet." Craig turned back to the medic. "*Are* you saying that the gunshot killed him?"

The equivocal look on the pathologist's face said his answer wasn't going to be clear.

"On the balance of probability that's the conclusion I'll most likely reach, but I can't reach it just yet."

"Because?"

"Although there was no blood that could either have been because he was cleaned up before he was left in the vault or because his heart had already stopped beating, i.e. he was shot after he'd already died from another cause, for example a drug OD. I'll need to view the histology along the bullet trajectory and get the tox screen before I commit."

Craig considered for a moment. "OK... let's say he *was* shot, I've never seen a suicide by shot where the wound was so perfect, John. Mike agreed there's usually some sign of angling to say the person was reluctant or afraid."

The pathologist nodded. "He's right. Often in temporal bone suicide shots the bullet ends up so angled that it embeds near the apex of the skull, but this one was textbook perfect. Burns, powder residue and stippling on the skin around a neat entry wound, bullet entry at a neat ninety degrees to the bone, which was bevelled to support that, and then straight through the temporal lobe of the brain and into the far side olfactory area where it lodged. Perfect. *Too* perfect in fact. As if someone or something was guiding your victim's hand."

"It also means there was very little momentum behind the shot or it would have gone straight through."

"That fits with the gun, boss. Both the revolvers looked old."

"Good point. And because the murderer's hand was on the outside forcing him to pull the trigger the GSR would still be mainly on *victim's* hand." Craig noticed his deputy pulling a face. "You think differently, Liam?"

"Sort of. I agree about the hand over his guiding the shot, but what if the boy wasn't a victim? What if he'd *wanted* to die and asked someone to help him?" He turned to John. "That wouldn't be murder but it could create an identical scene, couldn't it, Doc?"

John considered for a moment and then nodded. "Exactly the same. Marc?"

"Fine, we can add assisted suicide to our list of possibilities, but we can't rule out murder until we know a lot more so we continue to investigate as if it was. You said there was no sign of assault, but how about a struggle, John?"

"None. But-"

He stopped so abruptly Craig knew he was considering the wisdom of his next words. He urged him to take the risk.

"I promise we won't take whatever you say as fact."

It earned him a sceptical look.

"You *say* that, but we all know you will."

"Tell us anyway."

The medic's response was to open a second computer file and turn the screen around for them to see. A set of photographs of the back of their victim's body was displayed and the detectives stared at them for a moment uncomprehendingly.

"They're pictures of his rear view, Doc. So what?"

"Top of the class for anatomy, Liam, but look closer." Seeing that his best friend was looking blank too he added, "I'll tweak the resolution to see if that helps any."

After almost a full minute of staring Craig finally gave a slow nod.

"I think I can..." He pointed to the back of the youth's right thigh. "Is that early lividity?"

"*That's* the million dollar question. I think it could be, but if so it's just starting to become visible, and if *that's* the case then-"

Liam finished the sentence for him. "Jack Doe was killed

less than two hours ago! But that's impossible."

John nodded. "Exactly. I took these shots at four o'clock this afternoon, so a faint lividity patch of this size would put time of death at around two. Which is not only impossible, given the time that the body was discovered, but it doesn't work with his body temp and other indicators."

Craig dragged his eyes from the screen to look at him. "What are *they* saying about our time frame?"

"That our victim died between four and five days ago and not the few hours this early stage of lividity implies. But if he did die that long ago then why didn't his blood start to settle then and lividity appear?"

Liam interjected. "And is lividity going to show a pattern from the vault floor or somewhere else?"

"Well, the vault floor was the last surface he lay on, but I take your point. It could be secondary lividity but will a primary pattern develop as well?"

"Surely that's going to be impossible to tell, John? And if lividity *was* only in its first stage today at four o'clock, then now that he's lying on your table any pattern will match *its* surface."

"I've been turning the body frequently to ensure that doesn't happen, but I agree the whole issue of lividity's a mess and very unlikely to help you with where he was actually killed." The medic paused briefly. "There *may* be something deeper to see with black light so I'll check."

Liam was looking thoughtful.

"What if our perp ended the boy four or five days ago like your indicators say, but not at the bank 'cos he'd definitely have been discovered there before now. And what if they used some way to *stop* lividity settling till they brought him to the bank because they wanted to confuse us on timing? If we hadn't found the body till tomorrow like the killer'd probably expected, then full lividity *would've* developed to match the vault floor and mucked up our timings even more. Or at least confused the Docs enough to give the perp extra time to run."

Craig looked admiringly at his deputy. "That's almost brilliant, Liam."

"Almost?"

But his boss had already turned back to the medic.

"*Is* there some way of preventing lividity settling, John?"

The pathologist stared into space for a moment and then gave a decisive nod. "A spit."

Even Liam was revolted and he had a high bar. *"You mean they kebabbed him?!"*

"What? No. How could they possibly have done that without leaving marks? I don't mean a *literal* spit; I mean that if a body was rotated constantly and fast enough then how and where would the fluids and therefore the lividity settle? In theory it could have been evenly spread throughout the body, giving the boy a slight overall colour change that would have been very hard to notice *until* they left him lying in one position, for instance the vault floor. Secondary lividity might then have started to develop, to match *that* surface."

Craig gawped at them. *"Are you serious?"*

"I was, boss, but you can never tell with him."

The pathologist chuckled at being painted as an enigma.

"Liam actually has a point, Marc. I've never seen it done but constant post-mortem rotation *might* explain why the lividity development doesn't match Jack Doe's time of death."

His eyes glinted with curiosity.

"I wonder what they might have rotated him on and where... It would have taken special equipment to suspend him without touching anything. But then again, if he'd been very pale to start with lividity *could* have been evenly distributed and just made him look less so. That wouldn't be immediately noticeable..."

Craig rolled his eyes, knowing that he was about to lose his friend to the world of theory as he'd done so many times before.

"I'll leave you to play out that unlikely situation, John, but meanwhile, back here on planet Earth, what you're saying is that our Jack Doe wasn't killed in the vault."

"Highly unlikely."

"OK, forensics will confirm that, and we," he gestured at his deputy, who was looking inordinately smug about his theory, "need to find the primary murder scene. Two things before we move on. Liam, I don't think we're looking at a lone killer; the boy was too big for one person to carry. John, is there anything more you can say about our victim?"

"Not until his tests come back. I've sent everything I've mentioned plus his stomach contents to Des. He wasn't wearing any jewellery and had no tattoos, so there's nothing helpful there-"

Liam cut in.

"That's almost unusual in itself, with most youngsters

engraving themselves nowadays."

"Strict parents prevented him getting tattooed perhaps?"

"That'll be me in a few years, when I nail Erin's feet to the floor."

Liam's eight-year-old daughter was already showing signs of being a challenge, but rather than listen to his deputy's 'lock your kids up till they're forty' diatribe yet again Craig rose to his feet.

"You said Mike was PM-ing the girl, John?"

"What? Oh. Yes."

The pathologist reluctantly abandoned his rotation theory and a minute later the three men were standing in a dissection room watching Mike Augustus complete his PM notes to a soundtrack of Norah Jones.

"Her voice is very soothing," came by way of explanation as the deputy pathologist signed his last form and ushered them out into the corridor. "I don't like to talk in front of the deceased in case they hear me. Who knows how long their spirit or whatever stays around."

He was pleasantly surprised by the lack of teasing the comment provoked, all of them having seen far too much of death's strangeness to be definitive about *what* happened after the event.

Knowing that the detectives would soon grow impatient John took the lead to elicit the answers they needed, and in a short time they knew that the manner of their second victim's death had been almost identical to the first.

"So you've confirmed the girl's around twenty and it was a left-handed shot this time, again at a perfect ninety degrees into the temporal bone. The bullet lodged where?"

"The opposite temporal lobe."

"That's more laterally than with the boy's, but that's to be expected with the girl's thinner bone and smaller skull size. Easier travel. Again there were no signs of a struggle, she was well-nourished, similar age range, and without a single distinguishing feature that could help give us a name?"

"Yes."

"GSR?"

"Yes, but Des is checking how much and its distribution. He said he'd do it for your victim as well, just to give us an idea whether they actually pulled the triggers themselves or it was smeared on from someone else's hand."

"What about sexual activity?"

"Not a sign, but I've taken swabs."

"Good. Lividity?"

"First stages but very faint. I've taken black light images to see what's developing beneath the surface."

Seeing Liam was about to expound on the kebab theory again Craig cut him off with a shake of his head.

"John has a theory on that, so he can explain it when we've gone. Is gunshot your cause of death, Mike?"

"Too early to say until we've completed all the tests."

At least the medics were consistent.

"Whatever the cause was, how long has she been dead?"

"Everything points to between four and five days, so I can't fathom why there's no lividity."

"An identical timeframe to our other victim." Craig decided to say something that had been on his mind since they'd first seen the boy at the bank. "All things considered, and given there are very few martyrs in the west, there are enough similarities here for me to wonder whether this was a joint execution."

Liam's eyes widened. "Who the hell would do that?"

"To be confirmed." He turned back to the medics. "What do you two think?"

John puffed out his cheeks, perplexed. "Well, I certainly couldn't rule it out from my findings, and headshots are always evocative of punishment. What do you think, Mike?"

"I agree it's a valid theory, but then the question would have to be why."

John gestured to the detectives. "We'll have to leave that with this pair. The urgent thing now is finding our victims' IDs. Des can check the fingerprint database, but unless they've committed a crime..."

Craig nodded.

"We need to start running their photos, boss."

"Sketches will be kinder to the families, Liam. OK, I know it's late but get a police artist down here and call Ash in to set up some searches. Davy's on holiday so he's covering this week."

Ash Rahman was the squad's junior but very brilliant analyst and Davy Walsh was his vacationing boss.

Mike stripped off his gloves, asking a question as he did. "We're agreed that they were murdered then, and not at the bank?"

Craig's nod was emphatic. "With all due deference to

Liam's assisted suicide theory, I am. But as to *why* they were, that will take a bit more time."

Chapter Five

The Fraud and Robbery Unit. 6th Floor of The Coordinated Crime Unit (The C.C.U.). Pilot Street, Belfast.

When Andy Angel exited the lift on the C.C.U.'s sixth floor it was with both trepidation and excitement at the thought of visiting his old stamping ground of ten years before. Every day for the five years that he'd been first a detective sergeant and then an inspector there he had strolled through the squad-room's door at nine o'clock precisely, slung his second or third best suit jacket across his desk, the one first on the left beside the exit, and headed for the kitchen to make himself a coffee in his giant initialled mug; a quid from Pound Empire and it had never even chipped. Then he'd sat down, booted up his computer and read, and read, and read for the rest of the day.

Because that's basically what Fraud investigations had consisted of back then, before the squad had amalgamated with Robbery; endless hours of online searches and research, punctuated by, if you were lucky, a colourful spreadsheet or the occasional telephone call. There had been nothing like the excitement of a murder hunt and the genuinely evil perps that you met along the way, but then he supposed there'd been none of the risks of getting shot at, stabbed or pushed off a roof either.

It occurred slowly, accompanied by a sizable dollop of shock, to the easy-going D.C.I., who to anyone who'd known him pre-Murder Squad would probably have thought him perfectly suited to a peaceful office job, that he actually preferred, *really* preferred his current role on Craig's team to working in Fraud.

Andy supposed, no, to be fair he *knew*, that if Belfast had possessed a dedicated *Art* Fraud section then he would never have gone for D.C.I. rank and left the squad; the prospect of spending endless hours in galleries and auction houses searching for counterfeits and stolen artefacts too aesthetically satisfying for him to reject. But it hadn't and still didn't; the only counterfeits they'd dealt with back in the day had been ripped-off DVDs sold from carrier bags or market stalls and spending his days viewing those had been more boring than watching a sink drain.

All of these thoughts flashed through Andy's mind between the door and the squad-room's reception desk, where he found his first cause to smile. The secretary with her head bent low at her computer was Mary-Jane Murphy, a woman of almost sixty on whom he'd had a monumental crush as a D.I.

"Mary-Jane! I didn't know you were still here!"

Clearly unused to such familiarity the woman lifted her curly head slowly, preparing to give some cheeky scoundrel a meaningful rebuke. Instead she saw her old admirer and grinned, scanning him from head to toe as she did.

"Well, young Inspector Angel, as I live and breathe! You've hardly changed at all!"

"That's kind of you to say, but I've put on at least ten pounds."

"Good. You were so thin you could have blown away on the wind. But why are you here?" Her eyes lit up, clearly pleased at the thought of a returning crush. "Are you coming back to work on the squad?"

The Murder detective was saved from making excuses by Terry Harding walking on to the floor.

"Sorry, Mary-Jane, you can't have the D.C.I.. He's here to meet me."

The secretary looked impressed.

"D.C.I. now is it? Well, good for you. Are you two having a meeting? Because if so you'll have to use your office, D.C.I. Harding. The conference room's been taken by the Audit Group."

"On a Sunday night?"

"You know the auditors. Why else do you think *I'm* here at this ungodly hour?"

A rolling of both women's eyes said just what they thought of the oversight team.

"Fine. My office it is then. There are only the two of us anyway. Could we get some coffee and biscuits, please, Mary-Jane?" She indicated a small office in the corner, exactly where Liam's sat four floors up. "After you."

Andy lowered his voice as they walked. "Mary-Jane doesn't really need to be here, does she?"

"No, but she often comes in to work now her husband's dead. I think it fills the time for her."

His eyes widened in shock and he glanced towards the

secretary now entering the kitchen.

"When?"

"Two years ago. But don't mention it, will you. She still gets upset."

Andy shook his head, saddened by the news. It was easy to forget that other people's lives didn't pause just because *you'd* left them behind.

Two minutes later they were seated at Harding's desk with a tray of refreshments and Harding was playing mum.

"So you lead the Robbery half of the squad, Terry?"

"Yes, and Deidre Murray heads Fraud. The arrangement's only a year old but it's working well so far. Well, apart from a bit of a blip during Dee's divorce. She needed some time off so I had to run both sections, and *that* wasn't fun."

But Andy didn't want to hear about work, he wanted to know more about Murray's divorce, certain that there was someone on his squad who would find the subject riveting.

"She's completely divorced? Not just halfway or anything?"

She looked at him curiously. "Yes, completely. Why, do you fancy her?"

"Not me, but I know a man who did and probably still does."

He saw her gearing up for a gossip and shook his head.

"Let me make sure he's still interested before you say anything to her. I promise I'll keep you up to speed. OK?"

"You're no fun, but OK. Right. Work. What does Murder need from us?"

"Well, basically the chief wants me to dig into the Ferviers' wealth. He's got a real bee in his bonnet about it."

She gave a puzzled frown. "Why? There's a lot of wealth in Northern Ireland and sometimes wealthy people have things nicked."

"Yes, but it's the timing of the Vermeer's theft with our two deaths, and-"

She cut across him, shocked. *"Two?"*

He'd forgotten, and not for the first time, that just because one copper in the force knew something it didn't mean that they *all* did. Sadly their brains weren't connected like The Net. He was just about to speculate about the impact on crime rates if they had been when the sharp clink of a teaspoon against pottery reminded him where he was.

"Two deaths, Andy?"

46

"Yes, sorry. We found a second body in another of the vaults. The boss is at the labs about it now."

"And the deaths are definitely linked?"

Quite apart from the extremely low odds of two people randomly choosing the vaults as suicide sites on the same day, their methods had been identical, but Andy only verbalised the last part of that thought.

"Identical scenes and methods, so with that and the timing of the Fervier theft, especially as they died in the bank where the family keeps a substantial amount of art, the chief's got an itch."

Harding gave a slow nod. "OK... I suppose I can understand that."

"Not to mention that he gets these hunches."

This time her nod was immediate; *everyone* on the force knew of Craig's uncanny instincts for when something was off.

"OK. So how can I help then?"

"I need to get details of everything in the extended Fervier family's art archives, private and public, to see what pieces they currently own. Then I can start looking at their provenance, when they were purchased and from whom, prices paid and so on. I'll be looking into their family history as well. When the first Fervier left France, were they wealthy there, and if so where did it come from and when? All of that. But the main thing is I really need to do all this *without* the Ferviers finding out."

"Because?"

Andy tried and failed to keep a rarely used tone of smugness from his voice.

"Because in Murder we don't tip people off when they're of interest in a case."

Harding didn't tease him about how pleased he sounded because she was shocked again.

"You think Hortense Fervier killed your victims?"

Andy's smugness was replaced by surprise.

"*What?* No. No, not that. Well... not yet anyway. But if we make *her* aware then she might mention it at some family gathering and alert whoever did."

Harding rolled her rounded brown eyes.

"*Now* I'm picturing the Ferviers gathered in the drawing room of some huge country house with Hercule Poirot about to announce whodunit."

The image made them both laugh, especially when Andy substituted Craig for the diminutive Belgian 'Tec'.

"But seriously, the fact that we're checking on the Ferviers *has* to remain between us, Terry."

She reached for a biscuit, tapping it thoughtfully against her mug for a moment before speaking again.

"OK, if that's the case I'll see if I can get hold of a list of their artworks without them catching on. But if I can't, which is very possible with a private family like that, and you *definitely* can't ask for it, then I'd suggest you take a trip to London. The Met's Art and Antiques Squad has more info than we could ever offer, and their database of dodgy artworks and owners covers the whole world, including anything linked to France. If there's anything crooked attached to anyone by the name of Fervier they should know the name. Also, a lot of the main auction houses and galleries are over there so you're more likely to discover when pieces changed hands and for how much, so just thinking about it, it might be worth a trip anyway."

The Murder D.C.I. considered the suggestion for a moment. Craig wouldn't like him being away, but accessing the Ferviers' full inventory without asking them or their lawyers for it seemed unlikely so it might be the only way. Also anyone linked with the Ferviers would likely refuse the information or give only part of it *and* inform Hortense.

"When will you know if you can get the list, Terry?"

Her response was to leave the room, to return a full minute later.

"OK, Mary-Jane's on it now. So she'll give you a yay or nay on the chances before you leave."

Mary-Jane rivalled the Murder Squad's own PA Nicky Morris for efficiency.

"As for the Ferviers' family tree I'm sure you've got analysts who can dig on that for you."

"We have indeed."

Andy was moving to the edge of his chair preparing to leave when he remembered the painting taken earlier that day.

"Any progress on the Vermeer?"

"The gallery's CCTV footage has come through if you fancy a look." The D.C.I. turned to her desk computer and tapped some keys. "I'd be grateful for your thoughts."

Andy moved eagerly to stand behind her and watched as

three video files loaded up.

"OK, so the gallery has three cameras. Each normally holds twenty-four hours of footage, but obviously we removed the tapes early today. The tapes start at eleven last night. Saturday."

Andy raised an eyebrow. "Why eleven? Surely the gallery closed at five or six."

"Five, but apparently Hortense or one of her family always views the day's feed at home around eleven, just before they go to bed. Then they reset the cameras for the next twenty-four hours."

She moved her cursor to the first file and hit enter.

"OK, so the first camera's mounted on the ceiling of the gallery's front window, just above the display wall. It looks out on to the street. The other two give internal views; front of the gallery to its rear and vice versa. The internal cameras sweep regularly, so between them they cover every corner of the interior except the kitchen and bathroom. As the place isn't huge that seems pretty thorough to me."

Andy wasn't as easily impressed.

"Nothing over the back door to the street? And are there any street or traffic cams front or rear?"

"No to the first, which now that you mention it I can't believe the Ferviers *hadn't* set one up. The street and traffic cams I'll check tomorrow with Traffic and Aerial Support when everyone's in."

"Yes, sorry, I keep forgetting it's a Sunday. OK, fire ahead."

Harding clicked on the first file and they watched as a seemingly average dark winter's night on the Lisburn Road unfolded. Just the pavement and road immediately outside the gallery was visible in the fixed camera's field, with the limited scene illuminated only by street lights and the glow from the gallery's window, the rest of the retail strip shuttered and dark until the new week began.

As the detectives watched the tape, fast forwarded hours of dark night were followed by a sleepy early Sunday morning when the only people to pass the window were students doing the shuffle of shame cradling their hungover heads in their hands, the odd, very odd at that time of day, weekend runner, and some elderly people out walking their dogs, none of whom gazed in at the gallery's wares.

The latter half of the tape showed police cars pulling up

outside after the theft had been discovered and officers milling around on the pavement attempting to interview passers-by. The second and third video files, of the gallery's interior, showed no-one inside it at any time but cops.

Terry was the first to speak. "That's impossible! *Someone* must have entered the gallery and nicked that flipping painting."

Andy was astonished too, but not about that.

"Don't you find it odd that no-one even *glanced* in the front window as they passed? When there was such a beautiful painting hanging there. Not even someone elderly passing slowly with their dog?"

The Robbery detective was taken aback. "What? Well... I suppose... yes, now you mention it I do. But they obviously didn't. We both saw the tapes."

Andy wasn't sure *what* they had just seen.

Craig had chosen him to liaise on the art theft because of his visual skills and one of the strongest of those was his ability to recall everything that he saw in minute detail. It was so strong that he'd been dubbed a super-recogniser, a title given to someone who could memorise and recall thousands of faces often having seen them only once, and invited to join a dedicated unit that The Met had set up in twenty-thirteen, although he'd declined. Having the ability essentially meant he noticed things that almost everyone else missed; and he *never* forgot a face.

"Play the first tape again on quarter time, Terry."

They watched as this time dawn broke far more slowly on the wintry Sunday morning and the trail of students shuffled even more lethargically past the gallery's window, expressions of indifference, self-congratulation or boredom now clearly etched on their youthful faces. The elderly passers-by travelled sluggishly, the arthritis limited walk of one pensioner chivvying his small Collie to "Come back here" seeming like a crawl.

As the tape finished Andy shook his head, disgusted but also in some part admiring.

"The clever buggers."

The Robbery D.C.I. twisted to look up at him.

"OK, I'll bite. Who's a clever bugger and why?"

"Your art thief or thieves. They altered the tape, and I bet if we view the other two again they'll have done the same to them."

Harding motioned him to retake his seat before she got a sore neck and sat forward anxiously at her desk.

"Altered how?"

"Well, I'm no expert so you'll need to have Audio-Visual check the details, but I'd say that at some point before sunrise they put the camera on a loop. Watch it again and you'll see that the same students walked past that window three times. The old man with the dog ditto, before and between. Whether your thief did it with magnets or hacked into the cameras I've no idea, but *somehow* they deleted the segment where they nicked the painting and repeated other bits to fill the time. *That's* why no-one even looked fleetingly in the window. Because the Vermeer wasn't there when they passed. Whatever time it was when the first person passed that window, the painting had already gone."

The D.C.I. gawped at him in horror but recovered quickly.

"Yes, but what about the *internal* cameras and alarms? *They* would have picked up anyone inside."

"My guess is your thief did the same thing with those. But play them again on slow so we can check."

When nothing obvious revealed itself Andy shrugged.

"It's hard to see exactly when they did it because there were no people moving about inside to give visual clues, but in theory all your burglar would've had to do was stroll in, nick the painting, and then alter the tape to cut that section out and use repeat footage to fill the gap."

He paused for a moment in thought before going on.

"But that's the thing. There were no signs of forced entry and no alarms were triggered, were they? I'm presuming they would have been rigged to alert a security firm and the local cops?"

"Yes to both, but no alarm went off. We're interviewing the gallery and private security staff tomorrow, but Fervier says they've all worked for her family for years so she really can't see them being involved."

"Poirot wouldn't trust them so check. On the other hand, it's unlikely that someone who could hack cameras would have had a problem with alarms or locks. Was the painting itself alarmed?"

"Yes, there are pressure triggers on the mountings that should've gone off as soon as they lifted it. Clearly they didn't."

Andy shrugged. "Well, see what your analysts have to say

about the tape footage and I'll ask the chief if ours can check it as well."

Just then something occurred to him and he took out his phone.

"Thanks for this, Terry. I need to go but let me know what you find on the interviews and tapes. And could Mary-Jane call me when she's checked that other thing out?"

As she nodded him out Andy made the first of the three calls. One to get an update from Annette on missing persons, so far none; the second to ask Craig whether he'd thought any further about how their victims had accessed the vaults to a non-committal response, and to pass on Terry's suggestion about him possibly visiting The Met. As soon as Craig had given his provisional permission for the trip and Mary-Jane had called to confirm she couldn't access the Ferviers' art list without involving their lawyer, Andy's third call was to book a flight to London for early the next day.

****

Craig *had* actually started thinking about how their victims had entered the bank's secure vaults but had decided to leave that detail until the following day's briefing after Des had interrupted with some information; not only did the absence of even microscopic blood or brain spatter anywhere in the vaults definitely prove that their victims *hadn't* died there, but both had a sufficient quantity of correctly distributed GSR on their hands to confirm they *had* fired the guns that had caused their own deaths.

Whether they'd been forced to do so or not the scientist couldn't yet say but he'd confirmed the positions of the weapons in the vaults weren't where they should have fallen after suicides, even allowing for recoil or bouncing off the walls, meaning that someone else had been present and set them in place.

It gave Craig an outline of their two killings and the foundation of a plan for the next day. Until then he had a family to see, so he waved goodnight to his deputy and left to spend what was left of his Sunday at home.

Chapter Six

The C.C.U. Monday 16th December. 9.10 a.m.

"Right, get it together, everyone. We're about to start."

Energetic though Craig's words sounded, his 'Top Gun briefing' tone conveying dynamism and 'Let's get it done' zing, the man saying them actually looked like he'd been wrung out and left to dry. After a night of his teething son howling at a louder volume than by rights someone only a few feet long should have had the capacity to do, he and Katy had finally fallen asleep at seven a.m. only for his alarm to go off at half-past.

As he downed his third black coffee of the day in a single gulp and gazed pleadingly at the squad's second PA Alice for another, his deputy recognised the symptoms of sleep deprivation, now thankfully long ago memories with his own kids, and attempted sympathy in as quiet a voice as he could.

"Rough night, boss? Colic or teething?"

His kids' screaming sessions had always been down to one of those.

"The second. Is it that obvious?"

"Only 'cos your tan's gone green."

Craig's normally tanned olive skin had turned a shade that manufacturers of expensive paint usually called Sap or Lichen Green, far more attractive colours on a wall than someone's face.

"But my cold's feeling much better, boss, thanks for not asking."

The health debate was cut short by Andy belting into the squad-room ten minutes late.

"Sorry, chief. I was in the archives and lost track of time."

Craig's curiosity was piqued, knowing that only something genuinely fascinating would make someone delve into the force's dustiest files at such an early hour. He made a mental note to ask about it in a moment and kicked off the briefing by writing 'N.I. Bank' and 'Two victims' on the whiteboard before perching on a nearby desk.

"OK, we'll get to Andy's archives in a minute but first I'll give some context for the people who weren't around yesterday. First one then a second body was found in two of the six sealed vaults at N.I. Bank yesterday. Both victims, one male and one female, were between their late teens and early twenties and both had suffered single shots to their temples."

He was careful not to say that the shots had caused their deaths.

It brought a tut of disgust from Nicky.

"For God's sake! People don't know what to be at nowadays, do they?"

The detective acknowledged the comment with a phlegmatic smile.

"It isn't a common scenario, I'll give you that. OK, so the similarities between the two victims and the fact that we're now sure their bodies were moved to the vaults after they were killed, which was probably, according to Doctor Winter, four to five days before they were found, so last Tuesday or Wednesday, point to them having been moved there specifically to stage their deaths as suicides."

Annette raised a finger to interrupt.

"How are we sure they were murdered, sir, rather than that they killed themselves?"

He looked to his deputy to answer because Alice had returned with his drink, and while Liam outlined his assisted suicide theory and then grudgingly explained its low odds Craig drained his cup and then glanced immediately at his PA.

Nicky had anticipated a further drinks request and pre-empted it now by producing a mug as large as a flowerpot from her drawer, filling it from her newly bubbling percolator and then putting it in Craig's hand with such defiance that she might as well have said, "Try draining *that* in one gulp, if you can!"

The detective smiled his gratitude and turned back to the group.

"Anything more from forensics this morning, Liam?"

"Still waiting for all the prints at the scene to be processed for elimination, the Vics' dental X-rays and prints are doing the usual runs, and Des is finishing the ballistics and tox-screens this morning."

"OK, thanks. Right, back to our victims. The female victim was small, but our male victim was very muscular and it's unlikely he would've gone down without a good fight, yet there were no defensive or restraint injuries at all. That means we can't rule out sedation. We'll have more on that by the end of the day. The amounts and distribution of GSR on the victims' hands say they pressed on the triggers themselves, but even if they did it while alive Doctor Winter believes someone held their hands to force them, because as Liam's just outlined there was none of the hesitation or angled bullet entry that we normally see with headshot suicides."

He scanned the group for his junior analyst and found the flamboyant earring wearing, pirate-shirted IT expert at the back of the group, scrolling through his smart-pad.

"Ash, can you help with the print and dental searches? I know you uploaded the artist's sketches last night but keep focused on them, please. We need our victims' names ASAP."

In response the analyst gave a blinding white smile that prompted immediate recoil from Liam.

"Agh! What's happened to your teeth, man?"

"I had them whitened at the weekend. Cool, eh?"

"Only if you want to cause mass blindness!" The D.C.I. covered his eyes dramatically with a hand. "Bring me some sunglasses quick! The pirate's gone mad!"

Craig gave him a warning nudge. Liam had a habit of commenting on other people's appearance and not always positively, and he'd been warned about it before.

"Very nice, I'm sure, Ash. Just run the data, please."

The analyst held up his smart-pad in response.

"Already on it, but nothing yet."

"Fine. So, Doctors Winter and Marsham will have more for us on our victims later-" Craig stopped again as another thought occurred to him. "Annette, you were searching the missing persons' reports. Anything there?"

She shook her head glumly. "None that match, sir, but I only got through to the Belfast stations so I'll cover the others today. They know to call me if any new reports come in, although there are a couple of things on that. People don't normally register adults missing for several days, and Doctor Winter said our victims have only been dead for a max of five. Also, our victims' ages mean they could've been living alone, so they may not have been noticed missing by their families yet. Especially not just before Christmas. Their parents might just think they're off having fun with their friends."

Good points but they had to keep trying. Craig said so then wrote up 'Stolen art' on the board.

"OK, the other thing that happened yesterday is that a valuable painting by Johannes Vermeer was stolen from the

Fervier Art Gallery on the Lisburn Road."

Mary Li the team's constable perked up. "He painted Girl with a Pearl Earring. The one they made the film about."

"He did indeed. OK, so D.C.I. Terry Harding from Robbery, whom some of you know I'm sure, called to inform us that the gallery's owner kept many of her other artworks in the vaults of N.I. Bank. Andy, take that, please."

As the most artistic member of his team reported Craig drained his caffeinated flowerpot and went in search of even more coffee to keep himself awake, this time in the form of an espresso from the new machine in his office that Katy had gifted him a month before. This time instead of gulping he sipped the liquid, feeling his alertness returning to near normal levels as Andy outlined the magnitude of the family's art and valuables collection and range of properties, and then as the D.C.I. dug into the detail of the not always ethical world of art.

"The truth is the serious art world is sometimes more about money than beauty, and the view of an artist's skills can be decided by the zeitgeist. For example, if there's a particular trend at the time or some currently popular celebrity likes their work then the value of their whole portfolio could go up, or if an artist dies they may trend on social media and that can mean their paintings' values get a serious boost-"

Annette interrupted. "Because they'll never paint any new ones so those that exist become rare?"

"That and if they had a particularly gory or scandalous death it can push the weirdo interest factor up. The public are basically ghouls and the art buying public often more so. The other thing about art is that whether a piece is good or bad is purely subjective. What *I* love *you* might hate and so on."

Liam screwed up his face. "So how does anyone tell if an artist's good then?"

"Excellent question. Often it's just because a lot of people *like* their particular art so it's declared good by consensus, or if it fits with the times, so what was popular last century might not trend in this one and so on. But a clever art promoter can enhance the value of complete crap simply by asking their mates in the art world to give it good reviews."

Craig raised an eyebrow. "Sounds crooked."

It earned him a shrug from the D.C.I..

"I'm inclined to agree with you, but others call it good

business. It happens with movies, books, hotels and so on too. Have you never gone to see a movie because a reviewer raved about it, only to leave wondering what all the hype was about? *That's* why you should only ever buy art that you really like and forget trying to predict the market."

He tapped the board. "Except in the case of the Old Masters; that's a European painter of acknowledged skill before eighteen-hundred. They've stood the test of time and historically pretty much everyone agrees on the value of their works, although what they fetch at auction still depends on who's around on the day to buy."

"Right. So tell us about the Ferviers' collection."

The D.C.I. shook his head. "I can't yet, chief, not until I go to London in..." He glanced at the clock, "Two hours time. The Ferviers won't give up a list of what they own without us going through their lawyers, but that might tip them off if they're involved in something dodgy so I've arranged a meeting with The Met's Art and Antiques Squad. I'm hopeful that when I explain what we need they'll give me access to their archives and anything under the name Fervier. Our records are woefully thin."

"That's why you were searching earlier."

"Yes, but there's almost noth-"

A loud Belfast voice cut across him as Aidan Hughes, Craig's third D.C.I., spoke for the first time at the briefing.

"I've some questions, Guv. Were there any breaches in the vault walls? And I know the Ferviers keep stuff there, but why are we so sure that matters? And isn't the painting theft Robbery's job?"

Liam obliged on his first point. "The vaults are single smooth units made with no joints. My bet is they were the first things lowered into the build. No breaches in the walls or floors."

When he looked to Andy to pick up the rest of the questions the arty D.C.I.'s nod back to Craig said that he was leaving them to the boss, but before said boss could react his deputy spoke again.

"It's 'cos the boss has a hunch about the Ferviers, and for once I agree with him. The timing of everything yesterday *was* a bit suspect, *and* the Ferviers' link with the bank."

Craig smirked at the 'for once' but let it pass.

"That's right. The theft of a painting on the same day as we find two dead bodies in the vaults where the rest of the family's collection is held, plus the sheer size of the Ferviers' fortune, which makes me curious as to its origin, means that I want to dig."

"So basically you're just indulging your curiosity, Guv?"

Craig chuckled. "You *could* call it that, but it feels like more. But since you've mentioned the work with Robbery, with Andy heading over to London I'd like you to take that on please. Liaise with Terry Harding on her interviews at the gallery and then head down to the bank. Take Ryan with you."

Ryan Hendron was the squad's quiet but astute sergeant and had joined the team from Strangford after working with them on a case three years before.

"We only got a cursory overview of their security arrangements yesterday, so drill down there, Aidan. Andy, did you get a chance to speak to Mervyn Gambon?"

"No, sorry. I was at the gallery and then with Terry. I've stuff on the cameras to tell you about too."

"OK. In a minute. Aidan, liaise with Mervyn Gambon the bank manager, but remember he's still a suspect, along with the rest of the bank staff, although there's no need to point that out to them while we need their cooperation. Find out who the last person was in each vault before the bodies were found yesterday and at what time. Also, who had the codes and prints to open them, because they weren't broken into, and who keeps the up-to-date inventories? We'll also need the names of any clients who deposited or removed valuables from any vault in the past month. Most important of all, has anything on the inventories altered, either removed or added since they were last checked? Don't forget the security guards, CCTV, any outside firms linked with the bank, any temp staff employed in any role and so on."

"I know the drill, Guv."

Craig was confident that he did. Aidan was a good officer who'd led the Vice Squad for years before moving sideways to join them.

As Craig turned back to his coffee he noticed Mary stretched vertically in her seat like a meerkat. It was as close to raising a hand and shouting, "Me, me, me" as most adults ever got.

"Take Mary along with you too, please, Aidan. There'll be a lot of work so you'll need to split it up."

The order brought a smile from Ryan who had grown

quite fond of the sometimes, well to be fair often, difficult junior officer, and a pleading look from Aidan who hadn't. His pleas were ignored and his boss turned back to the group.

"The Ferviers are, as their name suggests, of French extract, but Hortense Fervier and her family were born and raised here. Can anyone suggest a reason why I might be curious about the family, other than me being nosy or having a hunch? And no, it's not because I'm anti-immigrant, I could hardly be considering I'm half-Italian myself. And it *isn't* because they're wealthy. If I was interested in wealthy people I would read The Ulster Bazaar."

Liam couldn't resist the opening. "You mean you don't, boss? I was *sure* I saw a copy on your desk last week. There you were, prancing around in a tux and drinking champers with the best of them. Baron Craig of Laganbank."

Craig chuckled at the image. "Thanks for that fantasy, Liam, but my social life is much more mundane. So, can anyone guess why I'm interested in the Ferviers?"

Annette had first stab. "Historical interest? Most of the French names in Ireland belong either to the Anglo-Normans who invaded in the twelfth century or Huguenots who fled here to escape religious persecution in France in the seventeenth."

"You're clearly a student of history, Annette, and it *is* possible the Fervier name is a corruption of the Huguenot Le Fevre which is still found down south. But, although we *do* need to find where this group of Ferviers originated that's not the main reason why I'm interested. Anyone else have any ideas?"

When he was greeted with nothing but head shaking and blank looks he allowed himself a small smile.

"OK then, I'm glad to see I'm still capable of the occasional mystery. Let's move on. Andy, you mentioned cameras."

Liam gave an aggrieved howl. "*What?* You mean after all that palaver you're not going to tell us why you're asking about the Ferviers?"

"Nope, not yet. Andy?"

The arty D.C.I. smirked. He thought he might have guessed the reason for Craig's curiosity but he wasn't prepared to say until he was sure. As he carried the thought through his face fell slightly; if his guess *was* correct then their investigation could be about to open a very murky can of historical worms.

He shook himself from the depressing thought and started to report.

"Right, I went to see Terry Harding in Fraud and Robbery. Did anyone else know they'd amalgamated the squads?"

Everyone but Craig and his deputy was surprised.

Annette shook her head. "It must have happened very recently, although when you think about it, it makes sense."

"That's what I thou-"

Aidan cut in suddenly, making Andy smile. He'd been waiting for the penny to drop on him.

"Has Deidre Murray left the squad then? I mean if Terry's the D.C.I. there now."

"No, she's still there. They've got two D.C.I.s now. But there's something interesting on that. I'll text you."

Sensing that Craig was growing impatient he hurried on.

"Anyway, Terry had files from each of the three cameras at the gallery. One camera's at the front of the gallery looking out on to the street and there are two internal ones: front to rear of the gallery and vice versa on a continuous scan, all usually taping for twenty-four hours. The family reviews the feeds every night at home before resetting them, so this footage only ran from eleven p.m. Saturday till the Robbery Squad seized it yesterday."

Craig's caffeine binge might have woken him up but now it was making his head hurt, so he waved the D.C.I. on sharply.

"And?"

"And nothing. Not a single sighting of the thief. The tapes had obviously been altered. I can go into the details if you like, but essentially segments, including the ones where the painting was nicked, were cut out of all three video files and other sections probably repeated and looped in to fill the time. Don't ask me how it was done."

Ash perked up. "I could take a look at them."

Ash was not only a skilled analyst but he was an ethical, or white-hat, hacker, who could get into almost any computer system that had been made. It was a skill they'd utilised on many cases, more often than not on the down-low.

"Excellent. I've already asked Terry if she'd mind and she doesn't, so please do. Their own people will be taking a look too and she's contacting Aerial Support and Traffic today to see if there's anything on the street and traffic cams-"

Craig interrupted the exchange. "Were the gallery locks intact? And the alarms? Any chance someone came in through the ceiling if the upstairs storey doesn't belong to the Ferviers?"

"There wasn't a mark on the locks and the alarms didn't sound, but I didn't think of ceiling entry so I'll give Terry a call on that."

Liam shrugged. "Someone who can mess with cameras and alarms won't have had any trouble with access."

Craig conceded the point with a nod.

Andy carried on. "Anyway, Terry's planning on interviewing the gallery and private security staff today, but apparently Ms Fervier said all of them had worked with her family for years so she really couldn't see them being involved."

Craig considered for a moment, tapping his finger against his chin very deliberately as if ticking items off a mental list before turning back to his analyst.

"Take a very close look at those tapes, Ash. If the killers accessed the gallery so easily and the thief there *is* linked to the bodies in the vaults, it might give us a clue as to how they broke into the bank as well. And yes I did say killer plural everyone. I think the likelihood of this being one person has dropped to nil. OK, good work, Andy. Anything else useful? Anyone?"

When no-one offered anything new Craig did a final, perfunctory scan of his team and rose, his mind already on the next thing he needed to do.

"You all know what you're doing so get on with it."

Just as he turned towards his office Annette had a last minute thought.

"Are you thinking that the main motivation here is greed, sir? That our killers are just thieves with some hacking ability?"

Craig kept walking as he responded, "I really wish that *was* all I thought about them, Annette."

****

N.I. Bank Reception Hall. 10.30 a.m.

Aidan wasn't certain at first how to deploy his small troop, but he knew that he needed Mary far enough away from him that he couldn't hear her. It wasn't the constable's voice that he objected to; in fact it was very pleasant: high, light and with more than a smidgeon of a southern Irish lilt, the complete opposite to his own hard Belfast growl. No, it was Mary's *words* that were almost always the problem, although the sarcastic rolling of her eyes and arm crossing that often accompanied them gave him a pain in the ass as well. *Why* she was always so cynical and difficult he couldn't fathom, and to be honest he wasn't interested in finding out; he had enough problems of his own without psychoanalysing the junior staff.

As for Ryan, well he enjoyed the sergeant's company so much they'd actually been out for pints together after work; in fact Ryan's other half had set him up on dates with a couple of her friends, although on both occasions they'd mutually agreed to leave things after the first date. Finding someone that you connected with seemed nearly impossible as you got older, although strangely not so much for everyone but him. He thought wistfully of Craig's recent marriage and Andy's relationship with Rebecca Wickes, a detective constable, which although it was no longer an engagement was still a good friendship. Whatever label their relationships carried, all he knew was that everyone seemed to have someone to spend their down time with but him.

His thoughts turned back to Ryan. The sergeant had one major flaw in his book; he seemed incomprehensibly fond of Mary and often took her side in arguments, so much as Aidan liked him, for the sake of his sanity he needed to lose *both* detectives for a little while.

"OK. You pair divvy up the security guard and staff interviews while I speak to the manager. You know what to ask and I'm told you can use the offices up on the first floor."

Far enough away to ensure he couldn't even *sense* Mary's sarcasm.

Without further ado the D.C.I. turned his attention to Mervyn Gambon, who today was wearing the standard professional man's uniform of suit and tie, a particularly expensive silk one if Aidan wasn't mistaken, which reinforced his belief that bankers got paid far more than they were worth.

"Do you have an office, Mister Gambon?"

In response the shorter man strode off across the bank's

marbled reception, his progress followed by the timorous gazes of several tellers hiding behind their Perspex windows and a security guard by the front door, whose planted stance and set jaw suggested that he was prepared to shoot *anyone* who made a false move with the Taser at his waist, a weapon that Aidan wasn't sure he was actually allowed to carry and made a mental note to check.

As pensioners who'd accessed their hard-earned savings and students living on loans stared unhappily at the printed slips in their hands that said they needed to eke out their funds in thriftier ways, Aidan followed Mervyn Gambon into his surprisingly sterile looking office and took a seat at the desk. He was just about to outline what he needed when the manager spoke first.

"*I'm shocked, Chief Inspector!*"

Whether it was a comment on his mental wellbeing or one of disapproval the D.C.I. waited with zero interest to find out.

"I can't *believe* that this has happened in *my* bank."

Gambon's irate tone annoyed Aidan but he tried to ignore the outburst. It was a challenge; the D.C.I. had no time for other people's petulance at the best of times but given his current relationship vacuum that best of times *definitely* wasn't today.

"Have there been break-ins before, Mister Gambon?"

Realising that his emotional needs were going to go unmet Gambon made do with a huffy sigh before he answered.

"Never. Well, not since the *big* one."

Oh, *that*.

It was pretty hard to forget the robbery a decade before that had relieved the bank's Royal Avenue branch of so much cash that it had been forced to shut its doors for a week, especially as no-one had ever been arrested for it and rumour had it the cash now lay in a pension fund for some of Northern Ireland's 'dark and dangerous men'.

"But apart from that one time, no?"

"No. Never in my twenty years working here, and not at any of our other branches."

"How many branches does the bank have?"

It took a moment's mental arithmetic before an answer came back.

"In Northern Ireland there are twenty high street

branches, the corporate offices and here. This is our headquarters."

The words implied the bank functioned outside Northern Ireland as well so Aidan asked.

"You're elsewhere too?"

"Yes. In the Irish Republic since two thousand and ten. And we have a small merchant banking branch in London. But Northern Ireland is where our heart is."

The manager looked so reverently at a plaque on the wall behind him that proclaimed 'N.I. Bank' in large font that Aidan half-expected a choir to sing. In its absence he carried on.

"How many of your branches have vaults for valuables?"

"None. We hold the only vaults."

"Three of them."

He was surprised when the manager shook his head.

"Six."

He'd completely forgotten Craig had mentioned that.

"We have two sub-basements where…"

The manager's sentence tailed off but they both knew he'd been about to say, "The bodies were found."

Aidan nodded briskly. "I'll need to see all the vaults, but first I have a number of questions. Who was the last person in each of the vaults before the bodies were found?"

The answer came snapping back. *"Me!"*

It was as close as Aidan imagined the slightly pompous manager ever got to being really angry; bad form at the golf club 'don't you know', but he knew that it came from fear and guilt. Fear that Gambon might somehow have missed the two dead bodies when he'd last checked the vaults, and guilt about how someone could have broken into *his* branch, and worse, or at least he *hoped* that Gambon considered it worse, might have murdered people there.

Perhaps there was a 'why?' and a 'what if?' in there somewhere too. Why here? Why now? And what if there was something he could have done to prevent it happening?

After a few seconds Gambon repeated the word more quietly.

"Me. It's always the manager of the day who checks the vaults before they leave, and I was that person on Friday. Our bank doesn't open at weekends so the only people here then are the guards."

"No cleaning staff?"

The manager shook his balding head. "No, not at the weekends. Not since the robbery. They come in at seven on Monday mornings to clean instead."

"Are *any* of your branches open at weekends?"

"No, we haven't adopted that practice..."

His tone implied that weekend opening was the Devil's work. 'Banker's hours' clearly wasn't just a pejorative trope.

"... but the branches do remain open until nine o'clock each night except Friday."

It was something Aidan supposed.

"All right, so the bank closed here at what time on Friday?"

"Five o'clock. I checked all six vaults with Miriam Bamford my under-manager just before then, and I can tell you that there were *definitely* no bodies in there."

"Does it require a code to seal each vault?"

"No, but it does to open them. A complex alphanumeric code plus a voice and thumb print from an authorised person is inputted and then they spring open. But to close the doors they have to be pulled shut, the rotating wheel turned and the lever handle pushed into place. The wheel's very heavy and takes two people to turn it, if that's of interest."

The D.C.I. nodded. Two people fitted with Craig's plural killer theory.

"OK, I'll return to the codes in a moment, but first I'd like to ask about the contents of the vaults."

Gambon's slightly downturned eyes widened. "I can't tell you *that*! Customers who store their possessions here are assured of confidentiality!"

The D.C.I. gave him a wry look. "That wasn't what I was asking, but I can assure you that confidentiality will get *very* short shrift if it impedes our murder investigation."

To a defiant look from the official he continued with his intended question.

"Now, do you always keep items in the same vault? I mean do you ever move them between vaults?"

The manager looked relieved to be back on safer ground. "No. When an item is lodged with the bank it's allocated a vault in order of the space available and it remains in that same vault until the owner retrieves it."

The detective threw him a bone of approval. "Good. Do owners ever ask to inspect their possessions *without* removing them?"

"Yes, but rarely and they're always supervised while they do."

Good idea, otherwise someone else's family jewels might end up leaving in their pockets.

"I'm assuming you keep a running inventory of each vault's contents?"

"Absolutely. It's held on our main computer database but it's also checked and signed off manually by my under-manager every morning, and by me every evening before we close."

"What time in the morning?"

The manager glanced at his watch. "Eleven. So, very soon in fact. Miriam will be starting her checks so she'll need me there."

"Why? I thought *she* did the morning checks."

"Yes, but I still have to open the vaults with my prints and help her to close the doors afterwards. Her check normally takes from eleven to one and mine from seven to nine in the evenings, except for Fridays when it's from three to five. Sometimes those periods extend when we're in a high content period, or if I'm called away to deal with something pressing."

"So Ms Bamford will know who deposited or removed their valuables at all times?"

"Yes, she'll have the computer inventory. But as I said before that's confidential."

To underline the point he tapped his desk three times. It was irritating but Aidan left his retort for another time. For now he was more interested in what the inventories might reveal.

"So, as of yet you have no idea if the contents of *any* of your six vaults has altered since last Friday, *including* the two that our victims were left in? Items could have been taken or left there during the crimes and you wouldn't know."

The question caught the manager off-guard, and as he realised its possible import he blanched.

"*Oh my Lord!* I was going to check the inventories yesterday, but what with your colleagues everywhere and people measuring and dusting for fingerprints and, and..."

Aidan watched him spiral for a moment, feeling smug because he was so irritating, then he realised that Gambon would be no good to him if he lost it completely and decided to rescue him, but not without adding a small barb.

"I understand. There were a lot of police around

yesterday and inventorying people's secret valuables in front of *them*, well..."

His message was clear; for 'secret valuables' read 'contraband and the proceeds of crime'.

The manager blanched even further and rushed to defend his employers.

"N.I. Bank would never-"

Aidan, who was tiring of his nice cop role, cut across the words.

"You mean to tell me you check the provenance of every single item that's deposited here?"

"Well, no. I mean how could we poss-?"

"But the bank *does* get customers to sign money laundering forms and declarations that the possessions are legally theirs of course?"

The astonishing size to which Gambon's pupils dilated said that either the bank didn't or he didn't know; Aidan had hit his mark and he was damn sure the manager *would* be checking, the moment they'd all left.

"We'll expect to see those declarations soon, Mister Gambon, so you have a few days to gather them. Now, take me back to the opening mechanisms on the vaults. My colleague says that there are no joins in the walls. Is that right?"

The manager was scribbling furiously on a piece of paper that Aidan knew would be flung at his PA as soon as he was gone so it took him a moment to respond. When Gambon did so it was briskly, impressing the D.C.I. with his recovery.

"Yes. Each vault is made of three foot thick steel and formed as one seamless unit, so there are no joints or weaknesses in their walls. They were set into the foundations inside specially created concrete rooms which are separated from the outside world by at least two other walls."

No tunnelled entries for this bank.

"OK. Now, please explain *exactly* how you access them, and is the method the same for all six?"

"Yes, it's identical. Thumbprint and voiceprint verification and a new randomly generated code entered into the keypad each time."

"Whose thumb and voice?"

"Mine."

Interesting. And potentially incriminating in their murders.

"And if you're away?"

"The prints are altered to my covering officer's, who is James Prince from our corporate office."

"And *have* you been away or on holiday recently?"

The implication made Gambon want to throw up. When he eventually responded it was prefaced by a dismayed sigh at his honesty being impugned.

"No. The last time I was away was in October. I've been here every day since then."

Unmoved by his hurt feelings Aidan removed his notebook ostentatiously from his jacket pocket and scribbled down a note of his own, which in fact said 'buy olive oil on the way home' but the manager didn't need to know that.

When he looked at Gambon again it was solemnly.

"So only *your* voice and thumb print could have opened the vaults this weekend?"

"Along with the correct code. Yes."

"And the voiceprint is analysed *how*?"

"I have to recite a particular phrase."

"Always the same phrase?"

"Yes."

Even as Gambon said yes he realised that had been a security risk, but it was too late to mitigate now.

"Which is? I presume it will be changed now anyway."

"We've already done so. The phrase has to be something that couldn't be said accidentally in conversation so we chose a line of James Joyce's from Ulysses; 'That one about the cracked looking glass of a servant being the symbol of Irish art is deuced good'."

Not something you heard said every day right enough, so how had it been copied?

In truth Aidan knew there were a million ways in which someone's voice and thumb prints could be copied and that even such an obscure phrase could be cobbled together by arranging randomly recorded words, so he was far less convinced that the man in front of him was a murderer than Mervyn Gambon appeared to be that he was about to be accused of being one.

But it served the D.C.I.'s purpose to keep the manager on edge a little longer and the vaults' codes turned out to be a more interesting topic.

"Tell me more about these codes. You said they were alphanumeric."

"Alphanumeric plus symbols to be precise."

"Who chooses the code?"

"It isn't chosen, it's generated using a random code generator."

Aidan had seen the devices being used by people logging on to secure government laptops and had always thought they were a faff. With those versions the generated code had only lasted for seconds before it had expired meaning it had had to be inputted quickly, usually while the frantic user was turning red in the face. Did the same apply at the bank?

"How long is each code valid for?"

"Each can be used for fifteen minutes before it expires. If the vault hasn't been opened by then you need a new one."

"Could different codes have been used to open the six vaults?"

Gambon seemed surprised by the question.

"Well...yes, in theory. I always use a single code to open all six for Miriam, but I suppose..."

The point was moot. If their killers had got hold of a code generator they could have produced any number of codes they'd liked.

Gambon produced a palm-sized device from his pocket. "This is my generator. I'll use it to produce a code before Miriam carries out the inventories this morning. After my voice and thumb prints I'll enter the code via each vault's keypad to open its door and then leave her to her work. She'll call me again when all six have been checked and we'll lock up. When I check the inventory again tonight I'll generate another new code."

Aidan rolled his eyes. It seemed like a real chore. But then if the valuables were worth a lot of dosh...

"OK, so Miriam never generates the code?"

Gambon unconsciously tightened his grip on the small pad. "Goodness me, no."

"Just you or your covering manager James Prince."

"Yes. Or a Board member. They hold generators as well."

The detective's ears pricked up. "You didn't mention Board members before! You said you did it! Tell me how that works."

The manager gave him an ill-advised pitying look.

"Of course all Board members can access the vaults; they're trustees of the bank."

His implied, "You silly man" remained mercifully unsaid.

"But that only ever happens in emergencies, for instance if I accidentally got locked in a vault. In the highly unlikely situation that I didn't have my generator on me and no covering officer had been designated for that day to release the lock, I wouldn't be able to open it from inside. As air is slowly withdrawn from the vaults in the thirty minutes after the doors close, to preserve valuables that are best kept in a vacuum such as paintings and parchments, I would die. Obviously the bank couldn't have its employees dying so we decided to use the Board members as back-up just in case. It was an added precaution decided on five years ago."

And a bloody big addition to their suspect pool.

Aidan's mood took a nosedive and it showed. *"How many Board members?"*

He'd been very tempted to add "sodding" before Board.

"Seven including the Chair."

"And they can *all* do this at any time?"

"Yes. I believe they tried a Rota originally but that just confused everyone. These are powerful people whose commitments change frequently. Any one of them could be called halfway across the world at -"

The D.C.I. cut him off.

"I get it. No Rota for the bigwigs. So, if needed, *any* of those seven members could come down here and do the business?"

"Well, they wouldn't need to actually *come* here. We already have their thumb and voice prints stored." Suddenly Gambon palmed his forehead. "Oh, how stupid of me! I completely forgot to ask them to record the new phrase."

Aidan was still on the practicalities of entering the vaults.

"Thumb and voice prints stored *where*?"

"What? Oh well, in our main computer of course. All Board members' thumb and voice prints are filed as e-signatures and they all have code generators at home."

The D.C.I. asked another question.

"But someone at *this* end would still have to input any generated code manually, wouldn't they?"

"No. There's a remote entry facility on the keypads, so a Board member could unlock the vault remotely using a code they'd generated and their stored thumb and voice prints and the trapped person could then walk out."

Aidan rolled his eyes, and not covertly. The bank had basically handed any halfway decent hacker the key to their vaults!

"All of which means that your computer can be hacked to access the e-signatures, so all it would take for a thief to break into your vaults is a code generator!"

And technology was supposed to make things safer too.

As Gambon's jaw dropped in horror the D.C.I. was tempted to press the point home and make him feel even worse, but there was no benefit to the case in beating the man up and that had to be the focus right now.

So how had their killer got near a code generator? The Board members needed to be contacted to check they all still had theirs.

A noisy howl from the manager shook Aidan from his thoughts. It was clear the administrator hadn't considered anything like this so they needed to move on quickly before he became unhinged.

"Focus please, Mister Gambon. You mentioned that when the lock is released the vault door springs open?"

The manager made an attempt to concentrate, wrenching his silk tie loose and opening his top button to cool himself down as he did.

"Yes, yes."

"But if no-one but the trapped person is present how can a Board member be *contacted* to release them? A mobile wouldn't work inside the vault."

"There's a land-line on the wall of each and a list of members contacts."

It answered something the D.C.I. had been wondering about since the briefing; why bother shooting their victims when the killer could just have left them to suffocate in the vaults? But it was clear now that if they'd been left alive they would have called someone to be released.

But even if they were dealing with a hacker talented enough to access a Board member's e-signature on the computer they would *still* have needed a code generator to open the doors and dump their Vics. There was no way around it; he needed to research every Board member to rule them out.

"Right, Mister Gambon, just one last question. Is there CCTV *inside* the vaults?"

He was relieved when the manager nodded, although not for long.

"Inside all six vaults and outside them on both sub-basements as well. But we've already checked and it's been wiped."

"It being?"

"Our main computer. That's where all the CCTV feeds stream to, twenty-four hours a day. I checked it yesterday, it was almost the first thing I did when I arrived here, and the feeds showed nothing but static. The bank's IT team has confirmed it today."

Damn.

"Do you mind if *our* analyst takes a look?"

"Not at all, but they'll have to come here to do so. The bank won't let anything go off-site."

Extra work for Ash. What a time for Davy to go on hols. Although, it *was* to Iceland with his fiancée, and pre-Christmas that was allegedly *the* romantic place to be.

But if much more computing stuff accumulated Craig would have to get the analyst some support. Aidan's eyes lit up as something occurred to him; *Mary* could help Ash out! She had a computing degree and obliged sometimes with basic IT work like database searches to leave Davy and Ash free for the more complex tasks. That's if obliged was a word that could *ever* be used where the D.C. was concerned.

But obliging or not helping Ash now would keep her out of *his* way.

He rose to his feet. "Right, I'll need the names and addresses of your seven Board members and Mister Prince your usual cover officer, and I realise your computers have been tampered with but I'll still need you to try to identify which one of those people has generated a vault code since Friday. I'm presuming you deny doing it yourself."

The manager shook his head hastily. "No. I mean, yes, I do. Didn't."

On a wry look from the detective he abandoned his verbal Gordian knot and moved on.

"But none of those people generated a code either or they would have notified me. They always do. It's the routine when any vault is officially opened, even if it's just to show potential investors how secure the bank is at a weekend."

"And that happens often?"

"Well, no. Perhaps once every six months when a trustee encounters a potential investor socially and wants to persuade them to deposit here. It's part of the Board's ambassadorial role to recruit new account holders, but only people who could benefit the bank in a major way. But that didn't happen this weekend or I would have been notified. I'm certain."

There was absolutely *nothing* certain about the case but Aidan let it pass.

"Well, *someone* opened the vaults so they got a code generator from somewhere. Get me those names and addresses right away, please. And if you even attempt to call any of the people on it to tip them off I'll consider it obstruction and you'll be under arrest."

He was handed the printed list a minute later by a now shocked into silence Gambon.

"Good. Now, take me to the vaults please and you can start your inventory. I'll need to check in with my two officers on the way past."

It was a very short chat. Get Ash down here ASAP, and everyone and anyone who could have had access to the bank since Friday needs to be checked out.

****

The Labs.

That morning's lab visit began with a quick dip of Craig's toes into John Winter's office followed by an immediate U-turn as the pathologist waved him and Liam towards the lift and a trip to forensics three floors up, with only, "That's where it's all happening" by way of explanation.

Craig usually objected to visiting Des Marsham because of the scientist's lack of decent coffee, his only version of which lay in freeze-dried clumps at the bottom of a jar with a worn gold label that harkened back to some cult TV adverts Craig recalled from his youth and looked just as old. The ads had boasted subtly of the drink's near-hypnotic seductive power, most notably and oddly over two attractive next door neighbours, and if he hadn't already been addicted to caffeine by then he would definitely have been sold.

But today the detective *didn't* object to visiting the forensics department because he'd had a substantial jolt of his drug of choice before he'd left the squad-room and even *he* had a limit to how much coffee he could ingest before he started to shake, so they entered Marsham's cramped, glass-walled office, which became even more cramped when Des summoned in his lead CSI.

"Grace has been doing your bodywork."

Even for Liam that was too much of an open goal so he let it pass. The dark-eyed CSI knew that had partly been for her sake so she gave him a demure smile as she tapped her smart-pad to bring up what they needed to know.

"Well now..." it was said solemnly, like the introduction to a sermon, "...your two victims may have died in an identical manner as you know, each from a single gunshot to the temple. The bullets' ballistics match their respective guns, and trajectory work plus the weapons' positions on the floors suggests that both guns were set in place."

Craig raised a hand to halt her. "They didn't fall there? So no recoil or bounce back?"

"No. And there were no prints but the victims on them."

"Are the guns known to you? Or us?"

"Unfortunately not. They're very old and the serial numbers have been filed down. I'll keep searching the databases of course but there's nothing so far. The weapons themselves are unusual so I'll research them further as well."

The detective nodded in resignation. It had been too much to hope there would be an obvious lead to their killers.

"There was also GSR on each victim's hand, the male's right and the female's left, in an amount and pattern that matches that expected from firing a single shot-"

Des interrupted his junior eagerly. "They know all that. Quick, tell them the rest, Grace."

Her stare at him over her glasses was a clear, 'Patience is a virtue' rebuke and she carried on at her own methodical pace.

"Our findings concur with Doctor Winter's belief that the victims were killed elsewhere between four to five days before, moved and staged."

Liam turned to John. "You got anything more on the lividity, Doc?"

"Nothing. Even with black light I could only find that developing patch on the male, and we know that doesn't give us a true timeframe for when they were left in the vaults, even *if* we assume both victims were left there together."

Craig's eyes widened in alarm. It hadn't even occurred to him that the victims might have been left in the bank at different times. He frowned; he really *was* slipping. Liam saw his concern and made up his mind to say something that had been on his mind since the day before once they were back in the car.

"The lividity suggests the bodies were left there around two o'clock, which is impossible-"

Craig cut in, determined to show *some* dynamism. "Because the security guard called us before then. The best we can say is that the bodies were left at the bank sometime between Friday five p.m. and Sunday noon."

Not a helpful timeline for solving a crime.

The pathologist returned to the point he'd been about to make. "Well, perhaps, although the lividity-" Seeing Craig's pleading look he moved quickly on. "So what Grace is referring to-?"

It was the CSI's turn to interrupt, with a staccato, *"Ah, ah, ah"* that told them *all* where to get off.

She took back the floor with a jibe.

"I'll continue *my* report, shall I?"

John had the good grace to blush.

"As I was saying. The scenes were staged, and although it's still possible the method of death was shooting-"

Craig took his life in his hands by interrupting anew, "Just possible? Nothing definite yet?" adding insult to injury by turning back to John on the second question, although in his defence he *was* a pathologist.

"Nope. I mentioned the possibility they might have been dead *before* they were shot, but I'm having a hard time confirming because the bullets made such a mess of the brains. Judging by Grace's expression that *could* have been what she was just about to say."

But Craig wasn't letting go until he had more detail. "Explain."

"I found *some* blood along both internal bullet pathways, which could mean their hearts hadn't quite stopped before they were shot."

Craig nodded briskly. "OK, that's clearer."

"Speak for yourself, boss."

"He's saying they might already have been ebbing away when they were shot."

Craig motioned the CSI to pick up her report, which she did with a ladylike sniff.

"As I was saying before I was so *rudely* interrupted, for all the reasons already outlined the person who shot both victims most probably wrapped their hand around theirs and forced the triggers down. The *reason* the victims were passive enough to allow that was because they were probably unconscious and *may* actually already have been dying from drugs. I found an opiod called Carfentanil in both their blood tests."

Liam's sandy eyebrows rose. "Like Fentanyl that's used after surgery?"

"A version of it certainly, but-"

The D.C.I. turned to his boss.

"Fentanyl's heavy duty stuff, boss, and it's on our streets. Killed fifty here last year. But it's not that common so we might have something here to follow up with the dealers."

Craig nodded. "Perhaps. Thankfully most of our addicts still seem to prefer heroin and coke, but speak to the Drugs team about it, Liam. We might be lucky." He turned back to the CSI. "Sorry, Grace, I know we keep interrupting. Do carry on, please."

Her disapproval faded in the face of his politeness.

"If D.C.I. Cullen had allowed me to finish I would have told you not to waste your time looking for Fentanyl. *Carfentanil* is what you need to find. Where Fentanyl is fifty times as potent as heroin Carfentanil is one thousand times as potent. It could easily have killed your victims."

Liam gave a whistle. "Not many repeat users with that stuff, and dealers killing their customers is bad for business."

"Which means it won't be sold on the street unless it's well cut down. Ask Drugs about imports and hospital thefts as well as street buys, Liam. How was it ingested? Grace? John?"

The CSI got in first. "It must have been administered orally because Doctor Winter didn't find any injection sites, but it wasn't present in either victim's stomach contents, only in their blood."

That was John's cue again. "So they must have been given a dose calculated to kill them so slowly that their stomachs had emptied of the drug before they died. Then they were shot just before or just after the drugs killed them, on balance I'd say before, and kept somewhere after death, somewhere where they were turned sufficiently often to prevent lividity settling until they were taken to the bank."

Craig thought for a moment. "Would they have felt the shots?"

"Nothing. Carfentanil's a powerful analgesic."

"So how long are we talking between being killed and dumped at the bank?"

"Death occurred on Tuesday or Wednesday for both, so that depends on whether they were left at the bank on Friday or Sunday. The other unknowns *are* how long they were held after their abductions before they were drugged, and how did the killers prevent lividity settling after death. But surely Tuesday or Wednesday would have put them out of circulation long enough for a missing persons report to have been taken seriously if one had been made?"

"And if it wasn't made then why not, boss?"

"Annette's point that they might not have been living at home is valid, and could mean they were working or students. My flat-mates used to disappear for days and I didn't worry. But that's all useful information, John, thanks."

It was, and yet it wasn't as far as ID-ing their Vics was concerned. All they could hope was that Ash or Annette got a hit. Craig made up his mind to call his inspector as soon as they'd finished and turned back to the CSI.

"Is there anything more, Grace?"

Her pursed lips said yes.

"If you all have the time to listen."

Des shot her a look that made her blush and hurry on.

"*I* may have an answer to the lack of lividity."

She was thrilled when all eyes widened.

"Doctor Winter, you've been working on a theory that the bodies were rotated continuously to prevent blood settling and lividity developing." She allowed herself a sceptical sniff before going on. "Well, quite apart from honestly being unable to picture what sort of machine could do that, there's a much simpler method which you would know about if you read the archives of Forensic Science CE."

Her chastisement was mainly aimed at Des but Liam's curiosity was piqued.

"What's CE?"

"Cutting Edge. It's has some really interesting information."

"Like what?"

Des broke up the exchange, stung by his junior knowing more than him. "How far back are we talking, Grace?"

"Nineteen seventy-three."

Who had the time or dedication? Her clearly.

"There was a report of a case in Canada where a woman

went skating on a frozen pond, had a heart attack and died. She collapsed on to the ice and ten minutes later a massive blizzard started and the snowfall covered her body so well that it lay hidden for a week. When she was found she showed no lividity at all because her blood and fluids had frozen in place almost instantly and so *couldn't* track down to her lowest point and produce the usual lividity pigmentation."

John's mouth had been hanging open since 'blizzard'. Now he gave an impressed nod.

"Very clever. Our victims were flash frozen to prevent lividity. But they must have been thawed out before they were taken to the bank, Grace, or we would have found at least some water on the vault floor."

"I agree. They were probably defrosted rapidly a few hours before they were moved. Of course we'll need to check the cell histology to confirm everything."

Liam's eyes popped like a startled cat's. He'd seen plenty of bizarre kills over the years but this one was completely new.

"You're saying they were chucked in a *freezer* after they died? Then defrosted, moved to the bank and staged?" He assimilated the mental image quickly and nodded. "Aye, well, I suppose a couple of chest freezers *could* have been used. We've seen that before, boss."

The scientists shook their heads simultaneously and Des outlined why.

"Normal household freezers would take too long, Liam, even at their top setting. The bodies needed to be frozen almost instantly and that takes special equipment."

"Such as?"

"Can't say off the top of my head but we'll check. Probably something used in the food industry."

Craig nodded admiringly. "Brilliant catch, Grace. Thank you. OK, this tells us two things; that our killer wanted us to believe the victims died more recently than they did, and that they wanted or perhaps were even compelled to stage things in the perfect setting. I'd say the first part was because they needed the extra time for some reason, and the second suggests the bank holds real symbolism for them."

Liam shook his head. "The vaults hold it, boss. They could've left the bodies in reception if they'd just wanted to draw attention to the bank."

"You're right, Liam. This is all about the vaults, or perhaps what's *kept* in them." He turned back to the CSI. "Is there anything more, Grace? Last meal, anything?"

"Sorry, their stomachs were empty."

"Ah yes, you said that earlier."

"And just while I remember, the test for steroids came back earlier than expected. It was negative. No signs of recreational drug use either."

"OK, good. Des, do you have any points to make?"

"Yes. Why shoot them? They could easily have killed them with the drugs, so why bother to go to all that effort? They *must* have known that we'd work out that everything was staged eventually."

John interjected thoughtfully. "The staging itself means something. It's almost as if they were recreating some event or tableau they'd seen."

Craig had been thinking the same but he wanted more input so he threw the forensic scientist's question back to the group.

"Sadists", "They're playing us" and, "They've watched too many movies" came back. But it was Liam who made the most important point.

"Didn't you say this felt like a joint execution, boss?"

"Go on."

The D.C.I. warmed to his audience, rearranging himself on his stool before he spoke again.

"So OK, there are passive ways to kill people and active ones."

"Methodology one-oh-one."

Des added a sceptical note. "Just choosing to kill in the first place sounds pretty active to me."

"Ach, now, that's not what I meant and you know it. We're talking about method not decision here, and if there are a hundred ways to kill then the method that the killer chooses tells us something in itself. Anyway, active ones are typically chosen by men and include stabbing, punching, strangulation, shooting and so on, but *not* a shooting like this."

He looked to his boss to pick it up.

"Liam's right in that most shootings are in the heat of the moment, shots in the chest, in the back and so on, but this method *was* very particular. A single shot to the head, almost like a military officer in olden days would have ended his life, or a prisoner might've been shot."

"Wouldn't they normally have been shot in the front by firing squad?"

"Or with a single bullet to the back of the neck?"

"Yes, but then our victims' faces would have been mutilated and perhaps our killer wanted us to know who they were. A firing squad's too much here."

"Honourable too, boss, don't forget that. Death by firing squad was considered a respectable way to die for officers and heroes."

Craig nodded at the implication and motioned his deputy on.

"Anyway, my original point stands. This way of killing our Vics means something."

Des summed up. "OK, so the killer didn't destroy their faces, meaning the victims' IDs could be important, they were executed which may be important, but not honourably, like by a firing squad, which may *also* be important, in the bank vaults which may have relevance, and they wanted to throw us off the timeline which could matter as well. Good luck sorting through that lot, you two."

Grace interjected. "Don't forget the guns might also be pointers."

"How?"

"Not only are they very old but I've never seen the models before."

John summarised. "And *why* were the victims killed is the question that ties everything together."

Craig slid off his stool and made for the door. "And when we can answer *that* one, we'll find our killers' names."

****

When Craig phoned Annette from the car there was no joy on missing persons, even though the D.I. had checked every police station but Newry's now. She was fast losing hope of a hit; if their young victims *had* had families and friends they either didn't yet know that they were missing or they didn't give a toss.

At Craig's request Annette transferred him to the team's analyst, trying to avert her gaze from where Ash had inserted a finger through his hoop earring and was bouncing it up and down nauseatingly on his lobe.

"Yo, yo, yo, chief, what can I do for you?"

The greeting made Craig smile and wonder if *all* of the youth slang in Western Europe had originated in the United States.

"Yo, yourself. What do you have for me on the gallery footage?"

"It was sliced, looped and spliced, that's what. SLS. Which means that a hacker got into all three camera streams, sliced out fifty-one minutes and then spliced in a repeat loop of later footage to fill the gap. I'm guessing fifty-one was the time that it took the burglars to enter, nick the painting and skedaddle."

"Exact timings?"

"Three-ten to four-oh-one on Sunday morning. Pure darkness outside, I checked. Sunrise wasn't till eight-forty."

Craig drew a hand down his face in thought before speaking again.

"OK, Robbery will uncover their routes in and out and find whatever prints the thief left on the cameras, although I doubt there'll be any, but sticking with the CCTV, I have a few questions. Is there any chance you can retrieve the missing footage?"

"Sorry chief, but no. They didn't just wipe it, they excised it. Whoever did this was no dork."

His tone said to be a dork was practically the worst thing in the world.

"OK, second. Was it done on site or remotely?"

There was a slight pause before the analyst came back.

"I'd say remotely. That way they could do all three streams without rushing." He grew increasingly confident. "Yeh. They *definitely* did it remotely because it was done hours after the event. Had to be, to have the later footage to splice in."

So much for finding prints on the cameras.

"Did the hacker leave an electronic trail?"

He felt the analyst's smile before he heard it.

"Hey, you're not bad, chief."

Both detectives heard the implied, *"For an old guy."*

"Thanks. Now enlighten me."

"Well, you'll know this 'cos Davy's told you before, but hackers have signatures. Bits of codes we leave behind or specific ways of doing things. It's like our tag."

Craig's eagerness got the better of him. *"And there's a*

signature here?"

His hopes were dashed right away.

"Sorry, no." Ash could feel the detective's heart sink from miles away and rushed to cheer him up. "But leave it with me. The SLS technique's unusual so I'll follow its trail. I mightn't be able to narrow it to a name, but if I could even get it down to a specific hacker conglom for you then that would help. Right?"

Hackers really formed conglomerates! He'd thought that was just a Hollywood movie trope.

Craig hid his alarm.

"Right. Well, just do your best, Ash. And if you need any help just yell and I can get someone up from IT."

The analyst tried hard not to laugh; the average public sector IT worker was like a Volkswagen Beetle where he was a Lamborghini. Still, he supposed they would be an extra pair of hands to do the scutwork of searching databases.

He heard Craig about to sign off and cut in.

"Just before you go, chief. Aidan's asked me to look at the bank CCTV feeds but I have to go down there to do it. Bank rules or something. It won't take me long but are you OK with that?"

"Whatever it takes. Just tell Nicky where you'll be and pass your searches on the victim IDs over for Annette to continue while you're out."

Just as Craig was wondering whether he should speak to Nicky himself the analyst said she needed to have a word and passed him across.

"HELLO, SIR."

His PA's foghorn-like voice invariably made Craig chuckle when he heard it isolated on the phone because it highlighted its incongruity with her slight, eight-stone frame, but he managed to contain his laughter and respond.

"Yes, Nicky, what can I do for you?"

"You won't like it."

The words made the detective roll his eyes. Why on earth did people think that prefacing bad news with an ominous warning would somehow make it easier to bear when it came? It reminded him of his grandmother in Rome who'd always told her gaggle of grandchildren not to get; "too excited" before they went to parties *just in case* they were disappointed when they got there, which of course guaranteed that they almost always were.

"Tell me anyway."

"Jack Harris has called through a murder in Smithfield."

Liam, who'd been listening to every word of the call as he drove, hit the brakes hard.

"Is it Tommy?"

Tommy Hill, a Loyalist paramilitary and convicted multiple murderer who was now *supposedly* reformed from violence, had emerged from retirement months before to take back control of UKUF, aka the UK Ulster Force, the terrorist gang that he had established in the seventies. After a period in East Belfast his 'office' was now at a betting shop on Smithfield's Gresham Street.

Craig rolled his eyes.

"There *are* other people in Smithfield you know! But whether it's him or not, you *can't* stop in the middle of the bloody road!"

"I just did."

The D.C.I. accelerated again smoothly, responding to the drivers honking their horns behind them with a flash of blue light that shut them up fast.

Craig sighed and turned his attention back to his secretary. "Any ID on the victim yet, Nicky?"

"Not yet. All I know is it's an elderly man on Gresham Street and Jack's team have asked for you to drop in."

As his deputy echoed, *"Elderly man?"* Craig responded in a resigned tone.

"OK, we'll head there now and I'll allocate it to one of the other Murder teams once we've checked the scene. We should be back around twelve. Thanks."

Liam wasn't appeased by anything he'd heard. "An old man on Gresham Street, that's *definitely* Tommy."

"Hardly. Jack would have said if it was since he knows Tommy almost as well as we do. Anyway, what do *you* care if he's dead? The pair of you slag each other off every time you meet!"

"Aye, but that doesn't mean I'm not fond of the wee shit. Murdering bastard though he is."

Although Craig rolled his eyes he did actually understand his deputy's reasoning. Liam and Tommy had formed that strange bond that often developed between enemy combatants, engendered by a shared memory of 'their' war which was often so vague as to be agreed between them even though they'd been on opposite sides. If Liam really had to

Craig knew that he *would* shoot the aging paramilitary, but woe betide anybody else who did.

Five minutes later they pulled up on Gresham Street and saw that their murder had happened in an old bric-a-brac and pawn broking shop of the kind the Smithfield area had once been famous for. Liam was relieved to see it was at the opposite end of the terrace from Hill's headquarters, although the ex-paramilitary *was* lurking, alive and as bolshie as ever and ordering the gathered crowd to be orderly and let some jump-suited CSIs pass.

When the aging gang master saw Liam emerge from his Ford he gave a huge wave. Whether from genuine pleasure or the street-cred Hill got from knowing detectives it seemed that the relationship between the pair was two way.

"Hi there, Ghost!"

Ghost had been Tommy's nickname for Liam for years because the D.C.I. was so pale, although usually an expletive preceded it.

"Come down fer sum tea after, Ghost!"

In return he got a smirk and a casual wave as the detectives ducked through the shop's low doorway into its dark interior.

As soon as they entered Craig knew he'd guessed part of the shop's genre incorrectly; it wasn't just selling bric-a-brac but antiques and memorabilia, and he recognised a few items near the front as having real worth. A moment's scan of the surprisingly large space after his eyes had adjusted to its poor light revealed a group of people gathered near the back.

He called out, "Jack? Who's in charge here?" and was surprised and amused when a voice that both he and Liam recognised from the past called back.

"That would be *you* now, so."

As a rotund man in uniform ambled towards them out of the gloom Craig's first glimpse said he'd been right in his ID. It was Sergeant Joe Rice, a Cork man who'd moved north on his second marriage, but had never forgotten the home county that held his heart.

Liam's greeting came in a mimic of the sergeant's still-strong accent.

"Ah now, is it yourself so, Joe?"

Rice had the Cork habit of adding 'so' after random words, and Liam's tribute act made him grin, which widened his round face to the shape of a rugby ball.

"I'd say that was clear so, ya big hallion."

The exchange ended in a shoulder thump, a grin and inquiries as to the other's health, but sorry as Craig was to disturb the reunion with messy facts they needed to get on. Dead bodies appeared to be piling up in Belfast this week.

"Good to see you again, Joe. Where's Jack?"

"Gone back to High Street, so. He was muttering something about someone asking him to send men to 'some bloody bank'."

Aidan was clearly being thorough.

"OK. So, why are we here?"

Liam decided to be literal.

"'Cos Nicky sent us."

As Craig rolled his eyes the Cork man concurred.

"To be sure. When Jack and I were called down he said he would ring through to your office and ask for whichever murder team was on call today, so. Is that not you then?"

Craig didn't answer for a moment, an idea slowly taking shape. So *Nicky* had decided to direct the murder to them, and if that was the case then she would have had a very good reason. His PA never did *anything* without one. That meant they needed to take a very close look at the victim before passing him to another team.

"In that case, lead on, Joe. But I'm afraid I'll need the CSIs to wait at the front until we're ready."

The suited scientists took the hint and shuffled back towards the street end of the shop.

"I'll tell you a few things first, sir, if you don't mind, so."

The sergeant produced a notebook that sank into his chubby hand, and began to read.

"This shop's been owned since nineteen-fifty by the same person, a Mister Horace Bolsover, and it's his residential address as well – there's an apartment upstairs, so. It does mostly pawn broking, loans and memorabilia. The opening hours are eight-thirty to six, seven days a week, which is really why we were called, so. The shopkeeper next door noticed that it hadn't been opened today and knocked on the door around ten. When he got no answer he entered using a key that Bolsover had given him for emergencies and found a man who he's ID-ed as the owner lying dead in the back room-"

Craig signalled to cut in. "This man's worked next door for a while?"

"Twenty-five years, and Bolsover obviously trusted him with his spare key, so."

"Is he still around?"

Rice nodded. "He is indeed. Back selling his wares. He runs a real record shop. Vinyl LPs, forty-fives and all. Proper stuff. He's there now if you need to speak with him, so."

Liam had been thinking about something else. "Bolsover's not a common name in Ireland, boss."

"Agreed. Anything on his background, Joe?"

"Well now, I know he was well into his nineties, so, because he told his neighbour he'd hit the big nine-oh quite a few years back. But I don't know any more than that about the man. I can dig if you'd like."

"Don't bother. Whichever murder team catches the case will do it."

Despite his secretary's clear steering of the case towards them Craig wasn't yet convinced that they would keep it, or at least he was pretending that they wouldn't out of defiance and sometimes the illusion of having control is all we really need.

He motioned the sergeant towards the rear of the shop. "Show us our man."

The clutter in the dimly lit and surprisingly lengthy shop forced the trio to progress in slow single file towards its rear, taking care not to disturb the precariously stacked books and dusty, glass-fronted cabinets that lined their way. The sergeant's leisurely amble delayed them even further so Liam used some of the available time to look overhead.

He was both amused and startled by the items hanging there, many large and heavy looking and suspended from the ceiling to only inches above his, admittedly high, head by what looked like significantly under strength ropes.

"Spot the low hanging fruit, boss."

Craig squinted up through the gloom and his jaw dropped when he recognised an antique guitar.

"That's a Gibson fifty-seven! It must be worth five grand. More depending on its age."

His knowledge came courtesy of having a professional musician mother, who although she'd played mostly classical piano had in her younger days been known to run the odd blues session at their home. He had also, like most young men in search of romantic props, flirted with playing guitar himself during his degree years. It had lasted only as long as it had taken him to get a date with the Sheryl Crow lookalike in his year.

But any further admiration of the shop's contents would have to wait, as, with a late warning of, "Step down" the detectives almost fell through a doorway into the shop's back room whose floor was set a foot lower than the rest. The detritus in it said that Bolsover had used the place for repairs, paperwork and to make himself tea, although the filth of the elderly Belfast sink set along one wall put even Liam off suggesting they had a cup.

Lying face-up on the grubby room's curling linoleum floor, halfway between the sink and a small Formica-topped table, was their victim. Horace Bolsover was as frail and thin as his age had hinted at, yet despite that he looked remarkably rosy cheeked and healthy for a corpse, although just as grimy as his sink. His clothes were stained with what they all hoped was food and his sparse white beard was stained a dull yellow-grey.

"Heavy smoker, boss."

Craig nodded. "And self-neglect."

He glanced around the walls and found a light switch, flicking it up and bathing the room in a dim twenty watt glow.

"Find me a brighter bulb, Joe. I can hardly see in here."

A trip next door and a bulb swop later the detectives were better able to examine both their victim and the space that they were in. The small room had clearly been an add-on to the main shop at some point, its width only a few multiples of the conduit created by the piles of stock earlier but this time defined by walls.

Craig's eyebrows lifted in surprise. "Are we in a Portakabin?"

Liam knocked hard on the wall behind him and nodded yes.

"He must've put it here years back, boss, judging by the state of the place."

"And without planning permission no doubt." Craig hunkered down beside the body. "Still, he's long past prosecuting now."

He lapsed into silence as he considered the man in front of him, searching for some obvious cause of traumatic death and finding none. Only Horace Bolsover's open-eyed horror and his hands lifted to his neck hinted that there had been anything shocking about the old man's death at all, and even those might just have been a natural response to the suddenness of a heart attack or the pensioner choking on some food.

"Why did Jack think this was murder, Joe? I must be missing something."

When Rice pointed at the window above the sink both detectives crossed to look, but they still failed to grasp what he meant.

Liam tired of the game first. "Ach, just tell us, man!"

The Cork man was unoffended and merely pointed again. "Look twice, so. The window's been taped shut."

He was right! And the masking tape that had been used to do it looked brand new.

Suddenly Rice realised he'd had the advantage of being a first responder and gave a sheepish grin.

"Ah now, sorry. I'm not being fair to ye. When we arrived the whole place was flooded with gas, so. It's cleared away now because we opened the front and back doors." He indicated a rear exit that they hadn't noticed. "When we came it was bad, so, but when his neighbour entered he said he'd almost choked on the fumes."

Liam eyes widened. "The old man must've seriously pissed someone off to make them go to all this trouble."

Craig didn't respond; too busy searching the room for gas appliances. When he found none, he raced through the back door to the shop's rear courtyard in search of a hose and car; also nothing. He re-entered the kitchen to discover that the on-call pathologist had arrived.

The doctor was one of what John called his 'newbies'; not long qualified and just out of their induction phase, so still with some eagerness in their step.

"Hello there. I'm Sigourney Montgomery."

From the young woman's very deliberate articulation of the words *she* clearly found her name a mouthful too.

"Siggie for short. Doctor Winter sent me."

Craig smiled down at her, aware that her CSI suit precluded wearing heels but still astonished by her less than five foot height. It made the suit look even more like a babygro than usual, and he was *really* hoping that Liam wouldn't point that out.

"Thanks for coming, Doctor Montgomery."

"Siggie."

"Siggie then. I'm DCS Marc Craig, and these two clowns

are Sergeant Joe Rice and D.C.I. Liam Cullen. Mister Bolsover was found dead by his neighbour at," he turned to Rice. "What time *was* he found, Joe?"

"The neighbour let himself in with a key around ten o'clock, so."

"OK. And apparently when he entered the shop was full of gas. Deliberately probably, given that the window had been taped shut. Obviously the gas has gone now, but any hint you can give us of what it might have been would be useful. There are no appliances that I can see."

"I'll check now."

She rummaged in her case and produced a gauge and air sampler, brandishing them in the air as she walked slowly through the shop.

Meanwhile, Liam had hunkered down and was peering hard at their victim.

"Don't you think he looks a bit healthy for a dead man, boss?"

"I thought that when I entered. You're thinking Carbon Monoxide?"

Carbon Monoxide poisoning can result in the formation of a compound called carboxyhaemoglobin when the gas combines with the blood and reduces its capacity to carry oxygen. In some cases this can give the skin a cherry red tinge.

"Maybe, except..." The D.C.I. turned to Rice. "Joe, was the connecting door between here and the shop closed when the neighbour entered?"

"Sorry, I didn't ask. I'll check now, so."

A minute later he returned.

"Nope, the dividing door between the shop and Portakabin was wide open, so."

"That means they would've had to flood the whole shop with gas too, boss, to get any real concentration. That's a hell of a lot of gas."

Craig considered the words for a moment and then surprised the others by shutting both the back and dividing doors and hunkering down to run a hand along each of their bases in turn. After a moment he beckoned them across.

"Feel the bottom of both doors. They're sticky. Our killer must have shut both the connecting one and the back door and taped them up before flooding this Portakabin part with gas. Then they removed the tape and opened the connecting door to the shop once Bolsover was dead."

Liam smirked. "*Then* the gas spread through the shop as well, which is why the neighbour copped it as soon as he entered. But he said it nearly choked on it so the amount that they pumped in *here* must've made the air like fog."

Joe grinned enthusiastically, enjoying the puzzle. "And they must've forgotten to un-tape this one window in their rush to get away, so."

Craig nodded slowly. "OK... that works. Then the question becomes, how did they get Bolsover to *stay* in here while they gassed him? There are no obvious signs of a fight on him or the room." He scanned the Portakabin as he said it and added, "Mind you, the place is a tip so it's hard to tell."

Liam shrugged. "I'd say they probably just threatened him, boss. He was old so it mightn't have taken much to scare him, and my guess is if they'd pointed a gun at his head he'd have been afraid to move. Maybe he didn't believe the gas would kill him so he thought he still had a chance of living if he did as he was told."

Craig nodded and re-opened the connecting door. "I agree that's the likeliest scenario. That means the killer must have worn breathing apparatus."

"So someone would have noticed it when they entered, so."

"Not necessarily, Joe. They probably carried it in a bag and put it on when they were already inside the shop. Once the job was done they opened the connecting door and then left, probably by the back door. At least the neighbour arriving when there was still gas to notice might help with timings."

Just then the pathologist rejoined them, looking puzzled.

"I take it you didn't get a straightforward reading."

"Yes and no. There are high quantities of Carbon Monoxide here."

She saw Joe's look of alarm and hurried to reassure him.

"No, don't worry, it's nowhere near danger levels, but much higher than I would expect for a building without gas appliances of any sort."

"You might want to check upstairs before you say none, Doc. It's where the Vic lived so he might've had a heater up there."

She shook her head. "I've already checked and he didn't. Everything's electric."

Craig joined the exchange. "OK, but your expression suggests you've found something *more* than Carbon Monoxide."

"I have, but it's a mixture of chemicals and particulates that I can't make sense of, so you'll forgive me if I have forensics do more tests before I commit myself."

He smiled at her politeness. John would just have said, "Wait," or even, "Bloody well wait" if it was a day when his relationship with Natalie wasn't going well.

"Of course." He glanced past her out at the street and saw the group of white-suited CSIs champing at the bit. "We'll leave you and the CSIs to your work now, but I'd be grateful for a report as soon as possible."

Liam gave him a knowing look. "So we're keeping the case then?"

Craig smiled and headed out to the street with his deputy in hot pursuit.

"It's not a bit of wonder you're always wrecked when you won't allocate cases to other teams, boss."

"I pass on plenty of cases that you never hear about, Liam, but there's something strange with this one."

The D.C.I. ignored another wave from Tommy Hill, who was now watching the proceedings from the comfort of a deckchair that he'd set up outside the bookies, the flask beside him hinting that he planned on being there for quite a while.

Craig gave the gangster a vague smile as he climbed into the car to the sound of his deputy's continuing rant.

"And pray tell me, what makes *this* murder any stranger than the others that happen every week in this mad wee place?"

Craig motioned his deputy to start driving before he replied.

"My gut and the fact valuables might have been involved, just as in the vaults. There were items in that shop worth a lot of money, so our killer may have come looking for something, yet this was a slow, calculated killing not a basic smash and grab. Why?"

"Like I said earlier, Bolsover had done something to piss the thief off."

"Exactly."

"But whether they came looking for something or not, boss, with the state of that shop there's not a hope in hell we'll ever find out. I'd be astonished if the old man kept an inventory except maybe in his head, and *that's* no use now."

They were on High Street when the D.C.I. spoke again. "Where are we heading by the way?"

"To the office. I need to think."

"OK, but go back to the valuables for a minute before you start. You're linking a stolen painting, vaults full of valuables and now a shop full of tat? Your head's full of sweetie mice, boss, you *do* know that, don't you?"

"I've no idea what that means, but if you say so."

The D.C.I. looked proud at having confounded him.

"It was one of my Granny's sayings. It means your head's full of rubbish, or mice nibbling away at it. I haven't a clue why they're always supposed to be sweet. But you've got to admit that linking this Vic to our others is a stretch even for you. Different ages, different locations, different methods, in fact there's *nothing* to link them but some maybe, maybe not valuable bits and bobs."

All Craig said was, "We'll see." And then he took out his phone.

"Now be quiet for a minute, Liam. I want to see what Aidan's got for us."

The D.C.I. shook his head. "Not yet. I've something I need to say first."

Surprise at his deputy's solemn tone made Craig's dialling finger freeze mid-air, and before Liam's first word had emerged he had already covered a list of things that the D.C.I. might be about to say: that he was resigning or was ill, and by that he didn't mean with a head cold, or that one of his team was having an affair with another one, leaving him with stretched loyalties and an almighty mess, *or* that one of them had done something so terrible that it was going to land them in jail. Note that *none* of those possibilities were good news, which said something about his current frame of mind.

When his deputy's, "You have issues, boss" hit the air Craig was almost relieved.

For five seconds that was, after which relief was replaced by annoyance and hurt pride.

"What do you mean I have issues? What *sort* of issues?"

He was just pumping himself up for a fight when the follow-up, "I mean you're too hard on yourself" made him deflate like a popped balloon.

"I am? How?"

Liam adopted a mournful expression that he liked to believe made him look sorrowful but wise, but actually, when accompanied by the slow nods he was now giving, it made him look more like a car window Deputy Dawg.

"Your problem is you're too clever. You see things most people miss, and don't even get me *started* on your bloody hunches. Mystic Meg had fewer of those than you."

Craig was bemused. "Thanks... I think. But I don't understand why that's a problem."

"It's a problem because when you're even a wee bit slow you think you've lost your flipping touch *forever* and start beating yourself up!"

Craig's jaw dropped at his perception. He'd thought no-one had noticed.

"Like now for instance when you've a screaming baby at home meaning you're getting no sleep, *you're* all ready to throw the head up and chuck in the job!"

When his boss' silence told Liam to continue he did, enthusiastically.

"That's why you have a *team*, because we can *all* bring something to the table. So for God's sake let us, will you? Just stop believing *you* have to think up every brilliant idea and do everything yourself!"

Did he really do that?

Craig was ashamed to admit that he probably did, although he would never acknowledge it out loud. Instead he gave his deputy a wry look.

"Finished?"

"No, not yet. If you *don't* let us feel like we're contributing then we'll start wondering why we're bloody well here at all!"

The D.C.I. gave a firm nod. "OK, *now* I'm finished."

Craig wasn't sure *what* to say about the diatribe, but the options running through his mind were: "Mind your own business", "sod off", and "thank you, Liam".

He decided that the last one was probably right, except that he wasn't quite ready to say anything yet but the "Hmmm..." he gave as he returned to making his call, completely missing his deputy's satisfied smirk as he did.

Aidan answered quickly and his loud voice bellowed, "Guv" down the line, making Craig really wish that he could attach volume controls to some of his staff. Nicky, Aidan and Liam could all benefit at times.

He set his phone on speaker before he got deafened and

asked what he needed to, receiving little useful information in return.

"Sorry, but there are more questions than answers at the moment, Guv, so I'll update you later when I've made sense of it if that's OK. I've borrowed some men from Jack and sent our lot back to the ranch, except for Ash who's here looking at the computers and CCTV."

"Fine. Nicky will call you with the briefing time."

He cut the call just as they were driving into the C.C.U.'s basement and a minute later the two detectives entered the squad-room, to find it remarkably quiet. Annette had her eyes glued to her computer, Ryan was typing, and Nicky and Mary were examining a book together and occasionally saying, "Mmm."

The scene disconcerted Liam so much that he followed Craig into his office.

"Did you see that?"

"What?"

"Nicky and the young one. They're agreeing with each other."

"So?"

"Well, it's not normal is it? I mean, those two were at each other's throats from day one and now all of a sudden they're holding hands!" He threw himself into a chair and continued in a tone of disgust. "Next thing you know they'll be braiding each other's hair!"

Since Mary's argumentative personality had made her the bane of Craig's life since she'd joined the squad eighteen months before and Annette had found a way to calm things down, he wasn't complaining.

"Thank God for it is what I say. Don't you remember what it was like here a few months back? Non-stop squabbling."

"At least it was lively! Now the place is like bloody Pleasantville!"

Liam had been forced to watch the utopian comedy-drama by his wife at the weekend and he was determined to pass his suffering on.

He threw in another pop reference he felt fitted his theme.

"What did Annette do to turn them into Stepford wives? Although *you're* as happy as Larry about it, I can see that!"

The background to the remark was that although Craig could face down gunmen while barely sweating, when caught between his pissed-off secretary and the bickering constable he had too often chosen discretion, well to be honest, retreat as the better part of valour. Eventually he'd begged Annette to sort things out; things meaning Mary generally but particularly her feud with Nicky, which had verged on violent at times.

The D.I. had solved the problem brilliantly but rather oddly six months before with the assistance of a book on astrology, a subject that seemingly fascinated both protagonists, and since then peace had reigned.

"You've mixed up your movie characters."

"Ah-ha! So *you* were forced to watch girly crap as well."

"I quite enjoyed Pleasantville actually."

"That's even worse! You went *willingly* to the slaughter."

"I'll ignore that. Anyway, back to your question. What's *happened* is that Annette found our foes a common interest. But anyway, who cares *how* she did it, she did it and I'm enjoying the peace."

The gleam in his deputy's eye said that he fully intended to disturb it.

"*Don't you dare, Liam.* We've enough on our plate with three murders."

"I didn't say a word."

Craig wasn't reassured. "Well, if they start fighting again I'll know who to blame. *And* punish. OK, get out now. I need to think."

What he actually needed to do was phone his builder, and then ask his PA why she'd sent the Bolsover case to them.

Chapter Seven

The Metropolitan Police Art and Antiques Squad Archives. London. 2 p.m.

Andy Angel gazed wonderingly around the enormous, high-ceilinged warehouse, finally understanding the hackneyed expression, 'Lost for words'. It was Hanukkah, his birthday and all the other exciting days of his life, of which there'd been many, including as it had done two weddings and his son's birth, all come at once.

The D.C.I. took a moment to let the reality of where he was sink in. The Met's Art Archives... a normally vacuum-sealed, inventoried and catalogued Aladdin's Cave of artworks, sculptures and manuscripts that even when crammed on to shelves and stacked haphazardly against walls were still the most beautiful sights he had ever seen.

But a moment was all he got to savour their glory before a loud cough behind him reminded the Murder detective that he was there to work not lust. The cough had come from the uniformed sergeant who ran and guarded the archive, and he followed it up by flicking noisily through the thick sheaf of pages on the clipboard he was holding, until finally, finding the set that he'd been looking for, he slipped them out.

"Right, so the Governor said you wanted to see the works from Europe."

Andy nodded mutely, his gaze still roaming the echoing hall.

"From anywhere in particular? 'Cos Europe's a big place you know."

He did indeed know. His grandparents had come from Austria and travelled back there frequently before they'd died, sending him postcards from every stop along the way.

This time he managed to vocalise his answer.

"France. Anything from sixteen-hundred onwards."

It wasn't a random date. He'd done some research before his flight and found that one branch of the Irish Ferviers *had* in fact been Huguenots and fled religious persecution in France in the seventeenth century. He'd asked Ash to keep digging and if any other branches were uncovered while he was in the Big Smoke he trusted the analyst to give him a call.

Andy's response prompted the uniformed officer to suck

his teeth hard, which made the detective wonder whether it was just that particular century that caused him angst or if he'd mentioned any other would it have had the same effect. But for once the D.C.I. was off in his judgement. The sucking wasn't from angst or even a sign that his guide couldn't be bothered searching for pieces from the period, but rather an indicator of the extensive knowledge that kept the policeman in his comfortable indoor job.

Sergeant Denis Struthers had worked in the archive for decades and watched items arrive post-seizure and rest there until the criminal trial involving them was over, which had sometimes taken years. Then he'd seen those valuables moved on to museums and galleries, auction houses, or on the rare occasion that the owners *hadn't* been up to their eyes in the original crime and fiddling their insurance, back from whence they'd come.

He *loved* art, absolutely adored it, favouring the old masters over the modern stuff himself but he revelled even in that, and every item in the vast warehouse was like his child, so he knew *exactly* what was in storage there at any given time and late renaissance France was a real feast.

So in response to Andy's, "Something wrong, Sergeant?" Struthers sighed and said, "Lovely period, sir."

The sucking of teeth had been admiration not angst.

"And we're full to the brim with stuff from then as well. But our system's not as neat as I'd like it to be, so we have to arrange pieces based on what we know about them. First the date the item was created or best estimate, then by the artist's or owner's nationality when we have it, and lastly by the country it was created in or likely imported from. So it's likely the ones *you're* looking for, that just *came* from France, will be mixed in with works by French artists and items owned by French people as well."

Far from being depressed by the information Andy perked up and discussion ended Struthers set off at a clip, marching up and down the warehouse's seemingly endless stacks and rows until he halted suddenly near the rear left hand corner and swept his clipboard around in an arc.

"There you go. France from the thirteenth Century on. That's as close as we'll get."

The whole corner was stacked and piled with valuables in boxes, on stands, in pigeonholes and in crates, leaving Andy in danger of being struck dumb again by the sight of more priceless artefacts than he'd seen in all the museums he'd ever visited in his life.

Instead he managed to squeak out, *"Where has it all come from?"*

Struthers reeled off a list.

"Burglaries, museum and bank heists, private collections where they shouldn't have been and seizures under Proceeds of Crime mostly. Others were just found at boot fairs and in antique and pawn shops, being flogged for a song because the seller didn't know what they'd got. Once it's pointed out an item's valuable ownership starts to be disputed, so we store them here until the lawyers sort it out."

"There must be millions of pounds worth here."

"Yep. And some of it here for years because the court cases take so bloody long." The sergeant glanced down at his pages. "Right now, we have an owner's name against some of them but not many, so who were you looking for again?"

"Before I tell you that, what dates exactly does this cover?"

Another glance and, "Thirteen-eighty to the present day" came back.

"They're the dates the pieces were created?"

"Best guesses by our experts, yes. But don't forget that as well as original pieces by French artists there are pieces by non-French artists that *came* here from France and those that just had a French owner too."

"Do you have the dates when they were seized by The Met? And when they'd originally been acquired by whoever was holding the pieces then?"

The sucking sound came again, but this time not from pleasure.

"You don't want much, do you? I can give you the date they came *here*, so that'll be the police seizure date or close, but as to when the owners first bought them you'll have to check back through the individual records or go and ask them yourself."

Andy nodded. It *was* asking too much and he had enough to be going on with.

"OK, then. The specific owner's name I'm looking for is Fervier. Are there *any* pieces in this corner, or *anywhere* in your records listed under that name?"

He crossed his fingers tightly as the sergeant ran his eyes down the clipboard, losing hope by the second when nothing was said. Hope soared again each time Struthers turned a new page, only to die as he moved on to the next. When he reached the end of the thick sheaf without a word Andy was ready to give up, until the sergeant returned to a page near the middle and tapped his forefinger midway down.

The D.C.I. held his breath for a moment until the copper's uncertain expression made him throw caution to the wind.

"You've found something?"

"Mmm... not sure. That's why I wanted to check right to the end."

How could he not be sure? Fervier was either written on the bloody page or it wasn't!

He bit back his sarcasm and employed his most emollient tone.

"Perhaps I could help?"

A shrug and the clipboard was turned for him to see a paragraph in the middle of the page that read 'Holbein: charcoal sketch of a young woman, title unknown. Estimated date of creation: fifteen-twenty. Entry date to archive: twenty-eighteen. Country of origin before importation to UK: France. Date of importation: nineteen-forty-nine. Ownership traced to Matilde Rosser née Fervier.'

Andy stifled the hope that had risen at 'Fervier' and kept his next question logical.

"So it's located in this section because the owner had a French name, even though the artist is German?"

"And because it came to England from France too. That's what you wanted, didn't you?"

Apparently it was.

"Yes. Thank you."

After a minute's careful searching the detective was gazing at the sketch itself and wishing that he owned it, or any of the works in the archive for that matter. But they were worth more than he would ever earn in his lifetime so a gaze was all he was going to get.

"Does it say anything more on your sheet about how the sketch ended up here?"

"Nope. But there's a file number so I can pull it for you upstairs."

"Great. Anything else here against the name Fervier before we do that?"

"Nope. I checked."

"Can we double-check your database for other Ferviers

when we go upstairs?"

"I suppose."

With that Struthers started walking back the way they'd come until Andy made a request that stopped him in his tracks.

"Any chance I could stay down here for a couple of hours to just look at the art? I'd be happy to be searched before I leave."

As the sergeant began to shake his head he hurriedly played his best card.

"It's just, well I'm an artist myself and I've never seen such wonderful pieces, so it would be a real treat." He hastily pulled his phone from his pocket. "I could show you some of my work if you'd like?"

Struthers leaned in to look as the D.C.I. swiped rapidly through photos of his paintings and sketches, including a recent charcoal one he'd done of Liam's wife Danni and their kids in payment for a favour months before.

Seeing the man was softening Andy made his final pitch.

"I could do a sketch of you now if you have some paper?"

It was the clincher and twenty minutes later Denis Struthers left the archive with his likeness clutched in his hand, issuing the instruction that Andy had one hour to wallow in the art then he would return and take him to Matilde Fervier Rosser's file.

An hour with the Old Masters; he couldn't think of better payment for a sketch.

****

Galway.

"They've found the old man."

Irina Tokár's words drew little response from her companions other than a shrug and a, "So what? We knew they would" from her other half, without him even taking his eyes off the TV.

The wiry, dark-eyed teen frowned and threw her legs over the end of the couch that she was sitting on, reclining on its threadbare purple velvet and staring up thoughtfully at the peeling, whitewashed ceiling high above their heads for almost a minute before trying again.

"Yes, but we haven't put the last piece in place yet,

Roman, and what if the cops work things out before we have?"

Roman Bianchi abandoned his viewing and moved to lie down beside her, encircling her small waist with his arm as he did.

"They won't, Rina, you *know* they won't. We worked on this for a year and ran every scenario so we're way ahead of them; even *with* the cop that we chose in charge. By the time the police get their act together we'll be gone and our message left behind loud and clear, just as we planned."

Her anxious gaze into his dark eyes said that she was less than reassured. "But what if they *find* us?" She gestured at their surroundings. "The longer we stay here the more chance there is."

"Without our names or photographs? Impossible. And they'll never find us through my hack; I didn't leave a trace *anywhere*. And no matter how good the cops' analysts are they'll *never* get the camera footage back."

He stroked his free hand through her thick black curls. "It will all be over soon, so relax. Everything that we're doing is right."

****

The Met. London. 4 p.m.

Andy didn't know *what* he'd expected to find in Matilde Fervier Rosser's file; preferably that she'd been a member of some international art theft ring who'd stashed the Holbein in her attic to admire in secret. The *minimum* he'd been hoping for was that she was someone he could have felt good about interrogating and who could yield some clues for Terry to follow on her gallery crime.

But as life rarely gives you what you want the D.C.I. had been half-expecting to be disappointed, although *not* to feel shamefaced in the way he did by the time he'd finished reading the woman's file.

He glanced dolefully at Denis Struthers.

"There are *no* other Ferviers in your whole art database?"

"Nope. I ran the name through our criminal ones as well. Nothing."

Andy sighed and set down the file.

"The Holbein was discovered at a boot fair being sold by a

healthcare worker. The theft case is against *him* for stealing it from Mrs Fervier- Rosser's home while he was caring for her."

"She's elderly?"

"And then some. Eighty-nine. It doesn't look like they found him selling anything else from *her* house, but he'd stolen from some of his other patients too so hopefully they'll throw the book at him when it comes to court."

Andy tutted in disgust. People who took advantage of the old were the lowest of the low in his book.

The sergeant tutted as well, but more about his archive. "Eighty-nine. She could be dead by the time the case is heard. That'll mean the Holbein will have to be auctioned off."

"Well, right now she's very much alive in a nursing home south of the Thames so I'd like to go and visit her. If that wouldn't be stepping on the case officer's toes?"

"You'd best check." Struthers pointed to a scribble on the front of the file. "That signature belongs to Bill Wainwright and he can be a touchy bugger. You should ask him to come along."

"Where can I find him?"

The office they were in was on a long corridor and by way of an answer Struthers jerked his thumb to the left.

"Three doors down. The fat inspector."

It would probably have been more politically correct to have said obese or even the 'horizontally challenged' favoured in some parts of the world, but Andy got his drift and went in search of someone fitting the bill.

He found Wainwright in the corridor on his way back from the staff canteen and the man's resting facial expression of a scowl didn't fill him with joy.

"Inspector Wainwright? I'm D.C.I. Angel from Belfast."

The D.I. continued past him into his office. "And I need to know that, why?"

"Because I'd like to chat to a victim in one of your art theft cases and I just wanted to get you on board."

The plate of nachos that Wainwright had been carrying hit his desk with a thud and his resting scowl became an active frown.

"On board? You mean you want me to go *with* you?"

The man was getting on Andy's nerves, and that took a lot. His cool tone reflected it.

"Not necessarily. I just thought it was polite to inform

you."

"Yeh, well, consider me informed. But I can't go with you, I have meetings."

Considering Andy hadn't mentioned when he would be going, either the D.I.'s calendar was a nightmare or he'd just lied. Either way a wave towards the door said he was dismissed; without a single question about which case he'd been referring to or who the victim might be.

If Wainwright had worked for him he'd have hauled him over the coals then and there, but worse, if he'd been so dismissive of *him* how had he treated Matilde Rosser? Depending on the answer to that question he could be having words with the head of the squad about his inspector before he left for home.

****

The C.C.U. 4.30 p.m.

"Right, everyone's up to speed on where we are and we'll move on to our next steps in a moment, but first I want you all to start activating your street networks and snouts. Just give them the bare bones of the case but set them hunting for anything they can find. Liam, ask Jack and Joe to do the same. OK, so..."

As Craig turned to the whiteboard to write up his first heading his analyst's smart-pad beeped.

"It's Andy, chief. He's face-timing us."

"OK, put him on Nicky's screen."

A second later the D.C.I.'s spiky-haired visage appeared at the front of the squad-room, five times life-size and in such high-res colour that it made the secretary jump.

"I *wish* you'd warn me when you're going to do that! I can't have people jumping out at me that way!"

Andy responded before anyone else could. "Sorry, Nicky. I didn't mean to scare you."

The bizarreness of the exchange made Craig smile, and he completely missed Liam moving until he was peering straight into the screen.

"You've got a zit on your chin that wasn't there this morning, Arty."

"Yes it was. You can just *see* it now because I'm magnified. Anyway, can I give my report or would someone else care to snark about my complexion?"

Aidan glanced up from his semi-recumbent position to make a comment that was more therapeutic in nature.

"Sunshine would clear it up."

"And give me cancer instead."

Deciding the cosmetic debate had gone on long enough Craig instructed his London located D.C.I. to move it along.

"OK, well, after hours spent searching The Met's Art Archives-"

Liam cut in, his face still close to the screen. "And loving it. Admit it."

"I'll admit it if you stand back. You look like a giant potato from this end."

Craig tried and failed to keep his chuckling in check. "Very witty, but hurry up, Andy."

"OK, the archives, which are spectacular by the way. Worth a trip for anyone who's ever at The Met."

"I know. I visited a few times when I worked there. Depressing in a way too though. All that art should be put on public display while cases are waiting to be settled. I really don't understand why they don't."

"Excellent idea. I'll start a petition. Anyway, it was always a long shot that we'd find anything linked to any Ferviers..."

Craig's heart sank.

"...by looking for anything that'd emerged historically from France. But actually I had a stroke of luck."

"What did you find?"

"A Holbein sketch that belongs to a woman called Matilde Rosser, née Fervier. I've only had a quick look at the case file," *because I was busy drooling over paintings instead,* "but it seems it was found being sold at a boot fair by her healthcare worker. He stole it from Mrs Fervier-Rosser's home."

Against a chorus of disgust Aidan asked a question. "Is she still alive?"

"Yes. She lives in a nursing home now south of the river, so I was planning to pay her a visit if that's OK, chief?"

"Yes, but bear in mind we've no idea whether she's a relative of Hortense or even part of the same Fervier clan yet. And make your visit as soon as possible in case we need you back here."

"OK. The lady is eighty-nine now and she married a Welshman called Milo Rosser and came to London from

France in forty-nine after the war. They brought the Holbein with them. Her husband died of cancer in twenty-fifteen and there are no children around to help her, which is probably why the thief took advantage."

"Did he steal anything else from her?"

"Not that the cops could find, but he *did* steal from some of his other patients as well so he'll go down for quite a while. Anyway, he obviously didn't know how much the sketch was worth because he was selling it for ten quid. The Met's estimate as of June this year is one point five million."

Liam, who hadn't moved very far from the screen because he was now scrutinising Andy's hair for grey, gave such a loud whistle that it hurt everyone's ears and nearly deafened the other D.C.I..

"What! For a sketch! I hope that one you did of Danni's worth that much after *you're* dead, Arty."

"Cheerful thought, thanks."

Craig rolled his eyes at the pair. "Move it along, please."

"Sorry, chief. Anyway, the Holbein wasn't catalogued anywhere that The Met could find, but depending on what Mrs Fervier-Rosser says I might need to check some auction houses, galleries and so on to find out where in France she and her husband bought it."

Craig thought for a moment. "Check Interpol's records too, Andy. A lot of art migrated around Europe in the chaos at the end of World War Two-"

Ash cut in. "The Allied forces set up the Monuments Men group, or to give them their full title The Monuments, Fine Arts and Archives section of the Allies, at the end of the war to search for valuables. They found a lot but said there was stuff still out there, so I'd be happy to check the Holbein out with Interpol and the FBI if you want, Andy?"

"Brilliant. I'll have plenty to do here."

Liam sighed wistfully. "It's so nice when everyone gets along."

Craig raised his eyes to heaven. "Thank you, Father Cullen. Right, you two clearly know what you're doing there, so anything else, Andy?"

"Nope."

"Fine. You're welcome to stay connected for the rest of the briefing but no more sudden movements or Nicky will faint."

As his PA arched an eyebrow at him Craig wrote 'Victim

IDs' up on the board.

"OK. We know the name of our dead shopkeeper, but anything on our two younger victims yet?"

Before anything was offered up Liam jumped in.

"So you're *definitely* lumping all three Vics together?"

"I am and *we* are, as you already know. And Nicky made the link before all of us, which is why she sent us there."

The secretary took a bow.

Liam needed more information. "Why'd you think they were linked, Nicky?"

"Three bodies in a couple of days is unusual even in this place, plus there was the commercial part – a gallery sells, a shop sells and a bank has loads of cash."

Craig nodded.

"Exactly. The link is the timings of the deaths and the valuables surrounding all three. Amongst all the junk in Horace Bolsover's shop there are items worth a lot of money, and although we've no idea yet if anything was taken, someone clearly had a motive for his death and theft could *easily* have been part of it. Plus, the method of killing used was too elaborate for it to have been a mere passing theft and assault."

A sharp turn towards the team's analyst signalled the end of his justification.

"Ash, you checked the CCTV in the vaults and bank. Anything that could put names on either our victims or killers?"

The analyst shook his head glumly. "Nothing yet, chief. Whoever did this was really good. There's not a single sighting of anyone on CCTV anywhere in the bank; outside or inside the vaults. One minute there's nothing on the footage then we're looking at our victims lying on the vault floors without any movement being recorded in or out. The killer even remembered to wipe the cameras on all six vaults' code pads which might have caught an oblique image of them, and that means they're *way* smarter than the average perp."

Aidan roused himself again, this time actually sitting up. "Not *that* smart. Everyone knows where the cameras are on ATMs."

Before the analyst could respond Annette threw in her ten pence worth.

"You mean you're surprised that the killers even thought of it, Ash, because there were obvious cameras on each wall and ceiling so they might have assumed *they* were the sum total of the surveillance?"

The analyst hemmed and hawed. "Yes and no. I agree with Aidan that most people know where to look for ATM cameras but the keypad cameras weren't positioned in the usual place. The lenses were set *in* the pads and trained straight up, and they were hidden within the bank logos so the killer couldn't have notic-"

Craig held up a hand to halt him. "Sorry, but aren't we talking about different things here? If they were going to wipe all the camera streams on the central computer anyway, why would the killer have *needed* to know or even cared where the keypad lenses were positioned, and how do we even know that they did?"

"We know because they took the time to cover all six pads' logos and therefore their camera lenses in Tippex. The two cameras on the vaults we're sure they entered *could* have caught full face views of whoever was opening them, but at best the other four might only have caught a glimpse because of their angles *unless* the killers had entered there too. As for why they did it when they were already wiping the central computer, I'd say thoroughness."

Liam shot him a look. "Why enter all six vaults?"

Craig shook his head. "We don't know that they did yet, but you're right that *would* seem logical now given the Tippex. They didn't leave bodies there so we have to assume they stole something from them, and we'll only know exactly what when the inventory checks are all done. Sorry Ash, you hadn't finished."

"Yeh, I was just going to say that as well as the Tippex thing they wiped themselves from the central streams too."

"Clever buggers, boss."

"Yes they are. But there's something else here. If Ash is right and the keypad cameras weren't visible that means the killers knew their locations before they arrived. So who told them?"

The analyst shrugged. "That's your job. But before anyone asks, they didn't leave prints in the Tippex. I asked the CSIs."

Craig smiled. "The Tippex wasn't just overkill, it was an error. By highlighting that they knew where the lenses were they've highlighted that someone with inside knowledge of the bank was involved."

Annette perked up. "A crooked banker?"

"Perhaps, but I doubt it was an inside job in the usual sense. All we can say for now is our killer made *some* connection with a bank insider, or the person who put in the key- pad cameras. Someone who knew that they sat behind the logos. OK, hit me with some better news, Ash."

A gleam in the analyst's eye said they might just be in luck.

"Well... I've checked all the bank's camera footage and I can tell you that our intruders used the same SLS sequence employed at the gallery. So that supports your theory that the gallery theft and bank murders are linked."

Craig wanted to whoop but his professionalism prevented it, so Liam slapped the analyst on the back in congratulations instead, knocking the slight youth clean off his chair.

When he'd regained his dignity Craig said, "Great find, Ash, and I hope you'll consider waiving your assault claim against Liam."

A pointed look at his deputy said it wasn't entirely a joke.

"Only if he buys me chocolate."

"Done."

As Liam's mouth opened to object, a glare from his boss closed it again. It was clearly time for their annual 'How to behave' talk; this year's emphasis would include a section on how not to injure your team mates.

Craig scribbled up, 'Continue checks for hacking - Ash', 'Vault inventories - Aidan, 'Fervier's Art - Andy and Ash' and 'Follow up on Ferviers- All'.

"Ash, when you're doing traffic and street cams don't forget Smithfield."

"On them already."

"Good. OK, Aidan, next steps at the bank, please."

"We need to follow up on the code generators, both the Board members and their portable devices, and find out whether the killer used the Board members' stored e-signatures to enter the vaults or not. The bank's checking their computers on that now. Also, like you've already written there, Ryan and Mary are checking the vault inventories to see if anything was taken."

He nodded Ryan to pick up on that.

"OK, so the vault inventories are checked every morning and evening on weekdays but never at weekends unless there's activity at the bank. It's always Mervyn Gambon or his designated covering officer who actually opens the vaults and then either they or a junior manager called Miriam Bamford checks the contents against a computerised list which is kept bang up-to-date. We know what was in all of the vaults as of five o'clock on Friday evening and we know that no-one *officially* authorised any vault being opened at the weekend, but there's so much stuff stored in each of them that we can't yet say if anything was taken. Bamford has been checking the contents all day. Normally it takes her a couple of hours because she's familiar with them but she's being extra cautious-"

Craig stopped him. "All six vaults?"

"Yes. That's their routine."

"Good. And the remainder of the bank?"

Ryan's startled and then horrified glance at both Aidan and Mary said that no-one had raised the issue before, so Craig's next scribble was 'Check all parts of the bank for missing valuables or funds.'

"It's unlikely but just possible that the thief might have stashed some of what they stole inside the bank for later retrieval, so there needs to be a complete search from the roof down. I would say check the contents of Bolsover's shop too but we doubt he kept any written inventory." He shifted his gaze to his diligent inspector who was busily taking notes, "Just while we're on that. Annette, how do you fancy leading on Bolsover? Liam can give you what we've got so far."

She grinned from ear to ear.

"Happy to, sir. I've got all the stations primed to alert me of any new missing person reports that match our victims, so I'll have time."

"Good. Liam, do that handover when we've finished." After scribbling a note to that effect he turned back to the group. "Anything else at the bank?"

It was Mary who replied.

"I interviewed all the daytime security guards and set up their background searches, but so far there's nothing. I've got the home addresses of the night ones, so once I've run their checks I'll visit them."

"OK, good. Take Ryan with you."

He'd known what was coming before his words had hit the air.

"I don't need a man to protect me! I'm perfectly capable of interviewing people alone" was accompanied by the constable drawing herself up to her full height in her seat.

Craig tried to conceal his weariness at the comment; he was all for feminism and equality, but fighting battles about it every single day, especially when they had no foundation, was enough to try the patience of a saint.

Still, he rose to the challenge in as engaged a tone as he could muster.

"This isn't about you not being capable, Constable Li, this is about *no* officer *ever* visiting potential suspects alone while we have killers on the loose. Sergeant Hendron *will* go with you. Now..."

To the sound of the D.C. spluttering he turned back to Aidan before a tit for tat could ensue. Even Mary found it hard to argue with the back of someone's head, although she would probably give it a damn good try.

"...Aidan. Any outside firms involved with the bank? Security, keypad manufacturers or otherwise."

"Yes, unfortunately. The bank uses a local security firm called, would you believe, Gird Security, to provide locums if they have a lack of cover or someone off from sickness, which unfortunately they did last week. Their people are mostly ex-military or cops."

"I suppose their name could have been worse. Bolster, Buttress, the list is endless, as are the jokes. But yes, they'll still need checked. If it looks like a lot of work ask Jack if you can use some of his men to assist."

"Will do. The chief guard Noel Lovett said they've used the firm for years with no problems and everyone undergoes extensive positive vetting, but of course that's no guarantee a guard didn't just take the head staggers and get tempted by all the loot. Mind you, why they would kill those kids and leave their bodies there I don't know."

"And until we do *no-one* does solo runs."

Craig didn't need to look at his constable for the barb to hit home, which is just as well as a horrified Annette saw Mary's tongue shoot out for a moment but it had happened too fast to get a pic for proof. Aidan had seen it as well but he couldn't be bothered with a fight.

"There's also an external catering firm that the bank uses to provide food for all its meetings and lunches, Guv, so we'll be looking into that as well."

Liam's eyes lit up on "food" and then his expression changed to one of pathos. "We *never* get catered for."

Aidan came back at him in a flash. "You mean at work,

don't you? Your wife caters for you every day."

"Here now, there's no need for *that* kind of talk!"

"Food! I meant food, man."

"Just as well." The deputy returned to his original point. "But I mean we never get lunches laid on for us at work, not even sandwiches."

Craig rolled his eyes unsympathetically. "That's why you have legs and a canteen a few floors down. Going back to the caterers, Aidan, any that have been to the bank will need to be checked for personnel backgrounds and access while they were there. I don't imagine they'll hold keys because they'll always be delivering food when someone else is there, but we need to rule them out. Also, see if there's been any maintenance or renovation work carried out at the bank recently and if so check out the workers. In fact check *anyone* who's been there at all."

The words made Annette drag her gaze away from her junior, where it had been fixed since the tongue incident in the vain hope of making Mary break down and admit her guilt.

"We can't check everyone, sir. There are customers in and out of the bank all day."

"Hopefully *they're* confined to the public areas. But that's a thought, Aidan. Can the public use the lift to get down to the vaults?"

"Nope, and only a handful of staff can. You need to have a key to use the lift up or down, and it takes different keys according to which direction you're travelling, so even the office workers upstairs can't get down to the vaults."

"Clever, but Ash, cast an eye over the reception level tapes from Friday to Sunday anyway. It shouldn't take long."

"Already done and it didn't. There was nothing on them. They'd been SLS-ed as well."

"OK, then check if there's any way the bank's pass and lift keys can be copied. Our killers got down to those vaults somehow."

"Sorry, chief, I've already checked that too. There's a normal keyhole that the chief guard and manager have metal keys for, but there's also a redundant key reader above it that hasn't been used for years but the bank didn't bother to remove. Same on the main front door. Any blank form like a plastic hotel key could have been programmed to fit them by a skilled hacker."

Craig sighed wearily. Their perps had thought of everything.

After adding any uncompleted action points to the board he stood back and scanned it.

"OK, if it looks like we have a lot of work to do that's because there is, so everyone carry on till six, please, then call it a night and get back in here at eight to start again. That's it."

As the others got on with it Craig nodded to his deputy and made for the exit. Liam caught him up at the lift.

"Labs *again*?"

"Yep. Let's see what they've got on Bolsover."

When they arrived there, or more precisely when they arrived at the door of John Winter's office, they found the pathologist staring at a sheet of paper spread out on his desk and secured rather oddly at each corner with improvised weights. The fixed manner in which the medic was reading the document told Craig straight away that it was important, just as his doleful expression said it was about personal business rather than work.

Craig motioned his deputy swiftly into reverse.

"Can you give us a minute, Liam?"

The D.C.I. nodded; *he'd* guessed what the paper was as well.

"I'll be upstairs."

With that he left his boss to what was bound to be an emotional talk. Craig did those well but he didn't, so horses for courses and all that stuff.

When Craig re-entered the office John was folding the paper into as small a square as he could manage before he potted it straight into the bin.

"A letter from Natalie's solicitor?"

The pathologist gave a resigned sigh. "Was it that obvious?"

"The ceremonial way you were reading it kind of gave it away. Bad news, I'm guessing."

John rested back in his chair with a shrug. "Do solicitors ever send anything else? She wants to make the separation official. After six months apart I suppose I knew it might be coming, but..."

"It still feels like a blow." Craig pulled up a chair and sat down. "She's still refusing to see the counsellor with you?"

"With an absolutism that would do a dictator proud. I've

said we can change to a new one if that makes her happier; we don't need to use Doctor Beresford. To be honest I'd be happy to see anyone Natalie chose, but she *still* insists that there's nothing wrong in her relationship with Kit."

"But surely the children's social worker-"

John's tut emerged louder than he'd meant it to. "But *they're* wrong as well, didn't you *know*? Everyone's out of step in this bloody world but my wife! It sometimes feels that even if Nat was never allowed to see Kit unsupervised again she'd accept it rather than admit that *she's* got issues. I'm actually beginning to think she can't."

His voice quietened suddenly, so much so that Craig had to strain to hear his next words.

"It's almost like Nat's whole grasp on the world depends on her being perfect, Marc, and in a way I'm frightened about what might happen if she realised she was wrong. What if I break her down and can't put her back together again?"

He shook his head sharply as if the thought was too much to face.

"Look, I know she *loves* Kit, but Nat's need for the child to be perfect is stopping her accepting that our daughter might just be a normal toddler who wasn't born to scale Everest or fly to the moon. I mean, I'll be happy if Kit decides to do those things someday of her own volition, but I'll be just as happy if she wants to be a farmer or a stay at home mum. I honestly don't give a monkey's as long as she's happy."

Craig sighed. "Sound like Natalie needs lengthy therapy of her own before she can accept joint sessions."

The medic's lips tightened. "Except that she's already said no to that and I can't force her, so round and round we go."

Craig wanted to reach out and touch his friend's arm in comfort, but he knew him well and right now John was wound so tight that would just make him walk out. It was better to keep things in their mutual comfort zone of action and facts.

"So what are you going to do about the letter?"

"Think about it for a couple of weeks."

"If you think too long Natalie might take things out of your hands."

The pathologist's sudden bolt for the coffee machine signalled the debate was at an end.

"Right, so you'd like to know about your victims, Marc? Three now according to Siggie. Coffee?"

"Always."

A moment later Craig had an espresso in front of him and John had withdrawn three files from his cabinet and set them on his desk.

He opened two and laid them out side by side.

"ID-ing your two younger victims is proving a real challenge, I'm afraid. Annette called through to say there are no matching missing persons' reports, and we've found no devices with serial numbers or unique marks that would help. None of their clothes were unique, so all we've really got to go on is that they were both probably middle-class and had had dental work, but so far there's no hit on that. Sorry not to be of more help."

Craig nodded. "We're only one day in so I'm not stressing about it, although I would like to put their families out of their misery."

"Even though it's a misery they don't yet know about, judging by the lack of reports. The families mustn't be aware they're missing yet, but that's understandable given their ages even if they were students still living at home. I did when I was at medical school and my folks still didn't see me from one week to the next apart from when I was raiding the fridge."

Craig nodded. He'd been the same. His friends had seen far more of him than his family back then.

It gave him an idea.

"Who saw most of you at college, John?"

"You probably. And the other medics in my group."

"Exactly. If our victims aren't reported missing by tomorrow we'll need to start showing their sketches around the Unis and colleges."

Of which there were eleven in the small city. Belfast was essentially a college town.

The medic's eyes widened behind his glasses. *"Not saying that they're dead!"*

"God no! Give me *some* credit. Finding out that way could kill their parents."

He had always been sensitive to families' feelings but they pained him even more now that he had a child of his own.

"We'll show the sketches to the staff to see if they match anyone in their records. I'll assess where we are in the morning and decide." He gestured at the files. "Nothing else on them at all?"

"Not from my side."

It had been too much to hope that the killers might've made things easy for them.

The detective knocked back his espresso in one hit and pointed to the third file. "What are your thoughts on Bolsover?"

To his surprise the pathologist picked up the file and headed for the door.

"Let's take it upstairs so we can cover the interesting stuff together."

When they arrived at forensics they found a tea party in progress in the outer office, with Grace passing around a plate of biscuits as if Liam and Des were her guests.

Craig chuckled as they joined the small group. "This place is a lot homier since you arrived, Grace."

Des nodded ruefully. "I don't suppose it could have been any less. My fault."

Craig didn't spare his feelings. "Yes, it was. The boss sets the tone and yours was at the level of no decent coffee, the lowest known civilisation level of all. I bet even the Neanderthals had a decent brew."

As the newcomers were handed drinks and whatever biscuits Liam hadn't already eaten Craig got to the point.

"Anything useful from the bank, Des?"

"Nope. No forensics at all. Grace?"

The CSI smoothed down her floral skirt before responding. "We found nothing. I couldn't believe it. There wasn't a single print or hair anywhere on the vault floors that didn't belong to an employee authorised to be there."

"Which keeps them in the frame for the killings, boss."

"In the frame, yes, but not centre frame. We have to rule everyone out, but I'm convinced that even if someone at the bank let something slip it wasn't deliberate. The gallery theft and now Bolsover say this whole case was an outside job. Did you hear anything interesting about the vault inventories while you were working, Grace?"

She gave a tentative nod. "I think I heard someone mention a missing harpsichord. They were still checking when I left."

John's eyes widened. "A harpsichord! You have a highbrow killer on your hands."

Liam made a face. "That's a small piano, isn't it?"

"Sort of."

The CSI rushed to caveat her words. "I can't be sure, it was just what I thought I overheard."

Craig smiled at her. "Don't worry. We'll know for sure soon." He rubbed his hands together. "Right. Who wants to go first with Bolsover?"

John volunteered, extracting some ten by ten photographs from the file that he'd brought.

"Sorry, these might ruin your tea party, Grace."

But the CSI gazed at the first photograph of Horace Bolsover's red, swollen face unperturbed, reminding them all that, floral dresses and china teapots or no, Grace was a seasoned forensic professional who'd seen worse things than many of them could dream.

John started his report, most of it detailing the routine degradation inflicted on a ninety-year-old body by time, before and after death, but with an additional tale of some scars in odd places.

"He has what looks like a burn on his left upper arm. Slightly odd position in that it's on the inner aspect and up near the axilla."

No-one noticed Craig turning pale.

"But more exciting than that, there are what look like old bullet wounds on his left shoulder and right calf. We can only speculate on how he got them. Wars, running from the cops, gangs-"

"Gangs? He was a bit old to have been running with a squad wasn't he, Doc?"

"All his wounds are decades old and he was young once, Liam. As for his cause of death..."

The pathologist paused and frowned.

"What's the problem, Doc? He died from suffocation didn't he?"

"Yes... essentially."

Craig cut in.

"Carbon Monoxide, John? He was cherry red and Sigourney detected it in the air."

"Yes... it's just... Oh, OK, here goes. Siggie brought her air samples back to the lab for analysis, so I'll leave the chemical composition of those to Des, but the effects on Bolsover's body, the torso in particular, resemble something that I've only read about in books."

He held the second photograph from the file to his chest and sounded a warning. "This is nasty. The skin is marked in a way that suggests the presence of something very different to Carbon Monoxide."

At a glance from Des he passed the image to Craig, who stared aghast at the dead man's body for a moment before exclaiming in an astonished tone.

"Are those green blotches?"

Liam craned his neck to see. "They are too! He's red with green blotches like some sort of alien! What the hell does that?"

As the image did the rounds, John motioned his scientific colleague to speak. As Des did so he screwed up his ruddy, bearded face in disgust.

"OK, here's what I can give you. The samples Siggie took had carbon, hydrogen, nitrogen and oxygen with some organic and inorganic particles suspended in the gas which we haven't yet ID-ed."

"All of which makes?"

Des shook his head. "In the right proportions those components could make any number of compounds from water to nitrous oxide to plastics, except obviously here they're in gaseous form. But..."

His voice faltered, something the detectives had rarely seen happen, so Craig repeated, *"But?"* in encouragement.

"But my best guess is this was some form of unsophisticated but effective chemical weapon."

All eyes widened in alarm, more than one of them mentally listing who they'd had contact with since entering Bolsover's shop. The thought that it might have included someone vulnerable deepened their alarm to dread as Des went on.

"The only thing we can say with any certainty at this stage, because of Bolsover's cherry redness, is that Carbon Monoxide *was* present in substantial amounts. Siggie called that right. But we've a lot more work to do before we can nail any other compounds down."

He paused to look at Craig. Curiously, as if the detective was some unlabelled specimen in his lab.

"You haven't asked if you or your team are in danger from the gas, Marc."

"I assumed we'd have felt its effects right away. But are we still?"

"No. The concentration was very low by the time you got there. But I'm interested that you didn't ask."

Craig shrugged. "When your time's up, your time's up."

Liam nodded emphatically. "Heroes, that's what *we* are. And heroes never whinge."

The remark earned him several rolls of the eyes.

"More importantly, could we have passed it on to anyone else, Des?"

"No, there's no indication of that. I'm fairly sure that only someone who inhaled a sufficient quantity of the gas would die, but I'll still be asking Porton Down for help to pin down what it is."

Porton Down in Wiltshire played host to the Ministry of Defence's Defence Science and Technology Laboratory (DSTL), and had been known for over a century as the UK's most controversial military research facility. However, its knowledge of chemicals could come in useful right now.

"Excellent, but could you arrange to have anyone else exposed at the shop checked out, please."

John raised a finger. "I'll do that."

"Thanks."

Des picked up his report. "Anyway, as for what the *non* gaseous components are, I haven't a clue yet. As I said, one of them looks organic, but the other seems to be a plastic of some sort. We'll need spectroscopy and more to pin them down."

Craig's earlier pallor returned and when John's eyes locked on his he knew that they'd both just had the same horrific thought.

Liam missed the exchange completely and returned to an earlier point. "You said you'd read about this red and green spotty look, Doc. Sci-fi novels or medical ones?"

A small shake of Craig's head reinforced the decision that the pathologist had already made to keep his thoughts to himself; if their embryonic thoughts *were* correct then Horace Bolsover's murder could turn out to be a societal nightmare as well as a criminal one and any careless words they uttered now could never be taken back.

The medic hid his feelings behind a shrug and casual words. "I can't remember. Sorry."

Seeing his deputy about to press the point Craig jumped in, "But I'm sure John will check and get back to us. Des, could you update Annette on Bolsover, please. She's leading from our side."

"Will do. I'll keep you up-to-date with the gas composition and Grace will keep looking into the guns."

The CSI interjected eagerly. "They're nearly one hundred years old, but I'm still trying to pin the exact models down."

"Great. Anything else for us?"

After a series of glances Des answered "No" for them all and then Craig stood up so abruptly he took everyone aback. But he knew he had to get Liam out of there before he began questioning John again.

"Right then, it's time to head home. I'll call you later, John."

They both knew the discussion wouldn't be about their kids.

Chapter Eight

Tooting, South London. Tuesday 17th December. 10.30 a.m.

The Restful Willow retirement home, a Jewel Company Home in case anyone was interested, wasn't half as bad as Andy had imagined it the night before. His vision had been of a characterless building with a maze of beige corridors floored with a dark, paisley-patterned carpet to save on shampooing and vacuuming, with a large communal sitting room where the elderly residents either sat in a circle staring at each other or in a line gazing at a TV with the volume turned down.

In real life the home's corridors were painted snow white and had prints by various artists dotted along their walls. The carpet was dark grey olefin, and combined with the white gloss woodwork everywhere it was clearly Jewel Headquarters' concept of a modern retirement, which was fine if your residents fancied aging on the set of a home improvement show.

The place had plainly been designed to attract or at least not offend future customers, in many cases the less than loving families of future guests rather than the guests themselves, something that struck the D.C.I. as odd coming from an extended family in which his grandparents had lived in an apartment at the top of their house until they'd passed away and he had enjoyed visiting them every day as a child. He hoped that the home at least allowed residents to personalise their rooms.

His hope was answered when a polite but officious manager knocked and opened the door into Matilde Fervier Rosser's bed sitting room, and he saw that its walls were painted a deep pink and dotted with silver-framed black and white images of four people whose resemblance was so uncanny they had to have come from the same family.

One particularly striking studio portrait took pride of place. It was of a slim, dark-eyed girl with matching hair curled and bouncing on her shoulders in a style linked firmly to the nineteen-forties, and when the slight, grey-haired woman writing at a small bureau turned in response to the manager's, "Matilde, you have a visitor. A Chief Inspector

Angel" the large dark eyes that stared straight at Andy gave the girl in the picture her name.

Matilde Fervier had been a real looker and the detective wondered whether that very thing, something that could be as much a curse in life as a blessing, had given her tales to tell.

On her graceful wave towards a chair he pulled it up opposite and sat down, keeping his eyes fixed on his hostess the whole time. Her gaze gave nothing away but her voice did. It was strong and as heavily accented as if she had only left her home in France that day.

"Thank you, Dolores. You may leave us now."

The tone was so imperious that Andy half-expected the official to courtesy on the way out, but she merely said, "The tea will be here in a minute" and left leaving the door slightly ajar, which made Matilde Fervier give a wry smile.

"She thinks men are not to be trusted. Even with someone as old as me." She gestured at the picture that he'd noticed. "Then I think, but not now."

Too much of a gentleman to agree that there was any difference Andy turned quickly to the reason he was there.

"Do you prefer to be addressed as Mrs Rosser or Ms Fervier?"

The question brought a gleam to her eyes.

"Ah now, that *is* a question. Fervier-Rosser I think. Milo was a good man and I respected him. He rescued me from my family you know. After the war."

Her family?

It made the D.C.I.'s antennae twitch and he thought he would quite like to find out why. He had been close to both his grandmothers and some of the tales that they'd told him about wartime still astounded him.

Not wanting to check how much time they had by his watch for fear of offending his hostess, Andy worked it out from the pattern of his morning so far. Up at eight and checked-out of his hotel in Victoria, coffee and brioche at a nearby patisserie because his call to the home the night before had said not to visit before ten, then a tube and a walk, a short wait in reception and here they were. That made it ten-thirty now or thereabouts. By that reckoning he could spend a good ninety minutes chatting and justify it easily.

His holding smile became more active.

"Rescued you from your family? Really? How did that

come about?"

After a brief pause while the tea was brought and poured, Matilde replied.

"Milo was in the Allied Army. A Captain you know."

As she indicated a photograph of a young man in uniform her pride was clear.

"He and his men were clearing houses in our area of Paris and they found me alone there, guarding what was left of my family's possessions from looters..."

The slightness of the young Matilde made Andy wonder just how effective a guard she could really have been, unless she'd planned on *staring* any intruders into submission. She was still speaking, in such precise English without contractions that elocution lessons had clearly been a feature of her youth.

"...I could not speak a word of English and Milo spoke no French, but the language of love is universal, no? We were married within months and remained that way for fifty years."

The words brought a lump to the D.C.I.'s throat and he thought of his own catastrophic love life: two marriages, two divorces, and now a broken engagement with an ex-fiancée who had placed him firmly in the friendship zone.

He was tempted to ask how Matilde and Milo had managed fifty years together, but they only had limited time and he was there to talk about art.

"What a lovely story. He was a very lucky man."

He expected to hear his maternal grandmother's unchanging response to the same compliment, "Yes, he was," but to his surprise Matilde shook her head.

"Non. I was the lucky one. Milo was a wonderful man. But now..." She gazed around her and gave a uniquely Gallic shrug. "Now I am just one more old lady waiting to die, and hidden away by the state in this rabbit hutch until I do."

"You don't want to be here?"

It earned him a sceptical look.

"*Would you?* Social services insisted I sell my house and move here after that bastard stole my Holbein."

The detective was taken aback by the expletive, although why *shouldn't* older people swear? Outrage and its accompanying medieval lexicon didn't belong exclusively to youth. In fact, now he thought about it, why didn't *more* pensioners swear? *He* would when *he* was eighty if his arthritis was aching and people insisted on patronising him like he was a kid. If old people weren't strong enough to hit their oppressors then maybe a few well-chosen four letter words would get the message across instead!

He realised that his hostess was still speaking.

"Of course, after he did *that* they said I was vulnerable. *Vulnerable.*" She snorted derisively and stared challenging at him. "Tell me, do I *look* vulnerable to you, young man?"

"Well, I-"

Too late Andy realised that she'd been daring him to say yes.

"*Of course I am not vulnerable!* I survived the war and guarded my family's Paris home for almost six months before Milo arrived! And there were *plenty* of nasty sorts roaming the streets then, I can tell you. Mashers were not invented in the present day you know."

Clearly not. He seemed to remember the Vikings had been keen advocates of the rape and pillage school of war.

But Andy was keen to steer her away from the violent topic and back to something else that she'd said.

"You said your family's *Paris* home."

"Yes. What of it?"

"So they had other residences?"

She sipped slowly at her tea as if considering what to say and settled for, "Yes. There were a lot of us Ferviers."

Sensing that he'd entered sensitive territory, the detective helped himself to a macaron, taking a bite and celebrating it loudly; the taste was fabulous and one he'd only experienced before in France.

"Good, non? I send to a patisserie in Kensington for them. They import them fresh from Paris."

When he'd savoured the last morsel Andy restarted his questioning in a deliberately casual tone.

"By a lot of you, is that a lot within your direct family, or including cousins, aunts, uncles and so on?"

"The second. At home there was only Mama, Papa, my little brother François and me, and we lost poor Frankie in forty-one." She gazed down at her hands, which Andy noticed were now twisting her skirt into a knot from angst. "He was caught in cross fire between our brave resistance and the enemy."

"I'm very sorry."

Matilde's large eyes filled with tears. "He was such a

sweet boy. So gentle. Perhaps it was better that he died then than to see what happened to our beautiful France in the coming years."

Andy gave her a moment to recover, and then he pressed on in a softer tone.

"You said your husband rescued you *from* your family. How so, if you were so close?"

"From my *extended* family, not my parents and Frankie."

Her sneer on the word 'extended' said he would need to broach the topic carefully, so he opted for a short diversion while he thought about how.

Trying not to show his pain about the suffering of his Jewish family at the hands of the Nazis in case it biased her response, he asked casually, "How were things in Paris with the Germans?"

It had clearly been more of a test question than he'd allowed himself to acknowledge because Matilde's immediate look of disgust made him want to cheer.

"Nazi pigs."

Her follow-on words added another dimension.

"*I* hated them."

Andy couldn't be certain but it seemed as if she'd slightly emphasised 'I'.

The speed of her looking away said that a further query right now would hit stony ground so he returned to his questions on family.

"So you had a wider family and they lived outside Paris?"

She answered with a brisk nod.

"But you all stayed at each other's houses when it suited, which is why you mentioned *your* family's Paris House?"

"Yes. Paris was where my parents, François and I always lived. My father was a bank manager. But we had relatives all over France and they might travel to us or us to them for many months in the year, especially in the summer when Paris grew too warm. My mother would always take us to the country then."

The twitch the D.C.I. had felt earlier grew.

"Where did the others live?"

Her glance away and casual tone hinted again that the topic of her extended family made her uncomfortable.

"The Alps, Nice and so on. I can't remember exactly. I was just a child."

It was clearly time to change the subject again; he could

examine the Ferviers family tree in detail when he got home.

To mark the transition he took out his mobile intending to show her an image of the Holbein, but the action had a startling effect.

"You are checking the time! You are leaving already! No-one wants to spend time with the old."

Andy reacted instinctively, reaching out a hand to touch her thin one in reassurance.

"I'm not leaving. I'm enjoying our chat so I'll be here until twelve, if that's all right with you? And I'm only leaving then because I have a plane to catch."

The words successfully halted her spiral and she gazed at him curiously. "To where?"

"Ireland. I'm over here to follow up on a case in which a piece of art was stolen."

"Like my Holbein?"

"A painting by Vermeer, but I'm hoping there might be a slim link." He turned his mobile around so she could see the screen. "This was what I was going to show you. It's your Holbein sketch."

He stroked the phone to light it up and watched her face light up as well.

"Ah, my lovely Holbein. Papa's cousin brought it to us for safe keeping with some other things but he never came back for it at the end of the war. But your police have said I cannot have it back until the criminal case is over." She gazed at him mournfully. "I will be dead before that ends and I would *so* like to hold it again, just once."

Andy made up his mind to see what he could do about it.

"Can you recall this cousin's name?"

"Frederick, Frederick Fervier. One of Papa's cousins. He was a ratty little man, and I always remembered his name because I thought it was silly having two names beginning with the same letter."

"I agree. My parents named me Andrew, so I've been Andrew Angel or Andy really all my life."

The giggle she gave was of the young girl she'd once been.

"I like it. Andy Angel. Angel is such a pretty name."

"Thank you. It was Engelmann originally, which in Yiddish means Angel Man, but when my grandfather came to Ireland in thirty-nine he shortened it. That's the family legend anyway. I don't really know. I suppose I should really ask my dad."

She nodded decisively. "I think Angel is nice."

He pressed the advantage created by their warmth to ask something else.

"Was the Holbein the only piece of art that you and your husband brought from Paris?"

She shook her head immediately.

"Oh no, there were lots of others. Some very valuable: a Monet, a Degas and I remember a small Renoir also. We brought them all here with us. But everything but the Holbein was sold when Milo was made redundant at the end of the nineteen-eighties. It took him three years to find a new job and we needed to live."

"Of course. Can you remember *where* you sold them?"

"Yes. We always used the same auction house. Mansours in Battersea. They were the largest at that time."

Andy sincerely hoped they were still around. If so they should have a record of all their past sales and might be able to throw some light on at least one Fervier clan's art collection, although whether Matilde Fervier's family had any links to Hortense Fervier still remained to be proved, and he didn't want to ask and raise Matilde's hopes of finding long lost relatives.

Matilde was still talking about her art.

"Of course all the pieces we brought over really belonged to my whole family. They had just been left with us in Paris by aunts and cousins and so on during the war because our house had a large strong room. Because Papa was a bank manager."

Which she could have hidden inside. That explained why she'd believed she could defend her home against raiders.

"Have you any idea where those aunts and cousins might have acquired the pieces from in the first place, Mrs Fervier-Rosser?"

The sudden and unambiguous aversion of her eyes told the detective that he'd just stepped back on to dangerous ground. It didn't matter. He'd discovered a lot, and a trip to Mansours on his way to Heathrow was definitely on the cards.

But before that there was a tea party to be had and stories to hear, then a quick text to update the chief followed by a lengthy call to The Met to cajole them into promising that Matilde would be taken to see her precious Holbein again.

****

The Ormeau Road, South Belfast. 11.30 a.m.

Craig glanced sideways at his chauffeur as they made staccato progress up one of the UK's most congested thoroughfares, Belfast's Ormeau Road.

"How many men can we spare this morning, Liam?"

The D.C.I. broke off his howl at a cyclist who'd just whizzed through the red light in front of them to reply.

"Just our lot, or did you mean including Jack's troops?"

"Preferably *not* our lot. They're all busy."

"Six uniforms then." He gesticulated in the direction of the law breaker, who was now nowhere to be seen. "We should've nicked them, running the lights like that."

"And by the time you'd kicked on the siren and the traffic had cleared enough to let us through they'd have been halfway to Bangor. *Focus.* Why only six?"

"'Cos Jack says we've been abusing his hospitality recently, whatever *that* means."

"Taking the piss, that's what that means, and to be honest he's probably right. We swan in and out of High Street like we own the place."

"Well we do, don't we? I mean, the same people that own us own it. Ach, you know what I'm getting at. It's not *Jack's* place anyway."

"Logical, but there's no accounting for feelings, and Jack's feelings tell him that *he* owns High Street. It's my fault really. I need to thank him more often."

"And me."

Craig rolled his eyes. "Let's just say I need to thank people in general more often. Look, I'll order a few bottles of whiskey and have them delivered to him. Maybe that will do the trick."

"It will all right, but it won't make him produce more than six men *today*."

Craig nodded in agreement and took out his mobile, and five minutes later they had the promise of six additional constables from Stranmillis Station. As he ended the call his deputy puffed out his cheeks and shook his head.

"*Now* you've done it. Jack *really* won't be happy this time. You've just gone and played the new girlfriend off against the wife."

Craig snorted. "You say that as if you'd know what having both was like, which before you try to bullshit me, you *don't*."

Realising the truth in his deputy's statement he sighed wearily. "I really can't win, can I? If I let Jack rule us today we'll only have six troops to show our young victims' sketches around the university departments, and if I borrow more uniforms from Stranmillis then I'm being a tart."

"Yep. That's you. A big Baron Craig tart."

With than Liam indicated right up University Avenue towards Queen's.

"I've had enough of this bloody traffic. At this rate we won't get to the gallery till the middle of next week."

Craig rolled his eyes. "*Finally.* I've been waiting for you to do that for twenty minutes. Why the hell you ever drove this far up the Ormeau in the first place I don't know."

The D.C.I. turned to gawp at him. "*Seriously?* You're trying *that?* When *you* didn't make up your fricking mind whether you were heading for the gallery or Queen's first until five minutes ago!"

Craig was saved from admitting it by his phone ringing. "Have to answer this, sorry. Good morning, Aidan."

His cheerful tone wasn't returned.

"Nothing good about it, Guv. They've completed the inventory on one of the vaults."

Craig put the call on speaker.

"Only one? What the hell have they been doing till now?"

"Gambon's being pernickety."

Liam snorted. "Anal more like. Probably doesn't want to tell some bigwig their tiara's been nicked till he can't avoid it."

"Whatever. Anyway, do you want to hear what's missing so far?"

Craig braced himself. "Fire ahead."

"A harpsichord from the court of Marie Antoinette of France, a solid gold carnival mask from Venice circa fourteen-hundred, and seventeen, *seventeen* emerald, diamond and precious metal items, including bracelets, watches and a diamond necklace. Gambon pitched a fit when he heard, and this is only the first of six vaults."

Craig's mind was on the practicalities of the theft so his response was vague.

"OK... and was that one of the vaults where we found a body?"

"No, they're starting on the first of those now."

"OK. Give Joe Rice a call, he's at High Street I think, and ask him to come down there to keep an eye on proceedings."

"While I do what?"

"Start at the top of the list of people who hold code generators and work your way down. Take Ryan with you and get background details on *all* of them from Ash before you visit the first. These people all know each other and they've the power to severely mess up our case if they want to, so before you question the first get your ducks in a row. Ask Mary to go back to the bank and keep an eye on the inventory checks with Joe."

He cut the call before Aidan had a chance to object and turned back to his deputy.

"Grace was right about the harpsichord."

"Bloody hell. I can think of lighter things to steal."

He was startled when Craig shouted *"Exactly!"* and followed it with a sharp slap to the dashboard. Liam automatically pulled the car to an emergency stop, throwing his boss hard against the door.

"What was *that* for?"

"You slapped for an emergency stop."

"That only applies in a bloody driving test!"

Realising his error the D.C.I. pulled off again smoothly and tried for a nonchalant tone.

"So what was the *exactly* about then?"

Craig allocated him points for his cool and carried on. "I meant you were exactly right when you said there were lighter things to steal, and they did that as well with the watches and jewellery. But a harpsichord *is* heavy, so why take it at all?"

"It could've meant something important to them."

"Exactly." This time Craig didn't risk a slap. "Which means perhaps some of the jewellery pieces did too, although others could have just been opportunistic thefts. Easy swag to put in their pockets while they were there. But not the harpsichord, that definitely *was* special."

Liam sounded a sceptical note. "Or they might just have fancied it."

"Possible but not likely, and it won't be easy to fence either."

"Unless some bugger wanted it for his private collection and they stole it to order."

"Good point. But either way, carrying a harpsichord any distance without smashing it means they must have had a secure container, packing materials and transport. So... where did they park their van?"

"Outside. Must've done. But that means they had to carry the harpsic thing up from the vaults in the lift, through the bank's main hall and out to Royal Avenue. Or maybe there's a rear exit, but either way the same transport needs apply. And that means something should show on the street cams."

"Ash is on them. Right. I need to make some more calls."

The first was back to Aidan, to add full forensics on any rear exits from the bank to his list of jobs, and the second was to the team's analyst, instructing him to drop everything for an hour and harass Traffic and Aerial Support until they found their killer's van.

When Craig looked up again they were outside the Fervier Gallery and Terry Harding was waiting by the kerb.

"What took you so long? You said you'd be here by eleven."

Liam gave his boss' arm a shove. "You mean you'd already decided we were coming straight here before we left the squad?"

Craig ignored his question and answered the Robbery D.C.I.'s instead.

"Liam decided to go sightseeing."

He left his deputy to bluster and followed her into the gallery, which looked just the same as two days before.

"OK, this all looks identical so what did you bring us here to see, Terry?"

A finger pointed at the ceiling explained.

"You're not serious!"

"I am, and as it was you who first suggested the upper storey might have provided our thief with access I thought it was only fair to give you a look."

Ignoring Liam's, "How did they get up and down?" and Craig's, "Who owns the upstairs?" Harding led the way to the gallery's staff kitchen and walked up to what she had originally thought was a broom cupboard near the back.

Craig chuckled. "This is the entrance to the upper storey? Talk about Narnia."

"It's been specially designed. Look."

She pulled open the door but at first sight all that greeted them was a vacuum cleaner and a floor brush, until, by pressing a button inside the cupboard, the front section slid out smoothly to reveal a set of stairs behind.

Within seconds they were on the building's top storey, a slope-ceilinged studio comprised of a bedroom come living space with a small kitchen and bathroom at the rear.

"This is someone's home?"

"It's not lived in. It belongs to Hortense Fervier, the whole building does, not that she bothered to tell me. I only found out when I checked the building plans."

Liam shook his head, stupefied. "What the heck does she use it for? Obviously not to rent out. It's bleak."

Craig arched an eyebrow at his deputy. "Maybe it's for the *girlfriend*."

Harding was surprised. "Hortense is gay?"

"What? No. Well, not that I know of. I was thinking more of Mister Fervier using it for that, referencing a conversation that Liam and I had earlier in the car."

Seeing her confused expression he added, "Just ignore me."

Liam seized his moment. "Can I ignore you too? 'Cos you're really getting on my wick today."

Craig didn't dignify the comment with a response.

"But why *didn't* Hortense mention this place existed, Terry? Especially when someone had broken in and stolen her painting."

Terry sighed. "I asked her and she just muttered something about completely forgetting that it was there."

"Bullshit. I take it you've had the CSIs go over it."

"Last night and there's nothing. If the painting thief *did* wait here until it was dark they knew enough not to leave a trace."

"That fits now we know they're linked with our bank case, boss. They were plenty stealthy there too."

Craig nodded and turned back towards the stairs. "So finding this doesn't move you any further on with your robbery, Terry?"

"No. And neither did the staff interviews. They all look just as clean as Ms Fervier thought. I'm as puzzled as I was on Sunday."

They emerged via the cupboard into the kitchen where Liam immediately set about making a cup of tea.

"Madame Hortense has contacted her insurance company of course, but I'm still hoping we'll get the Vermeer back. Did

Andy discover anything useful in London?"

"He's still there looking, and really enjoying himself amongst all the art. He'll be back sometime later today so I'll ask him to contact you."

With the caveat that Andy didn't mention Matilde Fervier in case it got back to Hortense. From what little update the D.C.I. had managed to text him there seemed to be branches of her family on which the old lady was less than keen. Plus they weren't even sure that she and Hortense *were* family yet.

"Did you get anything from the street or traffic cams outside, Terry?"

Her face fell. "Not a thing. Your analyst told me they performed the same hack on those that they did on the gallery cams. Although how they managed to access police cameras I've no idea."

Except that a gifted hacker could get at almost anything with a keystroke as Ash had demonstrated time and time again. It didn't bode well for them getting images from outside the bank either but before Craig could go down that unpleasant rabbit hole his phone rang with an unknown number.

"Craig here."

"Sorry, sorry, sir" came down the line in a barely broken voice, telling Craig that at least one of the uniformed officers currently roaming Belfast's colleges in search of IDs on their first two victims was very young, probably a probationer.

"That's fine. What's your name, Constable?"

"Edgar. Probationer Keith Edgar, sir."

"And where are you calling from, P.C. Edgar?"

"Queen's University. The History Department."

Craig tensed. "Which sketch did they recognise?"

"The young lady's, sir. Or at least they think they have, but I-"

Craig cut him off, already making for the gallery's exit. "Stay where you are and we'll be with you in ten minutes."

It *should* only take five, but with Liam's driving today...

"Give D.C.I. Cullen your number and we'll call you when we arrive."

He passed over his phone.

"Keys, Liam. I'll drive."

And with that they were back on the road.

****

Aidan Hughes stared at the list in his hand and allowed himself a quiet gulp. He wasn't impressed by money or titles, but when someone was a household name even a cynical Belfast man like himself could be forgiven for having a few nerves. And there was more than one of those names on the list of Board members Mervyn Gambon had given him, which answered something that the D.C.I. had always wondered about; where do older famous people go to graze?

It has always seemed to him that from the ages of twenty to fifty the rich and famous, and not just the showbiz celebrity kind, were *everywhere*. Splashed across the pages of magazines, tabloids or broadsheets depending on the 'seriousness' of whatever had generated their fame, and popping up on TV programmes from, 'I'm a star - leave me on/get me off an island', and 'Let me bake/skate/dance/tumble my way across your TV screen just to show that I don't have two left feet', to chat, quiz and topical discussion shows.

Then just as mysteriously as they'd become visible in the first place the process seemed to happen in reverse and all those who'd claimed "I was once somebody" faded into the background never to be seen again, unless they were an actor, in which case they were almost guaranteed to appear in ten years' time propping up a bar in some TV soap.

But now he at least knew where all the old newsreaders, bankers and politicians went; they became members of corporate Boards. He looked at the names again, two that he recognised in particular, one a Norwegian ex-TV presenter adopted by Ireland in the mid-nineties as their go-to gal on all matters mainland European, the other a man who had made millions in the fitness industry by establishing a chain of well-known gyms all over the UK. He at least Aidan was looking forward to meeting, given that he sweated his guts out every morning on a rowing machine bearing the man's name. As a treat he'd decided to bookend his and Ryan's visits with the pair, saving the Norwegian Goddess till last and resigning themselves to some boring hours in between.

The expectation was fully lived down to but took a lot less time than expected because several members' agents had got wind that they were coming and had obligingly lined their clients up for Nicky to arrange meets at High Street, so after six short, sharp interviews during which no-one had recognised either of their victims' sketches and each had accounted for their whereabouts at the weekend, although of course alibis would have to be checked but as most of them had been at events where their every move had been recorded by cameras, something which made Aidan wonder whether fame left people finding it difficult to be alone, they had then each produced their code generators and Ryan had checked them via a web tie-in with Ash, who had confirmed that none of the tested devices had created a new vault code that weekend.

As an exercise in striking things off a list it had been satisfying but as to enlightening them on how their killers had entered the vaults not so much, so as the detectives walked up the quite enchanting floral and trellised pathway to the Moira home of the last and clearly only person on their list not to get tipped off at around one p.m. Aidan prayed that *this* interview yielded something or they would be at a dead end.

The woman who answered the front door of the substantial flat-fronted Georgian residence looked so like his memory of the TV presenter that the D.C.I. introduced himself.

"Ms Pedersen, my name's Detective Chief Inspector Hughes and this is Detective Sergeant Hendron. Our office arranged this interview with your secretary earlier by phone."

The response was a flirtatious giggle and a shake of the woman's head. "It was me your PA spoke to. I'm Liv Pedersen. Marte is my daughter. "

Aidan was genuinely surprised and even more so when they were shown into a large, cream furnished room where Marte Pedersen was sitting; the women looked like there was barely five years between them, not a generation. After a gabbled exchange between them in their native language, Ms Pedersen senior brought in a tray of coffee and left again, closing the door.

The D.C.I. recovered his equilibrium although not completely, while Ryan looked on amused but not immune. Even at sixty, Marte Pedersen was a beauty and he knew that her tanned leanness made her just the D.C.I.'s type.

Aidan took out his notebook and hid his face in its pages for a moment as he tried to push away an image of them ski-ing down snowy slopes together and then enjoying a sauna before their *real* après-ski, until his lust finally under control he looked up again and met the Board member's green eyed gaze.

"Ms Pedersen."

"Marte, please."

The sauna started steaming again.

"Marte then. You're aware of why we need to speak to you?"

She nodded, throwing a lock of auburn hair forward across one cheek that made the D.C.I.'s fingers twitch to smooth it back.

"Yes, my mother said. Mervyn Gambon also called."

Ah... *that* explained how everyone had known what was up. The detective shrugged inwardly; he hadn't explicitly told Gambon *not* to brief them and he supposed the man was just looking after his job.

"I'm sorry to make you visit me but I just couldn't get back to town in time."

"That's not a problem. Right, there are a few parts to what we need to ask you. First, could you tell us your whereabouts at the weekend, please?"

Another tale of mass socialising plus a private appearance on the Saturday night came trotting out. It disappointed Aidan slightly; he'd always thought of Scandinavian women as soulful lone travellers like Greta Garbo; mysterious and all knowing. But it seemed that Nordic celebrities were just the same as those elsewhere.

"Thank you. Could I have the names of some people able to confirm each of those, please?"

As she dictated he scribbled down her words.

"Good. Now, could we see your code generator, please?"

In preparation for her fetching the device he took out his phone and pulled up the office number, only noticing that she hadn't moved when it was on his screen.

Ryan looked at her questioningly. "You *do* have it with you?"

A shamefaced shake of the head said not.

"I don't seem to have it at all, I'm afraid. I've been hunting high and low for it since Mervyn called, thinking that perhaps I'd moved it between handbags or something, but it's nowhere to be found."

She gazed at each of them apologetically, blushing beneath her tan. "I'm so sorry. This has never happened before and I really can't think how it has now. I carry that thing with me everywhere because you never know when you might get a call from the bank."

The loss saddened and excited Aidan in equal measure. He would be disappointed if his celebrity crush turned out to be a criminal of course, but on the other hand he *was* a detective and this might just progress their case.

He said none of that aloud of course, simply scribbled on his pad again, choosing to move on to the final matter they'd come about before deciding what to do.

"We'll return to the code generator in a moment, but I wonder if you could answer something else for us first."

He motioned to Ryan who tapped quickly at his smartphone, bringing up the image of their female victim and turning it for the celebrity to see.

"Do you by any chance recognise this young lady?"

Pedersen gave it her best perusal, but eventually ended with a shake of her head.

"No, I'm sorry. Who is she?"

"I was hoping you might have been able to identify her."

"I'm sorry. I can't help. Is she one of the victims found in the vaults that Mervyn mentioned?"

Was there anything that Gabby Gambon *hadn't* mentioned?

"We can't comment on that, I'm sorry."

Ryan tapped up the boy's image and held out the phone again. "Have you ever seen *this* person?"

The mobile was wrenched instantly from his hand and after a moment's wide-eyed silence the air was rent by a scream that brought Liv Pedersen hurtling in. She rushed to her daughter's side, glaring at the detectives accusingly.

"What have you done? What have you done to my daughter?"

Ryan gabbled out a defence. "We didn't do anything! She was looking at a sketch on my pho-"

When she turned to look at the image she gasped, *"That's Dylan!"* her shock transformed almost instantly into a perplexed frown.

"Why do you have a drawing of my grandson? What has he to do with *you*?"

But her daughter had already guessed, and as Marte Pederson doubled over sobbing the detectives knew they had one of their IDs.

With her code generator missing they could also guess how their killers had entered the bank.

****

Queen's University Belfast. The Vice-Chancellor's Office. 1 p.m.

Craig and Liam had been left alone in the Vice-Chancellor's small, warm office for so long that they were just about to go in search of its owner when the wood-panelled door behind them opened and three people walked in, one of them in the traditional black gown that some of Liam's schoolteachers had worn and which had always made him want to call them 'Batman' instead of 'Sir'.

It wasn't Batman who took a seat behind the desk but the tall, slim woman with him; the third, uniformed entrant Craig guessed as Keith Edgar, the P.C. they'd called on arrival and arranged to meet after he'd gathered whatever background on their possible female victim he could.

The woman, who introduced herself as Vice-Chancellor Marjorie Walker, sat down at her desk and steepled her fingers so hard that their tips turned white.

Craig wasn't surprised she was stressed; it couldn't be every day the cops came asking about a student.

After a full minute of watching her straining digits he tired of the silence and broke it himself.

"As you know, Ms Walker, this constable has been showing sketches of two young people to your academic staff, just as officers have been doing at colleges all across Belfast. And this gentleman," he indicated the superhero, "I'm sorry but I don't know your name, said that he might recognise one of them."

The academic nodded. "I'm Professor Ben Mooney, Head of History. Yes, I think I recognise the girl from my new intake. She's Sophie-"

He halted abruptly mid-name, his eyes, now fixed on his boss, widening to a glassy stare, making it clear that Walker had given him some secret signal to shut up.

Craig fixed *his* stare on her as well. "You object to Professor Mooney helping us for some reason, Vice-Chancellor?"

Clearly not used to being challenged the VC was instantly taken aback.

"*What?* No, no, no, not at all. Of course not. I mean, why would I?"

Liam, who had been listening in silence to the exchange, gave her a sceptical look.

"Probably because you don't fancy having to tell the girl's parents the police have been asking about her." After a quick glance at Edgar to confirm that he hadn't said either young person was dead the D.C.I. went on. "Well, never you worry about that. This is a serious case so we'll do any telling that has to be done." His tone hardened. "*When* you've given us her name."

The words galvanised the official and she almost flew to the door, yanking it open and murmuring something hastily to her secretary before retaking her seat. In what seemed like only seconds later the PA deposited a file in her hand and Walker placed it on the desk face down, setting her jaw.

Craig had been trying not to show his impatience with the woman but it had proven harder by the minute and now he let it show.

"Vice-Chancellor Walker. We *fully* understand that you have a duty of care and confidentiality to your students, but this is a serious investigation. We wouldn't be trying to identify this young woman without *very* good reason."

When there was no change in her expression, he took what he regarded as the action of last resort. He removed his warrant card from his pocket, set it face up on the desk and waited for the gasp.

When it came it was noisy and so were her words.

"MURDER SQUAD! *MURDER?*"

An echo of the sentiment came from Mooney but Liam was having no truck with it. If they hadn't realised detectives rarely paid social visits then they were both far too thick to be in their jobs.

"We told you this was serious."

Walker was spluttering now. "You're saying she was *murdered*? One of *my* students?"

Liam wanted to laugh at her possessiveness but he knew that it wasn't the right time. Everyone who died suddenly became *my* friend, *my* employee, *my* mate; it seemed like second nature to appropriate their pain.

Craig nodded. "We believe so. Now can one of you *please* tell us who you believe this girl to be? And preferably show us a photograph to demonstrate why."

Walker's response was to push the file across the desk at him and fall back into her chair.

He read the name on its cover aloud, "Sophie Adomaitis" and opened the file to see a photograph that almost exactly matched their sketch and *definitely* matched the girl that they'd found dead in the vault, although in this image she was smiling and full of life.

"It says here that she was twenty. A first year studying History and with an address in Rowena House."

Mooney commented in a weak voice. "That's a student hall on the Malone Road. First year students from abroad usually stay there."

Liam turned towards him. "Abroad where?"

"Lithuania in the Baltic States. A city called Klaipėda I believe. I recall her mentioning the name at our first tutorial when everyone was introducing themselves." He gestured at the file. "The details should be in there."

Walker found her voice again. "How was she killed?"

"I'm sorry, we can't disclose that. Did she have any family here in Northern Ireland?"

Mooney shook his head. "No, I don't think so. Foreign students often don't. But she was a chatty girl so I'm sure she'd have already made friends."

"Had she missed any classes?"

"Not mine, I saw her at a lecture last week. On the Monday. But I can check with her other lecturers."

Craig smiled his thanks. The man was obviously trying to help but this had to be done by the book.

"That's kind, but no. We need to do that. If you could just provide a print-out of her schedule and the names of the staff who took the sessions, please."

When he had both lists in his hand Walker gave an exhausted sigh.

"Her parents will need to be notified."

Liam shook his head quickly. "Just contacted initially and *we'll* do it. Until she's been ID-ed by them we can't be sure it's the right girl."

"Very well. Their address is in the file."

In the Baltic States. That meant the formal ID would be delayed for at least a day but waiting was the only moral thing to do. Craig passed his deputy the file and then looked at the academics in turn.

"I don't need to tell you that everything must stay in this room. Telling anyone else could risk causing pain to Ms Adomaitis' family and might even alert her killer and make them run. Am I understood?"

An emphatic nod from the lecturer and a more resentful one from the VC gave the policemen their cue to leave.

"I'll be in touch, Vice-Chancellor. Goodbye, Professor."

The three cops had barely hit the corridor before Liam gave a noisy sigh.

"God, I'm *glad* I didn't go to Uni if the bosses are like that."

"They aren't all, and Walker isn't deaf so keep it down, will you. But she's clearly out of her depth dealing with a death. OK, Liam, get on to the family and arrange for Nicky to fly them over. Do that now, please. You know what to say."

He turned to the young P.C., whose puppy fat stretched face said that he was barely more than a child.

"Our female victim is almost certainly Sophie Adomaitis, so very well done, Constable Edgar. Who's your boss?"

"Sergeant Harris at High Street."

It prompted a smile from the detective. Jack was clearly teaching his newbies well.

"Well, I'll be sure to tell him of your good work. Now, you still have a second victim to ID so on you go."

Craig soon discovered that they were two for two.

****

Mansours Auctioneers. Battersea, London. 1.30 p.m.

As auction houses went Andy had been in larger and more elegant ones, ones with high ceilings like the police warehouse he'd visited the day before but adorned with elaborate Plaster relief ceilings and chandeliers. Their walls had been lined with a fleece of expensive tapestries, heavy period furniture and the large paintings propped against it, creating an ambience that made the potential buyers seated at its heart feel cloistered and important, as if they were in some elegant club that awarded membership only to a wealthy few.

It was a clever marketing tactic; make your customers feel special and they would try to impress their companions by displaying the wealth that justified them being there. The fact that they did so by bidding on the very artefacts that had made them feel exceptional in the first place was both a win for the house and amusing to watch.

But Mansours' Auctioneers *wasn't* one of those grand places, and as Andy pushed at its half-wooden, half-glass door, with its upper half set out like a chessboard where instead of being black and white each square was a prism of differently coloured glass, he was transported back to somewhere very familiar; the primary school that he'd attended in County Down forty years before.

He glanced around him for evidence to support the memory and found a waist-height dado rail dotted with the plastered over remnants of hooks that had been removed, hooks where the coats and anoraks of small children had once hung. Other evidence, low-set windows for little eyes to peer through and door handles placed a foot below where they should have been, confirmed that he was right. Mansours was operating out of an old Victorian primary school, which was at worst a sign that the business wasn't prosperous and at best that they were performing a service to conservation by repurposing the building rather than have some developer knock it down.

Resisting his urge to go in search of a blackboard on which to scribble 'Andy Angel Wuz Here' the D.C.I. pushed through a set of inner doors and entered what seemed to be the auctioneers' exhibit hall. Paintings, sculptures, china and furniture were arranged throughout the space but not haphazardly, rather the pieces were clustered in small islands which when Andy looked closer were grouped according to either provenance or age. Clever; and attractive to a provenance nerd like him, as well as demonstrating instantly that the auctioneers knew their stuff.

He circled the clusters for a few minutes examining an occasional piece at close quarters, and had just arrived at a grouping of French glass when the narrowest elderly man that he had ever laid eyes on emerged from the back of the hall.

The suddenness of his appearance made the detective jump and then immediately think how unprofessional that must have looked; behold the police officer, keeper of law and order, calm in the face of threat and pressure blah blah, blah, who jumps out of his skin at the sight of an old man.

The pensioner stifled a smile as if he'd just read Andy's mind and said, "I'm sorry to have startled you" in a deep bass and an accent that the D.C.I. couldn't immediately place.

"I was in my office."

He indicated the corner he'd come from, where Andy saw what looked like a glass-windowed classroom, which it probably had been once. Failing to notice it made him chide himself yet again, this time for being so absorbed in the art that he'd missed a whole room, never mind the potentially machete wielding assailant standing in front of him now.

"I am Fareed Mansour."

The name above the door.

"I'm afraid the next sale isn't until Friday so there's little to see at the moment. If you return on Thursday most of the exhibits will be in place."

It was time to show some ID so Andy held up his warrant card.

"I'm sorry, Mister Mansour, I'm not here to look at the exhibits." He *was* sorry too. "I'm D.C.I. Angel and I need to ask a few questions about some items your auction house sold."

The man's greying eyebrows reached for the roof. *"We don't sell stolen goods!"*

Andy made soothing noises. "No, no, I'm sure you don't. Please don't worry, that wasn't what I was implying. These pieces were sold quite legally by your company on behalf of a family, but we're interested in their details, dates, prices and so forth. There's no implication of impropriety in any way."

Unimpressed, Mansour snuffled noisily before speaking again. "That's as may be, but we'll need their permission to disclose anything."

Thankfully Andy had anticipated the request and had had Matilde write a note for him to bring.

After staring at it for so long that the D.C.I. wondered whether the auctioneer somehow expected the letters to rearrange themselves, Mansour handed the paper back with a short, "Huh!" and at his insistence the next thing to be handed over was Andy's ID.

While the elderly man perused it Andy perused him, marvelling at his shape. Mansour barely measured two foot across and his shoulders were exactly the same width as his trunk and hips. It had the effect of making him look like a narrow rectangle with two feet sticking out at the bottom and a bump on top for his head. A caricaturist would have had a field day with the man.

Either unaware of what Andy was thinking or too used to it to remark, the proprietor finally returned the warrant card and waved the detective ahead of him into his glass den. Once inside the small office, whose windows and walls Andy could now see were streaked with dust baked in over several years and had, happy days, a blackboard on one wall, Mansour took a seat at his desk and unlocked a drawer, muttering, "Permission or not, this is most irregular."

"Yes, I'm sorry, but Mrs Fervier-Rosser was very particular. She said you'd always sold their pieces for them because they trusted you."

He'd added the line for effect but the auctioneer seemed mollified.

"We did sell their art. My father first and then me. They had some lovely items at the beginning. Fewer and fewer as the years went on."

The Rossers had sold their family jewels to live on. It was a tale of impoverished gentility and Andy felt sorry for them, but not as much as the families who'd never had any wealth to lose.

His socialist thoughts were interrupted by a large ledger appearing from the drawer, its patina of grime thicker but not quite as caked as that on the room's windows and walls.

"This covers nineteen-eighty to ninety. If my memory serves me right that's the period we're thinking of. When the Rossers were in here a lot."

Andy nodded in admiration; the man must have possessed an encyclopaedic memory to recall individual clients, their wares and dates.

The auctioneer began turning the pages one by one, so slowly that Andy wanted to scream. To fill the time he asked a question.

"Your accent. Where is it from?"

It brought a suspicious look before "B...Battersea" hesitantly hit the air, and despite the obvious sign not to probe further that's precisely what the detective did.

"Yes, but where before then?"

"What are you, the police or something?" was out before Mansour realised what he'd said, and the words brought first surprise and then a chuckle from them both.

"Sorry, I was just being nosey. Occupational hazard."

"Yes, you were. But I'll tell you anyway. I'm originally from Iran and came here in seventy-eight with my parents."

The answer and the man's reluctance to disclose it came together in the detective's mind and he realised that he was looking at a refugee. Mansour's family had obviously fled the Shah's rule just before the Iranian revolution of seventy-nine. The reason they'd left could have been one of many but Andy knew Iran's intelligence agency the SAVAK had been ruthless to anyone who'd even murmured dissent.

The old man read the question in the policeman's eyes and decided to put him out of his misery.

"My father was the editor of a newspaper and disagreed with the Shah's policies in print. He and my mother had been threatened, had their printing press destroyed twice and finally realised that if they didn't leave the country soon my younger sister and I might be orphaned." He shrugged. "We had to leave, but still we were the lucky ones. There were plenty of outspoken critics who ended up imprisoned or dead."

He shuddered and in an effort to move away from a subject that was clearly discomfiting, Andy motioned to the book.

"How's the search going?"

"Ah yes. Well, I've found the earliest items they sold through us."

Mansour turned the tome so that he could see and a who's who of artists and artisans from the fourteenth to the twentieth century appeared in front of Andy's eyes. The D.C.I. gawped at some of the names listed; Matilde Fervier's family had been worth a fortune, or rather her *extended* family had been but they'd failed to retrieve their valuables from Paris at the end of the war.

"Where did it all come from?"

The auctioneer stared at him blankly. "What do you mean?"

Suddenly remembering that *he* only knew the pieces had really belonged to Matilde's extended family because she'd confided in him Andy quickly shook his head.

"Sorry, what I meant to say is, I'm sure that when you receive a piece for sale you check where it's come from? I mean that it isn't stolen."

"Yes, yes, we do that. My grandson runs them through computer databases or some such for me."

"But in the period we're talking about that wouldn't have been possible."

"Well no, I don't suppose it would have been. But my father was an honest man so I'm sure he did the equivalent thing for that time."

Which would basically have been nothing. All Mansour Senior could possibly have done to check that an item wasn't stolen was ask the cops to carry out some checks, and back then that would have amounted to rifling through sheaves of paper crime reports and *perhaps* making a few calls. Even if the items Matilde Fervier had brought from Paris *had* been dodgy, neither the auction house nor Matilde herself could ever have known that when they were sold.

The D.C.I. dragged a hand down his face wearily, wondering what he would tell Craig. He'd been tasked to look into art belonging to Hortense Fervier and had found only an elderly and probably unrelated French woman in London and one Holbein sketch. Now he'd uncovered *this* treasure trove but it had already been sold on, and there was no information on where any of it had originated except for Matilde's Holbein from her uncle with the alliterative name. He'd steered himself right into a dead end.

Andy was just about to throw himself a pity party when he felt a tug at his sleeve and turned to find Fareed Mansour blowing dust excitedly off a page.

"Look at this."

The auctioneer jabbed a thin, arthritic finger at some words in tiny font that made Andy squint to see.

"A Manet. Brought for sale in August nineteen-eighty-eight by its owners Milo and Matilde Rosser. Police checks showed the item was reported stolen after the war by the Cassin family from the south-east of France, and the theft occurred in nineteen–forty-three. We withdrew it from sale immediately for checks and it was eventually returned to the Cassins by the police."

A prickle ran down Andy's spine. This was important, and something that Matilde had failed to mention.

"Can I copy this page? I mean, do you have a copy machine here?"

"Of course we have a copy machine! We're not completely last century you know."

That debate would have to wait, because ten minutes later Andy was on his way back to Restful Willows with a hot print-out in his hand.

****

The C.C.U. 2.30 p.m.

Craig was just getting ready to leave his office and start briefing when his desk phone started to ring. That was never good news. Anyone who he'd ever worked with closely or liked had his mobile number, so it had to be either the Public Prosecution Service, which fell into the first category but definitely not the second, the Chief Constable Sean Flanagan, who actually fell into both but was an old-fashioned cop who thought mobiles were the Devil's work, or someone who'd called Nicky first and given her so much grief that she'd decided to pass them on.

He found out it was the third option *and* the reason why when Hortense Fervier, emphasis on the tense part, yelled at him down the line. The conversation went something like this:

"Rant, rant."

"Yes but, Mrs Ferv-"

"Rant, rant, painting."

"D.C.I. Harding is dealing with-"

"Rant, rant, rant, and now my daughter hasn't come home!"

At that point Craig focused and cut across the gallery owner in a growl. "Ms Fervier, will you *please* let me speak!"

When the ranting turned to mumbling he went on.

"And don't interrupt. Right, the theft of your painting is being dealt with by Fraud and Robbery and D.C.I. Harding is your contact there, so please call *her* with all your queries on that. But I *do* want to hear more about your daughter. What's her name?"

"Angelica. She's eighteen."

"Is she at school, university or working?"

"First year university."

Craig felt a sudden chill. "Queen's?"

"Yes."

"Studying what?"

If she said History it would be too much of a coincidence.

"French."

But the fact that there was no coincidence didn't mean there wasn't something.

"When did you last see her?"

"Yesterday morning. She was going to her lectures and then spending the night with a friend."

"Someone you know?"

"Yes, Celine, a nice girl she went to school with. But that's why I'm worried. When I rang Celine at lunchtime to say I would collect Angelica after her tutorial she said that Angelica hadn't turned up last night. In fact, she hadn't seen her on campus yesterday either and they *always* meet at the Students Union for lunch."

"But your daughter *had* arranged to visit her last night?"

"Yes, at six o'clock. But when Angelica didn't turn up at her flat Celine just assumed that she'd changed her mind and hadn't bothered to call."

He'd hated people who'd done that when he was young. The only excuse for not calling to cancel was if you were lying unconscious somewhere with a hangover and Angelica Fervier would've had to have been going some to acquire one of those by six p.m.

Just then something occurred to him.

"Is Angelica's surname Fervier or something else?"

"*What?* Oh... I see what you mean. She's Angelica Swann after my husband. I've always kept my family name of Fervier. But what difference does that make now? We need to find her!"

"It could delay our searches if we get the name wrong. All right, so Angelica left your home yesterday morning, Monday, didn't go to university you think and definitely didn't turn up to see her friend at six as arranged. I'm assuming you've tried her mobile?"

"Ten times an hour since I found out! It's switched off."

"We can locate it anyway."

Craig took a deep breath. Normally missing adults weren't investigated until forty-eight hours after they'd been reported unless they were vulnerable, but with the stolen painting, Angelica's age similarity to two of their victims, and his uncomfortable feeling about her studying in the same university if not the same subject area as Sophie Adomaitis, he *was* going to move.

"Right, we're going to investigate. *Not* because I believe that anyone has harmed your daughter but because with your theft in the past few days we need to be cautious."

Better not to mention their two young corpses in case she had a meltdown. They'd managed to keep all three of their murders low key so far and that needed to continue until the parents had formally ID-ed their dead children, although in the boy's case Aidan's call to update him that he was the son of Marte Pedersen meant that one of their victim's names was likely to be plastered all over the Net in the next few hours.

Craig focused back on his call.

"I need you to do a few things for me, Ms Fervier."

"Yes, yes, anything."

"Take the most up-to-date photos of Angelica that you have to High Street police station. We need a clear face shot and a full length one, also a description of her height, build, the outfit she was wearing when you last saw her and a copy of her academic schedule including her lecturers' names. Ask for a Sergeant Jack Harris, he'll be expecting you. As soon as we have all of those we can get the word out and trace Angelica's phone. I'll need that number now, please."

She gabbled it out in an agitated tone.

"Good. Now, while we do all of that I want *you* to ring every friend of your daughter's that you can think of, and all her lecturers and tutors. Hopefully she'll just have chosen to spend the night with some boy."

He let the expected, "My daughter would never" rant run its course and then repeated his instructions firmly, ending the call as reassuringly as he could. Then he briefed Jack and went out to see his PA, who looked up apologetically as he appeared.

"Sorry to pass that Fervier woman on to you, sir, but she was melting my brain."

Craig smirked at the Belfast expression. Brain melt seemed to be a common condition in Northern Ireland nowadays. If he'd been an Irish artist Salvador Dali could clearly have gone further than melting clocks.

"It's fine, Nicky. I needed to speak to her anyway. Do you have that list of Sophie Adomaitis' lecturers and classes that I gave you?"

"I've put them in a table."

She indicated her screen.

"Excellent. Send it through to me."

On his way back to his office to look at it Craig changed his mind.

"Put in on the LED screen instead, please."

As the table appeared he thumped on his deputy's door.

"Get out here, Liam."

A copper who looked suspiciously like he'd just woken from a nap appeared.

"Can a man not get any peace around here?"

"You can sleep when you're dead."

"What do you want me for anyway?"

Craig pointed to the television and awaited his deputy's pearls of wisdom.

"What are we looking at?"

"Sophie Adomaitis' university schedule. Scan it for any classes in French or French history."

"Why?"

"Hortense Fervier's daughter Angelica's gone missing and I'm following a hunch."

The D.C.I. spotted the class first and pointed to the bottom of the display.

"There. Medieval French History. Sounds like a real bundle of laughs. The lecturer is a Doctor Mitt-er-and."

The pronunciation made Craig want to smile but he hid it well.

"Good. You know, I'm sure I remember hearing language students often study the country's history as well."

"So?"

Instead of answering Craig turned to his PA. "Nicky, get Ms Fervier back on the line and ask her if her daughter was taking any classes in medieval French history and if so who her lecturer is."

He beckoned his deputy into his office to explain and soon after the secretary popped her head around the door.

"Yes Angelica's taking classes in medieval French history. Her lecturer's called Suzette Mitterand."

The same as Sophie's.

"Thanks. Now call Ms Mitterrand and find out how many were in that class, please. Hang on here for a minute, Liam, I'll be back."

He followed her out and a minute later returned and started to scribble on his board.

"OK, Ash is tracing Angelica's phone and we need to think about this." He tapped on the words he'd just written. "Let's go back a bit. Ms Fervier's painting is nicked and her other stock is kept in the vaults where we just happened to find two bodies, both young. Actually, on that point, do we know yet if any of her other pieces were taken from the vaults?"

"Pass. They're wild slow checking the inventory so I'll call after this and see what gives."

"Good, and ask Mary if she'll come back up and give Ash

some help on the computing while you're doing that, will you? He's coped so far but things are heating up."

The response was an emphatic shake of the head. "Inventory, yes. That wee madam, *no way*. Ask her yourself, you big wimp."

Craig sighed. He should, he *knew* he should, but he would *really* prefer if someone else did it instead.

"I'll get Annette to ask her then."

He carried on speaking to the sound of chicken clucks.

"OK, so Ms Fervier loses her painting and she keeps other valuables in a bank where we find two dead. One of whom, twenty-year-old Sophie Adomaitis, we now know shared lectures in what's unlikely to be an over-subscribed subject with the daughter of said Ms Fervier, Angelica, who has herself now disappeared."

He paused for a moment to allow the information to sink in, not least to his own brain, but the quiet was disturbed almost instantly by his deputy exclaiming, "*Seriously?* What are the odds on that?"

"Zero. That's my point. This is no coincidence, but the question is what's the link? Fervier? Her gallery? The art?"

"Not to mention that our body count could be about to rise again."

"Sorry, yes, there's always that. We know Sophie was alive last Monday because Ben Mooney saw her, and John's estimated TOD was between four and five days when we found her on Sunday."

"That fits with her being killed on Tuesday or Wednesday last week."

"I'd still like an accurate last sighting to be sure how long she was held before she was murdered, and on the boy too. It could guide us as to how much time Angelica has left."

"It'll come."

"We hope."

Craig rubbed his temple hard as he considered their next steps.

"OK, the most important thing now is to find Angelica."

Assistance came a second later when Ash popped his head around the door.

"The phone's on Elmwood Avenue."

It was a busy thoroughfare near Queen's that connected the University and Lisburn Roads.

"Can you pinpoint where?"

"The Queen's end, but no tighter than that."

"It'll do. Good work. Ask Nicky to call Jack and get men there now on a door to door. The girl they're looking for is Angelica Swann. She's eighteen and her mother, Hortense Fervier, is on her way to High Street now with some photos, but I'm sure she'll have one on her phone too, so call her to send that through right away for the knocks. Those men aren't to come back until they find the girl."

Liam waited until the door had closed again to ask, "Swann?"

"Her dad's name. The mum kept the Fervier family name."

"Right. Women's Lib."

Liam's view of feminism was as old- fashioned as his term for it.

"Family tradition I think."

"Whatever. So are you really thinking they'll find the girl?"

Craig made a face and perched on the edge of his desk.

"Honestly? No. I think they'll just find the phone and maybe signs of a struggle, but we can always hope."

He glanced at the clock. They really needed a briefing to pick up on loose ends and see where everyone had got to, but with Andy still not back from London and everyone else busy he was starting to think the end of the day would be a better time.

Decision made, he re-opened the door.

"Let's head back to Bolsover's to see what Annette's found. Nicky, re-organise the briefing for five, please, and tell Andy I want him back for it if he has to sprout wings. Invite forensics and path to attend as well."

He ignored the "Do this, Nicky, do that, Nicky, make me coffee, Nicky, nah, nah, nah" muttering that followed them to the lift.

Chapter Nine

South London.

For Andy one of the main joys of London was its iconic black taxis, which, although perhaps less prevalent in areas south of the river like Battersea, could still be hailed within minutes on most streets. The *tragedy* of London was its traffic, as dense as a herd of the now extinct Bison that had once thundered in a dark throngs across the America plains and every bit as unwilling to make way.

But the detective's inventive driver, whose encyclopaedic knowledge of his home town's geography sat above even that required for 'The Knowledge', that university level requirement for joining the ranks of those deemed deserving of the title Black Cabbie, made sharp, frequent turns down side streets unnoticed by the D.C.I. and deposited him back at Matilde's Tooting rest home in under half an hour.

Andy was there to ask her about the Manet that the police had deemed stolen and, quite apart from her aging hearing, Andy didn't believe that was a topic Matilde would wish discussed on the phone.

He was right; a call would have yielded nothing but the five minutes of stubborn silence their visit became as soon as he mentioned his reason for being there, signalled by his hostess, initially smiling at the sight of him, setting her face hard and then turning it away.

It took Andy those five minutes to coax Matilde to look at him again, and when she did he saw that her stubbornness was mingled with pain.

"I'm sorry to cause you distress. This is obviously a sensitive subject."

She shook her head and followed it with a meaningful sigh.

"It comes from shame, and disgust at my wider family too. They left that item in my parents' care and they *must* have known that it was stolen when they did so." Her anguished tone told him just how ashamed she felt. "My father was such an honest man, so honest, and to bring something stolen into *his* house..."

She shuddered so violently that Andy felt it shake *his* frame.

"Thank God my parents are dead and never found out. Milo and I were horrified when we did."

The detective reached out a hand to take her frail one.

"You couldn't possibly have known. You trusted your whole family to be honest."

Her hesitant nod said that wasn't *quite* true, but when he saw her tense shoulders lower slightly he sensed that she was ready to answer some questions, safe in the knowledge that she wasn't being blamed for a decades old crime.

Keeping his tone as gentle as possible Andy outlined the details.

"The piece was by Manet and you and your husband brought it for sale at Mansours in August nineteen-eighty-eight. But can you recall when exactly the piece was left at your house in Paris and by whom?"

Matilde had nodded before he'd even finished the question, surprising him. Andy had imagined that after so many years it would have taken her a minute to recall at least. *He* could barely remember what he'd done a week ago!

"It was brought to us during the last years of the war by my Uncle Hubert and Aunt Aveline, along with some other items that it seems were *not* stolen. Or at least we were not informed they were when we put them up for sale."

They might have been but the police checks back then simply hadn't caught them. Andy wondered how many of the Rossers' items would be flagged if he ran them now.

The point was moot; the pieces belonged to other people now and Matilde and her husband hadn't known. He wasn't going to check them out and embarrass her; although once she was dead he would make sure The Met's Art Squad did.

He tuned back into what she was saying.

"I remember Hubert and Aveline specifically because I had never met them before and I never saw them again. They were a branch of the family that Papa did not mention, although perhaps I understand why." Her top lip curled. "Hubert was only a *very* distant cousin of Papa's and Aveline had been a dancer before they had married, and *not* the ballet sort."

The comment made the D.C.I. laugh. Not only did Matilde swear, she was a snob and judgemental; it made her seem younger for some reason and then made him wonder *why* it did. No-one ever expected the elderly to be anything but nice, as if at eighty people suddenly stopped being brave or bitchy or sexy or tempestuous or any of the million things that they'd been when they were young and instead developed an overwhelming love of toffee and biscuits and turned into identikit saccharin-sweet old ladies and men.

But Matilde swore and was sarcastic and cheeky, and good for her. The more that older people refused to morph into their movie stereotypes perhaps the more that society would acknowledge them as a real force.

Andy focused again on what she was saying.

"Aveline wore far too much make-up too." The words were accompanied by a haughty sniff.

"But they only came to your house in Paris once?"

"Yes."

"How can you be sure it was near the end of the war?"

"Because that is when not all but most was brought to us. Between forty-three and the winter of forty-four. After that it became too dangerous to travel at all."

"And everything that Hubert and Aveline brought, you and your husband transported here and eventually sold?"

For him to have referred to the couple as her uncle and aunt would have been an insult that Matilde hadn't earned.

"Yes, with other things. Only my Holbein is left now and it did not come from them."

He broadened the topic slightly.

"Police checks showed the stolen Manet was taken in forty-three from a family named Cassin."

"Yes. Milo and I never met them, but we wrote them a letter to say how sorry we were about their painting and we had not known."

"Did you learn anything about them?"

She nodded, making her soft grey curls bounce up and down.

"Yes. Even though they lived in France their father was a German, but he was very outspoken against Hitler. He was the owner of a large theatre and had been holding lectures and meetings there denouncing Hitler's rise since the early thirties. He must have been on a Nazi watch list somewhere because as soon as the Nazis invaded the area they closed the theatre and sent the father to a camp. Luckily the mother escaped with their children to Switzerland, but they had to leave everything they owned behind in their house and it was looted, and somehow Uncle Hubert acquired the Manet."

Somehow? It sounded off.

"Hubert got it from the looters?"

She shrugged and pulled her cardigan tight around her as if she suddenly needed its comfort.

"That was what he said. I thought it was as unlikely as you now do, but the other option did not bear thinking about. The shame would have killed my parents if they had guessed."

Andy's heart sank as he recalled the history of that period, and his next words came squeezing out.

"Where did Hubert and Aveline live?"

Matilde dropped her voice. "Vichy."

In June nineteen-forty France signed an armistice with Germany, and the parliament also voted to give Chief of State Marshal Philippe Pétain, a World War One hero, full powers, while Charles de Gaulle who disagreed strongly became head of the French Resistance and fought against the Germans. Pétain replaced France's traditional liberté, égalité, fraternité with travail, famille, patrie (work, family, fatherland) and an authoritarian regime ensued, ruled from the government's new headquarters in Free France, located in a spa town called Vichy. When the Nazis eventually took military command of the free zone in forty-two the Vichy government enacted anti-Semitic policies that removed Jews from civil service, seized their property and participated in deportations and arrests.

The timing fitted. The Cassins had fled because of persecution and Hubert and Aveline had been Nazi sympathisers. No, more like collaborators to have been in such good favour that they'd been gifted valuable stolen art.

The D.C.I. and his hostess exchanged a mournful look that said both were aware of the heinous deeds what had occurred at that time and he moved on.

"Why did Hubert need to hide his art with your father then? If he was protected by the Nazis."

She gave a tired sigh.

"Well, he could never have told Papa that of course, because he would have given Hubert up to the resistance."

"Your father was a member?"

"He didn't hold a gun but he allowed them to meet and hide in our basement and he funded them as well as he could."

The bravery it had required to take a stand against the Nazis when they were occupying your country still amazed the detective.

"And also because near the end of the war everything changed. The Nazis realised they were losing and that made them even more vicious, if possible, and *anyone* seen to have helped them became a target. Hubert must have believed that some of his art was safer in my father's care."

"Was Hubert's name Fervier?"

Matilde tutted in disgust. "Yes, unfortunately."

"And what happened to him and Aveline after the war?"

"They never returned to collect the pieces they had left with us, but we heard they got out through Spain and took a great deal of other art with them. But as to where they ran to I have no idea. South America most probably. That was where a lot of the Nazis ended up."

Andy sensed that he'd uncovered something interesting with Hubert and Aveline, but whether it would prove useful to their case only time and research would tell.

Even knowing that he needed to get back to Belfast the D.C.I. drank his tea slowly, reluctant to leave and not wanting Matilde to have to see him go. It led him to a decision.

"Mrs Fervier-Rosser, I have to leave now and fly back to Ireland, but if you wouldn't mind I'd like us to keep in touch."

Her large eyes lit up.

"By letter?"

"And phone call, if that suited you? We could ring now and then for a chat? If you'd like that then I'll speak to the nurse on the way out about getting you a phone in your room." Which he would fund.

He had genuinely enjoyed her company; both his own grandmothers were dead and he missed the peacefulness of those relationships. They'd compared very favourably to the tug of war over discipline and studying that he'd had with his parents at times.

To underline that he meant it Andy produced his card. "The number on there is my mobile number. Evenings are best because sometimes I mightn't be free to talk if I'm at work, but even then I'll see that you've called and phone you back that night. I studied French at university so we could try chatting in it sometimes if you'd like."

Then with a gentle squeeze of her hand the detective rose and made for the door. When he reached it he turned back.

"I've really enjoyed our chats."

"As have I, young man."

Both of them smiled, Andy partly because at forty-four

someone was still calling him young.

****

Smithfield.

Horace Bolsover was proving a challenge, in the way that people who died suddenly but not naturally often did when it transpired that they had no relatives in the world. It made Annette realise something that she never really had before; relatives were actually pretty handy things to have.

Not essential perhaps as they'd been when you were a child, to feed, clothe and educate you, but even as an independent adult and leaving love and affection completely out of the equation, handy is definitely what relatives were, especially after you were gone. They could identify your body, enlighten the police on the details of your day-to-day life, something that could often yield a clue as to whether or not and why you'd been murdered; they could also gather your possessions and dump or distribute them, perhaps even inherit them if you hadn't already left everything to the local home for cats.

In Horace Bolsover's case they already had an ID courtesy of his next door neighbour, but even *he'd* only known a fragment of the dead man's tale.

"Horace was quiet; he just ran his shop and watched golf on the TV. He didn't talk about himself but I never saw any signs of a wife or family. And we never went out for a drink and socialised, not even at Christmas time."

Computer searches had confirmed that Bolsover had had no siblings, no cousins, no spouse and no children. The shopkeeper had been a true island, one that looked like it was going to be the graveyard of all his secrets, including why someone had hated him enough to cause his death unless there was something to find in his paperwork.

But Annette was most troubled by Bolsover's apparent lack of parents, and as growing full-term babies in labs was so far impossible it made her determined to dig.

She stared at the small wooden table in his above-shop apartment, on to which she had just emptied *yet another* drawer filled to the brim with receipts, diaries, letters and old coins and decided that there *was* actually something worse than a dead person with no relatives; a dead hoarder with none. How could she possibly make sense of the papers in front of her? She didn't even know where to start.

The D.I. was still gazing trancelike at the pile five minutes later when a thundering of heavy footsteps ascending the stairs said that she had company, not necessarily a good thing when the likes of Tommy Hill worked just down the street. She'd just reached for her gun when Liam's large, pale face appeared at the door.

"Hello there, woman of the house! I hope that kettle's boiling?"

Craig appeared a second later and gave her an apologetic look. "Ignore him. We just thought we'd check on you."

He shunted his deputy out of the doorway and entered.

"They're up to their eyes in inventory at the bank too."

When Annette motioned Liam towards the pile of papers the D.C.I. shook his head right away.

"Noo... That's *not* happening. I stopped digging through rubbish two ranks ago."

Craig rolled his eyes. "Delusions of grandeur, but much as I hate to say it he's right. You shouldn't be wasting your time on it either, Annette. Get a constable to go through the papers and sort them into piles."

"That's all well and good, sir, but then I'd just have to check those. There isn't a single relative alive to tell us about Bolsover. He never even socialised with the guy next door, so if we want to get even a hint of why he was killed it'll be in this lot."

Craig pulled up a chair to think while his deputy roamed the apartment like it was the Serengeti until Annette got annoyed.

"Sit down, will you, Liam! You're making my head sore."

"Ooh... What's biting you then?"

"Well, if you must know Carrie's nursery's decided to close at Christmas, which means I have two weeks to find her another place and everywhere will be shut for the bloody holidays."

He nodded solemnly. "I blame Brexit."

"You'd blame Brexit for your flipping head cold if you could!"

Craig had finished thinking and motioned them both to be quiet.

"OK, here's how we'll tackle this. I'm presuming there's no computer here?"

"Nope."

"OK, then we need to gather every scrap of paper from the shop and up here and find a few constables to arrange them into letters, receipts and so on. Then they can scan them on to a database with their phones, Ash can design a programme to search for any potentially useful ones, and *you* can have a look at those. Simple."

As if she hadn't already thought of all that. But she hid it well.

"Good idea, sir, but where do we get the constables? The ones we managed to squeeze out of Jack and Stranmillis are all in use at the bank."

"Or searching for Angelica Swann."

"Who?"

Craig dismissed the question with, "I'll explain later" and returned to the topic in hand.

"The bank can spare you a couple of men, just call and tell them it's my order." He rose to his feet. "Now, let's head downstairs. I think I noticed something when we were here last."

Five minutes later he knew that he'd been right.

"OK, initially we thought this shop was completely disorganised, but it actually has a system."

He led the way to a set of shelves by the front door. "Look at the items here and hanging above us. What do they say to you?"

Liam snorted. "That they need a damn good dust."

An exasperated tut said that wasn't what Craig had had in mind so Annette stepped in.

"They're all from the sixties, sir."

"Very good, Annette. The items themselves are mixed, but the period they've originated from is the same."

The D.I. nodded eagerly. "There's an early Beatles Album, and look, hanging in the window, that dress has an original Biba label! That must have come from when they had the shop in Carnaby Street."

"Excellent. Let's check a few more shelves to see if we're right."

Further inspection revealed that everything on the opposite shelves came from the following decade, early to late seventies, and every shelf in the parallel row held items from the next. The pair were congratulating themselves on their discoveries when Liam rained on their parade.

"Yeh, but I mean, so what? It might tell us how Bolsover filed stuff but it's still a mess so there's no way of telling if the killer stole anything."

Craig was undeterred. "I agree, but I don't think that's what's important here." He started walking up and down the other rows, calling out, "Fifties... and here's some stuff from the nineties, Annette... The next row is nineteen-twenties... and now there's turn of last century Victoriana."

When he suddenly fell quiet the others rushed to catch up and found him in the corner furthest from the front door, where instead of items stacked on shelves or hanging from the ceiling there stood a tall corner cupboard that needed a good dust. A quick tug at its door said it was locked.

"Annette, did you find a key that might fit this? It'll be small."

A quick search of the ones she'd collected and a tiny silver key was passed across. It opened the cupboard door all right, but once inside they encountered a steel cabinet weighed down with one of the strongest looking padlocks Craig had ever seen. With no key to it found there was only one thing to do, and Liam, who always preferred short cuts when they were available in life, raced out to his car and returned a minute later with bolt cutters.

Annette looked at him wryly. "Do you *always* carry those?"

"Aye. Have you never seen inside my boot? There're things in there that could open Fort Knox."

Unlikely, but she took his point.

Craig nodded his deputy to do the necessary and a moment later they'd discovered two things. First, a neat collection of typewritten files that said Horace Bolsover hadn't been quite as disorganised as his surroundings made him appear, and second that the shopkeeper's collecting efforts from the nineteen-thirties and forties, those being the only decades not represented on the shelves, had struck gold. Quite literally. The reinforced bottom drawer of the cabinet was filled to the brim with gold bars, gold and silver coins and intricate gold jewellery heavy with precious stones!

Craig passed the files to his D.I. then lifted a coin and held it up to the light, swallowing hard when he saw the inscription on one side: 'Meine Ehre heißt Treue', in English 'My honour is called loyalty'; the motto of the notorious Waffen-SS. On the back of the coin were the organisation's lightning flash double 'S' runes.

He passed it to his deputy without a word and reached into the drawer again, this time withdrawing a slim gold bar.

"Either of you know anything about precious metals?"

Annette set down the files and gawped at the gleaming slab. *"Is that real gold?"*

"I'd say so. But take a look for yourself."

Liam was still staring at the coin. "This has to be someone's idea of a joke, boss. I mean, even Hitler wouldn't have minted coins with an SS logo, would he?"

"Who knows what that bastard did, but I wouldn't put anything past him. The Third Reich was very wealthy."

Annette's gasped, "This bar has a hallmark, so it must be real" made them turn. "And look..." she held it out for them to see, "...is that a *swastika* on the end?"

Liam dropped the coin back into the pile and reached out for the piece, staring at it for a moment and shaking his head.

"It is too. Those fuckers got everywhere."

Craig nodded him to put the bar back into the drawer and closed it.

"OK, we'll need everything in this cupboard transported securely, first to the labs to be tested and then into evidence. I'll call the C.C. and check what arrangements he needs us to make."

As he did that his officers speculated wildly.

"So, do you think they were brought to Bolsover like that, Liam, or did he buy or lend money against gold and have it melted into those coins and bars?"

The D.C.I. rolled his eyes. "What sort of eejit would do that? And who would have agreed to mould them for him? Everyone knows what the SS stands for never mind the swastika! They're hate symbols all over the world."

Craig came off his call. "Your question's valid, Annette, but I think Liam's right. There aren't many goldsmiths in Northern Ireland and I can't see any taking on that job. They'd know the risks."

She wasn't convinced. "If they were made for a private collector no-one might ever have known."

"Perhaps. Well, either way forensics should be able to tell us how old the coins and bars are. If they link them to the thirties or forties then the odds are that Bolsover acquired them with the symbols already imprinted and just decided to hold on to them. They can check out the jewellery too."

He nodded at the files. "OK, get the uniforms sorting and scanning those papers upstairs and the CSIs to dust everything in this cupboard for prints, please, Annette. Then send the valuables over to forensics and bring the files back to the office. The C.C.'s arranging an armoured car to transport the gold to the labs and I'll arrange an armed guard to stay with you until then. As long as word doesn't leak about the stash before it's moved you should be fine."

Liam guffawed. "Providing Tommy doesn't hear that there's gold in them thar hills!"

Craig laughed as well. "True. Actually that's an interesting point. If Tommy *had* known about the gold he would have nicked it ages ago, so Bolsover must have been good at keeping secrets. Clearly not even his killer knew the valuables were here or they would've disappeared."

Liam shrugged. "Maybe they just couldn't find them."

Craig shook his head emphatically. "No. Untidy as this place is it hasn't been ransacked, and the dust on the cupboard suggests it hasn't been touched for weeks. The killer can't have been aware of what was here." Something occurred to him. "And that means they definitely didn't kill Bolsover for his loot."

Liam nodded. "Like I've said before, he'd pissed them off."

Annette wasn't so sure. "Maybe they knew there *had* been gold once but thought the old man had already got rid of it, so they didn't search for it but still killed him on principle."

It was a possibility. She had another one as well.

"*Or...* maybe the killers knew *exactly* where it was but they left it because they wanted *us* to find it."

An excellent point.

"I like the way you're thinking, Annette, but whichever it was let's focus on what we know for now. Horace Bolsover annoyed someone enough to get him killed and those files could tell us how."

Liam raised an eyebrow sceptically. "His Nazi obsession would have done it for me. I'd like to dig those bastards out of their graves and kill them all over again."

Craig smiled at the image despite knowing that he should set a higher tone.

"OK, yes, but what exactly *was* the association between Bolsover and the Reich, Liam? I doubt collecting Nazi valuables alone would have been enough to get him killed."

Even Annette wouldn't commit on that one.

****

Galway

"Is everything arranged?"

The teenager stared down at the shorter girl sitting cross-legged on the windowsill, wondering idly as she waited for her to answer why *she* couldn't have had natural curls. Irina felt her stare *and* her envy and allowed herself a smile of pride in her Romany heritage, deliberately nodding her head in slow motion knowing the movement would make her curls oscillate and glisten in the afternoon sun.

Such were the simple triumphs that kept her rooted in the present when so much of her life, *their* lives, conspired to pull them towards the past; a past that carried with it a duty to complete unfinished work. It was a duty that all of them would have fulfilled even if the oaths they'd taken hadn't compelled them, but hopefully things would soon change and the world would pay attention to their cause.

Hopefully, between the finality of the lives that they'd ended and the clues they'd left to follow, the Belfast detective they had read so much about would find the path laid out.

They had researched Marc Craig very carefully, him above all the detectives in Europe because of his ability but also his lineage, poring over history books and the reams of newspaper columns and clips of TV interviews generated each time he'd added another successful conviction to his list. The interviews had always seemed dragged from him reluctantly, often half-averting his gaze as if determined that his matinee idol looks shouldn't distract from his real purpose in life; to follow the trails left by murderers and discover why they'd killed. He'd wanted to lock them away as well of course, but the assiduous Craig would be thwarted in that this time.

There was risk entailed in setting this particular cop a challenge and they knew it; of all the ones they could have chosen he was most likely to catch them before they could flee. But he was also the one most likely to uncover *why* they had killed and expose that reason to the world, and along with it the mission to which they'd dedicated their lives. Then *everyone* would know their reasons, and risking their freedom seemed a small price to pay for that.

Irina's thoughts were interrupted by a shove from her companion and, "*How* arranged?" in an Irish accent came in follow up. This time she responded not with a nod but words.

"The tickets will be waiting for us at the airport once our final task is complete."

She lifted her eyes to the other girl's aquiline face; a face that although technically pretty she didn't believe even a mother could love, such was the devious, selfish nature that shone through. She'd never agreed with Roman's decision to let the girl work with them, but as well as being her lover he was their leader so his word was law.

"But you must be sure. *Are* you sure? You know this will alter your whole family's lives-"

A snapped back, "I'm sure!" didn't deter Irina from finishing what she had to say.

"Your father's and his family's too. *They're* all innocent but they'll be hurt by association. Are you *really* prepared for that?"

The tight cry that came back startled her with its emotion, as did the taller girl's tightening fists and reddening face.

"*Shut up, shut up, shut up, SHUT UP!* Stop going over and over it, will you! My family made their choices and I've made mine, so BLOODY WELL LEAVE IT ALONE!"

The shouts brought Kurt Nilsen rushing in from the corridor, where he'd been gazing out one of the building's high arched windows and smoking a joint. He glanced from one woman to another and knew immediately what had just transpired.

Grabbing Irina's arm he dragged her down several flights of stairs and out on to the grass, where she finally managed to wrench away from him, rubbing her limb and venting her hurt pride noisily.

"*What was that for? I'm telling Roman!*"

"You know exactly what! And go ahead and tell your boyfriend, he'll agree with *me*. Stop poking at her guilt, for God's sake, Rina! If she changes her mind now our plan could be blown!"

The petite girl was defiant. "I don't trust her so I *need* her to be sure! She's giving up her family for us, Kurt, and *I* don't think she'll carry it through."

The young man's face darkened and he shook his head hard as if to erase a thought. A moment told her that it had been a memory, and the anguish it had caused him was obvious when his eyes met hers again.

"I understand that, Rina, and we all know she's a risk, but remember *why* we're doing all of this. *Our* families gave something up as well." His tone tightened as he added, *"Much more than we are now"* and when his gaze shifted sideways Irina knew they weren't alone anymore.

A clear voice came from behind her.

"I won't change my mind. This is my family's penance."

Irina didn't believe that was her motivation for a second, but the youth with her nodded, pleased by the words.

"Good. Then stop arguing, you two." He swallowed hard and added, "I'm sorry that I grabbed you, Rina."

Her snapped comeback of, "Let's just hope this Marc Craig's as good as his publicity" said she was far from appeased.

****

The C.C.U. 5 p.m.

"OK, we've a lot to get through, so each of you give an update on where you are and then we'll take our scientists."

The order of play was deliberate; Des and John might hear some things to give fresh context to their reports.

Craig nodded to the newly returned Andy to start and went in search of his favourite drink. By the time he returned the preliminary reporting had worked through and Liam was gawping at Des, who was perched on one end of the group.

"Cyanide gas! *Honest to God?* In this day and age?"

Craig retook his seat and sipped slowly at his espresso, waiting for the inevitable chorus of horror to die down before he said a word.

"You'd prefer Bolsover had been killed with something more modern, Liam?"

"I think there are *easier* bloody ways to kill someone, boss, that's what."

Smiling and setting his cup to one side Craig lifted a marker and wrote 'New Info' on the board.

"OK. Before we get to the gas that killed Bolsover, let's hear about other new things people have uncovered. Andy, what's the situation with the Ferviers' art?"

The D.C.I.'s response was to call out to Nicky and she

projected the image of a painting up on the TV screen.

"OK, this is a work by Édouard Manet, a French painter who died over a century ago. It was part of a collection of artworks sold off over the years by Milo Rosser, a Welsh ex-army officer now deceased, and his wife Matilde Fervier Rosser, through Mansours Auction House in Battersea. It was a large collection that had been amassed by Matilde's father, through extended family members leaving items of value for safe keeping at their Paris home during World War Two. Matilde and her new husband, they married not long after the war, brought all the art to England and sold pieces off whenever they needed a cash boost, and all of the transactions went smoothly except for this one-"

Craig interrupted. "Stolen?"

"Yes. The auctioneers did checks on everything they were asked to sell, but back in the day those would have been limited by whatever info the cops held on paper so God knows how much slipped through. But this piece *did* show up as stolen and was returned to the family."

"Did Matilde Fervier know it had been?"

Andy shook his head emphatically. "No. I'm positive she didn't, but what she had to say about it was fascinating. The piece had been left with her family in Paris towards the end of the war by her Uncle Hubert Fervier and his wife Aveline. To cut the story short, it had been stolen from a family in France called the Cassins whose father was a firmly anti-Nazi German, so when the Nazis invaded France they got their own back and sent him to a camp. His wife and kids escaped to Switzerland."

Annette shook her head glumly. "The administration in Vichy acquiesced to the Nazis." She shuddered at what that had meant for the people living there.

Andy continued without commenting; he'd gone through that once already today.

"Anyway, Matilde couldn't be certain how the Manet fell into her Uncle's hands but the suspicion has to be that he was either a Nazi sympathiser or an actual card-carrying member of the party."

Craig sighed. "Was he rounded up after the war?"

"No. He and the wife escaped, Matilde thinks through Spain on their way to South America, and apparently he took a lot more valuable art with him."

Ash nodded vigorously. "That's what I was saying the

other day. The Monument Men found a lot but a lot more disappeared." He indicated the screen. "I'll check out the details on Interpol's missing art database."

"See if Matilde's Holbein on there too, if you wouldn't mind. I really hope it isn't, but it's better that we know."

Craig thought for a moment. "So Hubert and Aveline Fervier slipped out through Spain around the end of the war."

"Yep. But they obviously couldn't reach Paris to claim back the stuff they'd stored with Matilde's family-"

Liam cut in. "They must have had plenty more to live on then, boss. No Nazi could have escaped the Allies without lots of dosh to pay bribes."

"Probably, although the Nazis *provided* a lot of people with funds to start new lives and got them out through pre-arranged transport routes called the ratline. I'd say whether they'd offered to help the Ferviers would've depended on just how loyal they'd been to the Reich-"

Des cut in. "So if Hubert had just been a collaborator instead of a loyal party member they *mightn't* have helped him escape? How would the French locals have viewed him and his wife if they'd stayed behind?"

"Turned on them. They'd have had to run."

Andy nodded emphatically. "Matilde was adamant that they left and I agree. Either way they took a lot of loot along."

Craig nodded. "OK, we need to find out where Hubert and Aveline disappeared to after they left the European mainland and what happened to the art they brought with them." He heard his analyst gulp. "Don't worry, Ash, you've enough to do. I'll get you some help."

All eyes turned to Mary, who responded just as Craig had expected.

"Computing's not my job! I'm a detective the same as the rest of you."

He was about to agree and say he would get a locum analyst from IT when Nicky's disembodied voice came from behind the board.

"But if you're in the office we could finish our discussion over coffee."

As everyone knew that all the pair talked about nowadays were star signs and charts and didn't want to risk that discussion starting now, no-one said a word. They simply watched as the expression of indignation on Mary's heart shaped face was replaced by interest, then stubborn refusal and then interest again, this time laced with acceptance.

Finally she gave a nod.

"OK. But I'm *not* making a habit of this."

Ash's cheerful, "Great, I'll send some stuff across for you to start on" thankfully drowned out Aidan's, not half as quietly muttered as he'd thought, "Thanks be to God" from everyone but Craig who was standing just in front of him. Sympathetic through he was to the D.C.I.'s obvious relief at not having to deal with the truculent constable in the field for a while, he thought it better *not* to acknowledge that fact right now.

"Thank you for that, Mary. You and Ash will have a lot to do. I'll need everything you have on the CCTV footage from the streets outside the gallery, bank and Bolsover's later today."

Ash shook his head, making his earring swing from side to side.

"You can have it now, chief. There was nothing on any of them."

Craig face dropped. *"Nothing?* You've checked with D.C.I. Harding? And the bank's rear exit if there is one?"

"Yep and yep. The only bit of good news is that now I can link the gallery theft with not only the bank murders but Bolsover's. All the cameras inside and outside each venue had everything of use erased by the same slice, loop and splice hack."

Liam was disbelieving. "The traffic cams too?"

"Yep. All of them were SLS-ed. Whoever did this was one ace hacker. Nearly as good as me."

Craig dragged a hand down his face in despair before speaking again. "Is there *any* hope of you finding out who they are, Ash?"

The analyst was tempted to play the moment for all it was worth and make like a computer genius on a cop show, shaking his head and arguing that what Craig had asked was impossible before finally having a miraculous last minute breakthrough. But by the time he'd finished the thought he was bored with it so he stuck to the facts.

"The only thing I've got is the SLS technique. They didn't leave any extra code or sign the hack. But like I said before, I posted a question about SLS on all my boards so now it's wait, watch and pray."

Liam eyed him warily. "I'm sure I was supposed to

understand all that but I didn't, so humour me."

Ash shrugged. "Boards are like chat rooms or special interest FaceChat pages. Places to discuss specific interests. I'm a member of most of the advanced computing ones. Anonymously of course, chief, before you freak your dog."

Craig had no idea what that meant and he wasn't about to ask.

"Good. Here's hoping that produces a gem, Ash. Anything else we need to know on your side?"

"The keypads in the bank definitely weren't hacked and I checked with the manufacturers who made them and they'd restricted knowledge of the cameras hidden beneath the logo to just two of their staff members, who I've cleared, and the bank's list of authorised people. That's the Board, Gambon and his cover officer James Prince, and they're all clean too."

Craig scribbled a note to that effect on the board and sat down again. "OK, before we go *there*, anything more on the vault inventories?"

"Yes. The killers entered all six vaults and took a total of thirty items, most small but some larger, like the harpsichord and a few paintings. I'll print the list for you and I've already sent it to the Republic and GB to check their fences, pawnshops and keep a general eye out."

"Humour me and send it to Interpol to search their databases too; and alert Europol and the other agencies in case the items are heading abroad. I want the current owners of every missing piece checked out as well."

The analyst made a face. "Yeh, that bit's proving tricky. Gambon's resisting giving us their names."

Craig turned to an officer who he knew wouldn't take any shit. "Liam, offer Mister Gambon a choice of giving up the names or being locked in a cell and see if *that* focuses him. I especially want to know if any of the missing items belonged to Hortense Fervier or any of our three victims and their families. And Ash, I'll need to know the provenance of each missing piece too."

"Will do."

After a short pause Craig turned to his third D.C.I., who was still looking smug at no longer having to deal with Mary.

"Aidan, you have something on our young male Vic as well, don't you."

The lanky detective nodded and shouted through the whiteboard for Nicky to put up his slide. A list of seven names appeared.

"OK, these are the Board members and the holders of all but two of its code generators, which are held by Mervyn Gambon and his cover officer for when he's away. Everyone had their generators and alibis for the bank break-in except one." A picture of Marte Pedersen appeared. "This is Marte Pedersen, a Norwegian presenter some of you may recognise from TV. Her code generator can't be found, and her son, although she didn't realise he was even missing till I showed her the sketch, was the young man that we found dead in the vaults. His name was Dylan Pedersen-Storey and he was her only child."

Ignoring the gasps from those who hadn't known Craig turned to their visitors. "John?"

The pathologist nodded. "She and her mother confirmed the ID an hour ago. She's divorced from Dylan's father so I've a call out to him too. The boy was at Ulster University, and although he lived at home he often stayed over with friends for days at a time so she hadn't even noticed he was gone. Typical student."

Craig nodded glumly. "How old?"

"Nineteen. Within the estimated range."

"Last time his mother saw him, Aidan?"

"Sunday a week ago. He had his own car so I've people out looking for that now."

"OK, good. So Dylan must have taken his mother's code generator or been forced to by his abductors, which they then used with her already stored e-signatures to enter the vaults."

"That's the likeliest scenario. They could have made passkeys to the bank and lift, but the mother was adamant Dylan couldn't have known where the keypad camera was so we still don't know how the perp knew to Tippex those."

Crag snorted. "Do you honestly think any of the Board would *admit* they'd gossiped about the bank's security details with their families?"

"So you think she *did* tell the kid."

"They lived together so they're bound to have talked."

"So the perp used her code generator to break and enter before they killed Dylan and the girl?"

"*After* they killed him. Both victims had been dead for days when they were left in the vault. And I'm sure we're looking at killers plural. There's no way one person dragged two bodies to the vaults alone, certainly not the boy's. But yes, Dylan took his mother's code generator and told them everything they needed to know about the bank's security-"

Liam cut in. "You're saying the kid was in on the robbery, boss?"

"No. I'm saying that after he was abducted he would probably have said or done anything to save his life like most people, but it didn't work. He might have been taken purely for his usefulness in accessing the bank, or there could have been an additional reason."

Ryan spoke for the first time since they'd started the new round. "Like what, chief?"

Craig shrugged. "We won't know until we dig." He lifted his cup to his mouth and realised that it was empty. "Liam, brief everyone on the girl while I get more coffee."

When he returned his deputy was saying, "The folks are coming over from Lithuania tomorrow morning, so we'll get a confirmed ID then, but if it is their daughter then she was called Sophie Adomaitis. She was twenty and studying history at Queen's. Her Prof saw her last Monday but we need to tie down if that was her final sighting and that could take a while."

Craig took a sip of his fresh coffee and gave a satisfied sigh before picking things up.

"OK, while we're on teenagers, Angelica Swann, daughter of Hortense Fervier, has gone missing. Ash, since you didn't call me to say she'd been found I'm assuming she hasn't yet."

"No, but her phone has. In a cubicle in the ground floor toilets at Queen's Students Union, lying behind the loo. She could have dropped it there or I guess it could have fallen if she was abducted."

"OK, I want the contacts checked and I want to know when the signal at the Union first appeared on her provider's system and exactly when the phone was turned off. Actually, geo-locate everywhere Ms Swann has been over the past week."

"Sure will."

"So... we now know Angelica and the dead girl were in the same medieval French history class."

It brought a gasp of shock from those who hadn't been informed.

Craig wrote up two names. "OK, victims one and two. Dylan Pedersen-Storey we have a positive ID on and Sophie Adomaitis is still to be confirmed."

He wrote up 'Angelica Fervier Swann' and drew a line from her to Sophie.

"Angelica, daughter of Hortense Fervier whose gallery was robbed on Sunday, was in a small history group of...?"

Nicky shouted out, "SIX."

"A *very* small group that probably met once or twice a week."

When his PA called out again with, "Twice weekly lectures plus a fortnightly tutorial, taught by a Suzette Mitterand," Craig slid the board aside and she came into view.

"You should become a detective, Nick." He decided to set her a little test. "OK. How many girls in the group?"

"Two."

"Angelica and Sophie. That means they probably chatted."

Annette smiled; his faith in female solidarity was touching.

"And then both girls disappeared. Sophie dead, Angelica we don't yet know. Ash, check out all their tutors and lecturers to weed out any weirdoes. Dylan's too."

He turned to his two non-deputy D.C.I.s. "And we need to find out *exactly* how close those girls were, and if there was any link between either of them and the boy."

Aidan made a face. "Dylan went to the University of Ulster, Guv, not Queen's."

"They might still have met. I knew lots of students elsewhere when I was at Queen's. Through clubs, sport-"

"And pubs."

He turned to see his best friend grinning as if he was remembering every single bar they'd crawled in their youth.

"Exactly. Pubs and bars, and we both dated girls from other colleges as well. Aidan and Andy, find me the link between Sophie, Angelica and Dylan if there is one. Two people don't die together unless there's *some* link, either between them or from both to their killer."

Ash cut in. "If you can give me all their phone numbers I can run a check for calls between them."

"Good. Aidan, sort that out, please. Ash, I doubt you'll find anything there but add Horace Bolsover's number to the phone tree too."

Liam decided to rain on his parade. "Bolsover's decades older than all of them so what's the link there?"

Craig shook his head, frowning. "I don't know yet. So far valuables seem to tie all the crimes together, as Nicky said. But we know there's probably something more significant because of Ash's find on the SLS. Tell everyone about the gold at Bolsover's, Liam, while I think for a moment."

The word, "Gold" produced the expected awe, and prompted the deputy to rise to his audience.

"Aye, gold... You've never seen anything like it. Bloody great lumps of the stuff there was. And coins. Jewellery too. But the weirdest thing was the SS symbols and Swastikas."

Speculation on the fascist symbols spread to Des and John, who suddenly discovered their heroic sides and described what they'd liked to have done to the, now conveniently dead, Nazis.

Craig allowed the discussion to run for as long as it took for him to order his thoughts and then he cut it off.

"Thanks for the Raiders of the Lost Ark sequel everyone, but we need to make some sense of this. So..." He wrote 'World War Two' up on the board and stood back. "Anyone with ideas, shout them out."

Annette was first. "Matilde Fervier lived in Paris during the war."

Andy followed up. "And one of her distant uncles may have collaborated with the Nazis before he fled with lots of valuable stuff. Could some of that be in Bolsover's stash?"

Craig's nod as he wrote up the links said it was possible.

"What about the painting nicked from the gallery, boss? Could that have been part of old Uncle Hubert's heist too? Maybe he passed it on to a relative here on his way through to South America."

"Good point, Liam, and we need to follow all that up. The SLS technique links all three murders and could also link the valuables involved as well. But whether the Ferviers *here* are linked with the Ferviers in wartime France we don't know, although Fervier isn't that common a French name. Neither can we say that either branch of that family knew Horace Bolsover. Who was looking at the Vermeer's provenance? Andy?"

"Terry. I'll chase her up on it."

Ash looked sheepish. "I was going to as well, but other things got a grip."

"It was Terry's job first, so don't worry. But we will need information on the items stolen from the bank and the stuff at Bolsover's, plus let's tie down the Fervier family tree as a matter of urgency. Annette, work with Andy on the valuables, please. Ash, I'll need that family tree ASAP."

He turned back to the board and noticed their forensic scientist staring hard at it.

"Something on your mind, Des?"

"A lot. Bolsover's stash arrived at the lab about an hour ago and Grace is trying to date the gold now, but we'll have problems if it was melted down and mixed with other metals at any point so don't get your hopes up on a definitive age."

"I have faith in you."

In other words, 'I want an answer and it had better be the right one'.

"I was just about to hand over to you and John anyway, so fire ahead."

The pathologist got in first.

"Basically Horace Bolsover was executed like the other victims were except in a different way, and I'm starting to wonder if the methods themselves had more significance than we thought. I mean, not *just* that they were executions."

Liam shrugged. "Dead's dead, Doc."

John gave him a sceptical look. "Now you *know* that's not true. In fact *you* were the one talking about passive and active methods of killing at the lab!"

Craig jumped in before his deputy could respond. "Is that what you meant, John? That the shootings were more aggressive than Bolsover's gassing?"

The medic shook his head. "No. I mean they were but that isn't it. It was the gassing that made me think of it really. The shootings were fairly straightforward apart from the Carfentanil and freezing of the bodies to try to throw off our timelines. In the first two victims' cases the *place* they were left is the more significant thing, especially since you've discovered that items were taken from the vaults."

"*Exactly!*"

Aidan accompanied his exclamation by dropping his feet off the desk they'd been resting on with a bang.

"Why a bank and why *that* bank in particular, when there are a ton of different ones in the north? And why all the effort to leave the bodies in the *vaults* when they could've been left up in the reception with a hell of a lot less fuss?"

Ash got in first. "There are no criminal or ethical charges pending against the bank or any of its major players, chief, and all their investments are above board. Nothing that would get a lobby or terrorist group up in arms that I could find. But Aidan asked me to check the bank's money laundering and declaration requirements and they're pretty lax, so some of the items in the vaults could be dodgy."

Craig nodded, perching on the nearest desk as he did. "That's useful, thanks. It points to the vaults' *contents* as the important thing. They'll need to be checked thoroughly, so put Fraud on that while we concentrate on the items that were removed."

A pointed glance at Annette and Andy said to get a move on with that.

Ryan, who'd been listening attentively to the various contributions decided to make one of his own.

"What if that bank was specifically chose because of the Storey boy?"

"Explain."

"Like you said. The killers wanted into the vaults because of something specific about the contents that we don't know yet, and the only way to access them was with a code which only nine people in the country had the means to generate. Two, Gambon and his cover needed to be *at* the bank to input everything, but the seven Board members' voice and thumb prints were stored in the computer so they would've been the ones *I'd* have aimed for."

Aidan nodded in agreement. "Patching together the key phrase by recording Gambon's voice would've taken time."

Craig frowned. "And meant being close enough to follow him around to record the correct words. OK, so it *had* to be one of the Board members' generators that was stolen and Dylan Pedersen-Storey was chosen because he could easily access his mum's. We already know that, Ryan."

Seeing the sergeant nodding eagerly, he stopped to let him finish his thoughts.

"Yes, but surely other people could have got close enough to a Board member to steal their generator too, so why did the killers choose *Dylan*? They could have abducted one of the Board members themselves, or their spouse to blackmail them into cooperating, so why *specifically* take Dylan and kill him? It wasn't necessary to get the information. A bit of torture and the boy or his mum would have given up anything to get him freed."

Ryan's words generated speculation on accessibility and

vulnerability that ended when Ash's clear voice rang out.

"Youth."

Craig turned to face him.

"Go on."

"I could, but I'm pretty sure Ryan already has your answer. That's why his last question was rhetorical."

When all eyes turned to the D.S. again he looked pleased.

"It was actually."

Craig could feel his patience starting to fray.

"So what's the answer?"

"Well, I *think* Dylan Pedersen-Storey was chosen because of his youth-"

John liked puzzles, so he sat forward eagerly and cut in.

"Because he was more vulnerable to abduction than an older person?"

"Yes, OK, he probably was. But that wasn't the *main* reason."

But the pathologist didn't take the hint. He was too busy thinking laterally.

"So are there kids in the other Board families? Does anyone know?"

It was Mary who responded. "I've got a list of them here."

Craig gestured briskly at the television. "On screen."

With a tap on her smart-pad they were looking at a list of names and ages, which showed that there were three people under twenty amongst the Board members' extended families, of which Dylan Pedersen-Storey was one.

Annette smiled. "Three. You might be right, Ryan."

The sergeant smiled wryly. "It has been known before."

Craig waved them down. "*Why* do you think his youth was relevant, Ryan?"

"It may have made him easier to access by the killers if they were young as well."

Liam frowned, confused. "Who said the killers were young?"

Craig had already turned back to Mary. "Tell me about the others under thirty."

After a moment's scanning of her screen the constable shook her head. "Nothing here makes Dylan the easiest target. There's one other male and one female. All three lived in Belfast, one drove and two cycled, Dylan was the driver."

"So why not abduct the cyclists when they would have been easier, boss? And Dylan was a big lad so he wouldn't have been easy to snatch."

"Exactly, Liam. There's something else we're missing that made Dylan Pedersen-Storey the *favoured* target. Yes, the killers needed the code generator and perhaps his youth *did* play a part, and if that's the case then why? But there has to be an additional dimension we're not seeing yet that singled him out of the three Board members' kids. We need to know more about his family."

The thought of possibly seeing Marte Pedersen again made Aidan perk up.

"I'll get on it."

Annette turned back to the pathologist. "What does this mean for *your* earlier point, that the methods of killing have relevance in themselves?"

Before his best friend could answer, Craig took back the floor.

"We'll finish with Ryan first, then go to John and Des. Ryan, how old was Dylan again?"

"Nineteen."

"So...out in the day at university and socialising in the evenings probably made him easier to access if someone wanted to snatch him, even though he had a car. We also have a young female victim, probably Sophie Adomaitis, and now we have another young woman who studied with her going missing, Angelica Swann. So why them? Was there anything that made Sophie stand out?"

Ash shook his head. "Other than her being an overseas student, no. Every report says she was a good student, lived in halls and was quiet."

"She was definitely alone in Ireland? No relatives here at all?"

Ryan shook his head. "None. Back to the issue of youth, chief. I was just wondering... what if Dylan wasn't abducted but seduced?"

"By Sophie Adomaitis?"

"To be confirmed."

Ash shook his head immediately. "Sophie didn't have a boyfriend. I checked with the students living on her floor."

"OK then, not necessarily seduced sexually but seduced by ideas perhaps? Students are always navel-gazing and putting the world to rights, so what if Dylan and Sophie were enticed to join a student group that was involved in something radical, and then disposed of when they were of no further use?"

Liam puffed out his cheeks, nodding. "We've seen that before, boss. And Smithfield was involved in that case too."

Five years before to be exact, in a case that had begun with a bookshop in Smithfield being blown apart and turned out to be about Islamic fundamentalism.

"But enticement and seduction take time, Liam. Abduction's still a hell of a lot easier. But OK, Ryan, you can assist Aidan on chasing up the links between our three youngsters instead of Andy. *If* Sophie, Angelica and Dylan all knew each other then someone on the university circuit might have seen them together."

Annette frowned. "If they did all know each other then we might be finding Angelica's body next."

"Let's cross that bridge if we come to it."

Ryan wanted the last word. "So like someone said earlier, once the killer got the generator they had no further use for the boy and bumped him off in case he ID-ed them."

Craig made a face. It didn't feel completely right.

"That still doesn't explain the dead girl or why they bothered leaving them both in the vaults. As Liam pointed out to me, the *vaults* are relevant somehow. Now, that may turn out to be purely because of the stolen items, but if theft had been the *main* motive then why didn't they clean all six vaults out? We think they had a van so they could have carried a lot. No, we're still missing something so keep digging."

He turned back to their guests and nodded to John first. "Go back to what you were saying about the methods of killing."

The pathologist had been tapping his teeth with his pen as he'd listened to the discussion and it had been annoying Des so much that now he seized his chance to snatch the implement away, knowing that John wouldn't take time to object or he would lose his tight reporting slot.

With a look that promised later retribution the medic started to speak.

"Yes, right, the methods. Well, basically I believe all *three* killings were executions, but the choice of methods is important. Two were either dead or in a coma from drugs when they were shot, which is a pretty peaceful way to go, and then they had a staged scene. We've already discussed the significance of them being headshots. The third, Bolsover, who was dying of stomach cancer already by the way, suffered an elaborate and very unpleasant suffocation by gassing when the killer could just have easily shot him within seconds and made good their escape."

He stared directly at Craig. "So...why take the time and risk of getting caught? Is your killer a sadist? And why not take Bolsover's gold? Did they not know it was there or did they deliberately leave it for you to find?"

Liam shrugged. "Gassing's slower and more painful so maybe the old man had done something to make the killers hate him?"

"Yes, suffocation's a horrible death. But the killer made it painful psychologically as well; because Bolsover would've had to watch them taping up the windows and doors knowing what was coming."

Craig moved to the board again, writing up 'gunshots' and 'gas' side by side. Under the first he wrote: drugged, dead or unaware, quick, humane; and the second: awake, aware, anticipating death, slow, tortuous. Above both he wrote 'punishment execution' with a question mark.

"Is that what you're saying, John?"

The medic nodded. "Yes. I think they wanted to torture Bolsover by letting him know what was coming, whereas with the kids it was more about disposing of them humanely to make a point. But there's another dimension too, from the weapons. The guns and gas mean something here but I don't yet know what." He turned to the scientist beside him. "Des has more."

The forensic lead stroked his unruly beard as he responded. "Well... the guns are both untraceable and both old. Manufactured in the early part of last century in Europe. One in Lithuania and one in Norway. So perhaps history's a factor here again. Like with Matilde Fervier's art."

Craig felt an alarm go off. "Can the weapons be tied to World War Two?"

"No. They're from years earlier. The Norwegian gun was a model from the twenties and the Lithuanian one could have come from anytime from the nineteen-tens to thirties."

Craig was still convinced there was something relevant there.

Aidan sat forward urgently. "Dylan was Norwegian on his mother's side. She's Pedersen."

"And we think the girl was Lithuanian. Were they shot

with the corresponding guns, Des?"

"Yes."

Craig sighed. "I don't know what that means yet, but it's definitely something. OK, Des, what about the gas? Any progress on that? Liam mentioned cyanide."

"Yes. The gas was made up of carbon, hydrogen, nitrogen and oxygen in various concentrations, with some organic and inorganic particles suspended in it. Porton Down's working on a long waiting list of things to try and prevent deaths, so as our man's already gone we're low priority and they said it could take another week. But... we know those elements can make a host of different compounds and from the appearance of Bolsover's body we're now focusing on Carbon Monoxide and Cyanide in its gaseous form, which John says can occasionally give the greenish tinge we saw."

Craig doubted the pathologist had elaborated further on that point. Not after their discussion the night before.

"No luck on the other particles yet, but we *did* find a print on the tape around the window that Bolsover's killer forgot to remove. We're running it now. It was the only print around any of the taped areas."

Craig said nothing for a moment, chasing an idea that seemed determined to stay two steps ahead of him. In the end he gave up and tapped the board.

"OK, good. It's messy at the moment but hopefully another twenty-four hours will tighten things up."

He glanced at his deputy and Liam knew that another job was heading his way.

"Liam's going to update you quickly on the Narnia we found at the Fervier Gallery. It's just for information at the moment but I'd like you all to think about its possible significance in our case, if any, and come up with ideas. Then go home and be back early tomorrow ready to shift. Liam, I need to make a quick call so just disperse the group when you've finished. John, could you hang around afterwards, please?"

With that he passed over the marker and went to his office to call Katy, to check how she felt about him not being back till nine and arrange a lift home, possibly with a drunken pathologist in tow. John needed someone to discuss his solicitor's letter with even if he didn't know it yet.

Late pass organised, twenty minutes later the two men were in The James Bar hoisting the first of what was likely to be quite a few pints. The medic drained his beer faster than usual and set the glass down with a satisfied sigh, signalling for two more drinks to be brought.

"I really needed that. How did you know?"

"Your expression when you had Natalie's letter spread out in front of you."

John's slim face fell. "Oh God, *that*. I know I'll have to deal with it at some point but I honestly don't know what to say."

Craig pressed himself back against the polished leather and wood wall of their booth and got ready to do something that his deputy did uninvited every day of his life but which he never did. Something that he *hated* when it was done to him. He was going to interfere in a friend's private affairs.

"OK, tell me to butt out if you want, John, but I'm going to ask you something."

He took the ensuing silence as permission to proceed.

"Do you *want* your marriage to end?"

The pathologist's eyebrows shot up. "*What?* No!"

Craig wasn't so sure. There was death by decision and then there was death by apathy. Doing nothing was often just as definite a life choice as making your move.

"OK, let me ask you that another way. Are you going to fight to *prevent* it ending?"

That brought a defeated sigh. "How *can* I prevent it? If Nat wants a divorce then I can hardly stop her, can I?"

There was a short pause while their fresh drinks arrived and then Craig shook his head.

"Ah, but Natalie hasn't asked for a divorce, has she? Just a separation."

"Yes, but everyone knows separation's the first step."

It was the turn of Craig's eyebrows to rise. But only one.

"*Is it indeed?* If it is then it's an unnecessary one. Nat could just have gone straight for divorce proceedings if that's what she'd really wanted and waited for a judge to say she had to wait a certain length of time. I think it's usually two years."

John's glass halted halfway to his mouth. "You don't have to declare separation first?"

"Well, I studied law over twenty years ago so I'm not an expert on modern divorce but I don't think so. I mean you've been physically separated for six months and the date of that can be proved by our rental agreement, so if she was just trying to start a clock she didn't need a lawyer's letter to do it. And Natalie knows as well as I do that you're not the sort who would block her if she really wanted a divorce."

The medic looked confused. "So why did she send it then?"

Craig decided that he'd been diplomatic long enough and responded to the question by knocking his friend's elbow off the table to wake him up.

"*Because it's a warning shot, Dumbo!* She's trying to get your attention! And even leaving aside that Natalie's *always* looking for attention, she's careful with money so she wouldn't cough up several hundred quid on a solicitor's letter just for that."

The pathologist gawped at him. "You honestly think she would do that? *Really?*"

"Yes. I agree it's an oblique way of getting a message across, but we both know how weird Natalie can be."

There was no argument from her erstwhile Romeo. In fact he warmed to the theme.

"She's as tight as a duck's ass too. Always has been. Did you know she even resented the money we spent on counselling?"

Craig rolled his eyes. Home economics wasn't the topic under discussion, and if the couple's differing attitudes to money had been the reason for their relationship breakdown they would never even have made it up the aisle.

"Whatever. That just makes my point. She wouldn't waste money paying a solicitor unless she had a damn good reason. She's trying to communicate with you."

John still wasn't convinced.

"Why doesn't she just pick up the phone then? Or come to the sessions with Doctor Beresford?"

"Because *they* both make her vulnerable. This doesn't. It's just her usual passive-aggressive approach."

The medic peered into his face. "Who *are* you and what have you done with my best mate?" He sat back again and folded his arms. "More to the point, when did *you* do a psychology degree?"

Craig smirked. "I'm not wrong though, am I?"

A lengthy silence ended in a grudging nod.

"Well then. If I'm right, what are you going to do about it?"

"Marry *you*, or make sure my second wife's a less

complicated soul."

"Ha ha."

"Well, what do *you* suggest I do about it, Doctor Freud?"

Craig drank another mouthful of beer while he composed his answer.

"OK. How about you ask Natalie to go on a weekend away, just the two of you, so you can talk things out far away from lawyers and psychologists?"

John's sceptical snort was so loud that it woke up an old man who'd been dozing in the next booth.

"There's *no way* she'll agree to that!"

"There is actually. She dropped the hint to Katy at work yesterday. She even suggested a venue. Ashford Castle."

The pathologist gawped at him, offended for some reason. *"Has she booked the bloody place too?"*

"Nope. I think she's hoping that you'll do that."

Craig drained his glass and signalled to the landlord to bring two whiskies, knowing by Joe Higginson's amused expression that he'd overheard their discussion and probably many similar marriage guidance sessions in his pub before.

As expected, by the time the drinks arrived John was in full obstacle mode, throwing them up for Craig to knock down one by one. The last and most easily dealt with was Kit.

"It's all right for you, *you* have parents who'll take care of Luca if you fancy a romantic weekend away. I'm an adult orphan."

Craig's snort of laughter was ill timed and resulted in his drink spouting up his nose.

When he'd stopped spluttering he retorted, "Except that Katy couldn't be separated from Luca by a tug of war team, so we'll probably *never* be alone again until he's eighteen. Anyway, you know mi casa es su casa and my mum would *jump* at having Kit for a whole weekend. She'd probably have taught her Italian and how to play the piano by the end of it so I wouldn't worry about her care. Now, do you have any *more* excuses for not calling Natalie?"

The medic muttered, "Let me think," into his whisky and fell silent, thinking about the fiery, irritating, bloody minded, unreasonable woman that he still unfortunately loved and giving his friend time to ruminate about his case, until after many more rounds of drinks and on the dot of nine o'clock Craig senior entered, to ferry the by then stinking drunk pair home.

Chapter Ten

Galway. Wednesday 9 a.m.

"It was a pity about Dylan."

Gretchen studied her female companion's face warily. "What do you mean?"

The response came in an accent far more local than her own.

"I mean he was sweet. *And* he was good in bed. Who will I sleep with now? You four have each other."

It was said petulantly and the teenager's gaze flicked past her companion to alight on the tanned Adonis across the room. She gazed at Kurt Nilsen in such an openly predatory way that his girlfriend erupted angrily.

"Dylan was guilty! They were *all* guilty! And being hot in the cot is no defence!" She turned towards the young man, who was typing studiously on his laptop. "*Kurt. Back me up here! They all had to die!*"

The young man murmured, "Yes, elskling, yes of course they did" soothingly while still keeping his eyes on his screen.

But it wasn't enough reassurance for his girlfriend so Gretchen pointed accusingly at the other girl.

"*She* should leave! I don't trust her. We don't need her now that we're nearly done." Her voice rose to a jealous screech. "*We don't need her anymore. We don't need her!*"

The tall brunette in question, who had been gazing hard at her during the exchange, first as if Gretchen was being childish and then as if she was insane, began to rise slowly from her chair and move towards the door. She was halted mid-flight by Kurt banging his fist on the table triumphantly.

"*There!* He's done it, just as we'd hoped. This guy's good but not as good as Roman."

Bloodlust instantly forgotten, everyone in the room rushed across to look, but a full minute of peering at the screen still didn't enlighten most.

Roman took his friend's place at the computer, tapped to enlarge a section and motioned them to look again. This time there was a series of nods and smiles.

"You see? The police geek posted a question on my slicing and splicing technique to lots of hacker boards. They must've worked out how I did it but couldn't follow my digi-dust, so now they're trying to crowd source people to give up my name."

Irina gazed at her lover anxiously. "But that's not good, Roman. Someone might tell them."

He slipped a muscled arm around her waist and pulled her close. "Don't worry, Rina. No-one will give him a name because I've never used that hack before now and I won't use it again. But while the cops are searching for me on here they might just give away something about their search for us, and forewarned is always forearmed."

The leader glanced around at his team.

"Look, I know it's not easy being cooped up but we'll only be here a little longer, so play nice, will you? It's sunny so go out and get some fresh air. And, Gretch, we're *all* in this together now, so you've *got* to stop this talk of getting rid of people. We wouldn't have got as far as we have if she hadn't helped us out, and remember that we still have our last job to complete."

He smiled at the brown-haired girl who still had one foot pointing towards the door.

"We can't do this without *any* of you, and as soon as our job's done we'll be on our way to somewhere there'll be *thousands* of men to replace Dylan Pedersen-Storey."

The brunette gave a tight smile and returned languidly to her seat, removing a brush from her handbag and drawing it slowly through her long hair in the way she always did to calm herself down. After a few strokes her eyes narrowed coolly.

"Wouldn't it be better not to take the *risk* of them tracing you, Roman?"

"What do you mean?"

"I mean, wouldn't it be better to post something that throws the police analyst completely *off* our track? Like say you post an anonymous reply to the question saying you're from Thailand or somewhere and you recognise the hack as coming from there. Or aren't you *able* to disguise your location?"

Irina's eyes widened in alarm at the taunt, knowing that it was an attempt to goad her boyfriend, whose ego was common knowledge. Why was she doing it? Because in her book the late addition to the group was just a devious, attention seeking cow.

She interjected hastily before the idea took hold.

"Roman can proxy serve to show we're anywhere in the world he wants! But it's dangerous to poke the bear."

She turned to the others for support and was gratified to see that they agreed with her, and then she tilted her boyfriend's face towards her and gazed into his dark eyes, for once unable to read his thoughts.

"Don't do anything, Roman, she's wrong. If this police geek is so good that he's worked out your technique then he *could* be good enough to break a geo-location hide."

She grabbed his hands and held them tight for emphasis, kissing him hard until she felt that the moment of danger had passed, then she freed her lips and hissed, *"Go for a walk"* to everyone else in the room.

A moment later the door closed and they were alone, but to be certain the deal was sealed Irina drew him over to their sleeping bag and only when they'd finished their love making did she quietly repeat what Gretchen had earlier screamed.

"I know we still need her for a while, Roman, but we *have* to get rid of her as soon as we're done. I don't believe she can turn her back on her family completely no matter what she says, and she's every bit as tainted as the others were. We need to dump her and disappear. Otherwise everything we've been planning for years will fail."

His murmured, "OK, Rina" and renewed kisses went some way to reassuring her. They mightn't have done if she'd realised her boyfriend had just decided to use the board as a shortcut to lead Craig to their hideaway.

****

The C.C.U. 10 a.m.

"OK, Hortense Swann, née Fervier. Who has the details on her family?"

Ash responded to Annette's question first, raising a finger and saying, "Yo" which prompted a "hit me" from Mary in response.

The D.I. rolled her eyes at them.

"You two sound like you're in New York."

"Yo, yo, Big Mama."

"I'll Big Mama you, young man."

Andy decided to act his rank for a moment and, "The names, please, whoever has them" emerged in a stern tone.

The analyst obliged hastily.

"Hortense Fervier's parents were Cyril and Marie Fervier, and Cyril's parents were Roger and Augusta Fervier."

"Roger's date of birth?"

"Eighteen-eighty-four."

The D.C.I. shook his head. "It's not far back enough. Who came before that? Just the ones with Fervier as their surname, please. I need the first Fervier to arrive in Northern Ireland, or Ireland anywhere."

"OK, that would be Emmanuel Fervier in seventeen-twenty. He was thirty when he landed and thirty-five when he married Faith Wilde, a Dublin girl."

"Where did he come from and was he Protestant?"

"Paris is cited as his place of birth, and yes he was Protestant. They both were according to the marriage cert. It says he was a silk merchant, so he may have had money. Maybe that's where Hortense's wealth comes from."

Annette nodded. "The early eighteenth was when the protestant Huguenots mainly came from France to Ireland, so that makes Hortense from a Huguenot line. But there were quite a few Huguenots who chose to convert to Catholicism to remain in France, so could a branch of Emmanuel's family have done that and could that be where Hubert sprang from? Near Vichy? Or even Matilde's family in Paris? And did any Fervier or even Le Fevre come here after World War Two?"

The room quietened while the techies scrolled through genealogy databases, giving Annette enough time to make everyone hot drinks.

Ash was the first to come up for air.

"Nope, no links between Emmanuel's French family and the Vichy area."

Mary concurred. "And no Ferviers or Le Fevres who moved here post-war. I'll check another database, just in case anyone called Fervier even entered Ireland then."

While the other three moved on to the provenance of the art and valuables the D.C. continued with her searches, until, just as Andy was about to speak again, she gave a loud whoop.

"Got them!"

Annette asked first. "Got who?"

"Hubert and Aveline Fervier. Look."

She tapped her smart-pad to shift the display to Nicky's television, making the PA swear about the lack of warning, *yet again.*

The small group gathered in front of the screen.

"OK, so H and A Fervier entered Dublin Port from Lisbon on the tenth of May nineteen- forty-five."

Annette gasped. "Ten days after Hitler topped himself! Hubert and Aveline saw the writing on the wall and ran."

"Yep. OK, so the manifest..." Mary tapped her smart-pad again and a ship's manifest appeared, "... says they brought a *lot* of luggage with them. Look."

She zoomed in on 'Ten crates, various sizes, eight large trunks and eight carryon suitcases'.

Andy sighed heavily. "What are the odds those crates and trunks were full of stolen paintings."

Mary shook her head. "I'm not taking *that* bet."

Ash was. "A tenner."

"Done. But you'll lose it."

"I doubt it. I think there was far more likely to have been gold in half of them. Look."

All eyes followed his finger to where the manifest's final column gave each piece of cargo's weight. Five of the Ferviers' crates had come in at over half a ton each.

"There's no way art is that heavy, not unless they brought some marble sculptures with them."

Annette gawped at the screen, astounded. "They managed to smuggle *that* much gold out of France?"

Andy shrugged. "End of the war chaos. Most people were too busy trying to find food and water to worry about gold. Mary, any clue to where they went when they got off the boat?"

A smug look said yes.

"I can tell you where they were booked to be three weeks later, but not where they went in between."

"Fire ahead."

When she displayed another official looking document, this time from a long defunct airline that had flown out of a now abandoned airfield on the rural south-west coast of Ireland, Annette had to squint to see it, too lazy to get her glasses from her bag. She really wished that she'd joined Mike in having eye lasering six months before. He still wore specs occasionally, just until he could get his second eye done, but already his vision was a king to what it had been.

"OK, here's Hubert and Aveline again. They didn't even bother to use aliases to book themselves on a first class flight from an old airfield near Cork to the USA on the thirty-first of May that year. Although as Ireland was neutral during the war probably no-one would have questioned them. It will take me a bit of time to confirm whether the U.S. was their final destination or just a connection to somewhere further south."

"OK. Good work. Keep on it."

As Annette kept on squinting at the TV, her poor eyesight didn't stop her spotting a discrepancy.

"All I can see listed on the airline booking is three suitcases, so what happened to all the crates, Mary?"

The constable looked startled. "Oh! I hadn't got round to checking that."

You mean you missed it.

Ash decided to help out. "There's no way even half the weight they brought to Ireland could have flown out commercial class. So unless they got rid of it between the tenth and thirty-first they probably sent it to the States by boat or cargo flight. I'd check those first, Mary."

He got the expected grudging sniff instead of thanks.

Andy moved the discussion on. "OK, so where did Hubert and Aveline go in Ireland during those intervening weeks? We're *sure* they had no family links with anyone in Emmanuel Fervier's line, Mary?"

"Not that I can find, but I'll keep searching."

"OK. But if *not,* it's possible they spent those weeks fencing some of the gold and valuables."

Annette made a face. "Would anyone legitimate have touched art coming out of mainland Europe at the end of the war?"

The comment made the D.C.I. smile. The notion that the art world was above criminality and venal behaviour always amused him; in his experience its dealers included some of the biggest crooks that there were.

"In a word, yes. Like Mary said, the Republic of Ireland was neutral in World War Two like Switzerland, and God knows how much war stash is still hidden in Swiss vaults so why not here as well?"

The D.I. pulled a face.

"But as to whether we'll ever *find* the stuff... I'd say it's unlikely. The pieces could be sitting in private collections or have changed hands several times since then. The only way they would ever be noticed was if they were displayed or came to public auction, which most won't. They'll be sold by private auction houses or through secret negotiations between dealers. People who can afford the kind of art we're talking about do things *very* privately."

Something occurred to Annette.

"But they *might* turn up during the commission of a crime, like *we* found Bolsover's gold."

Andy's jaw dropped. "Oh my God, you could be right! Bolsover *may* have been a fence back then and if his stash turns out to be part of Hubert's loot then happy days." The D.C.I. frowned. "Although proving it will be the challenge, of course..."

Annette hadn't finished. "And you *might* also get the odd modern art owner who doesn't know a piece was stolen because they'd inherited it and naively puts it on display."

Ash was keen to join in. "What about if they stash it in the vaults of a bank? Aren't banks here required to report stolen goods?"

"Yep. But that presupposes they or even the owner knows they are and most banks won't have an in-house art expert checking these things. Plus Aidan said N.I. Bank's money laundering approach was lax so I'm guessing their stolen goods radar is as well. Turn a blind eye seems to be their policy-"

Andy cut in. "This is taking us back to provenance. Mary, keep researching Hubert's journey while we get on with that."

Before they restarted Annette asked something that she'd meant to ask before.

"Where's Aidan? I haven't seen him this morning."

The question made Andy smile. "He volunteered to liaise with Terry Harding before heading to the universities with Ryan."

But only after *he'd* dropped that Deidre Murray was going through a divorce.

****

The Labs

Death notifications are never easy, but they're even more painful when they occur over the phone. Not that that had been Liam's intention the day before when he'd phoned Sophie Adomaitis' parents to request they travel to Belfast, but calls from police officers that contain the words, "We really need you to come" to a city with which your only connection is a child rarely fail to trigger a follow up, "*Has something happened to our son or daughter?*" in frantic tones.

At that point Rasa Adomaitis had dropped the phone, probably on the floor judging by the clatter that had followed, and the next person who'd spoken to the D.C.I. was a man.

"I'm Nojus, Sophie's father. Please tell me the truth, Officer."

Liam had, as slowly and kindly as possible, emphasising that they couldn't be certain that the girl they'd found *was* their daughter Sophie, their only child, until they identified her, and all the time pushing away his vision of *him* getting the same call about his own little girl. The thought had made him want to vomit, but he'd held things together as the pain of the man over a thousand miles away had seared down the international line.

Now that man was standing in front of him and Craig, pale and anguished, his pale eyes devoid of understanding about how some complete stranger could just have destroyed his world. And perhaps even worse, how he could tell his wife; seated in the relatives' room with a W.P.C. at that moment praying that her husband would return from the identification smiling and saying that it wasn't *their* daughter who had died.

Both detectives felt the father's agony, more so as each question he answered confirmed earlier assertions that his daughter had been a happy, quiet girl innocently enjoying student life. Sophie Adomaitis should have been looking forward to her future, but now her parents would return to Lithuania with only a body to bury and the horror of their child's final moments in their minds.

There at least Craig was able to give the man some comfort, ensuring them that their young daughter had felt nothing, slipping into oblivion on drugs. The details of the freezing and gunshot he left for the written report, the pathology technician having successfully masked the gunshot wound for the identification. It seemed the most basic kindness; why would he worsen the parents' grief now with such brutality when the inquest would be time enough for them to hear the awful truth?

When the couple had left and the detectives were seated

in John Winter's office sipping coffee the mood was unrelenting sombre, with not even Liam finding a quip to lighten the gloom. He did however turn to his boss with a lacerating observation.

"It feels different when you have a child yourself, doesn't it?"

Craig nodded, saying nothing. In truth he had always sympathised with the relatives of victims, even more than with the deceased who to his mind were free of pain, but since Luca's birth he *had* more than sympathised, he'd empathised, and that was a far, far deeper well.

After five minutes of no-one saying much something suddenly occurred to him.

"We forgot to ask them if Sophie knew Dylan Pedersen-Storey!"

Liam shook his head immediately. "We didn't. I asked them on the way back to the car. Sophie wasn't dating and she'd never mentioned anyone called Dylan. They'd never heard of Bolsover either. The dad *did* say he'd heard her mention a girl called Angelica, but only in passing and he thought she was just someone in Sophie's group at Queen's."

"Which she was. Well done."

"There's something else, boss. Dylan and Sophie were both only children. Angelica Swann is as well."

Coincidence? Neither detective believed in it.

"Marte Pedersen didn't recognise our victims' names, did she, Liam?"

"No idea. Hughesy took that ID."

John shook his head. "I was there when she came in to identify the body and I heard Aidan ask her. She said her son had never mentioned a Sophie or anyone called Horace or Bolsover, but she *did* think that Dylan might have been seeing someone for a few weeks. He never gave her a name."

"Get Aidan on the line, Liam."

They disturbed the most athletic D.C.I. on the squad mid-flirtation with Dee Murray, and just as he'd thought he was making progress too.

The poor timing was reflected in his barked, "YES? What do you want, Liam?" when he recognised the deputy's number on his phone.

"Less attitude from you would be a start, mate!"

The retort made Liam's audience smile and then the others tuned out for a moment, until the D.C.I.s' spat became an adult conversation and Liam eventually hung up.

"Apparently Dylan Pedersen-Storey had mentioned a girl with long brown hair, but his mum wasn't sure whether they were dating or just friends."

John's eyebrows rose. "Curiouser and curiouser."

Craig hadn't finished with the D.C.I.s' spat. "Yes it is, John, but we'll get to that in a moment. What was the narkiness with Aidan about, Liam?"

The deputy smirked. "He's on the pull down in Fraud and apparently I interrupted him at an important moment. I knew that would happen as soon as Arty said Dee was getting divorced, but I didn't give Hughesy credit for getting there so fast. Good man."

Craig smiled. He liked Deidre and if dating her improved Aidan's sometimes acerbic temperament then it would be a win win.

"OK, let's get back to the connection between Sophie, Dylan and Angelica Swann. Liam, we'll need background checks on all of them just to cross the Ts."

"The pirate's already on it."

"OK. So, right now all we have for sure is that Sophie and Angelica had a medieval history class together. Now it looks like Dylan was seeing a girl with long brown hair. Doesn't Angelica Swann fit that description?"

"Aye, but brown hair's dead common in Ireland."

The brown-haired pathologist gave him a *look*.

"Then we need to ask Hortense Fervier *specifically* whether her daughter was seeing a boy called Dylan. She denied that Angelica was dating, but if she and Dylan *were* an item it could be very important."

Even John sniggered at his turn of phrase. "*An item?*" He adopted a southern U.S. accent. "Why bless my soul, child, next thing you'll have him signing her dance card and fetching her a mint julep. You sweet old-fashioned thing."

"Bugger off. It's not *that* old-fashioned a saying."

"It is you know, boss. You need a tweenie like Erin to keep you up-to-date. They call it hooking-up now."

Craig rolled his eyes. "And *that* will have changed by next week. Well, whatever the hell you call it, if this brunette *is* Angelica Swann and she and Dylan Pedersen-Storey *were* a couple, one of them is missing and one's dead!"

Liam sighed, still on modern romance. "Youngsters don't seem to date long-term nowadays, not the way we would've."

It brought a snort from the pathologist. "Marc had a different girlfriend every week."

"So the Baron had a harem did he?"

He stored the point away as a resource for future slagging.

"Anyway, my point is that hook-ups are mostly casual encounters, so the pair of them might've just got together once or twice. But I suppose even that would've meant they were in each other's orbit, which seeing there are thousands of students in the six counties has to mean *something*, I suppose. I mean, what are the odds?"

"Slim to zero." Craig considered for a moment. "This means Ryan's comment about youth might hold some weight. Sophie, Dylan and Angelica were all around the same age, all at Uni, and all possibly mixing in the same circles."

"But Bolsover was four times their age, so what's the link there, boss? It *has* to be the valuables. The stolen painting was valuable, Hortense stored valuables at the bank where Sophie and Dylan were found dead and where there were more valuables, and Bolsover had valuables at his shop."

Craig pursed his lips for a moment and then added something else. "Matilde Fervier had links with World War Two, Bolsover's gold says he had too, so what if our dead students have links to that period as well?"

Liam pulled a face. "Their grandparents or even great grandparents maybe, but them? No way."

John jumped in. "And you've still no proof Matilde Fervier's relatives had anything to do with the Ferviers here."

But Craig had the bit between his teeth. "Humour me for a minute. What if... OK, what if we're looking at a 'sins of the father' scenario here? Someone who's taking revenge on our victims for something that their antecedents did?"

John shook his head. "Except Horace Bolsover doesn't fit with that."

"OK, so where it was *possible* our killers directly accessed the person they blamed, such as Bolsover, and where it wasn't possible they accessed their first living relative?" Craig shook his head immediately. "No, that won't work."

Liam had spotted the flaw right away.

"Yeh, because why not kill the kids' parents then? The older generation of Pederson and Adomaitis are obviously still alive."

Craig puffed out his cheeks for a moment trying to think

of a good answer and finally shook his head in defeat.

"OK, I admit that I haven't thought it through yet, but there's *something* here, I'm sure of it. I said at the briefing that there could be a few dimensions to this so let's think about them."

Liam considered the point as requested, leaning so far back in his chair as he did that John was waiting for it to topple over; but even deep in thought the D.C.I. was aware of his exact position and tipped his chair forward again just in time. It made the pathologist think Danni Cullen had to be the calmest woman on the planet or she would constantly be living on her nerves.

"What if..." Liam paused for a moment and then restarted. "What if you're right about the links with the bank and valuables and world wars and whatnot, but Ryan was right too, and the reason our killers chose to kill kids *is* because *they're* kids as well, so it made making contact easier? But what if they only killed kids from *very* special families, families linked with everything you've already said? That way one theory doesn't contradict the other. They'd both fit with your ancestor theory."

Craig's, "YES!" was so loud it startled the others, but not as much as the "I could hug you" that came next.

He'd moved on before anyone could comment.

"When you think about it, it's actually brilliant in a warped way. Young people killing young people. Bypassing their parents' generation for some reason to take revenge for something even further back."

John was sceptical. *"Really?* You don't think you two might just have read too many novels?"

"Give me an alternative theory and I'll be happy to look at it, John, but for now let's work with this."

The pathologist's shrug came just as Liam observed, "It's as much use as *any* theory of a murder, Doc. The wife did it, the gasman did it, they were murdered by some randomer who broke in. None of them hold water until we produce proof."

None of them knew that Ash's hacking might be about to do just that.

****

The Ulster University (U.U.) Campus, York Street, Belfast.

Aidan Hughes practically skipped his way down the modern building's lengthy corridors to its exit, or so it seemed to the sergeant trailing in his wake. In reality it was more of a swagger; skipping being difficult when your legs are three feet long, and anyway, the practice looks pretty stupid when you're anything over five years old.

But whatever was responsible for the D.C.I.'s cock-of-the-walk strut he'd been doing it since they'd left the C.C.U., so Ryan decided to ask what was up.

"Got a new girl, chief?"

Aidan hid the smirk that had accompanied his progress and turned towards the sergeant, feigning casualness.

"I don't know *what* you mean, D.S. Hendron."

The comment earned him a sceptical look.

"I mean that ever since you came back from the Fraud office you've been on cloud nine, and in *my* world that usually means a woman's involved."

He was dicing with death and he knew it; Aidan was almost as private as Craig and intrusive questions were usually met with a growl, but Ryan was bored so he thought he would chance it.

Their questions about Dylan Pedersen-Storey and his brown-haired girlfriend had hit a dead end at every college and now at the Ulster University's Jordanstown campus and its main one in Belfast, leaving only Queen's to try. Their call to Hortense Fervier asking if her daughter had been dating anyone had generated a stream of invective from the heiress that had made it clear that not only was Angelica Swann far too young for *that* sort of thing and was of course pure as the driven snow, but she was 'coming out' at a May Ball in Dublin with the rest of the island's wealthy debutantes and only *after* that would a 'suitable' match for her be sought.

Either Ms Swann was significantly more demure than the rest of Ireland's youth or her mother was living in ignorant bliss. On balance the detectives had agreed the second probably applied but decided not to challenge Hortense with it.

So Ryan was bored now, hence his 'woman's involved' quip. He held his breath while he waited to be slapped down, only to instead be gifted a rare smile from the athletic D.C.I.

followed by a, "Might be" that was a yes by any other name.

The sergeant *could* have pushed it and asked, "D.C.I. Murray?", there only being two female detectives working in Fraud and Robbery and Terry Harding having been blissfully married for years, but he thought that he'd gone far enough for one day so instead he just nodded and said, "Good luck."

He meant it. Aidan's fiancée Arela had died years before and he cut such a solitary figure on squad nights out that he deserved a break. Ryan didn't say that of course but instead returned to the subject of work.

"Hopefully we'll get someone at Queen's who knew Dylan was dating and can give us his girlfriend's name. That's if Hortense is right and it wasn't Angelica. Any sign of her yet, by the way?"

"Nope. I gave Jack a call when you were in the loo. Nothing on the posters and street interviews either, so they're thinking of doing a TV appeal."

"*I* would if it was my kid missing, and if I had the Ferviers' money I'd hire a troop of private investigators too. Hortense must be out of her mind with worry."

"Hard to tell with that sort. They're raised to have more front than Harrods."

They'd reached Aidan's car so he started driving towards Queen's, continuing the discussion on the way.

"OK, so we know Marte Pedersen saw Dylan last Sunday and that he played rugby and football for Ulster Uni, who often competed against Queen's. His mum mentioned he was into photography too so we'll need to split up and interview anyone from all those clubs to find who might've seen him, and we'll canvas the Students Union as well."

It could be their last chance of finding his mystery girlfriend's name.

****

The C.C.U. 12 p.m.

When Craig arrived back on the tenth floor, Liam having disembarked the lift on the fourth to meet a Drugs officer who said he had something on Carfentanil, he encountered near silence in his squad-room; surprising when all but three of his team were there. It reminded him of Queen's law library on the night before a big exam, when the only sounds had been the thick pages of leather-bound volumes being turned, followed by an occasional cough from their newly disturbed dust, and the clatters of random pencils hitting the floor as they rolled off polished tables, making every student there turn on the culprits in outrage as if, if they failed their exams the following day it would be *solely* because their concentration had been broken by *that* noise.

In that spirit, but also because he needed information, Craig tapped his pen loudly against his PA's desk, much to her disgust. Nicky had been reading an essay her son Johnny had submitted as part of his A Level course work and she'd just reached an interesting part.

Her irritable, *"What was that for?"* was greeted by a raised eyebrow from her boss before he turned to face his team.

"Right. I need an update on Angelica Swann. Call out anything you know."

Annette obliged him first. "Aidan said there's been nothing from the posters or street stops, so they're talking up a TV appeal. The mum's doubled down on her 'My daughter wasn't dating' position, in fact according to her Angelica's never so much as kissed a boy."

Mary snorted derisively. "She sounds as if she knows as little about her child's mating habits as most parents."

The D.I. screwed up her face in disgust. *"Mating?* Ugh. Let's stick with dating for now."

"Prude."

Craig waved them to be quiet. "OK. So where are Aidan and Ryan now, Annette?"

"Last heard of on their way to Queen's. They're trying to put a name on the girl Dylan was seeing and they struck out at the U.U. sites."

"OK. Thanks."

Before he moved on Craig shot a pleading look at his PA subtitled 'coffee' but wasn't that surprised when she didn't move; the price of his earlier arched eyebrow no doubt. After a moment's stand-off during which he added a coaxing smile she finally shifted, although so slowly that it underlined her point so in retaliation her boss sat defiantly on her desk while she was away.

Andy had watched the interaction rolling his eyes but not commenting, having been guilty of more than a few acts of childishness himself.

But Craig saw the eye-rolling and decided to pick on him next.

"Right, Andy, what more can you give me on the art?"

The D.C.I. obliged with a printed handout.

"This is?"

"A final list of everything taken from the six vaults plus the gallery Vermeer, and you're not going to like it. Around half of what was taken from the bank belonged to Hortense Fervier, including the harpsichord and the solid gold carnival mask. The rest of the items were the Pedersen-Storeys'."

"Dylan's parents?"

"Yep."

"Not a single stolen item belonged to a different bank customer?"

"Nope."

Craig was just about to speculate why there'd been nothing taken that belonged to Sophie's family when he remembered that they lived abroad. There might well be vaults in Lithuania being checked by the end of their case.

As he continued reporting Andy projected a slideshow of the stolen items on to the screen.

"The Vermeer has apparently been in the Fervier family for centuries, but that could be a lie of course. I can't find any date for its purchase. I'm digging into the other missing pieces now with The Met and Interpol, and they've promised me updates by close of play."

"Good."

Craig was just about to call for another report when the look on the D.C.I.'s face said he had more.

"Matilde Fervier's Holbein is clean thankfully, but Grace called through about the valuables found at Bolsover's. Not good news. Annette has the info on that."

Just then Craig noticed Nicky approaching with his coffee and sprang off her desk. He savoured his drink for a moment and then nodded his inspector on.

Annette displayed various items from Bolsover's stash on the screen as she spoke.

"OK, so the jewellery pieces found at the shop I'm running against the same databases as Andy. Some of them are old."

"Victorian?"

"Yes, and some even earlier that had obviously been passed down. Grace has managed to date the jewellery from hallmarks and testing their precious metals as dating from seventeen to nineteen-hundred and originating in Europe, Africa, Russia and the Middle-East. She asked a master jeweller to examine them too and he confirmed that the jewels are all still in their original settings."

"Any values?"

She nodded meaningfully. "Oh yes. We're talking upper hundreds of thousands for each piece because of their age and uniqueness, and two of the necklaces he said would fetch at least a million at a specialist jewellery auction."

Craig was surprised, not by the values, the gaudy jewels had impressed even him and he'd always preferred cleaner Scandinavian designs, but by the fact that there were specialist jewellery auctions at all, although he supposed it did make more sense than putting such precious items in a general sale.

"That's quite a haul."

"I'll say. In total he put the value of Bolsover's stash, apart from the bars and coins which he said he couldn't value other than by the weight of the metals, at nearly fifteen million pounds."

Nicky almost fell off her seat in shock. "And Bolsover was keeping them *where*?"

Craig gave a weak laugh. "In a cupboard in a rundown Smithfield shop."

"My guess is that's because they'll all turn out to be stolen, sir, so the old man couldn't sell or display them on without attracting attention. He *could* have broken the jewellery down and sold off the stones I suppose, but he obviously chose not to."

Craig nodded. "The pieces may have meant something to him intact..."

He was thinking of what that might have been when Ash spoke for the first time since he'd arrived.

"You mean like a serial killer revisiting his trophies and reliving his kills?"

The creepiness of the image made everyone shudder but Craig. He wanted to hear more.

"Expand on that, Ash."

The young man's eyes widened; he hadn't thought beyond his initial comment. But his quick intelligence showed as he did so now on the hoof.

"Well... what if Bolsover..." He paused for a moment and

regrouped. "Yeh, OK, let's say old Horace had a bad past. A criminal one where he'd stolen the jewels and gold. And let's say he didn't want to get rid of them because they reminded him of his youth."

It felt close but not right and Craig couldn't say why. There were pieces of a jigsaw floating irritatingly around in his consciousness but as yet none were close enough to fit.

He decided to play the cards he'd been dealt.

"OK, Ash, let's say for now that Bolsover was a thief in his youth, a serious thief, and the reason he held on to the pieces were because they reminded him of his heyday-"

Annette interjected. "Also, sir, if they were stolen he *couldn't* have sold them anywhere respectable without getting caught, not unless he'd broken the jewellery down."

"That still left criminal fences, Annette. No, the reason he didn't get rid of them has to be either because he didn't need the money or because the pieces held emotional value for him, either sentimentally or as trophies as Ash said. Unless Bolsover was a secret millionaire I don't think the first option applies." He turned back to the analyst. "*Was* he rich?"

"Nope. He owned the shop and had a few grand in the bank. That's all."

"OK, then for now let's go with the jewellery being trophies or perhaps even mementoes."

Andy had a different view so he shook his head firmly, stopping Craig in his tracks.

"You don't agree, Andy?"

"I think there's another option we need to consider, chief. That someone else sold Bolsover the stash because *he* was a fence."

Ash nodded excitedly. "What if Hubert and Aveline sold it to him during their missing three weeks?"

"What three weeks?"

Seeing that the analyst wasn't ready to say just yet Craig moved on.

"Tell me what that's about later, Ash, but good analysis, everyone."

The computer expert seized his moment.

"Before you move on, chief. I've checked Angelica Swann's phone and the only places she's been in the past month are the Malone Road, so probably her home, and around the University Road area, which would cover Queen's and the Union. The signal appeared at the Union on Monday around seven and it was switched off at ten-forty. There were no calls between her and any of our three victims. Also there are no crime reports on any of the Vics' lecturers."

Craig hid his disappointment behind, "Thanks for that, Ash" but he was still sure that the phone meant something. He parked it temporarily and turned to his D.I.

"Annette, we *need* the identity and origin of Bolsover's pieces so push hard on that. Meanwhile, has Grace managed anything on the bars or coins?"

"Not yet, sir."

"Right then, tell me more about Horace Bolsover the man. Anyone?"

Mary obliged. "Well, he wasn't born Horace Bolsover because there *wasn't* any Horace Bolsover registered as being born in Ireland or the UK *or* moving here in the past two hundred years. The only Horace Bolsover registered in Ireland anywhere was in Bangor in eighteen-eighteen. He died at the age of ten from TB, or consumption they used to call it, and he's buried in a small church cemetery there. But... checking *our* Horace Bolsover's tax records, it seems he adopted the birthday of the dead child and just changed the year to show himself born in nineteen-twenty-three, making him ninety-six at his death."

Craig sighed. Stealing the birth details of dead people was a favoured criminal way of creating new IDs.

"That could be false as well, but people often use their own birth date even when they're lying. He was definitely old, but he could have been anywhere from eighty to one hundred odds. It's hard to tell with a corpse."

John could probably narrow the age down further if they needed him to; he recalled the pathologist once telling him that as people aged various pieces of their cartilage slowly turned to bone. It was an unedifying thought.

Mary went on. "So basically I've no idea who Bolsover was or if he even came from Ireland, but he obviously wanted to hide his identity for some reason. If he didn't come from here it's probably impossible to say where he originated and when without speaking to him. I've asked the lab to run his prints and dental records so they might throw up something."

"John didn't mention anything about his teeth that would help with country of origin."

Annette frowned. "Did the shopkeeper next door mention Bolsover had an accent, sir?"

"No, and we didn't ask, so call him and find out, please. And if the old man did then try to pin it down to a country. Also, see if Bolsover ever mentioned anything about his childhood and so on in conversation. You know the drill."

Just at that moment Liam entered the squad-room, scanned the scene and immediately took the huff.

"You didn't say you were briefing."

"We're not. I'm just getting myself up to speed. And we haven't finished yet, so if you keep quiet you might learn something."

Craig ignored the fist that he knew was being shaken at his back.

"OK, Ash, you were digging further on the information side. Anything new there?"

The analyst nodded. "I've had a few responses to my message board post, but they've all traced back to legitimate posters so far."

"Did you think that they wouldn't?"

"Well, I was *hoping* our hacker couldn't resist answering me himself and leaving a digital trail."

Mary sniffed loudly. "It *could* be a she, you know."

Craig's frantic eyeballing told the analyst to deal with his omission fast.

He did, in his usual inimitable way. "He, she, they, I don't give a monkey's what gender the hacker is, but Dylan was big so there's someone with heft involved in these killings somewhere."

Nice save. Time for Craig to take his ball back.

"OK, so you'll keep looking on that."

"Yup. As for the print on the window tape and the flash freezing, Mary's been working on those."

Craig turned to his constable with as sweet a smile as he could manage considering she was making his head hurt.

"Anything?"

"No. The print on the tape's not giving us anything, so I think it might just be a useful comparator when you catch someone. The flash freezing's interesting though. It turns out there are only ten flash or blast freezers on this whole island. They're used in food production."

At that she tapped twice on her smart-pad and replaced the bling on the screen with a map of Ireland marked with ten red dots.

"These are the locations." Another tap and all but three

disappeared. "I've removed the ones that are too small to hold a body, and it only leaves one in Cork City, one in Armagh and one in Galway, near a river called The Clare. If the bodies in the vaults *were* flash frozen to throw off their times of death then it happened at one of those sites."

Craig moved over to the screen before speaking again.

"Andy, can your database checks run themselves?"

"Once I've finished uploading everything, yes. Why?"

"Do that and leave Ash to keep an eye on it then take Annette and hit the road. We need those three freezers checked for access and witnesses, just in case someone who shouldn't have visited them was seen."

Annette had a caveat. "Could we call on Bolsover's neighbour first?"

"Yes, do that. Then start in Cork and work your way back up. You'll probably have to stay overnight so make arrangements."

It brought a smile to both detectives' faces, particularly Annette's; she rarely got to work outside Belfast so it felt like playing hooky from school.

"OK, anyone else have anything?"

Ask gave a nod. "I cross-checked the phones and there was no contact between Sophie and Dylan, Sophie and Angelica or Dylan and Angelica. The middle one struck me as odd with the girls being in the same study group so I checked for common third numbers and there was one that came up on both Dylan and Sophie's phones; an unregistered pay-as-you-go mobile. I don't know what it means yet but I'm running its purchase details and geo-location."

"What about Angelica's phone that was found at Queen's?"

"Just what I already told you."

"OK, going. Anyone else have anything to say?"

A deep voice behind him said that his deputy had.

"Don't you want to know about the drugs then?"

Craig turned towards him with a humouring smile. "Why of course, Liam. If you'd like to tell us."

"Don't get cheeky, Baron, or I'll tell everyone about your student harem."

That sparked curiosity from everyone and a hasty wave to move things along from Craig.

"Aye well, Grace found our young Vics had been dosed with a drug called Carfentanil, which is twenty times stronger than the ordinary Fentanyl on the street. I asked Deke Rooney down in Drugs to look into it for us and he's just said they've never found the stuff on the streets up here, but it *has* been known down south. The Garda arrested a dealer about six months ago who'd smuggled some in from the States. He's in Killarney but he isn't the only one dealing it there Deke thinks, so I'd say that south of the border's probably where our killer got his."

Craig saw Mary's mouth open and added hastily, "Or her's. Good. Thanks for that, Liam. Leaving the drug-dealer's location aside for a moment, it's likely our killer would have used a flash freezer near where they were staying for ease of transporting the bodies, which gives us Cork and Galway in the south and Armagh near the border for possible hide-outs, say within twenty miles of the freezers-"

Liam cut in. "And we know they must have had access to transport to move the bodies, so they have a van. That fits with carrying that harpsichord from the bank as well."

"Yes." Craig thought again. "OK, this is where the dealer's location comes in. Deke's ruled out Armagh for drugs because it's in the north, but our perps *could* have their base near the freezer in Armagh and just nipped south to buy their drugs, so pay a visit to the station there anyway, but on your way back, please. When you reach Cork and Galway have a word with the locals and see what's what there with Carfentanil. Deke can name the best people to talk to. And ask him to put in a call to their National Drugs Bureau so you're not stepping on any local toes."

"Will do, chief." He turned to Annette. "So that means we visit Deke, Bolsover's neighbour and then home to grab our go-bags and get on the road."

"I'll need to organise the pickup for Carrie too, but yes, that sounds good."

"OK, you all know what you're doing so get on it. We won't brief again until the pair of you get back tomorrow."

As Craig turned towards his office, "Ah ha, so this *was* a briefing" followed him in, as did his gloating deputy in the flesh.

****

Queen's University.

Twenty-nineteen's Queen's University Students Union was a completely different building to the one where both Ryan and Aidan had misspent their youths. That one, with its subterranean Mandela Hall had heaved with hormonal possibilities and throbbed with the sweat of Northern Ireland's so-called gilded youth performing their various mating rituals to jive, rock, punk and trance only to regret them through a dull hangover the next day. *That* Union's vaguely grubby, long-walled corridors splashed with flyer covered paintwork had made their own scruffy teenage appearances fit right in.

But *this* Students Union was different; bright, modern, wholesome. It even smelt good too. It had had a different address as well since the year before, on Elmwood Avenue instead of its previously prominent occupation of the University Road, moved there in preparation for the demolition of the century old original that would grind generations of memories to dust to make way for a sleek new world.

It made Aidan feel mournful, and as he stood at the top of the old Union's steep flight of steps that he'd tumbled down often as a law student, with a little assistance from Jack Daniels and Jim Beam, Ryan was having similar nostalgic thoughts, although more of 'the girls I kissed here, and there, and over there' variety.

It translated into noisy outrage.

"*How can they knock this place down? It's part of Belfast's history!*"

The D.C.I. nodded glumly. "I'm guessing there's some history the great and good of Belfast would rather forget, namely their own misspent youths." He gazed across the street at the architectural masterpiece that was the Lanyon building. "They'll never knock *that* down, I bet. It looks as respectable as *they* all claim to be."

With a sigh that said 'The End of an Era', he turned his attention to why they were there. Having struck out at every club that Dylan Pedersen-Storey had ever associated with they were accosting passers-by outside the Union with images of their one missing and two dead students in what felt like a last hurrah.

After twenty minutes of terrifying young and not so

young stragglers by flashing their warrant cards, Ryan caught a break from a young man whose shoulders were as wide as he was tall.

"Hey, that's a photo of Dylan Pedersen-Storey, isn't it? What's he done?"

The sergeant greeted the ID with excitement. "It is indeed! How do you know Dylan?"

The whole do/did debate wasn't worth having unless he was prepared to tell the quickly gathering audience that Dylan had been murdered and deal with the excessive expressions of youthful grief that would inevitably follow, which he wasn't. Thankfully the young man's answer made the point moot.

"He scored the winning try at the intervarsity's cup last year. Hell of a run down."

Their victim's muscles had clearly been hard earned.

"Can you tell me anything more about Dylan? Have you seen him since then?"

"Oh yeh, I see him around the Union a lot." The boy smirked. "With a girl in the past few weeks."

Aidan finished up with a woman that he'd been speaking to and strolled across to listen in.

"Could you describe this girl?"

"Yeh, sure. Real thin, like *scrawny* thin, and tall." He glanced at the D.C.I.. "Not tall, tall like him, but pretty tall for a girl, like you."

The five-foot-nine Ryan wasn't sure whether to be insulted or not.

"OK. And her face and hair?"

"Long. Way past her shoulders. It was a mousey brown and kind of frizzy. But she had a *really* gorge face. A cutie."

The youth warmed to his theme.

"She must have been taking a language because I saw Dylan near the language labs a few times like he was waiting for someone."

The detectives exchanged a look. The description fitted Angelica Swann.

When the boy said, "Yeh" to her photo, Ryan concealed his thrill just long enough to take his details and say goodbye before exclaiming, "Angelica was dating Dylan Pedersen-Storey!"

They needed to take the discussion off the street so Aidan led the way to the nearest café and only when their coffees had arrived did he nod the sergeant to speak again.

"So Dylan Pedersen-Storey was dating Angelica Swann? Well, well."

The D.C.I. was less surprised than he thought he probably should be. Ever since Ryan had pointed out how young most of the protagonists in their case were a link between them had seemed almost inevitable.

"OK, so we know Angelica and Sophie were in the same medieval history class and now Sophie's dead. Now we find out that Angelica and Dylan dated and *he's* dead too."

Ryan set down his cup. "Yes, but what's the link between *any* of them and Horace Bolsover?"

"The chief called it right. There are lots of factors at play here. The camera hack says Bolsover's killing's definitely linked to the others somehow but his age says he's an outlier, and why *he* was killed mightn't come out till the end. I think we should look more at Angelica Swann. How did she meet Dylan and why did she date him?"

Ryan shrugged. "She probably met him at a dance or something. She's cute. It happens."

"Yes, but the odds of *this* particular cute girl knowing both of our victims and her mother having a painting stolen on the very day their bodies were found are *really* slim."

"What are you thinking?"

It was at moments like this that Aidan most missed smoking. Five minutes communing with his cigarette had been like pressing a five minute pause on the world allowing him to could think great thoughts in peace. He put a drinking straw in his mouth as he thought about the sergeant's question, but despite the oral gratification it just didn't have the same effect.

"OK, so... what if Angelica *isn't* missing? What if she left of her own volition because she's somehow implicated in these murders?"

Ryan shook his head instantly. "No way. *She* was the one who first noticed that the painting had gone."

Aidan gave a slow smile. "Why yes, she was. Great cover, isn't it? And what about that Narnia apartment above the gallery? Who else would have known about that but the staff, who we've cleared, and family? Angelica is family. She could have copied her mum's key to the gallery, hidden up there, come down in the middle of the night and nicked the painting. A painting she *really* liked, don't forget. The

Ferviers' have a house up the Malone that they use during the week so she could've stolen it, passed it on to someone else and been back in bed before she was missed."

The D.S. nodded grudgingly, knowing he could be right.

"And in plenty of time to go to church with her mum the next morning and point out the painting was missing as they drove past... It was the perfect diversion. She probably knew everything about the alarm systems and cameras so she might even have helped the hacker."

"Maybe we should go back there and look. It's only up the road."

Ten minutes later they were looking at the gallery's rear door, and more importantly the neat space to one side of it where a car or van could have reversed in, allowing the Vermeer to be deposited in its back unseen from the street.

Ryan had another 'No way' moment when he spotted a large floodlight above the door.

"That's a movement sensor, and..." he waved his hand beneath it and an immediate blue-white glare made them both avert their eyes. "...*that* would have come on and woken up the people in the flat across the road."

Aidan was undeterred. "OK, so, *my* bet is the thieves knew to cover the light because Angelica had warned them that it was there, but we should visit that apartment and ask what the occupants saw."

The answer was, on the early Sunday morning when the Vermeer had been stolen, nothing at all. The neighbours hadn't even woken, despite their bedroom facing the rear of the gallery and the light having roused them before many times.

Ryan was running out of arguments. "OK, so the thieves covered it. I'm not saying no way to the Swann girl being involved anymore, but I *am* saying we'd better get our ducks in a row before we tell the chief about this. He's going to want something substantial before he changes her status from missing teen to possible perp."

Aidan started walking to the car.

"Where are we off to now?"

"To get all this on paper before we face the Guv. And let's move it in case I'm wrong and the girl's in real danger, or I'm *right* and someone else is."

****

Craig's Office. 2 p.m.

Shakespeare once wrote 'There is a tide in the affairs of men', and as Craig grew closer to resolving a case he often felt an undercurrent sweeping him along in much the same way.

Stage one of a murder case always consists of bodies dropping and being discovered, and the overly obvious suspects being ruled out. Stage two is even messier, because the more you dig on a victim and their method of expiry the more loose ends are thrown up to either seal off or draw together into a single thread. How long these first two stages last can vary but once an investigation enters stage three and some, but unfortunately rarely all, of the answers come, speed and momentum suddenly become features of the case. That can lead detectives to believe they should know everything *now*, and coupled with the knowledge that their killer mightn't be finished and could kill again that brings the pressures of 'if only' to a case.

If only they were clever enough and *if only* they could solve the case instantly, then possibly, probably, someone out there could still be saved. And that means their death is on *you* the detective, or more accurately it's on your boss.

Marc Craig had just realised they'd entered stage three of their case and probably had less than twenty-four hours to stop their perps killing again and escaping scot-free.

For that reason he gathered his team together in his office, or those who were around anyway.

"OK, I know I said I wouldn't be briefing and this isn't one."

He ignored his deputy's rising eyebrow and turned to his whiteboard, where he'd already written up the numbers one to four.

"We've entered the final stage of our case sooner than anticipated, so I'm sorry but no-one's going home until we've sorted this out. Apologies if you had social arrangements but you'll have to change them."

The lack of objections said that his staff clearly needed to get out more.

"OK, one. Andy and Annette have gone in search of Horace Bolsover's accent, who's dealing the drug Carfentanil in the south, and to check the flash freezing units in Cork, Galway and Armagh."

Nicky raised a finger. "Andy phoned through. The

shopkeeper next door to Bolsover said his accent was European but not obviously French, Spanish or Italian because he would have recognised those."

"OK, good." Craig wrote up 'European' and left it at that. "Have we got anything from Grace on the gold yet?"

The PA made for the door. "I'll call her now and check."

"OK, number two. Aidan and Ryan were at Queen's trying to find more on Dylan Pedersen-Storey. Aidan, tell everyone what you found."

"We both found it." He motioned Ryan to speak.

A minute later both detectives were feeling gratified that Craig had taken their theory about Angelica's possible involvement seriously enough to scribble it on the board.

"OK, we can't be certain of this yet, and for obvious reasons I don't want it going outside this squad in case we're wrong, but I'm inclined to agree. It shouldn't affect the way we look for Angelica, just what transpires when we find her, so as far as the uniforms are concerned this is still a hunt for a missing teen."

Ash, who'd found one of the cosiest spots in the small office, in its left hand corner between the window and wall, signalled to speak.

"How does that affect the TV appeal, chief? Her mother's just recorded it and it's due to go out at seven unless we've found the girl."

"We proceed as if Angelica's an innocent missing girl, which Hortense Fervier clearly believes she is, and see what we get. Where's the mother now?"

"On her way to the family pile at Lough Neagh. She'll return if we need her."

Craig handed the analyst his marker. "Good. Write that up under number three."

Just then Nicky re-entered and passed him a note of some items, the first of which he read aloud in an unsurprised voice.

"Grace has dated the bars and coins to the nineteen-forties through something to do with the way the metals were smelted."

Liam whistled so loud that Mary shoved her fingers in her ears.

"Bloody hell, it *is* Nazi gold!"

"It *might* be Nazi gold or it might have just been stamped to look that way."

"Why would they?"

"No idea, but I'm not closing off avenues just yet."

"OK, so where did they *get* the gold to melt into the bars and coins?"

"That leads me on to Grace's second point. She found samples of several different carats of gold in each of the gold bars. That means gold from multiple different sources was melted into one mass and then shaped and stamped as we found it."

"It wasn't melted very well if the carats are still distinguishable."

"I'm sure she used some specialist technique."

A meaningful look said what Craig thought the sources of the gold had been originally and prompted looks of disgust from his PA and analyst.

"You mean gold taken from prisoners' teeth in concentration camps!"

"What? No! At least I hope to God not! I meant the Nazis looted valuables from every country they invaded so all we can safely say at the moment is that the gold belonged to several other, probably stolen items before it was melted down."

He turned to his deputy. "Liam, write that up under number four. Valuables." When he glanced back at the note in his hand, his tone moved another notch towards disgust.

"Grace has also confirmed that the print they found on the window tape belonged to Horace Bolsover."

He watched to see what reaction came from his team.

Liam was first. "They made him tape up the room himself!"

Aidan shook his blond head. "Nah. If they'd done that there would've been prints all over the tape instead of just the one."

The deputy's small eyes widened. "Then it's a signature!"

Craig gave a tight nod. "Explain to everyone, please."

Liam warmed to his theme. "OK, so like Hughesy says, that was the only print they found on the tape. That means the perps must've worn gloves. It's the only way to avoid leaving randomers. That means *this* print was left deliberately, and it was the old man's so they obviously took his finger-"

"Thumb. Even better."

"Thumb then, and pressed it deliberately against the

window tape, kind of like Bolsover signed his own death warrant. They had to know we'd find it, boss. That's the reason they left the window tape there."

Craig nodded. "But not only that. It shows they made Bolsover do it when he was alive. No-one's going to drag a corpse to a window to sign when a living man can walk there by himself. They also left the window tape in place because they wanted us to *know* they'd sealed Bolsover in the room when they'd killed him because that would then have led us logically to gas as the method of killing, just in case it had dispersed before we arrived. They'd left the connecting door open, remember."

Suddenly his dark eyes widened in realisation. "They *wanted* us to sample the gas! It has some special significance."

Nicky tutted in disgust. "They're animals."

"Perhaps. But I'd like to know why they thought Bolsover deserved it before I judge."

Ryan was curious. "Why did you say the thumb was better, chief?"

"It was the digit used most often in history to seal documents." Craig turned back to his PA. "Nicky, I need you to call forensics back when we've finished and emphasise how quickly we need that final gas analysis."

As she scribbled a note he turned to his analyst and was just about to speak again when Liam got in first.

"So the old man was executed like the kids but the killers hated him a lot more. No sedation and he was made to watch while they prepped the room to kill him, *and* sign his own death warrant before they did. It goes to motive, boss."

The fact it was a statement and not a question made Craig smile. Liam was almost ready to sit his DCS board, which didn't mean that he would of course. Ambition wasn't a big feature of his deputy's personality and there was always the risk that if he passed the Chief Con would move him somewhere new. He knew that Liam thought he'd broken him in as a boss now so that would *never* do.

"I don't disagree, Liam, but what is it?"

The D.C.I. snorted. "Bolsover must've done something to *really* piss them off."

"Like?"

"Ach well, I don't know, do I? But *I'm* planning on pissing everyone off in my old age."

Aidan's retort was dust dry. "Just rehearsing now, are you?"

Craig smirked but pressed his theme, trying to make his deputy really think things through.

"Yes, but even if we accept that Bolsover had offended his killer somehow, that could have just been something simple like ripping them off. People overreact all the time."

Liam shook his head emphatically. "Nah. Doing them out of a few quid or cutting them up in traffic wouldn't have earned *that* death. It had to have been something really big."

Aidan sat forward enthusiastically. "Actually, that's a fair point, Guv. Not about Bolsover, but why did they kill the kids at all? What had *they* done to the killers to deserve death?"

It was Ryan who answered. "Sins of the fathers."

Liam nodded to Craig. "You said that at the labs."

"I did, but we're still no closer to confirming it, unless," he turned back to his computer expert hopefully, "Ash has found something useful on his searches?"

The analyst was engrossed in scrolling his smart-pad when he heard his name being called again.

"You talking to me, chief?"

A flurry of De Niro impressions followed until Craig batted them away.

"I'm looking for anything new and useful, Ash. On people, art or anything else."

The analyst responded by rising and heading for the door. "The big screen's better for this."

They joined him out on the main floor just as he was projecting a family tree on to the TV.

"OK, so this is the family tree of Hortense Fervier back to seventeen-twenty when the first of her Huguenot line, Emmanuel Fervier, arrived in Ireland from Paris. Most of the family settled in Wicklow and Clare but some migrated north. Remember the north and south of Ireland was all one country in those days."

It sparked a noisy grumbling from Liam, whose unhappiness about Ireland being partitioned in nineteen-twenty-one was very well known.

Not fancying a political debate right now Craig waved his analyst on. Ash pressed a key that lit up the line from Emmanuel Fervier to Hortense and added detail along the way. There had been so many generations of impressive ranks, titles and achievement that Craig realised why the snobbish gallery owner hadn't wanted to lose the family name.

"And now," a tap produced a box in one corner of the screen which the IT expert populated with a second hierarchy, "here's the family tree of *Hubert* Fervier, uncle of Matilde."

As they watched he lit up a line from Emmanuel Fervier's father Charles to Hubert's hierarchy centuries before.

"As you can see, Hortense Fervier and Hubert Fervier had the same great great great whatever grandfather, Charles, but where one son Emmanuel remained Protestant and came to Ireland, another son Louis stayed in France and converted to Catholicism to survive. *That* branch of the family eventually produced Hubert who married Aveline and probably collaborated with the Nazis during World War Two."

Craig raised a hand to halt him. "Brilliant work, but the two branches wouldn't have known each other, would they?"

"We can't say whether they kept in touch through the generations or not, but there aren't that many Ferviers around so they might have done." He indicated his co-worker, who was sitting on a nearby desk examining the ends of her hair. "Mary has something on that."

The D.C. had clearly been listening because she joined him by the screen before "that" hit the air.

"OK, so," she gestured at Hubert Fervier's name, "we know that Hubert and Aveline fled France at the end of the war and arrived via Lisbon at Dublin Port with a lot of heavy luggage. We also know that they were booked on trains to Cork three weeks later. We *can't* know where they went in those three weeks, but now that we're sure that they were distantly related to *our* northern Ferviers they *may* have made contact with a branch of that family in the south."

She tapped her smart-pad and replaced the family trees with two tickets for flights from Ireland's south-west to New York dated for the day after the train trip.

"Hubert and wifey were booked to fly out on the first of June nineteen-forty-five but they didn't."

Craig's eyebrows lifted. "How can you be sure?"

"I contacted the airline. Well, its successor to be accurate. It's changed hands several times since World War Two and is currently a subsidiary of Lantic Air. They keep brilliant records and actually have an archive of everyone who's ever flown with them."

Liam gawped at her. *"Ever?"*

The thought made him uneasy. He'd always imagined his rare trips through the air as being recorded only for as long as it took the aircraft's vapour trail to disperse after landing. Someone being able to read about them in a century's time felt like Big Brother gone mad.

Mary nodded enthusiastically. *"Ever.* Brilliant, isn't it. I'm going to search for movie stars' names when I get the time."

Nicky perked up. "Clark Gable. My mum loves him."

Craig smiled. So did his.

"Search for whoever you like *after* we've solved the case, Mary. Just as long as you don't sell anything to the tabloids."

She took the hint and moved on. "OK, so not only didn't Hubert and Aveline get on the flight, which by the way was just the first step to their final destination of Argentina, but they'd also booked cargo on a ship out of Cork heading for South America and *that* never got on board either."

"So you're saying Hubert and Aveline Fervier remained in Ireland after the war and so did all their loot?"

Her reply was equivocal. "It seems so, but I'd need to check all the plane and boat cargo manifests since nineteen forty-five to be sure."

Her tone said 'please don't make me'.

Craig turned to his deputy. "What do you think?"

Liam shook his head. "I think it's a damn sight more likely that they got off at Dublin and their plans to travel on changed. I also think their wealth is still being held by some branch of the Irish Ferviers to this day."

Craig nodded slowly. "It's certainly worth consideration. If it is still here then there'll be war reparations to be made to the families who originally owned the items."

The possibility that some of Hubert's stolen booty might also be amongst Horace Bolsover's stash passed no-one by.

Craig straightened up briskly. "It makes checking the *whole* of the Ferviers' art collection, public and private, essential, but that will have to wait till we've solved our case. For now, what do we have on the provenance of the items taken from the vaults? Anyone?"

Ash took over the screen again and projected up Hortense Fervier's Vermeer plus the items that had been 'liberated' from the bank.

"The Vermeer's dirty and like *every* item taken from the

vaults is on Interpol's, the Met's or Germany's Lost Art databases as being stolen just before or during World War Two."

While the others' jaws dropped, Craig merely nodded. He'd been thinking it for days but hadn't wanted to believe it but now there was no choice.

"So every piece that was taken from the bank belonging to Hortense and the Pedersen-Storeys was dirty?"

"Yep."

"Details?"

"The items were stolen between nineteen forty and forty-four from all across the Nazi occupied territories: France, Poland, Czechoslovakia, Holland, the list goes on and on."

Aidan shook his head. "Taken as the Nazis rose to power."

Craig pulled a face. "Mostly, but some might have been stolen by their neighbours. Collaboration and opportunism occurred in several countries, and plenty of greedy locals saw their chance to loot houses when their owners were displaced or killed."

Liam shook his head sadly. "By displaced you mean sent to concentration camps, don't you."

Craig took a deep breath before responding. "Many yes, but others were initially herded into ghettos like the one in Warsaw. Mostly Jewish people, but others too. Some were put out on the street to make way for ethnic Germans that the Nazis wanted to resettle from the east."

Nicky shuddered. "So the stuff stolen from the vaults was originally stolen from people being sent off to be killed?"

"Mainly, yes. The Nazis hated a lot of people. The Jews and anyone who helped them; Polish, French, Czech and other dissidents and intellectuals who stood up to them; homosexuals, males in particular; anyone they suspected of being a communist; the mentally or physically handicapped; Romanies, Sintis..."

His voice tailed off as he realised it would have been easier to list the people that they *hadn't* hated instead.

Ash gestured at the screen. "We haven't got through all the vault stuff yet but we have managed to indentify the rightful owners of some of it."

Another tap and labels appeared below three of the pieces, revealing them to have been owned variously by people of Norwegian, Dutch Jewish and French origin.

"I checked the French family just in case they were linked

to the Ferviers, but they weren't. That piece is the emerald necklace and it belonged to a musician from Nice who was sent to Belsen in nineteen-forty-four."

"So the odds are Hubert Fervier acquired it from the Nazis and brought it here at the end of the war." Craig nodded. "Well done, you two. Find the true owners of all the stolen pieces and keep trying to find out exactly where Hubert Fervier ended up in Ireland."

Ryan was shaking his head and tutting.

"You need to say something, Ryan?"

"I'm just stunned at the arrogance of Hortense Fervier displaying war loot in the window of her gallery!"

"Perhaps she didn't know. To her the Vermeer may just have been another item from her family's collection."

The sergeant gave an uncharacteristically caustic laugh. "Yes, and the fact that their other war booty was hidden away in a vault was just coincidence."

The comment made Craig frown and turn back to his analyst. "Ash, did the Ferviers keep any possessions in the vaults that *weren't* stolen?"

"All the stuff that was stolen was dirty, but I'll need to check if there's anything else belonging to them still in the vaults."

"And, as earlier, we need to find out about *all* their other pieces, including the ones on public display."

If Hortense had stored a lot of items in the bank but only the looted ones had been taken that might mean she hadn't known their history. But it meant that the thieves very definitely *had*.

The next team member to emote was Aidan, who gave an uncharacteristically pained sigh.

"You sound bothered, Aidan."

The D.C.I. gave a sharp wave at the screen. "It's just, well the rightful owners had their art nicked once decades back and now it's been nicked again. The poor wretches are never going to get it back, are they?"

Craig's reply surprised everyone. "Aren't they?"

Liam's eyes widened. "You really think we'll catch our perps *and* the art, boss?"

"Was that what I said?"

Nicky gawped at him. "You're not saying the killers will do a Robin Hood and return the pieces to their rightful owners, *surely?* Why didn't they take Bolsover's gold then?"

Craig wasn't prepared to commit himself further at that moment so instead of answering the questions that started coming he said, "Keep your ears to the ground and check the local fences *just in case* the loot starts getting hocked around. OK, good work, everyone. You all know what you need to do."

He turned towards his office, beckoning his deputy to follow.

Once inside Liam gave a hearty chuckle. "Ah now, you just love that, don't you?"

"What?"

"Being all inscrutable. *'Was that what I said?'* indeed. Those poor buggers will spend the rest of the day trying to work that out."

"And I suppose you've done so already?"

The D.C.I. tapped the side of his nose. "Might have. I'll tell you when we've caught the perps."

By which time the answer would be obvious anyway. But Craig kept *that* thought to himself.

Chapter Eleven

Galway.

"So we're all agreed on the final stage?"

Roman scratched quickly at the tattoo on his forearm in the way that he always did when he was stressed, mentally reciting the numbers listed there like a mantra to calm himself down. Three of the others' hands flew to their arms in concert, all bearing similar tattooed memorials, even though in one person's case the tenets of their religion specifically prohibited marking themselves. They were living monuments to those gone before and their suffering, and even though unlike them *they* had been physically free all their lives they'd still never enjoyed a day of true peace.

Irina knew what her lover was thinking and took his hand, closing her eyes and recalling the stories she'd been told of her own people. The Nazis had driven a tank through her great grandparents' Roma encampment, crushing those children who hadn't run quickly enough beneath its tracks as if they were blades of grass. She heard her grandfather's voice as clearly as if he was still beside her. "I was a teenager and fast so the tank missed me, and I thought myself lucky until they took us to that camp and into hell. Never forget what happened to our people, girl, or it will happen again."

The knowledge was seared on her mind just as the numbers were on her arm and it was the same for the other three, all of them living legacies of Nazi oppression in one way or another, their grandparents or great grandparents shot, mown down, burnt, worked, starved or gassed to death. *Their* short years on earth had been defined by the lived experiences of people from generations before, and all but one person in the room had come from the victims' side.

Roman's dark eyes scanned the group, trustingly until he reached its final member. He'd never been relaxed about Angelica's involvement with their mission, but without her access to Sophie Adomaitis and through her Dylan Pedersen-Storey it might have failed.

It seemed that one advantage of living in a small country was that people often attended the same schools and colleges, just as Sophie's roommate's brother had done with Dylan. Once Angelica had befriended the Lithuanian girl in her history group it had been easy to engineer an introduction to the boy and youthful libido had done the rest, connecting them with the first two of their designated victims and providing them with a way to access the vaults.

Everything had gone smoothly so far but he still didn't entirely trust Angelica's motives. She *was* a Fervier after all. And who really hates their family so much that they're willing to help steal from them, even if they *have* learned some of their ancestors were Nazi collaborators in the past? After all, that had happened long before even Hortense Fervier was born.

Angelica said she hated her mother but what sort of girl would turn on her even if she did? Irina's response when he'd once voiced the question still echoed; *"The sort of girl who will turn on her mama will turn again just as quick."*

Unfortunately Angelica was essential to the next stage of their operation too so they were stuck with her for now, but she required close watching. She was manipulative and flirtatious and Roman knew his troops well enough to know that neither he nor Kurt should be left with her alone.

But time was short and they needed to get on the road soon so the group leader turned his mind to next steps.

"OK, does everyone know what they're supposed to be doing?"

A series of nods confirmed it.

"You all have your gear and passports and you've only left behind what we want found? Preserving your anonymity's essential for our future work so be sure. We're not returning here after this."

Yes again.

"OK, everyone except Irina go to the van."

Left alone, the long-legged youth and his girlfriend began their final walkthrough of the expansive space that they had called home for a fortnight, scouring it for careless clues to their true identities and pleased at finding none. Every inch had been vacuumed and scrubbed to remove residual DNA and sterile jumpsuits donned afterwards, and no prints could ever have been left because they'd worn gloves the whole time that they'd been there.

To make absolutely sure that nothing remained that didn't fit with their message they reversed slowly towards the exit spraying bleach over every floorboard, stick of furniture and foot of wall, one taking the left hand side and one the right, continuing as they backed down the staircases and then slammed the door at ground level hard. But Roman had completely missed his lover leaving the main room's left back corner unsprayed.

As he exited into the fresh air the group leader heaved a sigh of relief. Soon they would be finished in Ireland and move on to their next job. Until the day that all of the past wrongs had been righted and they would finally deserve lives of their own.

He turned to his team.

"OK, you all know the plan. Kurt and I go with Angelica to the gallery and Gretchen and Irina take the cargo to the boat and then catch their flight." He smiled at his girlfriend. "By the time you've landed and met up with the others our part will be done and we'll be in the air."

Who *we* would be was deliberately left vague.

****

Craig's Office. 3 p.m.

Craig gazed out at the undulating profile of the buildings between him and the Lagan, the lowest of them The James and the tallest, still thankfully five storeys lower than the squad-room and not in his eye line, an American computing company of some sort. The day the city planners allowed something to be built that obscured his view of the river would be the day that he would hand his papers in.

The town planning thoughts left the detective as quickly as they had come, his mind busy trying to make sense of the events of the previous three days. He'd got as far as laying out the theft, historical information and murder strands in preparation for plaiting them into the solution to their case when he suddenly realised that he was missing an essential piece. Everything they knew about Angelica Swann had come from her mother, and she was hardly an objective voice.

He was just about to go in search of better information when his door opened and Ash appeared wearing a grin. Instead of beckoning him in Craig exited and inquired what was making him so cheerful in a loud enough voice for the others to hear.

"I'm happy because I'm a genius, chief."

The policeman perched on a desk, smiling. "I don't doubt

that." From Mary's sceptical snort *she* clearly did. "But the question is, has your brilliance produced anything useful to the case?"

"Yep."

The computer whiz dropped the finger that Craig had failed to notice hovering above his smart-pad and an image appeared on Nicky's screen making her jump again and prompting muttered threats about where she would put his smart-pad if he repeated the offence.

Craig wasn't listening; he was walking towards the screen reading what was written there as he went. When he reached the end he thought he'd guessed the reason for the analyst's smugness, but being aware of his tech limitations he said, "Explain, please" to be sure.

"OK. So this," Ash lit up the text, "is the post I placed on the hacker boards."

Liam read aloud. "Hi. Uncovered new hack. SLS technique. Very cool. Anyone know who the white-hat is? It would be sick to chat."

He screwed up his face. "What the hell does *that* mean? *Sick?* It's nonsense."

"It's not nonsense, but I'll take it slow for the oldies in the room. OK, the first part's clear isn't it? The SLS technique is was what was used on all the cameras. Slice, loop, splice."

Craig nodded. "Yes, except if they understood what SLS meant, that in itself would give them away."

"Correctamundo! That was my first trap. OK, so then I say white-hat. Hackers are either white-hat and ethical like me, or black-hat and criminal like, well pretty much anyone involved in the big hacks you hear about on the news."

"So you're implying that whoever did this is a decent person, therefore not being judgemental."

"Yep. No point in pissing them off. And the sick part means good. It would be good, sick, to chat."

Liam tutted in disgust. "Why couldn't you just say it in English then? I admire your hack and would love to talk to you about it."

Mary's pitying glance spoke volumes and prompted a comeback from the D.C.I..

"Yeh, well, just wait till *my* kids grow up. They'll have *new* jargon and then *you'll* feel old."

Craig lifted his eyes to heaven. "Can you all *please* grow up?" He gestured back at the screen. "You wouldn't have got us here if there hadn't been a reply to your post, Ash. So what did it say?"

Another tap and more text appeared.

"OK, so out of twenty boards all I got was a few people asking what SLS stood for, and then there was *this* one. They didn't ask what it meant because as their answer shows they obviously knew." He read aloud. " 'No idea, bro, but my guess is they could wreak havoc with any camera they liked.' Except that I hadn't *mentioned* the hack was used on cameras or media in my post."

Craig peered at the screen to see if he could spot the place of origin.

"It's Albania, chief. Look down at the bottom right hand corner. They've shown their location in such a way that you're supposed to believe you're clever for working it out. The time difference and an advert for the Lek, a currency that's only used in one place in the world, Albania. This is our killer and they're playing with us."

"But it wasn't posted from Albania, was it?"

"Nope. And I finally worked through all the proxy servers to find out where it *was* posted. Galway."

Liam's eyes widened. "*Galway, Galway?* On the west coast?"

"Do you know any other Galway?"

"There's a Galway in New York State, smart ass."

Craig ignored the geographic debate, his mind on more important things.

"But why did they respond at all, Ash? They could have ignored your post and got away scot-free."

Aidan had a few ideas. "Arrogance because they're proud of their work? Or because they *want* us to locate them. Not to catch them, but... maybe..."

As he stopped speaking, unable to decide exactly why the killers might be leaving them a trail, Ash jumped in again.

"Just while we're on Galway, chief; I've been doing some work on that pay-as-you-go phone. It was bought with cash in a small store off High Street. They have no CCTV so that's a dead end, but the phone geo-locates to Belfast and Galway, and whoever owns it has been up and down between them several times in the past month. The geo-location isn't as accurate as with a contract phone so I can't say where they'd been in Belfast, sorry, but I bet the Galway address will turn out to be the same as our perps."

"Why would Sophie and Dylan have been calling a burn phone linked with our killers? That requires some thought." Suddenly something occurred to him. "Is that phone still operational?"

"Nope. It went dead on Monday around seven."

Craig smirked. He had a hunch why it had gone dead but he wasn't sure enough to share it yet.

"OK, good, let's return to Aidan's point. If they *do* want us to locate them then perhaps it's because they've left something there for us to find? Think that through, Aidan. It might be something."

Before then he needed to divert Andy and Annette.

"Right, Galway was one of our three possibles for the freezer but it's just become the favoured base for our perps. Ash, can you nail the location down any tighter before I redirect the others?"

"My geo-software's got it down to ten square miles already, chief, so by the time they're close I should be able to give them a street address."

"Good. I'll tell Andy to head for Galway. Ryan, call the Garda and ask them to have armed response and bomb disposal people standing by. We don't know what they might be walking into."

He turned to his PA.

"Nicky, phone Hortense Fervier, find out the name of her daughter's best friend and text the phone number and address to me." He glanced at his deputy. "First *we're* going to ask Marte Pedersen if she knows anything more interesting about her son's friend than that she had long brown hair." He missed Aidan's face falling as he turned towards the exit. "Time to go, Liam."

"Thanks be to God. I was going mad staring at four walls."

Mary's, "It's hard to tell the difference" made Alice, the main beneficiary of Liam's rants because her desk sat outside his thin-walled office, smirk, but Craig shot the constable a meaningful look.

There was banter and then there was cheeking up a senior officer in front of the team, and the latter wouldn't wash on his squad. He made a mental note that Mary needed a sharp refresher on the force's rank system and headed for the lift wondering what it would take to bribe Annette to deliver the rebuke.

225

****

The M1 Motorway.

The diversion advice reached Andy just as, despite Craig's advice, he'd been contemplating taking the A3 off the motorway to visit Armagh's main police station first, to ask a mate of his to put out feelers on the local freezer and drugs just in case Deke's sources weren't bang up-to-date. That way if they struck out in Cork and Galway the info would be waiting when they drove back north.

The fact that the station was on a main access road to the historic city's centre, otherwise known as the fifth circle of hell because of the fury generated by its narrowness and traffic jams, hadn't been filling the D.C.I.'s heart with joy. He'd taken his son to a kids' theatre event there the year before and while the show had been well worth the visit once they'd got there the ninety minutes they'd spent stuck in the car was something he would rather not repeat, even with Annette instead of a bored twelve-year-old.

Craig had made the call just as he and Liam were leaving Marte Pedersen's glossy home empty handed.

"Well, that was a waste of time, boss."

"Yep. But we couldn't have known that beforehand could we? I mean, I'd have expected a parent to know a *bit* more about the girl her son was dating than the length and colour of her hair."

"That's what Hughesy said she'd said. You should trust us more."

He tried for a hurt pout, but with his lantern jaw just ended up looking like Lurch instead. Craig didn't even notice, he was so busy with 'what ifs'.

"I just thought further questioning might... oh, forget it. Dylan clearly hadn't brought Angelica home or the mother would have known more."

Liam gave an understanding nod. "No-one got brought home to meet *my* parents unless we were thinking of marrying them, and only Danni fell into that camp with me."

"We brought everyone home. It was my mum's rule. I think she wanted to look into their eyes to make sure we weren't dating serial killers."

"In your case you'd probably have thought that was cool."

As Craig chuckled his deputy started the engine. "Where

to now?"

"Well, Nicky hasn't called with the best friend's details yet so let's head to the labs."

When the PA called five minutes later it was too late to divert.

"We're going to the labs first, Nicky, so just text me the address and phone number."

"OK. Her name is Gillian Pritchard and she lives in a student house in the Holyland. Fitzroy Avenue. I've checked her lecture schedule and she should be home now, but don't leave it too long or she'll probably be lying drunk in some bar."

The secretary's view of students had clearly been coloured by watching Animal House.

"OK, thanks. Call and tell her we'll be coming down in about thirty minutes, Nick, or she'll never let two strange men in."

He hoped.

Seeing that they'd arrived at the pathology building he ended the call and got out.

"The Doc first?"

"No, Des."

Two minutes later they were in the forensic scientist's office and Craig was playing a hunch that he'd had for two days, now reinforced by some internet research he'd done a few hours before.

"Des, you said the gas that killed Bolsover might be some form of chemical weapon but the only components you could be sure of were Carbon Monoxide and Cyanide."

The scientist nodded. "Yes. We know the inorganic particles are a plastic and we're looking at the organic material now. It seems to be mostly silica, with some iron oxide and alumina. Put together the whole thing doesn't really make sense."

Craig frowned for a moment, wondering if what he was about to suggest was so farfetched that he shouldn't bother. But then he often came up with wild theories and the only way to rule something out was to test.

Just as he was opening his mouth to do so John and Grace appeared.

"We heard you were here. Anything exciting?"

"I'm hoping Des will tell us, if he doesn't die laughing at my idea first."

The scientist nodded him on.

"OK, so Bolsover was cherry red and also had greenish blotches which John thought he'd read about somewhere. And Des, you've confirmed the gas contained Cyanide and Carbon Monoxide. On the basis of that and more information that's emerged during the case about the Second World War period I did a bit of research..."

He paused for so long that John sighed.

"Say it or I will, Marc."

"Be my guest."

"You think the gas used to kill Horace Bolsover was a mixture of Carbon Monoxide and Zyklon B, the Hydrogen Cyanide compound used in the gas chambers during the Holocaust. A greenish discolouration was occasionally recorded as attributed to it, and I thought I'd read about it because I had. In a report on genocides."

Liam's jaw dropped. Even he considered such a subject too sensitive to discuss, yet here they were.

Craig saw the horrified faces around him and picked things up.

"No, don't look at us like that. Listen. Zyklon B was essentially Hydrogen Cyanide, but absorbents were added to the canisters it came in and one of the most commonly used was diatomaceous earth, a naturally occurring silica based rock. Couldn't that be the organic component you found, Des?"

The scientist considered for a second and nodded. "I'll need to check, but yes. But why add Carbon Monoxide when the Cyanide was already lethal?"

"It was symbolic. The first Nazi murders by gassing were in nineteen-thirty-nine as part of the Nazi Euthanasia Programme. They killed Polish and Jewish people who were mentally ill and less able by using exhaust fumes, aka Carbon Monoxide, in the rear of what was called a Gas Wagon. Essentially a mobile gas chamber."

"And the inorganic particle? The plastic."

Craig and John answered simultaneously. "IG Farben."

Des frowned. "The chemical manufacturers?"

"The chemical and plastic manufacturing *Nazi Party donors* you mean. Farben used slave labour from Auschwitz concentration camp to work in the factory they'd built in a nearby satellite camp called Monowitz."

Grace glanced from one man to the other. "What did the

factory make?"

"Rubber and plastics - I'm guessing that's what your particles represent, Des. Also chemicals, amongst them Zyklon B."

The CSI wasn't the only person in the room who felt like they wanted to cry.

Des found his voice first. "If someone deliberately added the plastic particles to the gas that killed Bolsover that must mean he was at Auschwitz and his killers wanted us to know."

Craig nodded. "That would be my guess, but there must be a specific Farben link here too. Bolsover was certainly old enough to have been at the camp as a young man, but somehow he came here after the war, changed his name and carried on with his life."

Liam shook his head sombrely. "Dear God. He managed to survive the Holocaust only to get killed on our watch. We could be looking at a hate crime here, boss." His hands curled into fists. "I'd love to get my hands on just one of those fascist fuckers."

The normally prim Grace didn't even blink at his words, nodding sadly instead.

But Craig wasn't convinced that his deputy's perspective on the evidence was correct.

Until he had more information he just said noncommittally.

"Clearly someone had been on Bolsover's trail for some reason and they finally caught up with him."

Grace shuddered. "So the gold that I dated..."

"Must have been smuggled out of the camp. The jewellery too probably. The Nazis told the people they were transporting that they were being relocated, so they would have brought whatever valuables they could carry to help pay for their new lives. But of course-"

John cut in. "But if the war *was* why Bolsover was killed, your two young victims weren't even born then."

"If we've linked the case to World War Two, and things are stacking up that way, then they could have been killed for something that transpired with their grandparents or great grandparents during the war. We'll need a lot more information to be sure exactly what that was." He glanced meaningfully at his deputy. "Bolsover too."

Before Liam could comment he moved on. "So what do we know about Sophie Adomaitis' and Dylan Pedersen-

Storey's antecedents?"

"I notice you didn't say Angelica Swann, boss, 'cos we already know the Ferviers were up to the eyes in other people's goodies."

"That's *part* of the reason I didn't mention her, Liam, but also I'm not convinced that she isn't involved with our killers. That's partly why I'm not coming down on either side yet."

John gawped at him. "You think your missing girl isn't missing at all?"

"I think it's possible, but I'll need coffee before I explain."

Grace obliged and after a short interlude Craig's normal service was resumed.

"Let's think this through giving Angelica the benefit of the doubt for a moment. One, our killers needed Dylan Pedersen-Storey to access the valuables in the vault. Two, they may also already have intended to kill Dylan and Sophie anyway. Three, they knew who the Ferviers were and always intended to target their valuables in the vault as well as the Pedersen-Storeys', and perhaps kill Angelica the daughter as well. *But*, when they realised Angelica was in Sophie's study group and could be useful, they offered her a way to survive instead; the choice of helping them get close to Sophie and Dylan. Angelica seized the chance, befriended Sophie and dated Dylan to lead the killers to both."

John raised an eyebrow. "And *without* giving her the benefit of the doubt? Because your tone says that's not what you really believe happened."

Craig gave a tight smile. "Without the benefit, Angelica Swann was a willing participant in our murders from the get-go, and we," he glanced at his deputy, "need to uncover our killers' true motivation and prove which scenario applies. At the moment, precisely who the villains and victims are here feels a little murky to me."

He rose from his chair. "So let's get back to it, Liam. Meanwhile, can you confirm our theory about the earth and rubber, Des?" He turned to Grace. "Thanks for the information on the gold and thumbprint. We're fairly clear now that the killers pressed Bolsover's thumb against the tape in some symbolic signing of his own death warrant."

"And they wanted you to know that they'd done so."

"They did. I get the sense they'll want the world to know everything soon."

Liam gave a sceptical snort. "Except their names."

"Yes. But it's our job to find them anyway."

Fifteen minutes later the detectives arrived at Fitzroy Avenue, a long conduit connecting the streets behind Queen's with the busy thoroughfare of the Ormeau Road. The street of three and four storey Victorian terraces had been an elegant boulevard during Belfast's boom period of the nineteenth century, but now it was student rental land and houses of multiple occupancy had mostly replaced family homes, with the accompanying soulless, down at heel appearance that a lack of love often brings.

Gillian Pritchard had clearly decided to reinstate some of her home's original ambience, with multi-coloured houseplants lined up along the front windows of her ground floor flat and cheerfully draped floral curtains to match. The student herself carried the bright theme through by answering the door to the policemen wearing a bubblegum pink fluffy jumper over her artfully threadbare jeans.

Craig held up his warrant card and nodded his deputy to do the same. "Ms Gillian Pritchard? I'm DCS Craig and this is Chief Inspector Cullen. I believe my secretary phoned ahead to say we would be coming?"

By way of an answer the girl squinted hard at his warrant card and then his face, repeating the sequence for Liam with such suspicion that the D.C.I. was tempted to stick out his tongue.

Finally she nodded.

"Yes, she did. She also gave me a security question to ask before I let you in."

Nicky was clearly trying to teach the girl not to allow strange men into her flat. Good for her.

"Fire ahead."

"What are your wives' names?"

"Katy and Danni."

The suspicious look was replaced by a grin and, "Pass, friend" followed. It made her sound like a kid playing spies and made Craig feel very old.

She led the way into the flat's spacious front room which was, as Liam had suspected it would be, a cushion-stuffed, over-heated home from home.

"Coffee, Officers?"

"Yes. Thank you."

Liam got in fast in case the claggy taste of the caffeine that his boss loved was inflicted on him.

"Tea for me."

A minute later they were seated in a semi-circle and Craig started things off.

"Angelica Swann is your friend, yes?"

"Yep."

"How long have you known her?"

"Since nursery. We both went to one on the Lisburn Road."

"And what age are you now?"

"Eighteen, Angie too; we've known each other for fifteen years. I can't believe that she's missing."

Liam jumped in. "Why? Hasn't it ever happened before, even for a day or two?"

The girl shook her thick fair hair. "Never. Angie doesn't do all that staying out and walk of shame stuff. She's always been a good girl. Well, she's had to be really. She lives at home and her mum's really strict."

"And by good you mean?"

"No boyfriends, no booze, no cigs, no dope..."

The words faded away as she suddenly remembered that she was speaking to cops. But the list of 'no's was music to Liam's ears. Where could he sign his kids up?

Craig wasn't as convinced by the paragon of virtue defence. "Angelica doesn't *do* those things or she just tells her parents that she doesn't?"

The girl smirked. "*Definitely* didn't until we started Uni three months ago, but she's broken the rules on the first one since."

"Boys. So who is she dating?"

Confusion clouded the student's face. "That's what I'm surprised about really. I mean the first boy she gets serious with-"

Craig cut in. "Serious, as in loves?"

She was horrified. "God no! We're *far* too young for love." The words were accompanied by a sneer.

Serious in this case obviously meant sex.

"So Angelica and her boyfriend were sleeping together."

The question brought a blush to the girl's cheeks and she suddenly found the carpet fascinating.

"A yes or no will do, Ms Pritchard."

"Yes."

Moving swiftly on.

"OK, so Angelica got serious with a boy and that seems to

surprise you. Why? Because it broke her mother's rules?"

Her face screwed up in disgust. "Nooo. Because it was Dylan Pedersen-Storey. *I mean.*"

Craig was surprised. The boy had looked normal enough to him.

"What's wrong with him?"

He stuck to the present tense, not being sure whether she knew Dylan was dead or not. Also in case false grief moderated her true opinion of the youth.

Their hostess' disgust was replaced by laughter, indicating that she definitely didn't know Dylan was dead.

"What, apart from the fact he's a thick jock, you mean? All he can do is tell boring rugby stories and drink pints. Yawn. But I suppose Angie..." she gave a shrug, "whatever."

Liam thought he'd just spotted something useful so he asked another question.

"Are you saying Dylan isn't Angelica's *normal* type?"

It prompted a furious nod of the head.

"Defo. I mean she's never dated anyone before, but Angie *always* fantasised about poetic types. You know, the sort with great hair that reads Byron on top of a hill."

Craig could just picture him.

She was on a roll now.

"I know for a *fact* she had the hots for some long hair in her French class, and then all of a sudden she's snogging Dylan Neanderthal! I mean, what's *that* all about?"

Craig smiled at the descriptions, wondering how the girl would have described the pair of them when they were young.

"Did you ask her *why* she was dating Dylan?"

"DOH! Only every week. But she just said he had hidden depths so I left it. It had been going on for weeks so there must have been something there, I suppose."

And that something could have been Angelica setting the boy up to be killed.

"Do you know how they met initially?"

She sat forward eagerly, clearly in her comfort zone of gossip now.

"Some girl in her medieval history class had a friend who introduced them."

Sophie.

"And did Angelica ever take Dylan home to meet her parents?"

The question prompted a spluttered laugh.

"To meet Hortense the Horrible? No way in hell."

"Angelica doesn't have a good relationship with her mother?"

She pointed straight behind him. "About as good as mine is with that wall. Hortense isn't exactly what you'd call the cuddly sort. Angie hates her, like I mean red-hot hate. It's been pretty constant since she hit her teens and Hortense went all, 'this is how young ladies should behave' on her."

"What about her father?"

"Oh yeh, Angie loves *him* big time, but that causes problems too because she's not above playing him off against her mum to get her own way."

She'd just painted a picture of a dysfunctional family and they had learned a lot.

As Craig stood up to leave the girl suddenly looked serious.

"You will find Angie, won't you? I mean, she's a pain in the butt at times but she's my friend, and she'd *never* go missing like this without someone making her."

He wasn't sure how to respond so he made non-committal noises. The truth was if they found Angelica Swann alive it was looking increasingly likely that they might be locking her up.

****

The M1. En route from Galway to Belfast.

Roman Bianchi smiled to himself as he drove, satisfied at the progress they had made. Things were going smoothly, and if they continued as he predicted there would soon be Belfast coppers blue-lighting it to Galway as fast as they could. In fact, if their analyst was as bright as he thought they could be heading down the motorway already. Maybe they should wave at them as they passed.

The young killer allowed himself a moment to picture the computer whiz who'd uncovered his hack, deciding that as he, if it was a he, worked for the fuzz he was probably a real short back and side parting with Buddy Holly glasses, but still wishing that they could have met and hacked together in any case. It would have been a buzz. If Roman had seen Ash's shoulder-length black hair, gold earring and swashbuckling chic then he might have been more afraid of him; denigrating a stereotype is easy but the real thing can be more formidable by far.

But the group leader's mind was already turning to very different things and as he focused on the road ahead he was picturing his girlfriend and Gretchen, who would soon be at Dublin's port and then its airport on their way to Venezuela and the man who would meet them at the other end.

When Oskar had first contacted them one by one through social media they'd known nothing about each other, but within months he had melded four strangers into a loyal cell whose members would die rather than give each other up, *and* the cause in which they fervently believed.

Roman glanced sideways at Kurt listening to the dreadful Europop he loved through his ear pods and smiled, knowing that they would be friends for life.

After the melding had come the training. More than a year of extreme physical and mental challenges that had made them into what they were today: an elite covert force capable of taking on the best in the world. Better still, an elite force focused not by money like mercenaries or patriotism like armies but by history, trauma and love, determined to right the wrongs that had plagued their forebears' youths and had been passed down through stories, laments and empty chairs to colour their own.

Their grandparents and parents hadn't had sufficient distance from events to deal with them rationally and without pain, but *they* had a white hot anger that kept them sane and an unswerving belief that man's inhumanity to man could never be allowed to pass wherever or whenever it occurred or it would simply happen again.

Suddenly a female voice from the car's back seat made Roman jump, but the question that Angelica asked was timely.

"When should I call her? We've just passed Dundalk so we've only an hour till we reach the gallery and it'll only take her that long to drive back from the Lough even if the traffic's bad."

It was Kurt who responded, removing one ear bud and arranging his face in a smile before he turned around.

"Patience. I'll tell you when it's time."

As the girl slumped back against the cool seat fabric and began brushing her hair to calm herself Kurt focused back on the road, his smile dropping as he did and his distaste for the young woman behind them and having to work with her growing by the mile. Oskar hadn't been happy about it from the start, calling her the enemy, but he wasn't there and they'd had to think on their feet. Without Angelica the first part of their plan would have taken far longer and this final part mightn't be happening at all, so they would just have to suck up her involvement until everything was done.

He glanced at Roman, only to see that his eyes were fixed not on the road now but on his rear view mirror and yet a quick check behind said there was no-one on their tail. Kurt was just about to ask him what he was finding so fascinating when the group leader veered off the motorway and into a service station that no-one had spotted but him.

"Five minutes to stretch your legs and grab coffee then we're back on the road."

Just as he'd hoped Angelica jumped out of the car immediately and headed for the adjacent ladies' lavatories, but when Kurt went to do the same Roman gripped his arm to hold him back.

"She's having doubts."

It was said matter-of-factly, as if the idea didn't shock him at all.

His fair-haired partner was far less calm, thumping the dashboard and glaring at the girl's departing back.

"How do you know?"

"I watched her eyes as you turned face forward. There was doubt in them about luring her mother to the gallery to be killed."

"You're sure?"

"Positive."

"OK, we'll just have to kill *her* then. Oskar said no loose ends."

The dark-eyed driver shook his head. "No. There are other options." He opened his door. "Look, we can't stay here for long so let's talk on the way to the loos."

He waited until they had checked there was nobody lurking inside a cubicle before he spoke again, leaning his lanky frame against the convenience's white tiled wall and pulling an e-cigarette from his jeans.

"OK, as I see it we need Angelica to call her mum and get her to the gallery. If she hesitates we can pressure her to do that much just by waving a gun. She's a coward. We know that much."

The less than convinced Kurt frowned for a moment before responding.

"So you're saying we get to the gallery, set up and get her to call her mum. OK, I guess I can see that. She won't be brave enough to run-" He stopped suddenly, darting his eyes towards the door. *"She could have run already! Or told the guy in the shop. Or what if there's a phone-?"*

Roman waved him down. "Chill. I slipped a proximity tracker into her pocket before we left Galway. She's still in the ladies. Check it out." He passed his smart-phone across. "She's just on the other side of that wall, and as soon as she shifts more than six feet, like heading for the shop, it'll beep fast and we'll follow her out."

Kurt relaxed slightly and returned to their problem. "OK, so we can force her to call her mum but how do we make sure she doesn't warn her when she does?"

"Speaker phone. We'll hear everything she says and shut it down if we don't like it. Getting Hortense to the gallery isn't the problem; it's what happens if Angelica tries to run when she arrives. We can't chase two women down the street without being noticed, and if we mask up so people can't ID us some idiot will think we're terrorists and call the cops for sure."

"Well, what then?"

Just then the beeper went off and the youths were forced to move.

"We offer her the option of living as leverage." Kurt's mouth opened to object. "Yeh, I know you'd prefer to kill her to keep it neat, but no."

They exited the toilets to see Angelica heading for the garage shop and set off in pursuit, dropping their voices so they didn't carry.

"We tell her she either calls her mother or we kill her, and that if she betrays us at the gallery we'll do the same. She knows we're both great shots."

His companion frowned, perplexed. "Except we don't kill her? Not until we're almost at the airport?"

Roman shook his head emphatically. "We don't kill her at all, Kurt. She's helped us too much. Now, you take the left side of the shop while I take the right, and stay close so you can hear whatever she says."

By the time they were back at the car again both men were convinced they were going to be betrayed. Angelica's lingering gaze at the cheap pay-as-you-go phones that had ended as soon as Kurt had walked up behind her and her desperate glance at the checkout assistant who thankfully was too bored or preoccupied to see it gave her away.

Roman decided it would very soon be time to give little Ms Swann a choice, not as Kurt would like of living or dying but of coming with them or being left behind to take the rap.

****

Craig's Office. 4.30 p.m.

Craig's deputy exhaled noisily before he responded to his question, "Thanks for the updates, everyone, but does anybody have *anything* yet that could help ID our killers?"

"They're really good, boss. Three dead, three break-ins, a trail of stolen valuables and they're still ghosts. There's no sign of any of the stuff taken from the gallery or vaults being hawked around local fences, and all my snouts have come up with a big fat zip."

Craig turned to the other detectives seated around his desk. "Have *you* heard any word from the street? Even a whisper?"

Aidan shook his head. "I wish there was, Guv, but I've feelers out everywhere and nada."

"What about your man at the Diamond Traders? He's usually got his ear to the ground."

"I've had him asking around about new pieces and stones in case the perps decided to break down the vault jewellery, but there's zero word."

Ryan volunteered a thought. "So what if they haven't broken up the pieces because this isn't *about* money?"

Liam gestured at his boss. "That was his Robin Hood idea."

Craig nodded.

"It's still not out of the question that our killers could have stolen the valuables for themselves, but let's just for a moment consider that they *did* do it to return the items to their original owners."

As expected, it was Liam who responded with the greatest scepticism.

"Benevolence? They were hardly benevolent to their Vics, were they?"

Craig had to agree. "No they weren't. But there's a layer to this case that showed itself in Horace Bolsover's murder. *Context.* These aren't senseless killings, they're specific killings for a-"

"Cause" was drowned out by a knock and the door flying open to reveal a grinning Ash.

"Tell me how clever I am."

As Aidan scoffed, "What, again?" and Mary rolled her eyes, Craig decided humouring the computer expert was the quickest route to getting answers, so he ladled it on.

"Hawking would envy your brilliance and Einstein would be in awe. Now, what *particularly* clever thing have you done?"

The analyst set his smart-pad on the desk and glanced round for a chair. Finding none, he ignored Liam's offer of his knee in favour of propping himself against Craig's filing cabinet and indicated the pad.

"Heinrich Mueller."

The words begged for a question so Liam obliged.

"Who's he when he's at home?"

"*He* was called Horace Bolsover when he died, but before that he was a wanted criminal." He lifted the pad and turned it so everyone could see. "OK, so you know that aging-up software we've used in cases, chief?"

"Yes, and?"

"Well, a couple of months ago Davy and I worked out a way to use it in reverse. Taking people back to their youth. A bit like they did with De Niro in that new Scorsese movie, only not as cool."

Aidan shook his head hastily. "Don't let me catch you doing that to my photo! I've no desire to be shown how alcohol and cigs have ravaged my once smooth face."

Craig rolled his eyes. "Hopefully Ash has found a better use for it than vanity. Show us, please."

An image of an elderly but healthy Horace Bolsover appeared on the screen.

Liam frowned. "Where'd you get that from?"

"Driving license. He didn't have a passport, which isn't surprising considering what I found out."

With a tap the image started to age slowly backwards until it had reached Horace Bolsover at age eighteen.

"OK, so I ran *this* one through every international database I could think of and Interpol have just come back with a hit. Say hello to Heinrich Mueller."

A faded black and white photo of a youthful Horace Bolsover in uniform appeared; a uniform whose collar was adorned with the familiar lightening strike runes of the Waffen-SS.

Liam's outcry was noisy. "*Sweet Jesus!* The old man wasn't an Auschwitz survivor, he was a bloody Nazi!"

When Craig didn't even blink the outcry turned to accusation.

"You knew, didn't you? You knew at the lab and you said nothing!"

"I *suspected* back when John mentioned the burn on his inner left arm and again at the lab when we tied the gas that killed him to Auschwitz, but I couldn't be certain until now."

"What's the burn got to do with anything?"

"The SS had their blood group tattooed there in case of injury. Many of them had it removed at the end of the war so they could pass themselves off as ordinary Germans, but the Allies knew where to check for scars and arrested them. Somehow Mueller must have slipped through the net."

Ash picked up his report. "Yep, he was a Nazi, and an enthusiastic one according to the records I've been sent." He tapped up a new screen. "Heinrich Jan Mueller, born nineteen-twenty-three, joined the kiddies branch of the Hitler Youth at ten, long before it became popular, and volunteered to join the army early at sixteen. Mueller fought on the eastern front and was suspected of taking part in the shooting massacres of the Jews in Ukraine in nineteen-forty-one, after which he was basically headhunted into the SS and by twenty had risen to the rank of SS-Obersturmführer or senior Lieutenant and become part of the command structure at Auschwitz concentration camp."

Even Craig gasped at the information. Headhunted into the SS because of his talent for killing; there needed to be a special word for people as evil as that.

He closed his eyes for several seconds to get a grip on his emotions and when he re-opened them he homed in on the facts.

"Does it say anything in Mueller's records about IG Farben?"

The analyst's eyes widened. "How did you know?"

Ryan attempted to lighten the mood. "He's psychic."

Craig acknowledged his effort with a smile and gestured

at the pad. "Tell us exactly."

"Mueller was in charge of all Auschwitz's liaison with Farben's business at Monowitz. Amongst other things he organised for slave labour to be marched to work at the factory every day."

And doubtless shot anyone slow.

"And his other duties?"

Ash screwed up his face. "Interpol's a bit vague on that. It says 'sterilisation of arriving prisoners', but what exactly that means-"

Mary cut in. "It means Mueller herded people from the cattle trucks to the gas chambers, after all their valuables had been stolen of course."

Aidan grimaced. He'd always been interested in the World War Two period, and film imagery from that time was seared on his brain. As soon as Ash had said sterilisation, grainy black and white footage of trains arriving at concentration camps and the prisoner selection process had filled his mind.

"Mueller was probably on the Rota of soldiers who released the Zyklon B gas too, Guv. It was always a German soldier who did that; no-one else was allowed to. Probably some warped attempt to make the genocide appear like a legitimate act of war."

The room fell quiet until Liam broke it.

"It does explain the way Bolsover was killed, boss. Locked in a sealed room to mimic a gas chamber, and flooded with Zyklon B and some added plastic fragments to represent what the factory made."

Craig considered for a moment before responding. "This is what I meant by a cause. Despite the obvious thefts our murders weren't carried out for profit, they were driven by something."

"Revenge?"

"I think revenge is too... I don't know... vindictive perhaps? Retribution fits better here. Our killers believe what they're doing is merited, that their actions are just. They're locating people who committed wartime atrocities but escaped punishment and taking an eye for an eye. When the people themselves have died they kill whoever they can access in the family line."

"Even when they're innocent, boss? The kids didn't even have a fine between them."

Craig sighed and shook his head, "Clearly their forebears did something that made our killers think retribution was warranted, and I suspect we'll find out what that was fairly soon. Whatever they did will have involved shooting. That's why our younger victims were killed in the way they were."

Ryan interjected.

"But surely they'd *always* intended to kill the grandchildren of the perpetrators? I mean Sophie and Dylan's parents weren't touched."

"My guess is that was, as you said a while ago, about the killers themselves being young and therefore accessing the young grandchildren was easier. To access middle-aged people without raising suspicion, and they'd have *needed* that in order to kill without someone detecting it quickly, would have required middle-aged killers who could blend in and perhaps there were none available."

Liam wasn't as convinced. "Granted if you want to kill someone it's easier if you can mingle with them and get close, unless you're a sniper, but why would youngsters in their late teens to early twenties be *bothered* killing in retribution for a war that ended seventy-five years ago? I mean most of them are up to their butts in computers these days." He glanced at the two youngsters in the room. "No offence."

Before Mary could take some Ash jumped in. "None taken, although I don't actually keep a computer in my ass."

Craig motioned them both to be silent as he considered his deputy's point. It was valid. Why *would* someone kill for something that had happened so long before they were born, and risk their future by doing so? He was so deep in thought that he missed Aidan asking to borrow the smart-pad, and it was only when the D.C.I. waved a hand in front of his face that he remembered the others were there at all.

"Sorry, I was a million miles away. What was the wave for, Aidan?"

"This article."

He turned the pad around for Craig to see but he waved it back.

"Read it out for everyone."

"I'll summarise. I remembered reading a few years back about a thing called secondary testimony. They were accounts from the children and grandchildren of Holocaust survivors about their parents' and grandparents' experiences. Many of the generations were close and even lived together so they'd passed down the stories personally within families, but even if they hadn't can you imagine the trauma of learning about what had happened to someone you loved from a history book? And there've been a *lot* of books about that period, fact and fiction. Films too. So... psychological research found that some in those second, third and even fourth generations displayed symptoms of depression, fear, anxiety and addiction and eating disorders. Some even had their grandparents' camp identification numbers tattooed on their arms as a memorial, even some of the Jewish kids despite the fact it's prohibited by their religion."

Craig dragged a hand down his face in despair. "So you're saying our killers are descendants who might have suffered this impact and chosen to act."

Aidan looked pained.

"And *now* you're thinking, how could a bunch of teenagers have decided to organise and most importantly train themselves to kill so efficiently?"

"Something like that."

"So am I, and the answer has to be that they aren't acting alone. Our killers may well have had all the feelings of anger and depression and the urge to hit back that you describe, like we all might in their position, but few people act on those feelings and even fewer in such a coordinated way at a young age. Youth crimes are typically chaotic, impulsive and disorganised, whereas *these* murders were meticulously planned and smoothly delivered. And the methods used... execution shots to the head and gassing, say that *somebody* involved in this has a detailed knowledge of World War Two."

Liam nodded grimly. "There's a mastermind out there who set this up. A Svengali."

Mary sniffed loudly. "Young people *can* think for themselves you know."

"Yes, but it doesn't usually extend to mission *strategy*. That requires experience."

Craig nodded. "Liam's right. So, now we have more questions. Who is the planner, how many killers are we dealing with, and do we think they knew each other before or just came together for this mission?"

Ryan's eyes widened. "You're making them sound a terrorist cell, chief."

"Or the SAS."

Ash went one better. "Delta! Those boys are ace."

Craig gave a small smile.

"We could probably name crack forces for quite a few minutes but I don't think our killers belong to any government force. No government would sanction the killing of two kids who'd never been involved in anything criminal. This is strategised vigilantism. Right, now we need some facts to back up that theory so, Ash, use your contacts in the intelligence communities to put out feelers. But keep it diplomatic, please; I don't want some sniper taking offence. Mary and Ryan, can you assist with that?"

The sergeant was already glowing with excitement at the thought.

"OK, so we have young, skilled killers organised by someone older and more experienced. Definitely more than one killer because they carried two bodies into the bank, but not a large group for speed of responsiveness. So what are their next steps? Have they finished killing yet or not?"

Liam shook his head firmly. "Not. The Swann girl hasn't turned up dead yet."

"That's if she's actually a victim, remember."

As Craig said the words he knew that even if Angelica Swann *had* assisted their killers that mightn't protect her in the long run. These people clearly shared a cause and she wasn't one of them no matter how useful she may have been to date.

"OK, so we could be expecting another victim, who may or may not already be dead. What about the valuables? Ideas on what our perps will do with those, please."

Aidan responded first, passing the smart-pad back to Ash as he did. "Some of the items are bulky, the harpsichord and paintings, so they'll have to leave the country as cargo."

"Plane or boat?"

"Boat. Security's higher at airports so they'd want to X-ray everything and maybe even open a couple of crates. The items' details were circulated so they'd be spotted right away."

Craig scribbled 'cargo ships' on his whiteboard.

"OK, so the ship's going where?"

Liam jumped in. "International waters. They'd have time to split the pieces up from there."

"Perhaps, but let's keep our options open. Ryan, find the names and destinations of cargo ships leaving all Irish ports since Sunday. Check the ones in the south first. Start with

Galway and Cork. We'll need the ports watched and the ships' manifests checked."

Liam's eyebrows shot up. "You think they've skipped already? But what about the Swann girl?"

"I think some of the *valuables* could have left. OK, that's the stash but what about the players?"

"We still don't know how many there are, Guv. Or if the older strategist is with them."

Craig tapped the board marker against his chin for a few seconds before responding.

"I still maintain they'll keep the group small, so no more than five or six. And the planner won't be with them. Their expertise makes them too valuable to risk."

"All male?"

"No, but at least two are. They'd have been needed to carry Dylan Pedersen-Storey. But I think we'll find there's at least one female too. They'd have needed someone non-threatening as a lure. That's as much as we can say for now."

It brought a snort from his deputy. "It didn't sound like the Swann girl needed much luring. She hates her mum big time, so nicking the painting from her gallery was probably fun."

The words nudged at something in Craig's mind, but before he could explore it further Aidan spoke again.

"How about one of the gang leaving with the cargo and the others following by plane? Because they'll definitely split up now, won't they?"

"I imagine so, although it's hardly necessary to prevent them being recognised given we haven't a clue what they look like."

"Even if they haven't finished killing they would send the cargo on ahead, Guv. It's what I'd do. Cargo would just slow things down if they needed to make a quick getaway."

"Agreed, and some of our group might have left around the same time. Not on the cargo boat probably but flying from somewhere nearby."

He scribbled up 'Plane' and drew arrows to several 'X's representing unknown overseas destinations where a cargo boat and plane might link up.

"OK, Ryan, I'll need all of Ireland's airports and cargo ports marked on a map. And another world map showing every known destination where both cargo and air passengers can travel from here. Let's see where the boat and plane routes off this island overlap and try to narrow things down."

He turned to his deputy. "Any word from Galway? You gave them the exact location, Ash?"

"Pinpointed two hours ago."

"Good. So why haven't we heard anything? Liam?"

"Patience, man. It takes a good three hours to get there from Armagh and meeting up with the Guards could have slowed things down."

"Right ... OK, final thing for now, and I'd like you to take this one please, Mary. Look into the history of Dylan Pedersen-Storey's and Sophie Adomaitis' families, both sides."

"For?"

"Any links with the World War Two period. Family members, places they might have lived, anything at all. Interpol's probably your best bet."

Ash interjected, guessing the direction of Craig's thoughts. "The UN War Crimes Commission, the National Archives and the Simon Wiesenthal Centre too."

The detective nodded then set the marker down on his desk and rubbed the tiredness from his eyes.

"Right you lot, out you go. I need to think."

As his stomach rumbled loudly he realised that he probably needed to eat as well.

Chapter Twelve

The Banks of Lough Neagh. 6.15 p.m.

It wasn't a huge challenge. Take a woman distraught at her only daughter being missing and who'd lost a near priceless Vermeer that week, a painting that when Hortense Fervier had told her father and uncle about its theft she'd been startled by the vehemence with which they had demanded its return, and you had a distracted, vulnerable woman who was apt to act desperately, regardless of how formidably controlled some people might believe her to be.

Hortense gazed out the window of her family's granite walled... what? Home? No, it had *never* been that; no warmth or familial feeling had ever touched the place. Museum? Well there were certainly enough paintings on its walls to mimic one of those, but there were no paying visitors, no guided tours, no throwing open the doors to the public so that they could enjoy the art's beauty, so no, museum didn't fit either. She settled finally on mausoleum to describe the building in which she had been raised; an impressive, soulless monument to the dead.

Memories of them hung all around her: the dead artists who'd created the pieces, the dead auctioneers who'd sold them long before, and worst of all the dead owners, some of whom had doubtless auctioned their prized art to her grasping ancestors for a pittance in order to eat.

She shuddered at the thought and then pushed it away hastily as being nothing to do with her. Had she'd known just how atrocious the truth was her shuddering might never have stilled.

But that was her family's history and her ancestors' avaricious deeds were not her doing, not *her* guilt. Besides, she had plenty of personal deeds to regret without owning the evils of the past.

Her gaze returned to the Lough's lightly misted water and her mind to earlier thoughts. A creative person could capture her view in paint or words, perhaps even describe what was on her mind, but they would never *feel* it in the way that she did now.

Those feelings were thrust into the background by the ringing of a mobile and it took Hortense too long to answer, rushing inhibiting her ability to follow the sound and carrying through to fumbling and dropping the device when she did.

Finally she managed to gasp out, *"Yes?* Hortense Fervier here" and a calm male voice came down the line.

"Ms Fervier, this is Inspector Tarren of Malone Road Police Station. I wonder if you could meet me at your gallery. It's about your daughter."

Roman had decided against trusting Angelica to make the call. She clearly needed time to consider the options that Kurt was about to lay out for her.

Hortense gripped the handset hard enough to break it but only her voice did.

"Angelica! Y...you...you've found her? Is she all right?"

"Not yet, but we believe we may know how to, and it would assist us greatly if you could come to the gallery as soon as you can."

The group leader knew he'd been safe making the call from the flat above the gallery because a virus he'd planted on her smart-phone days before said she was at Lough Neagh and at rush hour it would take her a considerable time to arrive.

She confirmed as much a moment later.

"It will take me almost an hour to get there at this time of day."

"That isn't a problem. Just call me on this number when you're approaching and I'll come down from the station to meet you."

The panic in the mother's voice gave Roman hope that she wouldn't think to query why a police number had been visible when they were routinely withheld *or* to ring the station to check his legitimacy, and that believing the fictional Inspector Tarren had matters in hand she was unlikely to involve Marc Craig.

Even though they'd laid a trail for Craig to uncover the motives for their killing spree, the *most* important thing to them even more than the killings themselves, the last thing they needed was him doing so before they had time to flee.

But just in case Hortense Fervier did contact the cops Roman had a contingency plan. He'd hacked into every camera on the Lisburn Road so they could spot them approaching from miles away and beat a swift retreat.

When the phone call was over the swarthy youth allowed himself a celebratory whoop, fixing first his colleague's and then Angelica's gaze as he did.

"Your mother's coming!" His tone tightened and his gaze hardened to a challenge, "Think very carefully about what you'll do when she arrives, Angelica."

It was implicit that the decision would decide the rest of her life.

****

Galway.

Annette had never seen Andy really nervous before. No, she corrected herself, he wasn't nervous, he was impatient. The normally relaxed D.C.I. was like a horse champing at the bit to go but being held back by a combination of a Garda Chief Super whose leisurely approach to organising his armed officers seemed at odds with the strike squad's operating statement and a junior officer who insisted on buckling *them* into Garda-issue Kevlar vests like an anxious nursery school teacher, their own northern vests clearly not covered by the force's insurance regs.

Finally strapped into the navy blue contraptions instead of their own familiar green ones the Kerry born Simon Donovan waved them out his armed vehicle's door.

"Take your car and follow us." He waved the scribbled plan Andy had just drafted in the air, "And sure, we'll do this if we can."

It wasn't the most ringing endorsement the Murder detective had ever had of his efforts but he knew that it would have to do. They were in another country and that country's police force ruled.

As soon as he'd clambered into his Golf's passenger seat Annette pulled off, giving him time to look at the local map the Guards had supplied which showed the large industrial site to which Ash had finally traced the hack and a handy flash freezing facility two miles down the road. Plus the Garda Drugs Bureau had kindly listed the nearby drug dealers who were known to supply Carfentanil, their addresses marked as three dots around and between the two sites. The geography fitted their case perfectly, but that very perfection was making Andy itch.

"I'm calling the chief."

As the comment was clearly only for information Annette

merely responded with a nod. When his mobile rang Craig was nodding too, but only to himself and rhythmically because he was deep in thought. The maturity of their murderers' crimes pointed to what Liam had described as a mastermind but he hated the term, conjuring up as it did images of men in hoods and cloaks, or even top hats and cloaks if you were of a Sherlock Holmesian bent. Moriarty; an evil genius making plans and employing lackeys to carry them out. The analogy almost absolved the lackeys themselves of personal guilt, as if they were operating in a trance, and he very much doubted that was the case here.

Not a mastermind then, a facilitator, someone who'd assisted by cultivating and shaping the urges that had already existed in their killers and added strategic experience of his own. The only thing he could say for certain was that the facilitator wasn't here but probably in some inaccessible part of the world, and that was where their perps would head when they were done. Which he was sure that they weren't yet, although he couldn't logically have explained why.

The ringing of the detective's mobile, which for some bizarre reason Katy had set to play the tune 'Happy' by Pharrell Williams, probably to amuse the baby given that the bloody thing rang so often at home, cut across his thoughts and he saw Andy's number on the screen.

"Yes, Andy?"

"Hello, chief. We're with armed Guards and heading to the address Ash gave us, but..."

"Let me guess. There's a freezer place and drug dealers who supply Carfentanil just down the road."

"Yep."

"I'm with you. It's way too perfect. Our perps are long gone."

Annette cut in incredulously. *"Too perfect?* The right address and no murderers there to shoot us when we arrive seems like paradise to me! But of course there's no pleasing you two, is there?"

Craig conceded her point with a chuckle.

"OK, you're right on that bit, but as the object of your trip was to *catch* the bad guys, an empty nest isn't exactly what I wanted you to find. Except... Andy, they clearly set things up so we'd find their base which means there's something there that they want us to see. As soon as you have it locked down get a photographer to take shots of every inch of the place.

Forensics too, although I doubt they'll have been careless enough to leave any DNA. Send the images through to Ash ASAP."

Just as the call ended the Garda vehicle turned left into what they would later learn was an defunct Victorian Linen Mill estate complete with giant water wheel, but right now it looked exactly like the place where they'd done their advanced firearms training, full of dark corners and open doorways for snipers to lurk in and a high building with windows towering several storeys above them from which anyone who fancied could pick them off one by one.

"*Damn*. Look at the size of this place, Annette. It'll take us hours to find their setup."

He wasn't wrong, but if he was looking for sympathy the D.I. was fresh out, and, "Better start then, hadn't we" came back at him as she exited the car.

Still nominally in charge despite being on foreign soil Andy scrambled to catch her up, and with the Super heading up a third group they began the initial left, right and straight ahead strands of their search.

****

Dublin Airport.

It had gone exactly as they'd planned so far, but Irina was still uneasy thinking of her other half hundreds of miles away with Angelica, someone that she hadn't trusted since the day they'd first met.

Gretchen was having similar thoughts but with an added sense of pride that they'd accomplished all but the last leg of their mission, and the boys would soon see to that. There was wonderment too at how they'd actually managed it; fifteen months ago they'd been four complete strangers yet now she would love the others for the rest of her life. Especially Kurt, her miracle; who would ever have guessed that she would meet her future husband in such terrible times? The thought made her catch her breath as she recalled the things they'd left for the cops to find; people had fallen in love in circumstances *far* worse than theirs.

Suddenly she remembered her coffee going cold on the table in front of her and took a sip, glancing at her companion as she did. She liked Irina even though their relationship had been fractious at times recently; months cooped up in the squat hadn't always been good for the nerves.

But now she flashed her a smile of relief.

"The ship will have left by now."

The darker girl grinned and nodded, picturing the pride on Oskar's face when he opened the crates at the other end and the joy as he returned the contents to their rightful owners.

"Do you think the boys have reached the gallery yet, Rina?"

Irina glanced at her watch. Where others her age had dispensed with such things as anachronisms, preferring to use their phone's digital clock, her wristwatch was a reminder of a person long gone and she wore it with a bristling pride.

"Yep. Roman will have phoned Fervier and timed the setup to that. They should be at the gallery waiting for her in plenty of time."

Gretchen chewed her bottom lip nervously. "What about Angelica?"

A sceptical snort came back. "What about her?"

"I don't like her but she *did* help our mission, Rina, so I'm glad the boys agreed to give her a choice to stay behind or join."

The scepticism turned to hilarity.

"You believed that?"

Gretchen was confused. "Yes, of cour..." The darkening of her companion's face floored her. "You mean they're *not* going to give her the choice? *They're going to kill her anyway?*"

Irina's tone chilled. "Would that be such a bad thing? I mean, her family are just as bad as the others' so why should *she* live?"

"But we promised! We said as long as she helped us get her mother and the others-"

Tiring of teasing her soft-hearted friend Irina waved her down.

"Cool it, Gretch. They aren't *definitely* going to kill her, but Roman hasn't decided to bring her either. It depends how she behaves and if they get the mum."

"They'll free her though?"

All she got in reply was, "We'll see."

****

Craig's Office.

Craig was staring into space when he heard another phone ringing, but this time it was the one on his desk.

"Yes, Nicky."

She being the only person who should have been calling it.

"The Chief Constable wants to see you, sir, so I've booked you in tomorrow at nine if that's OK?"

"You say that like I had a choice in the matter. Any idea what it's about?"

Her silence said that he needed to come outside so he did, to be greeted by his PA glaring and pursing her lips.

"Well?"

"Well, what have you been up to? Donna was muttering something about a diplomatic incident!"

Donna Scott was the Chief Con's secretary and not usually given to hyperbole.

Craig frowned, puzzled. As light began to dawn he glanced around the squad-room, to see everyone looking up from their work.

"With any particular country?"

"Donna didn't say, but you've crossed some territorial line that's for sure."

"OK, no doubt I'll find out which one tomorrow. Don't expect me back for a while."

He turned to gaze at each of his team members in turn.

"OK, so the C.C. wants to see me, which is never good news. But this particular mess appears to be something to do with a diplomatic incident, so I need to know if any of you have been rattling cages. And before you answer, I'm *not* saying you were wrong for doing so, even if it *has* upset the brass."

As everyone tried to look innocent and then threw accusing glances at everyone else, Ryan remained as unfazed as an Easter Island statue.

Liam called it first.

"Ah, Ryan lad, it was yourself then, was it?" He stuck out his hand. "Put it there, mate, and congrats on pissing off the big boss. So, what did you do?"

Craig was waiting for the answer as well.

"Well, you remember that Rabbi Andy and I interviewed during the McClean case?"

He was referring to a case six months before where finding their killer's identity had required them to interview amongst other people a Rabbi and a priest.

Craig nodded. "Rabbi Moskos. Yes."

"Well, he was from Greece and it was invaded by the Nazis, so I thought he might have heard stuff about the war that wasn't common knowledge. He had, and one of the most interesting things was that there'd been groups in pretty much all the countries invaded *really* unhappy about the number of war criminals who were set free at the end."

Liam nodded firmly. "That's a fact. The big fish got caught at the Nuremberg and follow up trials but there were a *lot* of lower level scum who got off. It wasn't right."

Clearly a lot of people agreed. Hence the recent trials of ninety-year-old concentration camp guards.

Ryan nodded solemnly. "Rabbi Moskos quoted a shocking figure to me. Apparently of the almost eight hundred staff that operated Auschwitz only around fifteen per cent *ever* faced justice. The majority returned to their normal lives as if nothing had ever happened."

Like Horace Bolsover? But if Bolsover *hadn't* been a person of interest to the Allies then why had he bothered leaving Germany at all? Even if some of the loot they'd found in his shop had been stolen from prisoners at the camp the old man could have had it melted down just as easily there as here.

Craig grimaced at what it meant. Bolsover must have been an especially enthusiastic killer who the Allies *were* hunting for, and if anything he'd stolen from the war lay amongst the stash they'd found then the shopkeeper had kept them as trophies of his 'glorious' youth.

The thought made him shudder. He'd heard firsthand accounts of the war from his Italian grandmother, that was when she could even bring herself to speak of the heinous acts she'd witnessed the Nazis perform.

He refocused on his sergeant's report.

"The Rabbi said he'd heard from his parents that there were a lot of vigilante groups active back in the late forties and fifties. Some Christian, some Jewish, but many with no religious affiliation at all. Descendants of the various communities destroyed by the Nazis. After the war things were pretty chaotic in mainland Europe so they managed to cross borders undetected. They scoured the land for Nazis and collaborators, and rumour had it many were executed without trial and buried in forests."

Alice surprised him by not knowing what communities he was referring to.

"But I thought it was mainly Jewish people who suffered under the Nazis?"

The sergeant nodded. "The majority were, but the Nazis hated anyone who didn't fit their warped view of humanity. They targeted Jewish people, the Roma and Sinti, that's a form of Romany, and Slavic people – mainly Poles, Serbs, and later also Russians. Millions of Russians died in the war between fighting and the camps. Gay men were forced to work in the mines to supply the Reich with raw materials and then executed once they got worn out, or they were medically experimented on with hormones, anyone ill or disabled was killed, and then there were political dissidents of all religions plus anyone who protected *any* of the previous groups by hiding them from the Nazis. *They* were sent to the camps as well. That's if they weren't summarily shot in the stree-"

Craig's hand shot up to halt him. *"That's why!"*

Liam sat forward eagerly. "What?"

"That's why Sophie and Dylan were shot. The Gestapo and their local allies would walk up to people in the street and shoot them in the head-"

"And at massacres like Babi Yar at well."

"Yes. No trial and no reason except they belonged to one of the groups you've just listed." He tutted in disgust. "So if *all* of our victims' deaths are linked with their perceived crimes and not just Bolsover's, and if their methods of killing are relevant, then Sophie's and Dylan's relatives *must* have assisted in Nazi shootings."

Liam pulled a face. "That's pretty shitty symbolism all right, but I don't see how anything here constitutes the diplomatic incident the Chief Con's hauling you in about." He gestured to the sergeant. "I mean, all he did was talk to a Rabbi."

Craig smirked. "That's not *all* you did, is it, Ryan?"

The D.S. looked sheepish but before he could answer Ash jumped in.

"I cannot tell a lie. It was me who chopped down the cherry tree."

Liam rolled his eyes. "Oh aye, you *had* to be in this somewhere, didn't you."

Ignoring the analyst's generous confession Ryan re-entered the fray.

"I started it by asking the Rabbi if he remembered the names of any of the vigilante groups. He didn't but he put me in touch with a member of his synagogue who used to be a historian, and he contacted some people abroad. Not sure which countries."

Hence the diplomatic incident(s).

"The upshot was I got the names of four groups that were still known to be active until the early eighties."

"Jewish?"

Craig had visions of pissed off Mossad agents abseiling into his bedroom that night.

"Only two of them had any Jewish members at all and they were as part of a big mixed group. He said all the groups were mixed, with members from the backgrounds you mentioned as well as other people the Nazis enslaved. Czech, Hungarian, French, Dutch, Norwegian, you name it."

"And?"

"And all the known groups disbanded in the eighties, but I gave Ash their names anyway to do a bit of digging."

Liam snorted sceptically. "*Allegedly* disbanded you mean."

Craig turned back to his analyst. "And you found?"

"Not much yet." The computer expert winced apologetically. "But I *have* been rummaging around in a few databases that might be considered sensitive."

"Clearly they are since I'm being carpeted by the C.C."

Craig scribbled 'Vigilantes: past or present?' on the board.

The words made Ash smile. "You think one of the groups is having a revival, chief?"

Aidan rolled his eyes. "You make them sound like KISS."

Craig chuckled. He'd always liked that band.

"I think Liam was correct. *Allegedly* disbanded is about right. Does anyone *really* believe that all those group members just put down their weapons and said, 'Right, that's enough revenge now, lads, let's go home and get on with life'?" He shook his head. "Grief and vengeance aren't neat like that, so either some went underground immediately and continued killing, or they *did* retire but decided to start up again." He turned to his deputy. "It would make sense that's who's running this, given the maturity of our crimes."

"But even someone in their mid-teens at the end of the war would be ninety now!"

Aidan shrugged. "Does their age matter if they're just imparting advice to younger recruits and planning their strategies?"

Craig agreed a little with both of them. "I think it *would* have taken someone younger and fitter to have trained our killers up in the physical skills for the work, but there's nothing to say that one of the original groups isn't behind things. Perhaps the originals handed the group on to their kids, who'd be in their fifties or sixties now, and *they're* leading the training side."

He shook his head briskly to clear it. "OK, we could speculate about that all day, so let's just stick to the theory that *someone* has decided to recruit and train a new generation of assassins."

Aidan waxed philosophical. "We always say there's no statute of limitations on murder, so does an amnesty alter that?"

Liam was adamant that it shouldn't. "Just 'cos some wrinkly politicians announce a war's over doesn't make it over for everyone. You agree, boss, don't you?"

Craig did agree, but only partly. Who did have the right to say when the line was drawn in the sand? There was no statute of limitation on murder and the current trials of war criminals decades after their transgressions showed that feelings ran long and deep; he couldn't be sure that if one of his family had been butchered he wouldn't have joined one of those vigilante groups.

He pulled himself up short. It was peace time now and he was paid to uphold it. So even if he could empathise with the pain that might have driven their killers' acts, they were killers and he was a cop. There was a mechanism for punishing people like Horace Bolsover and assassination wasn't it.

"They're murderers, Liam, whether we understand their justification for killing or not. Whatever that actually turns out to be once Ash has uncovered it," the analyst smiled, knowing that he'd just been given the green light to keep rocking diplomatic boats, "is a matter for the courts. *Our* job is to find them and arrest them, so get back to whatever you were doing, please."

He signalled his deputy to accompany him into his office and updated him on Andy's earlier call.

"OK, now we're waiting for Arty do his thing, so..." the D.C.I. stared pointedly at the clock, which read six-thirty, "do we wait here or at home?"

Craig ignored the hint and gazed past him into space.

"The question is what will our killers do *next*? Have they already left the country and taken Angelica with them? Have they killed her and we'll find the body in a few days' time? Or have they still got loose ends to tie up, and if so how many have stayed behind to do that?"

"You're thinking Hortense?"

Craig focused on his pale face. "Yes. We need to find out where she is." He took out his mobile and dialled the number, only for the phone to ring twice and then be turned off.

"She switched off her mobile!"

"Maybe she wants some peace while she watches the appeal go out. It's on at seven."

"Maybe, but ask Ash to ping her phone anyway. I'm going to try the family homes at Lough Neagh and Malone."

"She went to Lough Neagh, boss."

"She might have changed her mind."

When both landlines dialled out it raised even more questions. Had Hortense Fervier pulled the plug out of the wall seeking peace as Liam had suggested, or had she gone out and if so to where and why? He had seen photos of the family's Lough Neagh mansion and it was enormous. They couldn't possibly have run the place without staff so why wasn't one of *them* picking up? Unless of course they all went home in the evenings instead of living in.

Craig's racing thoughts were stopped short by another possibility; that there might have been foul play at the house. Dialling a different number he connected with Lurgan Station and requested officers be sent there to check. That just left the Malone house and gallery to cover. If any of their killers had stayed behind their reason would be linked to the Ferviers.

Craig's next call was to Lisburn Road Station asking them to go to the house and gallery and check they were secure. The desk sergeant asked a reasonable question.

"Should we enter, sir?"

He did a swift calculation.

Hortense Fervier had recorded her appeal at two o'clock and said she was heading to Lough Neagh, but she *could* have changed her mind and gone straight home or to the gallery after the appeal instead. No-one would have questioned her appearance in either place so they would never have been informed.

If she'd gone to Lough Neagh she would have been there by three and even allowing for traffic if she'd turned around immediately she could have been back in Belfast by four. But... as the gallery was open until five their perps couldn't have entered it unnoticed before then, so that meant they'd either gone to her Malone house to lie in wait or used the ninety minutes *since* the gallery's closure to set up an ambush there. If they hadn't already got Hortense she was still vulnerable at either place.

Just as Craig reached the unhelpful conclusion his deputy re-entered.

"Hang on a moment, Sergeant." He covered the phone with his hand. "Anything on Fervier's mobile yet, Liam? We need to know where she is."

"Not yet. Should we phone the gallery?"

"No, it closed at five so she's unlikely to answer, as are our killers and I don't want to risk tipping them off. Chase Ash again."

As Liam went to do that his boss began drawing a possibility tree on his whiteboard. He'd completely forgotten there was someone hanging on the phone until Desk Sergeant Elsa Kavanagh did something she normally only did when she went to watch football; she put two fingers in her mouth and whistled as hard as she could.

The high pitched noise jolted Craig from his theorising, and after glancing around for a non-existent boiling kettle he realised what he'd done and snatched up the phone from the desk.

"Oh God, I'm sorry, Sergeant. I got distracted. You were asking if I wanted you to enter the house and shop."

The twenty-year veteran cop smirked. It was good to know that even bosses suffered brain blips now and then.

"Yes, sir. Do you?"

"Hang on just one more minute."

He brought the phone back to the board with him and followed through a strand of his earlier thoughts which took an even less helpful direction than before. If the killers *were* planning something more with the Ferviers it could happen at their Belfast home, the gallery *or* Lough Neagh.

At that moment Liam re-entered. "He says her phone's off now but her location five minutes ago was somewhere around Aghagallon. That's not far from the Lough. He'll keep trying to pin her down."

Craig smiled to himself. Hortense had been near her Lough Neagh home five minutes before, so even if she was on her way to Belfast now she wasn't anywhere close yet.

"Tell him not to bother, he's close enough. Call Lurgan Station back and see if they've reached the house yet, and if so if Hortense is still inside or anything's out of place."

As his deputy exited Craig spoke into the phone again.

"Sorry again to keep you, Sergeant. No, don't enter either location or park outside them; we just need drive pasts for now."

The last thing needed if their killers *were* inside was them spotting a cop car obviously standing guard.

"Just occasionally, to cast an eye out for anything suspicious, but *don't* make it obvious. If there's anyone inside the last thing we need is them being warned. Let me know if anything at all looks amiss."

"Yes, sir. I'll do that."

Just as she was about to sign off Craig added, "Spectacular whistling by the way."

He'd already returned to his whiteboard before Elsa Kavanagh hung up pink cheeked but Liam disturbed him again a moment later.

"The uniforms are at the Lough Neagh house. No signs of any disturbance but there's no-one home."

Damn. He'd been right. Hortense *had* been at Lough Neagh when he'd called her but now she'd left to go somewhere. The fact she'd turned off her phone implied something important was up, something in which she didn't want them involved.

He tutted in disgust.

"I think our perps got in touch and are using the chance of saving her daughter to lure her. *The* idiot. Why didn't she just tell us they'd made contact?" But they didn't have time for recriminations. "Right, we need to know how much time we have to play with. Tell Ash to do *anything* he has to, to track her phone."

Their resident hacker had tricks they couldn't and

probably didn't want to guess at, and fingers crossed he could employ one of those now.

When Craig was alone again he drew two dotted lines from 'Lough Neagh' to 'The Gallery' and 'Malone Home' and scribbled 'sixty mins' along each, fervently hoping that one of them *was* where Hortense Fervier was heading because if she'd been enticed to an unknown location there was no way they would reach her in time.

Summoning his last ounce of optimism he followed through his train of thought.

If their perps *were* waiting at one of the locations to kill Hortense then how did they intend to escape after the deed? They wouldn't want to travel any significant distance to get out of the country so they had to be leaving from somewhere very near Belfast. That meant flights out of either Belfast City or International airports and on balance it had to be the latter; the City flew mainly regional routes and travelling to *anywhere* in the UK could still see their murderers nicked just by him lifting the phone.

He was just about to leave his office in search of a map, when the door knocked and Ryan entered with one.

"Right. Good. Irish airports. Spread it out on the desk."

"Not just airports, chief. Ports too. And I've included anywhere that a private jet can leave from as well."

Craig pored over the paper for a moment, his eyes fixing first on Lough Neagh and then Galway before settling on Belfast. As he was thinking through the options Ryan gave his report.

"I've checked the manifests for cargo and a smallish boat left Dublin Port this afternoon carrying something you need to take a look at."

He passed Craig a page and watched as he scanned it and then jabbed at a line halfway down.

"This crate. It's big and heavy and it's the only piece on the manifest listed as fragile. Any more details?"

"I called the port authority and checked. It was marked 'Fragile. This way up only' and the instruction was to place it at the front of the hold." He smirked. "The perps obviously don't want their harpsichord cracked."

It earned him a nod and a sighed, "What name was it booked in?"

"You won't believe it."

"Try me."

"The buggers only paid the bill in the name of R Hess."

Rudolf Hess was Hitler's notorious deputy, one of the few Nazis actually tried and convicted after the Nuremberg trials.

"They have a sense of irony anyway. What's the boat's destination?"

"Stornoway in the Hebrides apparently."

Craig frowned. "The Hebrides are part of the UK so what's the point of sending the stolen goods there to be seized?"

"I was going to request the Scottish police do just that, chief."

"If it ever gets there, which I doubt. Did anyone travel with it?"

The D.S. shook his head.

"Nope. There are flights to Stornoway but as you said they'd still be in the UK."

Craig shook his head. "They weren't travelling with the valuables. Someone's already been arranged to collect those at the other end, but I very much doubt it will be in the Hebrides. Don't waste your time trying to guess where our killers have gone or who they are at the moment, Ryan. That boat could divert anywhere, and we don't even have certainty on our killers' numbers and genders to check flight manifests."

He handed back the page and stared at the map again for a moment, pressing his finger hard on Belfast.

"If any of them *are* still here they'll be leaving soon and probably through the International." He peered more closely at the area. "What does that symbol mean?"

"It marks a private airfield near Aldergrove. It's owned by some horse racing millionaire. "

Aldergrove is a townland in County Antrim, and Aldergrove Airport was the old name for Belfast International.

"I need to know what planes are due to leave there. Get hold of their flight plans too."

The D.S. pulled a face. "That'll be tricky, chief. Private fields are jealous of their privacy and we won't have jurisdiction for anything without a warrant."

"Get one then and ask Mary to dig on their flight manifests while you're out. I want to know if *anyone* has a jet ready to leave within the next twenty-four hours and who or what it's carrying."

It was a good move, but not quite enough to compensate for the bad one that Elsa Kavanagh was about to make. Or perhaps it was *his* fault, for always assuming other people thought like him.

****

Galway. 6.50 p.m.

It had taken almost an hour of reconnoitring and scoping the layout of the mill and its outbuildings from what he deemed a safe distance before the stubborn Garda Leader was prepared to risk his men making an entry, with Andy growing so impatient that by the time the go signal finally came he was practically chewing his tongue. Sod the fact that *he* was in charge of the detective side of the operation, he was on the Kerry man's turf, and *he'd* said, in no uncertain terms, that if Andy wanted the Garda assault team to storm the place with him then, "He. Just. Feckin'. Well. Had. To. Wait."

The Belfast D.C.I. *had* considered just strolling up to the mill's front door and knocking it, hoping that their killers were either long gone or inordinately polite and would invite them in for tea, but Annette had put paid to that idea, threatening to call Craig if he set one foot past the invisible boundary erected by the Kerry Kommando. So all they could do was wait, and wait, and wait.

By the time the, "We're on" call finally came Andy was all foam and frustration and stomped angrily ahead of the others to launch a kick at the street level door. Annette would have laughed at his snit had she not been gripping her Glock like a vice and scanning every corner waiting for a killer to leap out.

When they reached the building's top floor without hearing a single sound not generated by a booted Guard it became obvious the place was deserted. Which didn't mean that it had been a wasted trip; what Andy found on the mill's open-plan top storey could have filled a book.

The immense space, with its whitewashed stone walls and worn oak floorboards, resembled a Manhattan loft apartment minus the designer fittings. At one end sat a pair of large, worn sofas and a table, television, kettle and microwave that would keep forensics busy for days; while piled in the far corner were several sleeping bags, doubtless full of hairs, cells and fluids that, gather them as they might, would mean bugger all without perps to compare against.

But the really interesting stuff was at the other end of the space completely; four large cork display boards, three of them dedicated by their headers to a victim in their murder case and covered in photographs, papers and maps. The fourth was a different kettle of fish; completely covered with paragraphs of dense writing, each in a different tongue.

As Andy's degree had included French and Greek Annette looked to him for enlightenment.

"Can you understand any of those languages?"

The D.C.I. squinted at the writing, then stood back and looked again from a distance as if his ignorance might have something to do with focal length. Finally he shook his head.

"Not a single one. Some are European but not the languages I speak, and I can tell from the alphabet that the top one is Cyrillic. I think *that* one," he pointed to the paragraph in the middle, "could be an African language of some sort, but don't hold me to that."

Annette pulled out her phone and photographed the board methodically from top to bottom.

"I'll send them to forensics and Ash to make sense of."

That done, the detectives turned their attention to the first three boards, which were written in English, first scanning them and then stopping to read their detail, and the more they read the more they both wanted to throw up. Yes, Sophie and Dylan had been innocent, but their genetic lines had been a chronicle of the bad, the worse and the unspeakably evil.

Not only had both their young victims' great grandparents *and* grandparents been involved in acts of betrayal and slaughter in World War Two, but *their* children, Sophie's and Dylan's parents, had continued to profit from those actions, building fortunes without any thought of making restitution for what their forebears had done, and even worse, deliberately perpetuating bigotry and racism by amongst other things contributing to banned far right groups even now.

In Sophie's case her great grandfather Azuolas and grandfather Jokubas on her father's side had been members of a Lithuania auxiliary unit that in nineteen-thirty-nine had enthusiastically helped the Nazis expel eight thousand Jews from their homes in Memel, now Klaipėda in Lithuania, where the Adomaitis family still lived. Then in forty-one they'd assisted German killing squads in shooting eight hundred Jews and the one hundred locals who had tried to save them at Gargždai during what became known as the Garsden Massacre.

Dylan Pedersen-Storey's great grandmother Bodil had informed on Norwegian resistance fighters involved in sabotaging the Nazis' production of heavy water at Telemark in Norway, resulting in several people being shot. Her daughter Liv had been raised in her ideology and held membership of a far right group even now.

All of the collaborators had been rewarded for their actions by the Nazis with position, homes and wealth stolen from the dead, and after the war had used their corrupt fortunes to create luxurious lifestyles without a single backward glance.

Many of their possessions were hidden in vaults and private collections, but their profits had increased from generation to generation and now the newest generation had paid the price.

Annette finally found her voice, a very quiet one. "Sophie and Dylan had done nothing wrong except be born into those families."

"Just like their victims had done nothing wrong but be born Jewish, Romany, Polish..." Andy pointed to a line at the bottom of each board: 'We waited and hoped for them to show remorse but none came.'

"There's your answer, Annette. After so many generations someone obviously reckoned the families would *never* apologise for their relatives' actions or voluntarily make restitution, so they took what they believed was owed. Their valuables and lives."

"And because Sophie and Dylan were only children the corrupt family lines end."

Andy nodded and turned to the board dedicated to Horace Bolsover. "Now, *he's* a different story."

That was clear. Horace Bolsover, aka Heinrich Mueller, had been exactly as Craig had texted them. An SS officer at Auschwitz involved in slave labour provision for IG Farben and the selection of prisoners for the gas chambers, administering the Zyklon B himself at times. Their dead shopkeeper had been a genocidal maniac.

They read on slowly, Annette's eyes sliding sideways at times to check her teammate's reaction. Andy was reading about someone who had murdered countless people of his faith with impunity and if it had been her in the same position she would be crying, as well as cheering that Bolsover was dead. But what she saw on the D.C.I.'s face was a shocked grief so profound that it was palpable several feet away.

She wanted to put an arm around his shoulders in comfort, and after a minute of dithering about personal space and over familiarity and rationalising why she *shouldn't* do that to a grown man and a senior officer that was exactly what she did. Andy didn't detach himself politely or move away but simply closed his eyes tight for a moment, then he re-opened them, Annette dropped her arm and they continued reading side by side.

Eventually their silence was broken by a yell from the other end of the floor.

"THE CHIEF SAYS DEE YE WANT YUR FORENSIC LADS AR OURS?"

The young Guard's Dublin accent was so strong it made Andy chuckle.

"It had better be ours, I think, but I'll ring our boss to check."

He caught Craig still thinking about the airport map, and after ten minutes detailing what they'd found at the mill they agreed that Des should send a team. Craig was just about to end the call when he decided to ask the question he'd wanted but hesitated to ask when he'd heard the D.C.I.'s voice, inhibited by the same foolish constraints as his D.I.

"How are you, Andy?"

They both knew he wasn't inquiring about the D.C.I.'s day-to-day health.

"I'd braced myself for it, chief, but it's still grim." He brightened up. "Still, no better person to have with me than Annette."

"You're right there."

Craig would love to have taken the credit for anticipating the D.C.I.'s need for support and sending the ex-nurse with him for that reason, but he couldn't; it had simply been the way the staffing chips had fallen that day.

"OK, do your stuff while you're waiting for forensics and then leave them to it. But take plenty of images to send back. I want to read what's on those boards ASAP. Especially if you find anything about the Ferviers. And don't forget to thank the Guards for me. Tell Chief Donovan I'll be writing to his boss with fulsome praise."

He made a note to do it before he forgot and then returned to the ruminations that kept getting interrupted just in time for them to get interrupted again. This time by Nicky entering with a takeaway that she'd had the sense to order for everyone, something that had never even occurred to him.

It was a good job someone on his team had people skills.

****

The Fervier Art Gallery. 7.20 p.m.

One of the main risks of delegating is that the delegates sometimes, as we say in Ireland, lose the run of themselves. For everyone else in the world that translates as them getting *rather* carried away.

And perhaps because it was quiet at the station that evening, either the thrill of possibly nailing a criminal, which let's face it isn't an everyday occurrence on Belfast's leafy Lisburn and Malone Roads, or a desire to impress the big boss and see her name writ large in notes that might just, if she was *very* lucky, make their way to the Chief Constable's desk, the enthusiastic Sergeant Elsa Kavanagh proved to be one of those carried away people that day.

The upshot was that Craig's instruction to "do the occasional drive past" of the Fervier Gallery, a constable having been dispatched to observe the home, was expanded to her traversing the Lisburn Road so frequently in her police Skoda that several late opening shopkeepers paused what they were doing to speculate to their customers that, "Something must be up! The cops are fair wearing a hole in the road."

Unfortunately the vendors weren't the only people in the area with eyes, and Kurt Nilsen's, locked as they were on to the road's CCTV feeds via his laptop inside the gallery apartment, had grown ever wider with each pass of Kavanagh's liveried car. After three trips he was no longer persuaded by the casually averted eyes of the uniformed officer inside and beckoned Roman to one side to talk.

"They know we're here."

The leader's lips tightened in a clear 'shut up' signal and he turned to their uneasy companion.

"Make some coffee will you, Angelica? The stuff's in that plastic bag I left in the kitchen."

As the girl moved reluctantly towards the small room, knowing they were going to discuss her, a million thoughts flashed through her mind just as they had been doing all day. She settled as she always did on the only important one in her opinion; how could she save her skin?

She was in danger from two killers but knew the law wouldn't view her as a victim because she'd been an accessory in their crimes, driven just like them by revenge. *Her* revenge was against a mother who'd controlled her all her life and showed no signs of ever relaxing that grip, not like theirs against the descendants of murderers from decades before. Did that make her worse or better than them? After all, *she* was fighting for freedom just as their ancestors had, so didn't she deserve *some* allowance to be made for that?

Such was the depth of her selfishness that the difference between a struggle for survival and being forced to attend a debutantes' ball bypassed her completely, but self was all Angelica was thinking about right now. OK, so she did feel a *little* bad about luring her mother to her death but not as much as if it had been her own, and by the way Roman had just excluded her she was starting to believe it soon could.

She glanced around the small kitchen, searching for windows she knew weren't there and knives that were never kept in the drawers while trying to eavesdrop on the men's discussion, and in parallel frantically outlined the loft's floor plan in her mind. The studio room had the only exit and two fit young men stood between her and it, so without a substantial weapon she didn't have a hope in hell of escape.

If Angelica had been able to hear the words being exchanged in the other room perhaps they would have calmed her, or perhaps not. As the young men watched the CCTV for another minute and saw Elsa Kavanagh whiz past again they exchanged a nod.

"They don't *know* we're here but they think we might be."

"And they're looking for Hortense."

Roman locked his hands behind his neck and considered for a moment, glancing periodically towards the kitchen as he did.

"We can't stay here any longer. We'll have to forget the mother."

He was answered by a reluctant, "Okay..." and Kurt's

thumb jerking towards the kitchen. The subtext was, "What do we do with her?"

The response came typed up on Roman's smart-phone and after a brief pause they agreed with a smile and turned towards the kitchen, only to see Angelica standing in its doorway with a steaming kettle gripped in her hand.

The standoff lasted for less than a second. As she made to throw the burning liquid at them and run past to the exit Kurt body swerved and hooked a long leg around her shins knocking her to the floor, while his ally barely jumped out of the way before the water showered the floorboards where he'd been.

Grasping her wrists in one hand Roman hauled the girl to her feet and pushed her against the wall in disgust.

"What the fuck was that for?"

"You're going to kill me, I know it! I heard you talking!"

The group leader sighed heavily, shaking his head at his partner above her head.

"We can't take her with us now. She's nuts."

"You were taking me with you?"

Kurt shrugged. "It was either that or leave you here to carry the can, and we thought since you'd helped us that wouldn't be fair-"

Roman interjected. "But now we will."

Angelica was still on her imagined death. "You were *never* going to kill me?"

Kurt rolled his eyes. "We can if you like. Maybe you'd prefer that to life in jail?"

She wasn't sure whether the Norwegian was serious or not.

"NO! Don't kill me! Take me with you, *pleeease*. I was just scared that you were going to kill me. That's why I tried to run."

Roman met his friend's eyes and read the firm 'no' in them.

"Sorry, no can do now. How could we trust you after you tried to give us first degree burns?"

Angelica spat out her reply. "If you leave me behind I'll tell them everything about you! I know your names, ages. I can describe you. *Everything!*"

To her dismay it brought nothing but smiles.

"You *really* think we told you our real names, or even nationalities? *You?* A stranger? You know nothing about us except our faces, Ange, and as soon as we leave the country we'll disguise ourselves and go underground."

He signalled towards his rucksack. "Throw me the duct tape."

As he set to work tying her up his colleague withdrew a page of writing from his pocket and waved it in Angelica's face.

"*We'll* be somewhere no-one can ever get at us, Angelica, whereas you'll be here when the cops arrive, with *this* detailed outline of your crimes."

Roman chuckled. "When did you write that?"

"Last night."

"You *thought* she'd betray us?"

"Fifty-fifty, but be prepared is my motto. This tells the cops everything, Ange, from when we first hooked up with you to how you agreed to target Sophie and Dylan for us, and then came here today planning to help us kill your mum. She'll disinherit you after she reads this. Never mind, you can always go on social security when you get out of jail." He gestured at her bindings. "Secure?"

Roman smiled at his work. Bind the ankles, the wrists and then secure them both tightly to a fixed point, in this case a radiator. Oskar had taught them well.

He ripped off another strip of tape and was just about to place it over their ex-ally's mouth when she issued a last plea for mercy.

"Please don't leave that page, Kurt." She smiled up flirtatiously at him, knowing that had Gretchen not been around he'd found her attractive enough that he might have given their relationship a go. "If you don't leave it the police might believe I was just a victim, but that information could ruin my life. Please don't. *Please.*"

The men exchanged a lengthy look and she read a glimmer of doubt in their eyes. Finally Roman the more generous of the pair spoke again.

"Let's give her a fighting chance, Kurt. Fold it up and put it in her jeans pocket, then if she can manage to destroy it before the cops get to it fair enough."

Grudgingly his companion agreed, secretly hoping that Angelica would try to eat the paper and choke on it. He folded the page in four and slipped it into her front pocket, leaving a small corner visible as a tease.

Roman sprang to his feet. "OK, check the CCTV and see

how long the cops are leaving between passes."

Two more trips by Elsa Kavanagh put the answer at three minutes and their decision to leave immediately after the next one was made. As the team leader slipped on the duct tape gag his deputy gathered everything, and a second after the Skoda passed again they slipped down the stairs, through the gallery's rear exit and disappeared into the maze of unsurveilled back streets behind the Lisburn Road.

****

It's a funny thing about small cities like Belfast. During the day the traffic is hell because the original town planners packed the streets tightly to take advantage of the city's compactness and make it walkable, but after the Armageddon of the four to seven p.m. rush hours they miraculously empty as everyone but the young indulges in the small town traditions of sitting at home and watching the box. Said young are out pubbing and clubbing in search of mayhem and mates, but as that mostly happens around the universities even *they* tend to walk.

The upshot is that the roads are almost eerily clear and even an airfield twenty miles outside the city can be reached in under thirty minutes by car. Sadly, getting a search warrant signed by a judge in that same short period only *ever* happens on TV.

Nonetheless Craig had made a decision and it was comprised of three parts. Part one: if Hortense Fervier *was* on her way to the art gallery then she couldn't possibly have reached it yet, so they were going to intercept her before she came to any harm. To that end he'd sent Aidan and Armed Response to breach the premises. As the D.C.I. had long legs that leant themselves well to kicking down doors it was one of his favourite pastimes, and one that he didn't get to do half enough of in his opinion, so he'd greeted Craig's order with glee.

Part two had been telling Elsa Kavanagh to knock at the Malone house, something she'd duly done and informed him that Hortense's husband had answered and happily shown her around.

Part three of Craig's plan involved Liam and himself and had become more important when their perps weren't found at either the gallery or house. Research had revealed two

Cessna Jets were scheduled to fly out of the Aldergrove airfield in the coming twelve hours, but with no names, destinations or exact flight times yet filed, the only hope of preventing their killers fleeing was to ready themselves to react quickly to the warrant by driving out there to wait.

Just as Liam pulled up beside the airfield's wire perimeter fence Craig's mobile rang. He passed it to his deputy to answer and focussed his binoculars on the field's small departure building, scouring the area around it for anything that looked amiss but seeing only two small jets parked a runway apart and two men in pilots' uniforms conferring, one of whom was scribbling on a clipboard in his hand.

"Who is it, Liam?"

"Hughesy. They're inside the gallery but there's no-one."

"Tell them to try the flat upstairs."

Liam listened as heavy boots thundered up the narrow stairs and they kicked their way into the hidden space shouting, "Armed police! Stay where you are."

There was a series of shouts and a minute of mumbling before Aidan came back on the line.

"We've found the Swann girl. She's been tied up but she's alive."

"The girl's alive, boss."

He swopped the call to speaker so Craig could hear the rest.

"The Swann girl's saying she was kidnapped and held by four people, Guv. Two of them left her here a while ago; she's not sure how long. They were definitely skipping the country but -"

Craig cut across him. "How?"

"No idea. She said the other two left four or five hours ago. By boat she thinks, or maybe plane as well. From down south somewhere."

"*Damn.* That means the others might head south as well. Can she describe any of them, Aidan?"

"They taped her mouth so she's pretty groggy. The medics are giving her oxygen."

"Keep at her once they're done and call us back. And keep an eye out for Hortense Fervier. She could still turn up there."

He cut the call and returned to his scan of the airfield.

"Where's Ryan with that bloody warrant, Liam?"

The D.C.I. pulled out his own phone commenting as he waited for it to be answered, "It's good they found the girl alive, boss."

The words pulled Craig up short; he'd got so tied up in the hunt for their victims' murderers that he hadn't taken time to celebrate that they hadn't had a fourth death.

"Yes, sorry, you're right of course. At least the Ferviers won't be mourning anyone tonight." His voice hardened. "But after Ryan answers call Aidan back and tell him I don't want the girl released. I'm not convinced she didn't play some part in this thing so we need to interview her."

As he spoke he watched the two pilots clamber into the small jet nearest the building and begin running through what had to be their pre-flight checks. As they were doing so another three people in uniform marched out of the building and turned left towards the second jet.

"Damn! Both jets are about to take off by the looks of it. We have to stop them."

"Ryan's just said there's only one judge at the courts and he's busy signing something else."

Craig barely heard the words.

"Now an older man's walking out to the second jet. Obviously a passenger."

Suddenly he threw the binoculars on the dashboard and motioned his deputy to switch seats.

"What're you doing?"

"Warrant or no warrant, those bloody planes aren't taking off!"

Liam gawped as his Ford's engine was suddenly gunned and they began hurtling down the road.

"You're mad, boss! If you block them without a warrant you'll find yourself back pounding the streets!"

"I can't just sit here and do nothing! Unless I'm completely wrong, one of those planes is carrying our killers. Keep the line open to Ryan and shout the second that warrant's been signed."

As they accelerated along the perimeter fence towards the field's entrance Liam frantically fastened his seatbelt. It didn't stop him being thrown hard against the door as Craig swerved right towards the field's entrance, completely ignoring the guard in the booth who'd been reading with his feet propped against its window and tried to leap up so quickly to stop them that his face collided with the glass.

Thankfully the entrance barrier was up, although Craig would have ploughed through it anyway as he skidded on to the airfield and took at guess at which plane was more likely to play host to their perps. The one without the elderly passenger seemed like their best bet.

As Liam held his phone in one hand and gripped the dashboard with his other he watched the speedometer hit one hundred as Craig belted after the two pilot jet that had begun taxi-ing away.

Kurt Nilsen watched the granite grey Ford approach on the jet's left hand side and gave a running commentary to his co-pilot.

"He's doing the ton, Roman. Definitely Craig. I recognise him from our photos." He laughed gleefully. "We obviously chose the right man."

The team leader acknowledged the words with a nod, his black eyes fixed firmly ahead. As he accelerated so did Craig, but the detectives had the disadvantage that their top speed was a damn sight lower than a plane's.

Liam lifted the phone to his ear again and after a few seconds he gave a whoop. "It's signed!"

"Too bloody late! We're losing them. Can't this heap of yours go higher than one-ten?"

The D.C.I. ignored the insult and grunted, "Yes," adding unnecessarily, "but the bloody thing can't fly." As Craig accelerated to one-fifteen he post-scripted, "Do you want me to shoot at them? I could hang out the window and get the pilot if you pull up close."

Craig was indignant, in large part because *he* wanted to be the one shooting at the men, although that wasn't what he said.

"We can't go shooting people just on a search warrant! We haven't even ID-ed them as our perps!"

"Then kiss bye-bye, boss, because they're about to go wheels up."

The words galvanised Craig and he swerved hard right aiming for the small jet's wheels but missing them as just at that moment they were retracted into its hull, the plane's velocity out-stripped theirs and gaining several car lengths ahead of them within seconds Roman Bianchi eased its nose into the air. Tempted to give Craig a thumbs-up the group leader let his companion do it instead and contented himself with tipping the aircraft's wings as they disappeared into the sky.

Two very pissed-off detectives followed the jet's vapour trail into the distance and then Craig pulled the car to a juddering halt that Liam just *knew* hadn't done his brakes any good.

"Bugger that, Liam! If we'd just got the warrant ten minutes earlier... that pair were part of the gang for sure." After a moment's inventive swearing he restarted the engine and turned back towards the departure building. "We need to find out where they're heading."

"What's the point, boss? I mean, I've no doubt they lodged flight plans to somewhere just for appearances, but there's nothing to stop them changing direction mid-air. They're hardly likely to stick to aviation rules when they've already broken bigger ones than that."

Craig couldn't argue with his logic, but it left them with three deaths and no killers to prosecute. When they reached the building he went through the motions of checking the fleeing jet's flight plan, which said, more irony by their killers no doubt, that it was heading to Berlin, but his thoughts had already moved on to Angelica Swann and exactly why their killers had let her live.

"Right, you're driving again."

Liam didn't bother pointing out it was *his* car.

"Where to?"

"The gallery. I need to make some calls on the way."

The first was to Aidan, who confirmed that the Swann girl was on her way to St Mary's Hospital for a check-up, under guard. Craig's next call was to his analyst who confirmed that he'd just tracked Hortense Fervier to the outskirts of Belfast and by the look of it she was on her way to the Lisburn Road.

"You switched her phone on remotely?"

"Yep."

"OK, call her on someone's mobile. She won't answer an unknown number because she'll think it's us. Tell her Angelica's safe and just being checked over at St Mary's. She's in the care of D.C.I. Hughes."

Ten minutes later Liam, being skilled at spotting new orders even when not phrased as such, pulled off the motorway towards the hospital where they linked up with Aidan in the ED.

Craig's phone rang again just as they were entering so he stepped back out to take the call.

"Craig."

"It's Ash again, chief. I thought you'd like to know something. Andy sent the images through, and boy do they tell some story. You're part of it."

The detective's eyebrows shot up. "Me? Explain."

"Well, Andy was right that the stuff on three of the boards was mainly about our victims or their families, but there was stuff on the back of them too that he initially missed. One was covered with information on Hortense Fervier's family, mainly Uncle Hubert but not exclusively. It seems collaboration was rife amongst the French branch of the Fervier clan during the war, but I'll tell you about that later. The best stuff was about *your* family."

Craig froze, his grip on the phone tightening so much he thought his fingers might snap and cold sweat suddenly flooding down his back.

Had his Italian ancestors assisted the Nazis? No, he couldn't believe it. But then perhaps that was just vanity, perhaps they'd all been bastards a few generations back and he'd just never been told? His mum's family had been artists and musicians for generations, so what had happened? Had one of them joined Mussolini's private orchestra? And his dad's family were all from Belfast, so what if it was them? He knew some of them had been in the British Army during the war, so what if they'd swopped sides and committed atrocities?

As Craig's thoughts spiralled into nonsense his oblivious analyst kept on talking and finally a few of his words began to seep through. 'Castle' and 'hid' were the first ones the detective really heard.

"*What?* Sorry, I completely missed that, Ash. Say it again."

"I was saying it seems like Liam was nearly right with his Baron jokes. From the seventeenth to the early twentieth century there *was* aristocracy in your mum's family, but your great great grandmother was the only living member left by the time the war broke out. She must have been quite something because although a lot of the wealthy sided with Mussolini and backed Hitler she refused."

Craig's sigh was so loud it made the analyst laugh.

"God, *you* thought I was about to say you were Hitler's love child or something, didn't you?"

"I'm not *that* bloody old!"

"Sorry, your mum then."

The detective didn't bother correcting the timeline, agreeing with the general gist.

"I have to admit you did have me worried for a moment. So what did my great great granny do then? I'm presuming she got in trouble for going against Mussolini."

"She did, but it didn't stop her hiding half the people from three nearby villages. She was a Countess in Fiumicino on the coast and had money, so she concealed them in the cellars of her castle for the duration of the war. Jews, homosexuals and most of a nearby Romany camp."

Craig felt a flush of pride at her heroics that he had no earthly right to, just like the shame that he'd felt a moment before. But facts and logic had nothing to do with emotion, and it made him wonder how Sophie, Dylan and even Angelica had felt when they'd learned about their antecedents' pursuits.

The analyst hadn't finished.

"She was some girl your great granny. You should read this stuff. Anyway, that's not all there is about you. They had newspaper clippings about your successful cases since way back plastered on the back of another board. They knew exactly who you were *and* that you would probably end up with this case."

Craig was stunned. Was that why they'd got the thumbs-up from the plane? Had the killers *wanted* to be investigated by his squad? And by him especially because of his ancestry, hoping he would be sympathetic to their cause? Or because they'd thought the squad would manage to solve the case and expose *why* they'd done what they done?

Those questions would have to wait because he needed to interview Angelica Swann, but Craig's mind was still churning as he entered the steel and vinyl ED, its design so modern that it always reminded him of the set of a sci-fi movie. He preferred the old-fashioned, homelier casualty unit of his childhood. The one his parents had been obliged to bring him and Lucia to every other week courtesy of his tendency to jump off higher and higher platforms on to concrete and his sister's to put every object she encountered into her mouth. Such was the current erratic nature of the policeman's thoughts that he suddenly wondered whether Luca might inherit one of those tendencies, that's if there wasn't something even more bizarre lurking on Katy's side.

His deputy's brisk thump to his arm made Craig focus and he followed Liam's gaze to where a flapping Hortense Fervier was fussing over her bedraggled looking daughter while a doctor who looked even younger than Angelica attempted to insert an IV into her arm.

As his deputy moved to advance towards them Craig shot out an arm to hold him back, motioning him to observe the family interaction from a distance while he retreated a few steps to read a text that had just arrived. It was a cryptic follow-up from his analyst, 'There was a fourth board too. But that can wait.'

After a minute of watching the family reunion, Liam joined his boss in an empty cubicle and murmured in as quiet a tone as he possessed.

"Boyso but that wee girl hates her mammy! I thought her mate Gill was exaggerating, but she wasn't."

"I agree, although Hortense obviously can't see it. The question is does Angelica hate her enough to have set her up?"

"You think that's why she was at the gallery?"

Craig gave an equivocal shrug. "I think we need to find out what was said to entice the mother back from Lough Neagh and who said it."

"Yeh, but even if it *was* the girl those pilots could have forced her to."

"Mmmm... How much duress would it take for *you* to entice someone you loved to their death?"

"Well, I wouldn't. But I'm not a kid."

"Even so. I'm willing to bet you wouldn't have done it even back then. The problem is how do we *prove* Angelica colluded to make that happen?"

He rubbed his chin hard, thinking about their killers' obvious desire for him to take the case. It was clear they hadn't wanted to take Angelica with them, and equally clear that they'd wanted to leave her alive or she wouldn't have been. But alive for what reason? To tell their story? Unlikely; the boards in Galway had already done that. Because the girl had pleaded to stay because she loved her mother? The disdainful interaction they'd just witnessed nixed that. Angelica's love for her father then? But if so, why would she have got involved with murderers in the first place *knowing* it would have distressed him? Unless their killers *had* abducted her after all and it was only after that she'd joined their cause?

Knowing that he was thinking himself into a hole again Craig shook his head hard to clear it and noticed his deputy was staring at him amused.

"What's so funny?"

"You. You've just run through a load of scenarios, haven't you? And without a single shred of proof to say which might be right."

Craig shrugged. "What do *you* suggest we use to narrow them then?"

Liam leaned against the cubicle wall and folded his arms. "OK, they left the girl here for one of three reasons. One, to tell their tale, two, out of the goodness of their hearts, or three, so she could carry the can."

"One doesn't work because the stuff Andy found in Galway already tells us why they did what they did."

"Does it indeed? I'll need to look at that. OK, number two then, the goodness of their hearts... aye well, pigs might fly. We're hardly dealing with big softies when they bumped off two other kids. No, my money's on number three. Angelica was up to her eyes in everything and they want her to do time. They killed the other kids painlessly because they didn't want them to suffer, but it obviously tickles them to think of our Angelica in the nick." He whistled quietly. "She must've fairly pissed them off."

Craig couldn't fault the analysis so he followed it through. "OK, so let's just say they *did* leave her here to carry the can. We can *speculate* that she voluntarily enticed Dylan and Sophie and maybe even her mum to their deaths, but without evidence that she wasn't being coerced how can we ever prove it for sure? She's hardly going to confess, is she?"

The D.C.I. propelled himself off the wall and was just about to hit his boss' arm again when Craig swerved out of the way.

"Will you *stop* thumping me to make a point!"

"Ach, stop whinging. It's what men do in Crossgar. Anyway, I was going to punch you to *underline* something this time, but you've ruined the effect so I'll just have to say it instead. The way we'll *know* if she took part in the killings voluntarily is because our killers will have left something behind to prove it."

Craig's eyes widened. "That's brilliant!"

The D.C.I. flushed. "Yes, well, I am you know."

But his boss was about to damn the praise.

"Except that if it's not at the gallery then they must have left it on her, but she's not under arrest and we can't insist on searching her on a hunch. That's if she hasn't already got rid of whatever it was."

He was right; the detailed note Kurt had put in Angelica's pocket was long gone. As soon as her constraints had been removed at the flat she'd insisted on going to the bathroom, and the page had been torn into a dozen pieces and flushed down the loo.

But Liam's "Tsk, tsk" told Craig that all was not lost.

"All right, spit it out."

"Well, if *I* were our killers I'd have a backup plan."

"*That* assumes they'd decided they weren't taking Angelica with them long before they arrived at the gallery."

"You think they hadn't?"

"I'm not as sure of it as you. If Hortense had reached the flat and Angelica had been willing to kill her then they *might* have trusted her enough to take her along. But they left before Hortense arrived so our killers had to make a choice. Give Angelica a choice of leaving with them, kill her and leave her body there, or settle for discrediting the Ferviers by exposing their ill-gotten gains and leave something incriminating on Angelica that would put her in jail for a long time."

He sighed heavily. They were in a maze and the prizes at its centre had just skipped the country. Interpol and the in-country agencies would continue the search based on information they would provide of course, but all *they* had was a teenage girl whose involvement in the murders they couldn't prove.

Craig made a decision.

"OK. Once the Docs sign Angelica off tell the mother we need them at High Street to get their statements on paper while everything's still fresh, Liam. Just straight retellings of their versions to help us catch our killers and kidnappers, you know what to say. I'll brief Aidan on what we're thinking and to use kid gloves. Mary can interview the girl; they're around the same age and the mother's likely to accept her better. Ryan can take the mother with Aidan moving between the two rooms. Meanwhile, we'll head back to the gallery to see what we can find."

An hour later they were standing in the gallery flat staring at its toilet, or to be more precise at a piece of white paper on the floor beside it that the CSIs had tagged with the number twenty-one.

"It looks like printer paper but there's writing on it. Liam, see if anyone out there has a magnifying glass and a pair of tweezers, please."

A moment later both men were staring at the fragment while Craig held it up to the light.

"b.e.f.r. All lower case."

"Blue ink. Although that probably doesn't matter."

"I wouldn't dismiss anything yet."

Liam squinted at the fragment.

"It makes no sense, boss."

"Not on its own, I agree. OK, let's look at it logically. The b is lower case so it's obviously come from the middle of a sentence."

"Or the middle of a word?"

"No, the whole word would be on that line then. It's rare to split a word between lines."

befr, befr, befr....

Craig ran through possible words that the letters could be linked to and found there were remarkably few. In fact the only common one that he could think of was befriend, but he wasn't going to trust his internal dictionary.

"Liam, take a shot of it and send it to Ash. Ask him to generate all the words in the English language that start with befr. I'm off to get an evidence bag and then we're taking it to Des."

"At home?"

"What?"

"It's nearly nine o'clock!" The D.C.I. sighed meaningfully. "Normal people are home eating or watching the box."

Craig ignored the pathos in his voice.

"Well, Des will just have to stop eating!"

He disappeared into the studio room and returned with an evidence bag and a correction.

"Apparently Grace is on call and she's at the lab. What did Ash say about befr?"

"Nothing yet, he hasn't come back to me."

"OK, let's go. Give me your keys and I'll drive."

Liam shook his head emphatically. "Oh no, not this time. *You* won't stop for fish and chips on the way."

Twenty minutes later the newly-fed detectives were at the

labs and Grace was staring down a microscope at their fragment humming to herself.

"Nice tune. What is it?"

"Night and Day. Cole Porter. I'm singing it at The James on Friday night."

Grace had a beautiful alto voice that she normally employed in her church's choir, but occasionally she indulged her other pleasure, singing blues and jazz.

After a full minute's examination the CSI stepped back from her scope and placed the fragment on a slide, scattering fingerprint dust on top of it and nodding her head.

"There's the top half of a fingerprint there, just one, but it's small so it could be the girl's. You'll need to eliminate her anyway."

Liam nodded. "We can do that by saying we need to eliminate her prints from the others we've found at the flat and Galway. I'll call Hughesy to take them now."

Craig waved him to hold off as Grace continued reporting. "The paper is common A4 printer paper that you can buy in any store and this fragment came from the edge of the page. About halfway down judging with how thin the paper is."

Craig frowned quizzically so she explained.

"Pages tend to be thickest at the top and bottom. It's to do with the machinery that's used to make them. You wouldn't notice if you didn't know. Also, this piece was ripped off not neatly torn. You can tell by the shredding at the edges."

Angelica, if it was indeed her print, had wanted to get rid of the page pretty damn quick.

Liam made his call and after a muttered exchange passed his phone to the CSI.

"Hughesy'd already printed her for elimination so here you go."

A swift comparison later they got the nod. The prints matched.

Craig looked around for a clean board and a marker and found one in Des' office.

"OK, so" he wrote up the number one, "one, this fragment came from halfway down a common printer page which was ripped apart by someone. In a hurry, would you say?"

Grace nodded. "That feels right. Rushing would also explain the fact they missed this piece when they were flushing the rest away."

"Two, we know Angelica Swann handled the page because

we have her print on it. Three, because the print's on a ripped piece she must have done the ripping. Actually hold on that one, I'm not so sure of that conclusion. Four, the fact this piece came from halfway down the page and befr was in lowercase means there were words before and probably after it, and five, we need to find out what on earth befr could mean." He looked at the CSI. "Have I forgotten anything?"

"Well no, but I *would* like to perform chromatography on the ink. There are over two hundred shades of blue ink available commercially but most people use one of five, so it might tell us nothing but..."

"It might. OK, thank you, Grace. But remember we may need that fragment in court so don't destroy it, please."

The withering look she gave him made Craig drop his eyes in embarrassment, and as they exited the office Liam's deliberately loud, "Teach your granny to suck eggs often do you, boss?" added heat to his cheeks.

Just then the deputy's phone rang and he put it on speaker.

"It's Ash, chief. I've got that list for you. The only words in the Oxford English Dictionary that start with befr are variations of befret like befretting and befretted, which basically mean to fret greatly about; befringe, with means to decorate with a fringe, and befriend which we all understand."

"It has to be befriend, boss. I mean, who the hell's ever heard of befret or befringe? The note had to be about Angelica befriending the other two kids to get them killed and that's why she ripped it up. That means the core team left it behind deliberately so we could find her out."

"I agree, Liam, but without the whole letter or witnesses our only hope of proving it is if you're right about our killers leaving a backup or to get her to confess." He glanced at his watch. "OK, let's head to High Street and see what Aidan's managed to get so far."

Liam held out his hand for his keys. "I'm driving again."

Mainly so he could nip into a garage to buy some doughnuts for dessert.

****

In-flight Mid-Atlantic.

"Do you think it's done yet?"

"You mean the mother?"

Gretchen's light eyes widened in alarm. "Yes, of course the mother! Angelica won't do anything stupid to make the boys hurt her, will she?"

Irina responded with a smirk and turned to gaze out the window beside her, smiling at the night sky's brightening as they moved west.

The viewing was cut short by her elbow being shoved sharply off the armrest and Gretchen asking again, *"Well, will she?"*

"How would *I* know? I'm not a bloody mind reader". A more caustic, "Anyway, what do *you* care? You said we didn't need her the other day" followed.

When she saw she was getting to her companion, Irina added a teasing, "Maybe she'll *choose* to stay behind."

"But she can't stay! She could ID us!"

"As we were when *she* knew us, not as we usually are."

She glanced down at her grunge girl outfit and fingered her shoulder-length hair. "I can't wait to get back into my leathers and have my hair sheared again." She nudged the glasses she was wearing up the bridge of her nose. "Never mind get shot of *these* bloody things. You've no idea how heavy they are, and how bloody annoying when your eyesight's twenty-twenty like mine."

"You're saying Angelica's descriptions *won't* ID us?"

Irina's response was shrugged. "Scruffy youths are ubiquitous. And anyway, we'll be halfway across the world before they start to look. Actually, I hope the boys *do* leave her behind alive."

The meaningful look she gave her friend filled her with dread.

"What have you done, Irina? Have you done something that will lead them to *us*?"

"Wise up, Gretch. Why on earth would I do *that*? I've just made sure that little Ms Swann won't walk away scot-free."

"But she helped us."

"Not for the right reasons! It was just venom for her mum. Besides... she flirted with our men. *Big* mistake. And Kurt agrees with me by the way, she *shouldn't* get to just walk away; not coming from a family like that!"

Her companion's lips curled in disgust. "You're a real bitch, Rina. And if you've done *anything* that could jeopardise future missions Oskar will make you pay!"

Irina's eyes narrowed menacingly. "Don't threaten me, Gretch, or I might just forget to watch your back next time we're in a fire-fight!"

Before her friend could hit back she brushed the disagreement away with a laugh.

"Besides, what I did won't lead the police to anyone but Lady Angelica. You'll see."

****

High Street Station. 10 p.m.

After a quick read of the mother's and daughter's statements and a listen to their brief recorded interviews, which were, as instructed, basically step-by-steps of the day's events, Craig asked Jack Harris to have the pair taken home.

"To their Belfast house, please. We'll need to interview Angelica again tomorrow to see what more she can recall."

Hortense Fervier was *not* impressed. "But she's traumatised! She's just had a dreadful experience!"

"We'll be respectful of that and have a doctor available as required, Ms Fervier." A doctor who would just happen to be John. The detective's voice hardened slightly. "We *need* Angelica's help to catch these kidnappers before they harm anyone else."

Cynic that he was he found the girl's immediate martyred glance amusing, symbolising that no matter how she had suffered *of course* she would do anything to help them find the bad men.

As the women departed the station in a patrol car, Craig rolled his eyes.

"Quite the performance. Let's see how it holds up under real questioning tomorrow."

Liam gazed pointedly at the clock hanging on the staff-room's wall.

"What time tomorrow? 'Cos I'd *really* like to see my wife and kids at some point."

The words made Craig chuckle and feel guilty all at once; *he'd* only thought about Katy and Luca once in the previous ten hours. He comforted himself that it wasn't due to a lack of love but an excess of focus, and that if Katy had been dealing with a patient she might have been exactly the same; *might*. He smiled to himself. Well, she might not have thought about *him* anyway.

"Point taken, although Danni's probably been glad of the break from you. Come in at ten tomorrow and we'll plan things out."

He wished that he could come in at ten too, but at nine o'clock the next morning he would be wearing two holes in the Chief Constable's carpet with his knees.

Chapter Thirteen

Police Headquarters. Thursday 9 a.m.

As luck would have it there was a queue for Sean Flanagan's burgundy carpet the next morning; an overnight stabbing and a P.C.'s unfortunate gloveless handling of the knife had resulted in both the pale-skinned constable and his equally pale and almost as young sergeant joining Craig on the chairs outside the Chief Con's office, all on their way to a bollocking.

To be honest Craig felt positively relaxed about his coming encounter, pretty sure that he could justify his team members ruffling a few diplomatic feathers, whereas, judging by the rapidly jumping knees of the men beside him, his companions weren't feeling half as cool.

The detective decided to give them the benefit of his years of getting reamed out by higher ups and, ignoring a warning gaze from Donna that screamed, *"Don't you dare calm them down or they'll never learn!"*, attempt to calm them down he did, before one of the pair passed out on the floor.

"Don't worry, the boss will be fine. Just take the bollocking, don't argue, and above all be polite."

As Craig spoke the constable stared straight ahead, the bulge of his eyes the only sign that he'd heard him, but the sergeant's knee pumping slowed to a mere wobble and he turned to the Murder detective with a pleading look.

"Really?"

"Absolutely. Just make sure *you* take the blame and don't pass it to your constable even if he *was* the one who did it. The Chief won't like that. Disloyalty."

"Detective Chief Superintendent Craig!"

This time the PA's words were audible to everyone so he turned and shot her a grin, quite enjoying himself now. He'd spent the night tossing and turning about the right questions to make Angelica Swann cough to everything and had a headache as a consequence, so sitting on a chair unable to do anything but chat was as close to relaxation as he'd experienced for days.

"Yes, Mrs Scott? What can I do for you?"

The secretary pursed her lips disapprovingly. "You know exactly what you can do. You can-"

The ringing of her desk phone left him to add his own

ending.

"Shut up" perhaps? No, probably not in front of the children. "Be quiet" or "Stop interfering" were more likely. But he might never know because after a quiet, "Yes, sir", "are you *sure*, sir?" and a disapproving frown the PA hung up with a martyred sigh.

She said nothing for a long moment, which Craig half-suspected was deliberate, and when the words, "The Chief Constable no longer needs to see you, Chief Superintendent" came, he *knew* that it had. Designed to make him sweat. Donna and Nicky had clearly attended the same samurai school for PAs.

He decided to push his luck a bit so he sauntered over to her desk and smiled down at her.

"No reason given?"

"The Chief Constable doesn't need to give reasons!"

She followed the words with a disapproving clicking of her tongue.

"Fine then. I'll just be on my way then. I'll tell Nicky you said hello, shall I? Unless this year's ninja reunion's coming soon?"

Before she could retort Craig turned to the men he was leaving behind, as solemnly as if they were his troops going into battle.

"You'll be fine. Just remember what I said. Take it on the chin and call him sir."

A quick, "Bye, Donna. It's been a blast" and he was in the stairwell chuckling to himself and switching on his mobile to find three messages to return, two from his inspector and one from his deputy. He took Liam's first.

"What are you doing in so early? I said ten."

"Ach, well, Danni started to hoover around me so I thought I might as well shift."

"OK. What do you want me for then?"

Liam was curious; Craig sounded more cheerful than a man waiting to go to the guillotine had any right to be, and it was only ten past nine so he couldn't possibly have been in and out.

"What did the C.C. say?"

"Cancelled. What did you call me for?"

"*Cancelled?* That means he's had news about our case from someone important."

That possibility hadn't occurred to Craig.

"Interpol! Of course. Ash must've got on to them after the Galway discoveries and they've told Flanagan something that's validated our work. Anyway, you still haven't answered my question. Why did you call me?"

"Oh, right. Just to say Annette wants to talk to you."

Hence the other missed calls.

"Fine. I'll call her now. Contact Ms Fervier and say we'll need them at High Street for eleven, will you."

"That'll give them time to arrange a flash lawyer."

"There's no way around that. We'll just have to be well prepped. Meet me at High Street as soon as you can so we can plan. Now, I'm off to call Annette."

He walked to his car before he did, his head full of the questions he'd devised during his insomnia. Each of them alone was fine but not the money shot, and if they didn't ask them in the right order the interview could simply weaken into a chat.

He struggled with the interview's structure for another five minutes before giving up and making his call. It was answered by a jeans-clad Annette sitting cross-legged on the floor of the Galway squat as she sifted through papers removed from the four boards. Post-forensics the CSIs had sealed those from each board and side in separate transparent evidence bags with photos of their original arrangements on the front, and distributed them around the room in eight large piles.

As they'd been doing it Annette had hardly been able to wait for the printing and swabbing to be over to read what had been written in more detail, but now she could barely cope with what she'd read: the detailed manifests of the transport trucks to the extermination camps, the lists of street executions, the thousands of people summarily shot at massacres, diagrams of family trees, last letters from those being sent to die and photos of murdered children and pensioners, all non-combatants and none a possible threat to anyone. It made her want to cry.

Andy couldn't bear to look that closely at the papers but she'd felt she *needed* to read every single one as a tribute to someone lost. An interesting discovery had made her pleased that she had and try to contact her boss.

She was just about to open a fresh evidence bag when somewhere beneath a set of papers to her left her phone rang and made her jump.

She jabbed it on and snapped out a furious, *"Yes?"*

"It's me, Annette. Just returning your call. Everything all right there?"

"Sorry, sir. I was just... I was just surprised by the phone. We're almost finished here so we should be back later. But that's not why I called you. I was sifting through the papers from the boards and found something interesting. Our killers left you a note in a sealed envelope."

For him? It confirmed that their killers had expected and indeed wanted them to find their trail.

"Have you opened it?"

"The CSIs did for prints. But I didn't like to read it when it was addressed to you."

"Do so now, please."

She lifted an evidence bag in front of her.

"OK, so apparently there were no prints or DNA on it or the envelope. It's written on lined white paper, like the sort you'd pull from a file pad, and it's in black pen. Looks like felt tip."

Whereas the other note had been on plain paper and written in blue.

"I know it's impossible to say for sure but it looks like a woman's handwriting. It's on some of the other exhibits too-"

Craig cut in, "Hold on a second" and scribbled a reminder to compare the handwriting to the 'befr' slip they'd found.

"Can you send a shot of it through to Ash?"

"As soon as we're off the phone."

"Good. OK, on you go."

"It's quite long, sir, but the basic gist is that our killers didn't abduct Angelica Swann, they approached her with an offer because she was the only other girl in Sophie's medieval history group and they reckoned she could get close. Sophie was the target. In exchange for Angelica's help they agreed to steal the painting she loved from the gallery and then they threw in the killing of Hortense if she would approach Dylan for them too. They'd obviously picked up on the fact Angelica hated her mum."

"But Dylan was a clear target too?"

"Yes, that's obvious here. Sophie, Dylan and Bolsover were who they really wanted and the stuff on the boards outlines why. But *then* they found out Angelica's family was linked to the Ferviers who'd worked with the Nazis in Vichy, Hubert and Aveline are actually named here, and they were left with the decision of whether to just kill Hortense or her daughter along with her."

Craig wasn't convinced.

"That might be what they want us to believe, Annette, but they *could* equally have known all about the Ferviers before they got here and always planned to kill Angelica and Hortense, then realised the daughter could be more use to them alive and gave her a reprieve."

"Actually everything I've read here so far makes it look like they really *were* only here to kill Sophie, Dylan and Bolsover, sir. It looks like they didn't even know the collaborating Ferviers had links with Ireland before they arrived, and only realised it was the same family when they'd already engaged Angelica's help to get to the others. This letter definitely says Angelica helped them willingly."

For the price of a painting and bumping off her mum.

Craig sighed. Without Angelica's avarice and hatred they probably wouldn't have linked her to the killings at all. Foolish girl.

"Right, so Angelica made her mum a target, and probably prompted them to steal her possessions from the vault along with Dylan's family's hoping *she* would profit from them probably."

"There's another interesting thing on the thefts, sir. We found plans for a raid on a bank in Vilnius in Lithuania, so I called it and it turns out their vaults were cracked early this morning."

"*Damn.* But not by our group because they were still here."

"Yes. Anyway, they stole items owned by Sophie's family and two other families as well, so I told the local police what happened here and to give the families protection, in case the next thing is more deaths."

"Good. Hopefully they'll act in time. But that means we're dealing with something bigger than just our murders." He thought about the wider possibilities for a moment and then returned to their case. "So they were definitely trying to lure Hortense to that gallery to be killed today. What else does the note say?"

"That they didn't trust Angelica generally and they knew she didn't believe in their cause."

"Do they say anything specific about killing Angelica or taking her with them when they left?"

"It says they considered the first option and they let her *think* the second was a possibility, but whoever wrote this letter definitely didn't want to take her along. They favoured killing Angelica or leaving her behind to carry the can."

Craig frowned. "As did whoever wrote the note they left at the gallery. It looks as if the group couldn't agree on a plan for Angelica but we're unlikely to get confirmation with the other note being destroyed. Either way our killers seem very sure Angelica won't ID them to try to save her skin."

"I don't think they care, sir." The D.I. read out the final paragraph. "We know Angelica will try to barter our descriptions for a shorter sentence, but we gave false names, look nothing like the way she saw us and wore gloves at all times so as not to leave prints. Also, where we are going you can not follow us."

"Can not, not can't?"

"Definitely can not."

"Then English isn't the author's first language."

"The rest of the letter's written like that too, sir. Quite formal. Anyway, the last line's very interesting. It's addressed directly to you. 'Goodbye, Marco Craig. We wish you and the whole of your family well.'"

A small smile tugged at her lips. "They definitely like *you*. And they must have been watching you at some point, because there was a photo of you on the boards that wasn't from a newspaper report. Luca's in it so it must have been taken in the past few months, and it had to have been at a weekend because you're in jeans and Katy's beside you holding the pram."

A prickle ran down Craig's spine. It was a risk that they all lived with, a killer stalking them, but being photographed made it feel a little too real. He didn't care for himself; he'd accepted that he might be killed by a perp when he'd joined the police, but the thought of his family being at risk...

He gave a violent shudder, knowing that there was no way of preventing it if someone was truly determined. Katy had already been attacked by one of his 'clients' when her car had been hacked and crashed years before, and his parents had suffered threats. But Luca...

Annette's warm voice cut across his chill.

"So that's all it says, chief. But I thought you should know about it before you interviewed the girl."

Craig forced himself to focus on the job ahead of him.

"Yes, thank you, Annette. That's great work. I'll get a printout from Ash, and you and Andy get yourselves back here as soon as you can."

"Andy's gone to interview the estate's caretaker, but we will."

"And don't forget to ask Ash to get the handwriting compared with the fragment."

"Will do."

Craig cut the call and stared out of his car window for a good ten minutes, blind to the people parking and walking around him, his mind engaged in searching for ways to keep his family safe until in the end he realised that there weren't any, short of digging a moat around their new house and filling it with piranhas and forbidding Katy to ever leave home. The mental image of her as a surrendered wife who might agree to such constraints included a lot of gingham and flat shoes and made him laugh out loud; Katy wouldn't be separated from her four inch heels even in her grave.

Far better to think about the things that he *could* control, so he started the car and headed for High Street where he found the Ferviers not yet arrived and his deputy in the staff-room with his feet up on the coffee table. He shoved them off on his way to the kettle by way of saying hello.

"Liam, call Ash and get him to send through the letter Annette's just found so we can print out a few copies. I need to call John."

He'd primed the pathologist the night before that they might need him, so after a quick exchange John got on his way.

When there were three of them in the staff-room Craig passed around the printouts and fresh drinks, giving the others a moment to read the letter before he spoke.

"OK, it seems you were right about a backup, Liam. This implicates the girl in the murders of Sophie Adomaitis and Dylan Pedersen-Storey. But we still need a confession. The only evidence we really have against her is her print on that piece from the flat, and it's not enough."

John interjected. "Des says her prints were found in the squat as well, but only in one corner at the back."

The corner that Irina had deliberately left unbleached.

The words made Craig frown. "That's odd, because the others left nothing there at all. But then they did wear gloves."

"Not that odd, boss. If the arrogant wee madam never thought we'd make the link to her she was probably careless."

"I'm not so sure, Liam. It's unlikely Angelica would have noticed the others wearing gloves and not insisted on some too, which makes me think that our killers planted her prints in that area deliberately before they left."

"You think they didn't like her?"

"At least one of them would be my guess. But what matters now is that Angelica believes she's flameproof, and she *could* stay that way if she argues convincingly enough that she was abducted and couldn't escape because they kept her under constant watch. Their surveillance *was* very good."

John's curiosity was piqued. "How do you know that?"

"Because they got a shot of me at a weekend and I had no bloody idea I was being watched." He saw another question coming and waved it away. "The point is, proving that Angelica was a willing volunteer is going to be very hard without a witness. Any good defence barrister would claim the prints and this letter were planted by someone who hated her. If we'd managed to put a name on the pay-as-you-go phone that might have helped."

"You think it was hers, boss?"

"Yes. It had travelled between Belfast and Galway several times and went dead just at the time Angelica arrived at the Union on Monday."

"Clever little Madam. She used a burner the whole time and left her own phone in Belfast to cover her ass."

"Yes, she *is* clever, so... suggestions on how to prove her involvement anyone? Short of thumbscrews I mean."

John's face brightened. "I have some antique ones in my collection."

The pathologist collected curious historical implements, not all medical.

Liam frowned in thought for a moment and then nodded decisively.

"We face the girl with this letter and watch her try to cover her ass. She could dig herself a big hole with her mouth."

Craig considered the tactic.

"I agree she won't be expecting it. Whoever wrote this letter clearly didn't like Angelica so they're unlikely to have warned her they were leaving it. John, what do you think?"

The pathologist puffed out his cheeks for a moment and

then shook his head.

"What Liam's proposing *could* elicit surprise or shock and she *might* let something slip, but if she doesn't then you're basically left playing human lie-detector. I know you do that every day with criminals but, 'I *think* she was lying, M'Lud', is hardly evidence for court is it? Also she could just call your bluff and say you wrote the letter yourself."

Sadly he was right, although Craig didn't dismiss his deputy's idea completely.

"We *could* ask so many questions that she gets stressed and then hit her with the letter's contents rather than the actual paper. If she blurts out anything at all then we could base more questions on it."

John shrugged. "Perhaps. What did her initial statement say?"

Liam recited the tall tale from memory.

"That she was at the Students Union on Monday evening and someone must have slipped something in her drink and abducted her."

Craig frowned thoughtfully.

"Monday was when Ben Mooney last saw Sophie as well. Did we manage to tie down Dylan's last sighting?"

Before his deputy could reply Craig had pulled out his phone and dialled another member of his team.

"Aidan?"

"Guv. I was just about to phone you."

"About?"

"Dylan Storey. Uniform found his car on University Street, and handily enough it'd got a ticket."

"On?"

"Tuesday lunchtime. I had Traffic pull the nearest camera footage, and we've got the boy parking there at seven on Monday night and walking to the Students Union on Elmwood."

Where he no doubt met up with his girlfriend Angelica.

It explained a lot. Why take one person when you could snatch three at once? Or at least two genuine victims and a third who needed to be taken at the same time to give her an alibi, although Angelica had conveniently failed to mention she'd had Sophie and Dylan as company on her trip.

"Anything else useful around the Union?"

"A white panel van on Elmwood later that night. It was parked near the Lisburn Road end for a while doing nothing, then it drove around the back of the Union around ten-thirty and twenty minutes later it was on the Malone Road heading west. The plates were smeared with mud so it got lost pretty fast."

Liam nodded. "Smeared deliberately. West would have taken them to the M1 south, boss. There are plenty of back roads to Galway off that."

Craig nodded, torn between annoyance at the van's elusiveness and elation that they were finally starting to make some links.

"Angelica wasn't slipped a roofie, she gave one to Dylan. And ten-forty was when her real phone went dead. She planted it at the Union just before they left with our killers. God knows where she dumped the burner." He paused for a moment before speaking again. "But Sophie sounded a bit quiet to be hanging around the Union on a Sunday night."

It was Aidan who answered.

"Maybe they grabbed from her hall on the way past. It was on their way up the Malone."

"Good point, and we'll need to interview people there to confirm, but for now, thanks, Aidan. Good work."

With that he cut the call and turned back to his deputy.

"What else was in Angelica's statement, Liam?"

"OK, so she was in the Union and reckons she must have been roofied, because next thing she was in a car with a hood over her head on her way somewhere."

"A car? And just *somewhere*? She didn't know she was in the south? Then or never?"

"She could say she was confused about car or van, but she *must* have known she was in the south. She told Hughesy some of the killers had probably skipped from the south, remember."

Without warning the D.C.I. raced out of the room, returning a minute later with a copy of the girl's statement from the night before. He scanned the pages quickly and then pumped the air.

"Yes! I *knew* she'd mentioned Galway! Here, where she said she was hooded and driven on a smooth road, a motorway, over the border. Then later she says she realised she was in Galway."

Craig sat forward urgently. "What are the routes to the mill from here?"

Liam pulled up a map. "M1 then M6 or M1, N52 then M6

are the main ones. But there's a clatter of shorter ways cross-country using back roads, and why would any kidnapper take the long way round?"

"They wouldn't when back roads without cameras would've been safer. Even if they *had* hidden the van's plates they wouldn't have wanted to take any risks. But they *would* have driven on the M1 out of Belfast for at least a few miles so Angelica *could* argue she meant that. Read me that bit about the border again."

Instead the D.C.I. turned the typed statement so he could read it himself. Crossing the border was there in black and white.

Craig gave a satisfied nod.

"OK, make a list of all the possible routes from Belfast to the squat, Liam, and then do the necessary."

John had been listening with interest but now he looked perplexed. "But why bother mentioning the motorway over the border at all if she didn't actually travel on it? Unless she got to know the killers earlier than she said and that's the route *she* got used to taking when she was working with them to abduct Sophie and Dylan and driving herself around."

Craig registered his point with a smile.

"Well spotted. OK, let's play Devil's Advocate for a minute. Befriending Sophie and Dylan and gaining their trust would have taken time."

Liam glanced up from his note making. "Aye, it would."

John shook his head. "It couldn't have taken that much time. The Uni year only started nine weeks ago."

"Well, she was obviously a quick mover because her mate Gill said she'd been dating Dylan for weeks, Doc."

"And she'd have had to persuade Sophie to introduce them first. Pass me that statement, will you, Liam. I want to check something."

Craig tapped his chin thoughtfully before he spoke again. "Angelica *could* argue that she'd already known and socialised with Dylan and Sophie *before* she was abducted by our perps, rather than that she'd deliberately befriended them at their request. She could also argue that she knew about Galway and the motorway because one of our perps mentioned them after she was abducted and she got confused as to when exactly she'd known about both. But... she was allegedly abducted at night groggy and hooded so how did she know she was crossing our, *completely invisible,* border at all? The only way *I* ever know I'm across the border is when the signposts change, and according to her own statement about the hood she couldn't possibly have seen those."

His deputy grinned. "But she *would* have known if she'd been wide awake and a willing passenger, because she could've looked out and seen the signs."

John shook his head. "If she says the killers mentioned they were in Galway she could say it was logical to assume that meant crossing the border."

"I agree none of this is perfect, John, but that border crossing's a definite weakness."

The medic sighed heavily. "As it is with us all."

Craig chuckled at the political commentary and returned to his point. "But you're right, we can't be cocky. She *could* say that it was a logical assertion or that her captors mentioned the border at some point, in which case they were pretty bloody talkative around her. Where did she say she was held exactly?"

The pathologist obliged by reading from the statement. "In a storeroom on the top floor of the building they lived in and they only let her out when they needed her to do something for them."

Craig frowned. "*Are* there any storerooms on the top floor of the mill? I'll need to call Annette and ask."

Just then his deputy rose, waving the note he'd written. "And I'm away to give Hughesy a shout back about roads."

After five minutes of Annette exploring the mill Craig's answer came back as no. Each floor of the building was a single open plan space with the only storeroom in the whole building downstairs near the front door.

"Good. We've got her in some dodgy facts so we can pick those apart. As her prints were found in the main room we need to ask specifically if her abductors ever took her in there. Also, if she was abducted from the Union why was her phone found in the loo?"

The pathologist shook his head. "She'll say her kidnappers took her from there or else dumped it there to throw you off track. "

"When in reality she probably did it herself."

Just then Liam rejoined them.

"OK, anything else either of you can think of?"

The D.C.I. scanned one page of the statement as the

pathologist did the same with another and commented first.

"Look at this part. Where she says she was cuffed all the time even when she was asleep, unless they needed her free to show her face at home and make friends with Dylan and Sophie, and then there was always one of them watching her."

"That's a neat explanation of why she didn't need to disappear completely during those weeks, boss."

"Yes it is. What's your point about the cuffs, John?"

"Well, there are two really. Angelica's statement says that she was cuffed for long periods of time and yet the hospital doctors recorded no marks on her wrists except an imprint of the duct tape used at the gallery. I've read their reports and seen the pictures."

"Bingo! Another lie. That's the border geography, the storeroom and the cuffs. What was your other point?"

"Well, doesn't all of this point to your killers having been in the country for weeks?"

A grimace said Craig had already spotted that.

Liam signalled for attention. "She says here that there were four in the group, boss. Two male, two female and all young."

"As Ryan surmised. We saw the boys at the airfield but the girls must have left with the cargo. Actually that's a point, Liam. What happened to the Vermeer from the gallery? Was it found at the squat or did they export that as well?"

"I'll need to check, boss. If it was supposed to be the girl's payment like the printout says then we might have to search her homes."

John shook his head. "Surely keeping it would incriminate her in, at a minimum, the gallery theft?"

Craig sighed. "You're right. Save yourself the work, Liam. Angelica will either have it so well hidden that we'll never find it or it's already been sold on and she's pocketed the cash."

"Fair enough. But there's another thing, boss. If she *was* being watched, the watchers couldn't actually have gone into her tutorials and lectures with her, could they? So why didn't she report to university staff that she was being coerced? Or ask them to call the police? And Dylan or Sophie themselves, why couldn't she have warned them that they were in danger when they were alone? It would only have taken her a minute. Or she could have passed them a note."

Craig made a face. "She *could* say she was terrified of her abductors even when they weren't there, and we've seen that before with kidnap victims and battered wives being too afraid to confide in anyone in case it gets them killed. Mind you, if they go on to *kill* their captors we always distrust fear as mitigation until it's been proved, so actually you're right, Liam, the question does need to be asked."

Just then the D.C.I.'s mobile rang. He listened to the speaker for a moment and then cut the call.

"OK, that was the pirate. Des did a graphology course last year apparently so he took a quick shufti at the 'befr' slip and the letter Annette found at the squat, and he says there are enough differences to say they were written by different people. Also, he says the author of the letter was almost certainly female. I can't see the logic of Angelica writing either note because they'd incriminate her but we're to send a sample of her writing across if you want him to say for sure."

Craig nodded. "I agree that it's very unlikely she wrote them, but let's just keep things tidy for court. As soon as she arrives get her to write 'the quick brown fox jumps over the lazy dog' sample."

The standard text was a pangram, which meant it included every letter of the alphabet, and it was a test used for handwriting comparisons all over the west.

"I'm pretty sure I just heard her arrive, boss."

"Take a look, will you."

A few seconds later the D.C.I. returned, grimacing. "She's got her mum and a snotty looking solicitor with her, and I'm guessing *he* won't like a handwriting sample being done."

"Tell him we need it to rule his client out as the author of any the papers we've found at Galway, in case they're incriminating. It's unlikely Angelica wrote any of them, so she might agree to it for that. Leave her with it and come back, Liam." Suddenly he had a thought. "How long is it likely to take Aidan to do what you've asked?"

"I'd give him a couple of hours to be sure."

"The Ferviers won't like waiting, but tough. OK, tell the solicitor that our graphologist will need three hours to do the handwriting comparison so if they wish they can go home and we'll call them back. But we'll definitely be seeing Angelica today."

"I'll be back" in a Schwarzenegger boom accompanied the D.C.I.'s exit and made John laugh.

He *was* back, but only after getting an earful from Hortense, and another thirty minutes of discussion saw the trio finally run out of steam. But at least when they began Angelica's interview they would have the Galway letter in the background and the geographic slip-ups, storeroom, cuffs and 'watchers' to help pile the pressure on.

****

Galway.

It took Andy forty minutes to locate the cottage that groundskeeper Dáithí Stronge called home, such was the size of the linen mill's estate. He eventually spotted the tiny stone-walled structure down by the river, whose water had for centuries flowed into the mill to assist the washing and dying of fabrics and then been re-circulated by its giant wheel to carry the residue of God only knew what chemical pollutants down past the millworkers' village a few short miles away.

The D.C.I. pictured the people who had once lived there, born into poverty and never schooled out of it they would have worked in the mill just as their parents had, led there by tradition after a few short years of the three 'R's to risk their health and lives. The millies, doffers, spinners and porters would have had their hands stained by noxious chemicals, risked injury from heavy equipment, and spent every day but Sunday breathing in the preservatives used to protect a fabric more valued than any of them, soon to be exported worldwide to make the mill owner rich. Welcome to practically any century including this one; filled with the routine and unquestioned abuse of someone poor somewhere in the world so that another could get rich.

He and Annette had driven through what was left of the workers' village on their way there and gazed at the shells of cottages, overgrown now with weeds and ivy yet each one marked 'For Sale' at an exorbitant price. Fixer-uppers for the coming generation; a little piece of Ireland's history for those with more money than sense.

Stronge's cottage at least had a roof, although not a picture-postcard thatched one. Instead sheets of corrugated iron met in a peak above the walls, and another smaller sheet with a makeshift levered handle attached acted as its front door.

The D.C.I. knocked on it tentatively, unsure how much weight the thin metal would take before caving in. It withstood his taps to be tugged back a moment later by a red-faced whippet of an old man with the thickest thatch of grey hair the detective had ever seen.

"What dee yee want?"

The groundskeeper's west coast accent was so thick it took Andy a moment to realise he was speaking English and another to understand his question, then he produced his warrant card, which made the wary pensioner gawp and recoil.

"I've dun nathin' tee bring the guards an me!"

Andy waved him down with a smile. "I'm not here for you, Mister Stronge. I'd just like to ask you a few questions about the mill."

The old man's next words were accompanied by a frown. "What business is the mill of yourn? It's nat been worked in manys a year."

"I know that, but I also know that there were some people staying there recently and it's them I need to know about. Did you see anyone around?"

The man's defensive posture, which had included both feet still planted inside his house and one hand gripping the door as if ready to slam it in Andy's face, relaxed slightly and he folded his arms and answered the question in a conversational tone.

"Might have. Might nat."

The D.C.I. recognised the caution of the countryside where everyone knew everyone and protected their neighbour, and he admired it. It was also a pain in the ass when he was trying to work.

"Did you or not, Mister Stronge?" He came over all Liam for a moment. "Because if you withhold evidence I *can* arrest you."

He couldn't actually because he was out of his jurisdiction and he doubted any Guard would oblige on such a flimsy charge. Still, it was worth a punt.

Surprisingly it did the trick and the elderly caretaker backpedalled swiftly.

"Ach now, man, keep yer hair an. Sure, I was only actin' the lig. Aye, I seed them all right. Three girls an two boys, nat much older than twenty, maybe twenty-five. A fine lukkin' bunch they were too, but definitely nat from around here."

"Why not?"

"Too dark an too blonde." He screwed up his face, reconsidering. "Well, wan af them might've been from the island I suppose. A girl wi' brown hair."

Andy produced a photo of Angelica Swann.

"Aye, that's her all right."

"Was she friendly with the others?"

"Surely."

"You never saw her being restrained in any way? Her hands cuffed or tied?"

The caretaker snorted. "Get away wi' ye! They played that game with the bat in the grounds fer hours at a time, an that wan was bowlin' more often than nat."

Angelica Swann had been a willing companion to their killers.

"And you knew they were staying in the mill?"

Suddenly the ground became of more interest to the pensioner than him.

After a moment of foot shuffling Andy added, "I don't care if they gave you a few quid to stay there, Mister Stronge. I just need to know how long they were here for and what else you saw."

At the fiscal release the caretaker quickly looked up again, but instead of relief the D.C.I. saw defiance in his eyes.

"What did they dee to put ye after them?"

Calculating that only the truth would get him answers, Andy responded, "We believe they killed three people."

The shake of Stronge's head was immediate and sharp.

"I don't believe ye fer wan minute! They were nice kids an I'll say no different. No, I won't. The first time they saw me they had me in fer tea an gave me... well, let's just say they were more open handed than most."

"What did they ask for in exchange?"

"Just tee sleep in the mill fer a few weeks. They said they were touring Europe on the cheap an run out af hotel money." He shrugged. "Sure, it was no harm tee me so I turned a blind eye. The mill's been empty fer years. I even helped wan af the lads rig up the aul generator tee give them some heat an light, though I let them carry their bits of furniture from their van themselves." He placed a hand on his hip and winced. "My arthritis aches somethin' shockin' this time af year."

Andy made a few notes and then dug into the detail. "You said very blonde and dark. Was that the girls or the boys?"

"Both. Wan girl was dark haired wi' wild pale skin. Tiny wee thing wi' a head full af curls. She might have been from down around Clare where the Armada wrecked till I heard her speak, then I knew fer sure she was foreign. Dun't know from where. The second girl was a bit taller wi' that dirty-fair type af hair, an she was Dutch fer sure. I was a sailor fer a while when I was young an I know the accent well. The third girl is in yer photo. She was the tallest af them."

"What about the men?"

"The Dutch girl's boyfriend was tall an built up wi' blond hair. Tanned too. He looked like a Viking. Well, from somewhere up north anyway. The other lad was like him only in reverse. Tall an dark with black eyes, an tanned skin this time. A bit leaner but wild strong. He did them one-armed press ups an the grass. He was I-talian I think, although they only spoke English to me." He smiled as if something had just come to him. "Aye, aye, the more I think af it that girl in the photo *was* from here. Her accent wasn't thick, but posh Belfast maybe."

Andy smiled as he completed his notes. Things were falling into place.

"Thanks for that, Mister Stronge. Now, we might need you to help us with some sketches."

It brought an immediate shake of the head. "There'd be no use in that at all." The groundskeeper pointed to his eyes. "I'm growin' cataracts, so I can see big shapes an colours but my detail's hopeless." He peered at Andy's face. "I know you've got two eyes, a nose an a mouth, an your hair's short an kind of dirty fair, but that's about all I could say."

That's all he *would* say he meant. Judging from his detailed descriptions of their perps the groundskeeper's vision couldn't be all *that* bad, but whether from obstinacy or because he'd really liked their killers Dáithí Stronge had clearly gone as far as he was prepared to go. For now. If he was called to give evidence he had no doubt the caretaker would change his tune faster than snow off a ditch.

Accepting defeat temporarily Andy waved a cheerful goodbye and headed back to the mill, calling Craig to update him on the way.

****

High Street. 2 p.m.

There was a lot riding on their interview and Craig was well aware of it; three people had been killed and two of them had families who wanted justice. Their main perps had escaped and judging by everything they knew, confirmed by Andy's phoned through info from the mill's caretaker, they were clever so Interpol could be searching for them for years. That just left Angelica Swann to prosecute or not, a young woman who by Dáithí Stronge's report had been living quite happily with their four killers, which was something her solicitor would no doubt try to frame as compliance under duress but Craig *still* believed that he could use that new information to score a few hits.

As expected, Angelica's handwriting hadn't matched either the Galway letter or the torn fragment from the gallery, and the evidence that she had deliberately 'befriended' Sophie and Dylan to lure them to their deaths was thin. Even the detailed information in the letter confirming what they'd already guessed, that Angelica had been up to her baby blues in everything, *could* simply have been their perps framing her because they hated the Ferviers overall. Finally and inevitably, any good barrister would rip holes in their circumstantial evidence in court, although *they* would challenge any Stockholm Syndrome defence hard.

But all they were really left with was the girl's faux pas on the border, her prints in the main room, why she hadn't at least passed a note to the others to warn them and the lack of markings from the cuffs, supported by the caretaker's evidence that he had never seen her restrained. That *also* gave a lie to her tale of always being held in a small storeroom whichever floor she said it had been on.

They'd gone to court with less and won before but it wasn't his favourite thing, and definitely not in a case with so many victims and possible international links.

Suddenly Craig became aware that the other men were staring at him.

"Do you two have something to say?"

Liam answered first. "Aye. What are we charging her with?"

"Nothing until I get a feel of things."

But he knew his deputy was right. If it came to the moment when it was charge or release he had better have something lined up.

He pulled out his mobile and reluctantly dialled the Public Prosecution Service, only to have the phone answered by the Director himself. Eric Maynard, a man who could best be described as an awkward shit and with whom he'd crossed swords a few months earlier about the P.P.S. reneging on a witness agreement, something which after a shouting match with the C.C. Maynard had grudgingly backed down on, while signalling clearly that he would harbour a grudge.

"Mister Maynard, this is Chief Superintendent Craig. Could you put me through to whoever's on call for charging, please."

"*Director* Maynard, and you can ask me."

Damn. He needed a pissing match right now like a hole in the head, but needs must.

"Right."

Craig outlined the situation swiftly and waited through two minutes of, "Tsk"s and muttering before any decipherable words came back.

"It's far from ideal."

You don't say.

"And any decent barrister could pull it apart."

Apart from the obvious oxymoron Craig was forced to agree.

"But if you can get a confession that she actually took part in the murders then she'll have to be charged with murder just as the others would have been, and if you believe she didn't do that but she assisted before or after the fact then a charge of assisting an offender should be applied. Just on the first two victims, mind you. It will be impossible to prove she was involved in the shopkeeper's death."

Two murders or assisting on them it was then. It would all depend on what was said at interview. Now they just had to pray that Angelica Swann wasn't as devious as they thought she was and put her foot firmly in her mouth.

Craig hung up without saying thank you and ignored an immediate mental image of his mother wagging her finger at him for being rude. Maynard was a bastard so she would just have to deal with it this time. As if Mirella Craig would ever actually know.

****

Interview Room One.

Ten minutes into the session they had completed the formalities and John and Jack Harris, seated in the viewing room with coffee and a large box of doughnuts that, along with several bottles of whisky, Craig had gifted the sergeant for his infidelity two days before, dough being too soft to make the same crunching sounds as biscuits that could, and they knew this because they'd tested it before, be heard through the wall, were willing Craig on and champing at the bit for the 'Gotcha!' moment that always came in TV cop shows.

The detectives in the room were aware of the expectation but ignored it, knowing that if they didn't crack their prisoner now they might never get another chance and aware that they needed to move forward with extreme caution in case they missed a vital point.

Craig worked his way through the background evidence slowly and methodically, circling his opponent, because that was undoubtedly what Angelica was now, and viewing each new fact as another step towards the core where lay the few precious lies that they had caught her in.

Liam would have smiled at the process, one that he'd seen his boss follow many times before, except that he was wearing his serious face; a hard stare tinged with disapproval and disappointment that his father had used on him many times as a kid. It had been far more effective than shouting and made him confess to many misdemeanours, including some he hadn't even committed such was his eagerness to please.

Angelica however was avoiding both his gaze and Craig's, staring down at her long nails as if she had a script inscribed on them and occasionally drumming them against the wooden table top. The solicitor accompanying her was a grey-haired, white-faced man who had announced with some pomp at the start of the interview that he, "had been with the family for years" as if it was some recommendation of his competence in criminal matters. More likely the man had drawn up the Ferviers' Wills and dealt with their art and property purchases, and that difference in experience gave the detectives hope.

Throughout Craig's quiet setting-out of the case the lawyer's only comment had been, "Yes, my client feared for her life." But Liam, who knew his role right now was to observe what his boss couldn't while Craig concentrated on formulating questions, was seeing welcome signs that the girl's edges were starting to fray.

As Craig had spoken the nail inspections had grown shorter and more frequent and become interspersed with finger tapping of increasing speed and force, so that the initially light and barely audible sounds made at the beginning were soon replaced by sharp clicking and on more than one occasion the imprint of a nail being left in the table.

Craig's focus was such that the D.C.I. knew he hadn't registered the change so he gently pressed his foot down on top of his. Not hard enough to make his boss jump and give them away, but in a signal that they'd used in the past of, "Any minute now..."

John was watching the session wide-eyed, leaning forward eagerly in his seat and shovelling lumps of dough into his mouth faster and faster, until Jack finally wrenched the box away from him and swallowed what was left in a gulp.

When they saw what was happening beneath the table the sergeant whispered, "That's a signal the girl's on the ropes."

Before the medic could react Craig lifted his eyes abruptly from his page and stared straight into their suspect's eyes.

"Why did you lie about the border, Ms Swann?"

Her talons locked in place instantly and Liam watched as, although Craig had made his weakest point first, they dug deeper and deeper into the table's soft wood.

"*What?*" Her eyebrows knitted in fury. "I didn't lie about anything!"

"Yes, you did. It's all here in the interview you gave yesterday. Please tell me how you could *possibly* have known that you were crossing the border, when by your own admission you were hooded and drugged and it was night time so you *couldn't* have seen the road signs change."

Everyone including her dumbfounded solicitor watched as Angelica's fury became first panic and then defiance and then as she settled on a smug smile and invented another lie.

"I felt the road surface change."

Yet in her statement she'd said that the road was smooth, a motorway even.

But they'd anticipated the surface argument and in the previous few hours Aidan had arranged for patrol cars to drive every cross-border route that Liam had listed, as well as a few more that he'd missed. Even when the tarmac had been a different colour because of age or provider there'd been no distinguishable rise or fall at any north-south junction, not even one that could be felt with a hand never mind from inside a van. The two Departments of Infrastructure had done a smooth job.

"There *are* no north-south surface changes, Ms Swann. We checked every possible route across the border and there was no way of you telling a difference from inside a vehicle unless you could see the road signs."

She backtracked hastily. "Yes, well I mean I could see *them*. I could see them through the hood. That's how I knew I'd crossed the border."

Except that Aidan had checked that as well by wearing one, and they'd also had Annette search the mill for the mooted hood. Something like a hood *had* been found at the mill, most probably used for Dylan or Sophie, and now Craig intended to test Angelica on it.

"What material was the hood made of?"

Her eyes shot up and right in a classic sign of deceit. "It was dark and really thick. Coarse. I remember the rough feel of it."

Yet the one that Annette had found had been cream and made of light linen.

"Thick? But you said you could see the road signs through it. At night, in the dark, and while you were drugged."

The solicitor lurched forward, deciding to earn his money.

"I don't like your tone, Superintendent."

Craig clamped his jaw so hard that Liam winced inwardly at the crack, but neither of them took their eyes off the girl.

"And I don't like being interrupted, sir, so sit back."

As the lawyer retreated hastily Craig shifted slightly towards his suspect.

"You weren't hooded at all, *were* you, Ms Swann? And I very much doubt that you were drugged either. I believe you saw the signs changing because you were looking out of the window and completely free to do so."

Her hands clamped the table like a vice as she spat back.

"I'm not telling you again! I was hooded and drugged, and they kept me cuffed every minute except when they forced me to lure Sophie and Dylan! Even then they watched me constantly." Her eyes lit up as if she'd just thought of

something, "And, and they threatened to shoot me all the time!"

John's jaw dropped as her solicitor's disbelief was writ large. "She's lying and he knows it!"

Jack smiled at his shock that bad people were sometimes less than honest.

Meanwhile Craig had jumped on the new words. "You didn't mention that point in your statement. How could you possibly have missed it out?"

"I've just remembered. I was traumatised."

Liam bit his tongue to stop himself retorting, "Traumatised my ass."

"OK, we can return to that in a moment." John was sure he saw the solicitor heave a sigh of relief. "Tell me about being handcuffed again. They were cuffs, weren't they?"

Angelica relaxed her claws slightly and rested back in her seat, clearly feeling on more certain ground.

"Yes, metal ones, with a chain in the middle connecting them."

Her description was of standard forties' movie handcuffs, nothing like the modern ones used by them, but Craig let it pass for now.

"Were they tight?"

"Yes. Very." She gave her solicitor a pained look. "They cut the blood off sometimes, they made them so tight."

Made? Adjustable cuffs hadn't existed in the forties; she was even getting her movie props wrong.

"Did they ever remove them, even when you were in Galway?"

She shook her head vehemently. "Never. They kept me wearing them and hooded, and only lifted the hood if I was being fed." The violin grew louder. "They wouldn't even let me feed myself, and when I went to the bathroom one of the girls always had to help. They wouldn't even unlock the cuffs then. It was *awful*."

"You said you were kept in a storeroom. Was that all the time? Did they ever take you into another room?"

"Only the bathroom."

Except your prints were found in the main room.

"Your statement says the storeroom was on the top floor. May I ask how you knew that?"

"I was walked up loads of stairs when I arrived and down again when they wanted to use me. The same every time after that until they'd got Sophie and Dylan. *Poor* Sophie and Dylan. I really liked both of them."

She gazed at him so mournfully and for so long that a less experienced cop might have been fooled, but after a brief pause Craig merely continued, visibly unmoved.

"How did you know that it was a storeroom when you couldn't see?"

"I felt my way around it and it was small with loads of shelves on the walls, so what else could it have been?"

The girl's imagination certainly stretched to detail.

"And you say the cuffs and hood were only removed when you were sent to meet Dylan and Sophie?"

"Yes, because I couldn't wear them then, could I?"

"Ms Swann, what would you say if I told you a senior doctor has confirmed that you couldn't possibly have worn cuffs for the periods you state, because of the lack of marks on your wrists?"

"I'd say he was stupid."

John's eyes widened indignantly, "The cheeky pup!"

"Why didn't you try to escape when they un-cuffed you?"

"I told you they were watching me. With guns."

"But they didn't come into the university tutorial room with you, did they? So why not tell Sophie or your tutor then?"

Panic filled her eyes to be replaced quickly with guile, and her tone became coy. "I was too afraid. Even then."

Craig nodded slowly, humouring her. "Afraid... yes, of course." But only for a moment. "So you couldn't even have passed your tutor a note asking them to call the police? *Really?*"

"NO!"

The eyes shot to the right again. By the time they'd centred once more Angelica had fabricated the perfect excuse.

"I couldn't because they said they'd kill my mum if I told on them." The words tumbled out increasingly quickly as her fairytale progressed. "They were planning to do that from the beginning. It was only because they knew they could use me to get Dylan and Sophie that they held off."

Liam was tempted to applaud. *Quick thinking, lassie.*

Except that the caretaker's evidence, her lack of wrist marks, the layout of the mill, the border roads and the note that Annette had discovered contradicted everything that she'd just said.

With so many inconsistencies in her story Craig decided that he'd heard enough. He met her eyes flintily and his tone changed to match.

"You've lied several times during this interview, Ms Swann."

"I haven't!"

He continued as if he hadn't heard her.

"About crossing the border wearing a hood, the location of the storeroom, and being restrained constantly in cuffs. The only storeroom at the location where you say you were kept is on the ground floor, but we did find your prints in the *only* room on the top floor; an extensive living area that has no shelves anywhere on the walls. True, the hood you describe couldn't have been seen through but none of the cross-border road surfaces fit your story that you 'felt' the change in road. We also know that you weren't cuffed all the time in Galway because you have no wrist marks to prove that, and also you were witnessed playing ball games with your so-called captors several times in the grounds. That witness also said that rather than you being afraid you were actually friendly with them."

He watched the girl's mind racing as she tried to think who might have seen her, until bereft of an ID she plumped for point blank denial.

"*I was never outside and I never played any games! I was locked in a storeroom, I hated my kidnappers and they hated me. They tried to kill me!*"

Craig fixed her gaze and continued in an even tone.

"You were friendly with them and assisted them willingly. They left you in good health at the gallery with a note that they wanted us to find. We found your fingerprint on a fragment of paper in the bathroom that we believe was part of it. It bore four letters that could only have formed the beginning of the word 'befriend'."

He moved forward another inch, not breaking his stare.

"We believe that you ripped that note up and tried to flush it away deliberately, so *we* wouldn't see it, but unfortunately for you, you left a piece behind. We also found another note in Galway that had been left marked for my attention. It outlined your willing assistance in the murders of Sophie Adomaitis and Dylan Pedersen-Storey for two rewards. The Vermeer stolen from your mother's art gallery and her death. It was your intent that she should be lured to the gallery last night and murdered."

The revelations galvanised Angelica. Her eyes expanded wildly and her next words were a screech, *"THAT BITCH IRINA! SHE WROTE THAT! YOU NEVER WOULD'VE KNOWN WITHOUT HER!"*

Before her solicitor could stop her she was up on the table and clawing for Craig's throat. Her nails had just connected when Liam leapt up, grabbed the student around the waist and whipped her backwards into the air. Then, fighting the urge to just hurl her on to it, he set her slowly but firmly back in her chair, cuffing her hands and hissing at her dumbfounded solicitor as he did.

"Sort your client out, man! Unless you want assaulting an officer on her rap sheet as well!"

He turned to see blood spreading rapidly down Craig's collar but the man himself looking unperturbed. With a grateful nod to his deputy Craig motioned him to sit and began intoning the charges against their prisoner in a solemn voice.

"Ms Angelica Swann, you are being charged with two counts of assisting an offender, each of which will carry a sentence of up to ten years in prison, in that between the dates of the ninth and the fifteenth of December twenty-nineteen the you did unlawfully assist in the murders of Ms Sophie Regina Adomaitis and Mister Dylan Lars Pedersen-Storey at an unknown location and thereafter attempt to conceal your crime."

They would never be able to prove she actually took part in the killing of either victim or that she would have gone through with her mother's if Hortense had arrived at the gallery in time, but two stretches of ten years, and he was certain she *would* get the top tariff because the victims had gone on to die, could see her in prison for longer than she'd currently been on the earth.

As a stream of expletives screamed around the room Liam kept a close eye on the girl, ready to intervene again in a heartbeat if she moved an inch.

The seriously out of his depth solicitor had a final stab at limiting the damage.

"Surely you can do something if she gives up the others?"

Craig had no intention of 'doing something' for his client, but neither did he want evidence withheld.

"I can't promise anything specific, but obviously *any* cooperation would speak to good behaviour. Consult your client about it and let me know before she's arraigned tomorrow morning so that I can put in a good word with the judge."

Not *too* good though, and certainly not enough to get Angelica out on bail.

The detectives rose simultaneously and Liam's sideways nod at the mirror told their audience to, "Get thee to the staff-room and put the kettle on."

Jack stayed behind to return their prisoner to her cell, initially wondering whether Angelica had exhausted all her swear words and then learning some new Generation Z ones while the other men were savouring their drinks.

John took a few sips of his coffee and then busied himself ministering to Craig's gouges.

"They're deep, Marc. You'll need a tetanus booster and some antibiotics." He swallowed hard before adding. "And you'll have to be tested for Hepatitis and HIV."

Craig rolled his eyes. "Oh, brilliant. Katy will love that."

"I can do it at the lab if you come down now, but you'll need another test in three months."

Liam made a face. "Wouldn't it make more sense to just test the girl, Doc? Either she has them or she hasn't, in which case the boss is in the clear with no three month wait."

John hit his forehead with the heel of his hand. "You're right! I'm stupid. We can compel the blood sample because she attacked you."

Craig sighed in relief. "Let's do that then. She's probably low risk, but if you could do it today I'd be very grateful."

"Right after my coffee. I'll nip to St Mary's and grab the tetanus and antibiotics too. Where will you be?"

Craig rolled his eyes. "The office. Where else? There's going to be a *lot* of report writing on this one."

"Pity about the other scrotes getting away, boss."

"Yes it is, but they're Interpol's and the in-country agencies' problem now. Just on that, Annette says there's been a vault raid in Lithuania and valuables belonging to Sophie's and two other families have gone."

Liam whistled. "There'll be bodies dropping there too then."

"Possibly. Annette warned the local cops as soon as she found out, but whether they'll reach the families in time...

Anyway, it confirms that there's an international dimension to all this, and I suspect the C.C. became aware of that this morning."

"Certainly explains why he let you off the hook."

Craig gave a small smile, remembering Donna's annoyance.

"At least some people will be happy at the end of this. From what Annette and Andy found at the mill there's no doubt the original owners will be getting their valuables back."

John shook his head. "They'll never replace their dead relatives. *That* pain will fester for generations."

Craig sighed meaningfully. "Which is exactly what started this whole thing."

****

The C.C.U.

By the time the detectives arrived back at the squad-room, with Craig wearing a shirt he'd bought hurriedly on the way and with a wad of white bandage on his neck that made him look like he'd been in the wars instead of scratched by a girl, there was a pile of phone messages waiting from Des.

He ignored his PA's gawping at his appearance and took the message slips and his deputy into his room.

"Grab a pew, Liam. Des wants a call back so let's find out why."

Five minutes later the detectives found themselves in a six-way call with Des, Grace, Andy and Annette, the content of which shocked them all. As his geographically distant detectives explained about the fourth board they'd discovered at the mill, something he'd completely forgotten about in the interview haze of the previous few hours, and Grace added her thoughts on it, both Craig and his deputy listened in disbelief.

"So when Annette sent through the images I recognised one of the languages as Rwanda-Rundi. I visited the country on a school trip in the eighties."

Craig found his voice. "Rwanda had a genocide in ninety-four. Seventy percent of its minority Tutsi population were killed."

Des interjected. "Exactly. So then we ran *all* the

paragraphs through our language database and they came back as the languages belonging to the victims of genocides in East Timor, Iraq, Cambodia, Bosnia-Herzegovina, Libya, Bangladesh, Nazi Germany, the list just goes on. All countries where there have been genocides in the past century."

"Shit! I'd no idea there'd been so many, boss."

"Neither had I. God but we're a pathetic species." He sighed wearily. "What did they say, Des?"

"It's best if you read the translations for yourselves. I'll send them to your smart-pads now."

When they appeared Craig motioned to his deputy. "Liam, ask Ash to put these on the big screen and I'll transfer the call outside."

In a short time everyone present in the office was looking at them and listening to Des' commentary.

"OK, so basically each paragraph refers to a different world genocide over the past one hundred years and each account was written in the indigenous language of the victims so our translation's a bit clunky at times, but they essentially list dates, numbers of people killed, methods used, and give information on the victims and perpetrators. I'll shut up now so you can read."

It took several minutes to absorb the details of human beings' seemingly endless cruelty to each other set out in front of them and Craig's overwhelming thought was 'such a waste'.

So deep was his focus he didn't register the forensic lead's next words, but on their third repetition they cut through.

"I said it's what was written on the back of the fourth board that really chilled me, Marc."

Ash changed the screen to one where there was only a single paragraph, written in English far too perfect to have been a translation, something that Des confirmed right away.

"This part was already in English."

Liam was curious. "Arty, Annette, you saw this?"

Annette's warm voice came down the line. "Yes, but we couldn't put it in proper context until we understood what the other stuff said."

She wasn't wrong. On their own the words read like the mission statement of a fanatical movement, but now set in context their implication made Craig freeze. His deputy was having no such trouble with his thermostat and read aloud.

"We are the descendents of genocide. The generations

living with that legacy and tasked with vengeance. Your people were not the first to see retribution and they will not be the last. We are in and from every country of the world."

As he finished he gawped at the board. "What the fuck? Are these guys serious?"

Craig was too busy thinking to respond. He ignored the clamor that immediately broke out and searched for a word to describe what was going on. What he came up with seemed too fantastic to believe and silenced the noise right away.

"A cell. Our killers were a cell."

Ash's eyes brightened with interest. "You mean like terrorists?"

"More like avengers."

"From where, sir?"

"Not just where, when. In our case nineteen-forties Europe, but from what we've just heard they could have come from any time in the past century and from any country. *Our* killers were descendants of people who died in the Holocaust."

"Jewish?"

Andy's voice came down the line. "Yes, but not only. They've left details here about the killing of the Roma, the Poles, political dissidents, homosexuals, the disabled, the Russians, the French and Norwegian Resistances and more who were killed by the Nazis. It was all laid out on the boards without actually naming our assassins or the others they're working alongside."

"Some of whom are clearly in Lithuania at the moment."

"Yep. It also details exactly what Bolsover and Sophie's and Dylan's families did in World War Two, chief."

"I'll hear about that later. Let's go back to the fourth board. That tells us that this cell is just one of many active across the world, killing in revenge for what was done to their ancestors during genocides." He turned to his analyst. "You know what I'm going to ask, Ash."

"Can I start looking for mysterious deaths and thefts in all those countries? Yeh, I can, but just to point out that they killed people here for something that happened in mainland Europe, so there's no guarantee that geography will help the search that much. Also, it'll be a few days before I can start. Info's coming back thick and fast from Interpol on Bolsover's stash, the vault stuff and the Ferviers' art collection. It seems a lot of that, inside and outside the vaults, came from Hubert and Aveline, who incidentally settled in Wicklow and are both long dead, and it will all need returned to its rightful owners. Although we did find some clean stuff Hortense owned still at the bank."

"So she mightn't have known the provenance of the stuff that was taken, sir."

"Maybe, maybe not, Annette. OK, Ash, focus on that for now. If anything was sold by the Ferviers and they made a profit from it then the Proceeds of Crime Act might come into play, so, Andy, how do you fancy leading on that with Ash?"

"Happy to."

The D.C.I. grinned at the possibility of spending another few weeks up to his eyes in art.

Craig took a final look at the screen for now and drew things to a close. "Perhaps Interpol or the agencies will catch them."

Liam chuckled. "Try not to sound so hopeful that they won't."

Craig was saved from incriminating himself by the arrival of John, brandishing his medical bag.

"Good news. The girl was clear on the biggies so you're out of the woods there." The medic opened the bag and withdrew a needle. "Now, would you like me to jab you in the backside here or in your room?"

Putting on a strip show for his team wasn't high on Craig's bucket list so as it was getting near home time he invited everyone to The James for pints. They would meet them there in ten minutes and he intended to have *at least* three whiskeys before he started the antibiotics that would doubtless force him to be teetotal for the whole of Christmas week.

****

Venezuela. Near the Atlantic Coast.

It was perhaps fortunate that neither Craig nor any his team had any *real* concept of what they'd just dealt with, believing in their small cell of youthful assassins being controlled by others with dark memories and a thirst for vengeance, and some similarly tiny cells operating elsewhere in the world. Not that that was inaccurate exactly, just that the truth was on a far larger scale than they could ever have guessed.

As Oskar Nowak stood at the front of his enormous auditorium he allowed his sharp gaze to travel up from the rows of seats at eye level, through the middle tiers and on and on to those far higher, perched loftily in the Gods. Each row packed full of enthusiastic young recruits of differing ethnicities; all fit, all in fatigues and with guns at their hips, and all leaning forward eagerly to catch every word that their leader said.

The weathered, battle-honed veteran allowed himself a moment of pride at what had been created from the legacy and funds of those who had deep and painful memories but no longer the physical strength to act themselves, before calling on four young people from the front row to come and stand beside him, to a spontaneously raucous round of applause that he allowed to run and run.

When the last echoes of whooping and feet stomping had died away he raised a hand for silence and spoke in an authoritative growl.

"Three vermin are now dead by the efforts of these good soldiers and two evil dynasties ended to prevent their progeny doing further harm. The property that their ancestors stole and profited from is being returned to its rightful owners and I have no doubt more will soon be on its way."

He paused and gazed achingly slowly around the arena, so silent now that people could hear their breaths, before he continued in a voice that became a roar.

"FINALLY THEIR LOVED ONES' STORIES HAVE BEEN TOLD!"

The cheer that erupted ricocheted off the walls and built until it was almost deafening, but as Oskar opened his mouth to speak again the wave of sound halted as abruptly as if it had hit a dam.

"More loved ones' stories will follow and more evil descendants will die. At this minute soldiers just like these four are on missions in Lithuania, Russia, America, Brazil, Rwanda, Turkey and Sweden pursuing other parasites who have evaded justice. *They* will be equally successful, as will you new recruits once your training is complete."

He gripped the arms of Roman and Irina standing on either side of him and hoisted them into the air, to be joined by every arm in the hall, but his next words were slow and sombre not the rallying cry that had gone before and they sent a chill through everyone there.

"To those who were slaughtered, we will remember you. And from now into the future's future our good work will go on."

Chapter Fourteen

The James Bar. Friday. 9 p.m.

It's a wise person who knows their limitations and Craig thought he could lay claim to that label this week, even though, regardless of how accepting of losing four out of five of their killers he might *appear* to his team, he was actually as frustrated as hell.

If he'd known which country their killers were holed up in he would have gone after them himself with SWAT, but he didn't. As they'd suspected, the private jet's trail had gone cold mid-flight as if it had suddenly gone stealth to the surrounding countries' radar, and when the Hebrides-bound cargo boat *had* surprisingly been found, although a day after departure and floating in the Norwegian Sea, not one item of interest from its manifest still lay in its hold and the crew had been roofied and couldn't remember a thing after leaving port.

Liam's assertion that his boss had harboured a slight hope their executioners might get away had been partly correct, because Craig really *did* understand their urge to right historical wrongs. But they both knew people couldn't just go around assassinating other people, not even ones like Horace Bolsover who'd deserved it. Ireland's history, north and south, had been peppered with such revenge agents and what it had got them was, yes, *some* change, but far more innocent people dead and that wasn't a price worth paying in Craig's view.

But right now the detective's mind was empty of *all* meaningful thought, courtesy of his third glass of wine of the night. The combination of alcohol, Christmas cheer and Grace's astoundingly melodic singing was mellowing his mood very satisfactorily, although he did wonder whether deferring his antibiotic course so he could get pissed that night was really a good idea no matter *how* brilliant it made him feel.

John's earlier pointed look had said that was probably a no.

Seeing the pathologist approaching Craig drained his glass swiftly before the health police could stop him, and was surprised when his friend merely poured him another and then held the bottle up to read.

"You're not going to tell me off for not starting my tablets yet?"

"What? No, well I mean you should have done, and you *need* to start them tomorrow, but it isn't as bad as drinking *with* the ones I prescribed for you. One sip and they'll make you throw up."

"Lovely. Thanks."

The medic nodded appreciatively at the bottle's label, "Malbec. Nice. By the way," he leaned in conspiratorially, "I took your advice."

Craig rummaged quickly through his mind for whatever wisdom he'd accidentally dispensed in the previous week and landed on, "Oh, you mean you and Natalie *are* spending time away?"

"We are. You were right about why she'd sent the separation letter, so we're off down south tomorrow until Tuesday to talk. It's make or break though. Either she agrees to have therapy or we'll have to divorce." He crossed his arms determinedly. "I'm *not* letting her have unsupervised access to Kit until she stops pushing her to be perfect."

Suddenly a deep chuckle came from the seat behind. "Get away with you, Doc! You won't talk at all, it'll be non-stop nooky all weekend and you know it."

The pathologist gave Liam his best disdainful look. "Not at all. We have serious matters to discuss."

It earned him an exaggerated wink."Aye, that as well. Of course."

Debate over, the D.C.I. moved into their booth and on to more important things. "Where are you staying?"

"Ashford Castle."

"You're kidding! That's arm and a leg territory anytime, but the weekend before Christmas? What the hell, Doc?"

The ensuing discussion about what price people put on romantic gestures was cut short by Andy joining the group and nudging Craig's arm.

"Have you seen what's going on over there, chief?"

He indicated the darkest corner of the bar, where Craig could only make out some vague shapes.

"I'd need binoculars."

"It's Aidan and Deidre Murray. They're getting *very* cosy now she's divorcing."

Craig ignored John's wince at the 'D' word, although it

did renew the pathologist's determination to make his weekend as fruitful as hell. He really didn't like the idea of Natalie dating someone else; she might be as difficult but she was *his*.

Just then Craig noticed his deputy rising, and knowing he was about to go over and tease the lovebirds he shook his head.

"Give him a break, Liam. It's the first time in ages Aidan's really liked someone."

The D.C.I. rolled his eyes but sat back down. "OK, I'll let him off the hook for Christmas, *but that's all*. Then it's open slagging season so he'd better toughen up. Meantime, I haven't finished slagging you about being royalty yet, Baron."

Andy shook his head. "Count. Haven't you heard? More than one too. I dug back a few generations."

Craig tried for a diversion. "How's your cold, Liam? It seems a lot better."

It was desperation and sounded like it, and his deputy decided to turn it to his advantage.

"It's grand, thanks. So, I hear you think my advice in the car on Monday was right?"

If Craig hadn't been drunk he would have spotted the trap immediately, but all he was thinking of was cutting the aristocracy discussion off at its knees and he would have agreed to pretty much anything to stop that.

"Absolutely right, oh most wise and benevolent one."

Liam looked around the group. "I was right. You're all witnesses that he said that. And in vino veritas don't forget."

As the others looked bewildered, not having a clue what he was talking about, Craig clambered to his feet, hopeful that the earlier lineage discussion was now dead.

"Let me buy everyone a drink."

But his deputy was about to shatter his hope.

"I'll have a pint, boss, but if you're trying to divert us from your family tree it's no dice." He turned theatrically to Andy. "A Count? Really? Well, don't spare us the details, man."

So as Grace sang the first chords of Blue Moon Craig conceded defeat and climbed into his fourth glass of wine, listening as the Italian dynasty that he'd known nothing about was laid out.

THE END

Core Characters in the Craig Crime Novels

Detective Chief Superintendent Marc (Marco) Craig: Craig is a sophisticated, single, forty-eight-year-old of Northern Irish/Italian extraction. From a mixed religious background but agnostic.
An ex-grammar schoolboy and Queen's University Law graduate, he went to London to join The Met (The Metropolitan Police) at twenty-two, rising in rank through its High Potential Development Training Scheme. He returned to Belfast in two-thousand and eight after fifteen years away.
He is a driven, compassionate, workaholic, with an unfortunate temper that he struggles to control and a tendency to respond to situations with his fists, something that almost resulted in him going to prison when he was in his teens. He loves the sea, sails when he has the time and is generally sporty. He plays the piano, loves music and sport.

His wife of one year, Katy Stevens, is a consultant physician at the local St Mary's Healthcare Trust, and they live with their baby son, Luca, in Katy's old apartment on the River Lagan.

Craig's parents, his extrovert mother Mirella (an Italian concert pianist) and his quiet father Tom (an ex-university lecturer in Physics) live in Holywood town, six miles outside the city. His rebellious sister, Lucia, his junior by ten years, works as the manager of a local charity and also lives in Belfast. She is engaged to Ken Smith, an ex-army officer who has now joined the police.

Craig is now a Detective Chief Superintendent heading up Belfast's Murder Squad and Police Intelligence Unit. The Murder Squad is based in the thirteen storey Co-ordinated Crime Unit (C.C.U.) in Pilot Street, in the Sailortown area of Belfast's Docklands.

D.C.I. Liam Cullen: Craig's deputy. Liam is a fifty-two-year-old former RUC officer from Crossgar in Northern Ireland, who transferred into the PSNI from the RUC in two thousand and one, following the Patton Reforms. He has lived and worked in Northern Ireland all his life and has spent over thirty years in the police force, more than twenty of them policing Belfast, including during The Troubles.

Liam is married to the forty-two-year-old, long suffering Danielle (Danni), a part-time nursery nurse, and they have a seven-year-old daughter Erin and a five-year-old son called Rory. Liam is unsophisticated, indiscreet and hopelessly non-PC, but he's a hard worker with a great knowledge of the streets and has a sense of humour that makes everyone, even the Chief Constable, laugh.

D.I. Annette Eakin: Annette is Craig's lead Detective Inspector who has lived and worked in Northern Ireland all her life. She is a forty-eight-year-old ex-nurse who, after her nursing degree, worked as a nurse for thirteen years and then, after a career break, retrained and has now been in the police for an equal length of time. She divorced her husband Pete McElroy, a P.E teacher at a state secondary school, because of his infidelity and violence. He has since died. They had two children, a boy and a girl (Jordan and Amy), both at university, and Annette also has a baby daughter, Carina, with her new partner, Mike Augustus, a pathologist who works with Doctor John Winter.

Annette is kind and conscientious with an especially good eye for detail. She also has very good people skills but can be a bit of a goody-two-shoes.

Nicky Morris: Nicky Morris is Craig's forty-year-old personal assistant. She used to be PA to Detective Chief Superintendent (D.C.S.) Terry *'Teflon'* Harrison. Nicky is a glamorous Belfast mum married to Gary, who owns a small garage, and she is the mother of a teenage son, Johnny. She comes from a solidly working-class area of east Belfast, just ten minutes' drive from Docklands.

She is bossy, motherly and street-wise and manages to organise a reluctantly-organised Craig very effectively. She has a very eclectic and unusual sense of style, and there is an ongoing innocent office flirtation between her and Liam.

Davy Walsh: The Murder Squad's thirty-one-year-old

senior computer analyst. A brilliant but shy EMO turned Hipster, Davy's confidence has grown during his time on the team, making his lifelong stutter on 's' and 'w' now almost unnoticeable unless he's under stress.

His father is deceased and Davy lives at home in Belfast with his mother and grandmother. He has an older sister, Emmie, who studied English at university.

His girlfriend of seven years, Maggie Clarke, is a journalist and now News Editor at The Belfast Chronicle newspaper. They became engaged in early 2017.

Doctor John Winter: John is the forty-eight-year-old Director of Pathology for Northern Ireland, one of the youngest ever appointed. He's brilliant, eccentric, gentlemanly and really likes the ladies, but he met his match in Natalie Ingrams, a surgeon at St Mary's Healthcare Trust, and they have been married now for three years and have a toddler daughter called Kit. John and Natalie are currently separated because of discord in the marriage.

John was Craig's best friend at school and university and remained in Northern Ireland to build his medical career when Craig left. He is now internationally respected in his field.
The pathologist persuaded Craig that the newly peaceful Northern Ireland was a good place to return to, and he assists Craig's team with cases whenever he can. He is obsessed with crime in general and US police shows in particular.

D.C.I. Andrew (Andy) Angel: A relatively new addition to Craig's team and its second D.C.I., Andy Angel is a slight, forty-four-year-old, twice divorced, perpetually broke father of an eleven-year-old son, Bowie, who lives with his mother. A chocoholic with a tendency towards lethargy, he surprises the team at times with his abilities, particularly his visual skills, which include being a super-recogniser, a title given to a small number of individuals who possess exceptional visual recognition abilities. It is something that has proved useful in several investigations.

Andy's spare time is spent sketching, painting and collecting original Irish art. He is also constantly on the search for a new relationship, but without much success as romantic subtlety isn't his strong point.

D.C.I. Aidan Hughes: Originally seconded to the Murder Squad in twenty-sixteen from Vice, Hughes has now become a permanent addition to Craig's team.

Single, mid-forties, tall, thin, and with a broad Belfast accent and a tendency to tan so much at his parents' home in Spain that he resembles a stick of mahogany, Hughes has known Craig and John Winter since they were all at school together. A newly reformed heavy smoker, exercise addict and joker, he is a popular member of the squad.

Doctor Des Marsham: Des is the Head of Forensic Science for Northern Ireland and works with John Winter at their laboratories in a science park off the Saintfield Road in Belfast. They often work together on Craig's murder cases.

Instantly recognisable by his barely controlled beard, Des is married to the placid and hippyish Annie, and they have two young sons, Martin and Rafferty. The scientist is obsessed with Gaelic Football, both playing and watching it, and spends several weekends each year metal-detecting with his university friends on Northern Ireland's Atlantic coast.

D.C.S. Terry (Teflon) Harrison: Craig's old boss. The sixty-year-old Detective Chief Superintendent was based at the Headquarters building in Limavady in the northwest Irish countryside but has now returned to the Docklands C.C.U. where he has an office on the thirteenth floor. He shared a converted farm house at Toomebridge with his homemaker wife Mandy and their thirty-year-old daughter Sian, a marketing consultant, but Mandy has now divorced him, partly because of his trail of mistresses, often younger than his daughter, so Harrison has moved to an apartment in south Belfast.

The D.C.S. is tolerable as a boss as long as everything's going well, but he is acutely politically aware, a snob, and very quick to pass on the blame for any mistakes to his subordinates (hence the Teflon nickname). He sees Craig as a rival and is out to destroy him. In particular, he resents Craig's friendship with John Winter, who wields a great deal of power in the Northern Irish justice system.

Key Background Locations

The majority of locations referenced in the book are real, with some exceptions.

Northern Ireland (real): Set in the north-east of the island of Ireland, Northern Ireland was created in nineteen-twenty-one by an act of British parliament. It forms part of the United Kingdom of Great Britain and Northern Ireland and shares a border to the south and west with the Republic of Ireland. The Northern Ireland Assembly, based at the Stormont Estate, holds responsibility for a range of devolved policy matters. It was established by the Northern Ireland Act 1998 as part of the Good Friday Agreement.

Belfast (real): Belfast is the capital and largest city of Northern Ireland, set on the flood plain of the River Lagan. The seventeenth largest city in the United Kingdom and the second largest in Ireland, it is the seat of the Northern Ireland Assembly.

The Dockland's Co-ordinated Crime Unit (The C.C.U. - fictitious): The modern high-rise headquarters building is situated in Pilot Street in Sailortown, a section of Belfast between the M1 and M2 undergoing massive investment and re-development. The C.C.U. hosts the police murder, gang crimes, vice and drug squad offices, amongst others.

Sailortown (real): An historic area of Belfast on the River Lagan that was a thriving area between the sixteenth and twentieth centuries. Many large businesses developed in the area, ships docked for loading and unloading and their crews from far flung places such as China and Russia mixed with a local Belfast population of ship's captains, chandlers, seamen and their families.

Sailortown was a lively area where churches and bars fought for the souls and attendance of the residents and where many languages were spoken each day. The basement of the Rotterdam Bar, at the bottom of Clarendon Dock, acted as the overnight lock-up to prisoners being deported to the Antipodes on boats the next morning, and the stocks which held the prisoners could still be seen until the nineteen-nineties.

During the years of World War Two the area was the most bombed area of the UK outside Central London, as the Germans tried to destroy Belfast's ship building capacity. Sadly, the area fell into disrepair in the nineteen-seventies and eighties when the motorway extension led to compulsory purchases of many homes and businesses and decimated the Sailortown community. The rebuilding of the community has now begun, with new families moving into starter homes and professionals into expensive dockside flats.

The Pathology Labs (fictitious): The labs, set on Belfast's Saintfield Road as part of a large science park, are where Doctor John Winter, Northern Ireland's Head of Pathology, and his co-worker, Doctor Des Marsham, Head of Forensic Science, carry out the post-mortem and forensic examinations that help Craig's team solve their cases.

St Mary's Healthcare Trust (fictitious): St Mary's is one of the largest hospital trusts in the UK. It is spread over several hospital sites across Belfast, including the main Royal St Mary's Hospital site off the motorway and the Maternity, Paediatric and Endocrine (M.P.E.) unit, a stand-alone site on Belfast's Lisburn Road, in the University Quarter of the city.

Thank-you for reading this book. If you enjoyed it, why not leave a review on Amazon and recommend it to your friends?

Discover the other titles in the series at:
www.catrionakingbooks.com

Printed in Great Britain
by Amazon